CW01375967

VROLOK

by

Nolene-Patricia Dougan

AuthorHouse™ *AuthorHouse*™ *UK Ltd.*
1663 Liberty Drive, Suite 200 *500 Avebury Boulevard*
Bloomington, IN 47403 *Central Milton Keynes, MK9 2BE*
www.authorhouse.com *www.authorhouse.co.uk*
Phone: 1-800-839-8640 *Phone: 08001974150*

This book is a work of fiction. People, places, events, and situations are the product of the author's imagination. Any resemblance to actual persons, living or dead, or historical events, is purely coincidental.

© 2006 Nolene-Patricia Dougan. All rights reserved.

No part of this book may be reproduced, stored in a retrieval system, or transmitted by any means without the written permission of the author.

First published by AuthorHouse 9/28/2006

ISBN: 1-4208-8154-X (sc)
ISBN: 1-4208-8163-9 (dj)

Printed in the United States of America
Bloomington, Indiana

This book is printed on acid-free paper.

VOEVOD
WARRIOR PRINCE

PROLOGUE

It was a religious time, and like all other religious times, religion was the excuse for war but not the reason. Muslims and Christians fought against each other, invading each other's land, destroying each other's homes, causing utter devastation whenever they encountered their declared enemy.

The Muslim and Christian soldiers on both sides were hypnotised by their religious fervour and their religious leaders. Each side believed it was fighting the Devil's own warriors.

During this feral hostility there sprang up various warlords, usually rich men, who wanted to use their idle time either to become richer or to write themselves into the history books. One such rich man was Vlad Dracula, a young and vicious prince, whose brutality was renowned amongst his followers and his enemies, many of whom lacked the courage to face him.

The few who did regretted it.

This story begins over five hundred years ago, near the Romanian border. A battle had just been fought and a young Slovak soldier was wandering through the battlefield. With his raven hair and luminous, viridian eyes, he was quite a striking young man, not more than seventeen.

Behind him were the flickering lights of the campfires. There were fewer than there had been the night before, and beyond him lay the blood-soaked ground of the battlefield, where broken, battered, lifeless bodies stretched as far as his eye could see. In the near distance, the Danube glistened in the moonlight. It was the only peaceful view, untouched by the murderous events of the day.

The young soldier soon caught sight of a cart where two Wallachians were gathering up corpses for burial and looking for survivors. As he watched them, he saw one of the Wallachians try to remove a ring from a dead soldier's hand. The man seemed to be having some difficulty excising the ring. His compatriot handed him a shiv; the Wallachian then cut off the finger and took the ring.

The sight of this was not at all abhorrent to the Slovak; despite his youth, he was used to brutality like this. As far as he was concerned, the man was dead, no longer in need of trinkets—or fingers, for that matter. The young soldier started to look around, to see whether there might be anything he could salvage.

He quickly espied the body of a Boyar Knight. The Slovak approached the corpse slowly, not wanting to draw attention to himself or to the dead warrior. As he drew near, he was startled; not only were the Boyar Knight's eyes still open, he was looking straight up towards the young Slovak with an expression of terror. He almost seemed alive, with blood still gushing from an open wound on his neck. This man was dead, yet he hadn't been dead for long, and his death had come as a surprise to him. He was probably attacked from behind, unable to see the face of his killer before he died.

The Slovak's attention was quickly drawn from the Boyar's penetrating stare to what he was wearing. An embroidered cloak of crimson velvet eclipsed the Knight's body. The Slovak looked at his own torn cloak and promptly decided to take the Boyar's garment for himself. As he untied the cloak and pulled it from the body, he uncovered the Knight's right hand, which still tightly clasped the jewelled hilt of a magnificent and imposing sword. It was the grandest thing the young soldier had ever seen and he felt compelled to take it.

He put on the cloak and strapped the sword to his body. Then he made his way back to the Slovak camp. When he arrived, he headed directly towards the first campfire he saw.

Three other Slovak soldiers were already sitting beside it. They were a strange mix and looked odd together. One was reading a book, which obscured his face. The second was a portly, rosy-cheeked individual who looked more like a farmer than a crusader; this man was chatting away to his two companions and being ignored by both. The third Slovak was sharpening his sword on a stone; he was a daunting and frightening sight. His arms, hands and face were covered in scars; he was missing an eye and a few front teeth. The mere sight of him would terrify the enemy, never mind having to face him on the battlefield.

The young Slovak stood and warmed his hands at the fire. The portly soldier, noticing him, stood and saluted to acknowledge the presence of a knight. The battle-scarred soldier simply grunted to acknowledge the young man, and the third did not even lift his eyes from his book.

At first, the young soldier was surprised by the salute, but then he remembered what he was wearing. The young Slovak was not afraid to explain his unintentional deception to his fellow countrymen. These men would find no fault with his conduct. They were not members of the privileged classes; in a similar situation, they would probably have done the same thing. The young man knew that only rich men would be repulsed by his actions. Men who had never wanted for anything, he had learned, found it easy to pass judgement on those who had.

The young Slovak sat and gestured to the other man to sit, also.

"That's quite a convincing disguise you have there," remarked the plump Slovak. "Did it fool you, Goran?"

Goran, still sharpening his sword, grunted again.

"That means yes. My name is Dmitri. This is Goran and Nicolae."

"Alexei," said the young soldier, and nodded to acknowledge the introduction.

"We were just talking about Vlad, our eminent leader," said Dmitri. With pride, he pointed to a figure standing with his back towards them, a hundred yards or so in front of the camp. "He has been standing there for three hours. I have seen him stand in that manner all night and then be able to fight all of the next day like the most courageous and strongest of soldiers. He never seems to rest," Dmitri said with a sense of awe, his admiration for the man clearly apparent.

"They say he is descended from Attila," remarked Alexei.

"He says he is descended from Attila? He is no Szelely," Nicolae muttered under his breath, not even bothering to lift his eyes from his book.

Dmitri ignored him and continued: "The Wallachians call him Dracula. It means great warrior."

Closing his book, Nicolae fully joined the conversation. "It is also the word they use for the Devil," he said.

"Forgive my friend," Dmitri interrupted, worried for Nicolae, for to speak out against Vlad meant death by impalement.

Nicolae continued anyway, not caring who was listening. "There is no need to ask forgiveness of anyone for me! I will not sit here and listen to praise for any of us who fight for such ignoble reasons!" Nicolae sighed. "Ten years ago I was a farmer. I cared nothing for war. The village where I lived had arranged a hunting trip. We left the women and children behind to prepare for our return. But the Turks invaded as soon as we left. Every woman and child in the village was brutally slain. We could not even give them a decent burial; the bodies had been stacked up and burnt. Many of us were made ill by the stench. That day changed our lives forever. Some stayed behind and tried to rebuild their broken lives, but I could not. I couldn't face life without my family—I left and joined the Crusades. When I started fighting, I was filled with hatred for the Turks, but since I joined this war I have seen many brutal acts, most of which were performed not by the enemy I have been fighting against but by the men I was fighting with."

All four men sat in silence for a few moments and then Alexei turned to him: "If you are so disheartened, why are you still fighting?"

"What else do you suggest I do, go back to my family?" Nicolae retorted sarcastically. "This is the only thing I know how to do anymore. I joined this war to avenge my family, and every day I have become more like the men who killed them." He lifted his book and started to read again.

Alexei interrupted Nicolae's reading one final time: "Who taught you to read?"

"My wife." With this said, Nicolae closed his book and walked off towards his tent. Goran also removed himself, leaving just Alexei and Dmitri beside the fire.

"My young friend, pay no attention to Nicolae. We have all seen many horrific things which we would have chosen not to see, had things been different. Let us discuss your situation, instead. If I were you, I would use your good fortune at finding that sword and cloak to your advantage. I would use this opportunity to go and talk to Vlad. For ordinary soldiers like us, this could be the chance of a lifetime, a chance to be close to greatness, to converse with our noble leader as an equal. This could be a story to tell your grandchildren."

Alexei did not respond to Dmitri's comments. He simply got up and left the Slovak camp in silence.

Alexei had always admired Vlad from afar. Indeed, everyone admired him. He was not more than ten years older than the young Slovak, but it seemed to Alexei that he had been hearing of Vlad's exploits for as long as he could remember. Alexei was from a village in Transylvania. He could see the prince's castle from where he lived. A year ago, he had left home and followed Vlad into his first battle. He remembered how his mother had been, the day he left. Tears trickled down her cheeks as she begged him not to go. His father had been killed in battle, and even Vlad himself had been captured and imprisoned, along with his brother. Alexei's mother was convinced that she would lose her son, as she had lost her husband.

But Alexei had been determined to follow Vlad into war. He was mesmerised by Vlad and the tales of his adventures, how he had escaped from a Turkish prison and returned home to take back his kingdom from the Turks and to avenge the deaths of his father and younger brothers.

Alexei was not discouraged by what Nicolae had said. The young man had met a few men who talked like Nicolae, men who had once been farmers, who would have been happy to live out the rest of their lives with their families, had not tragedy struck. These men had become bitter and angry at the world. The only thing they could do was kill and weep for their lost lives.

The other soldiers he met were often just cold-blooded killers who would kill anything or anyone for the sheer pleasure they got from it. But this was war. Each soldier had a different reason for fighting, and all soldiers, no matter what their reason for killing, were needed to win a war.

Alexei had witnessed Vlad's treatment of the Turks who were captured alive. He did not envy them their fate. He always remembered something his father had told him: "To win a war, you have to be just as brutal as the enemy. To show mercy is to show weakness."

It was rumoured that Vlad had received firsthand experience of just how brutal the Turks could be when he and his brother were captured. The Turks' methods of torture had proven to be too much for his older brother—he had become a Muslim and an enemy.

There were also stories of Vlad's brutality towards his own men. One of the stories that Alexei heard most often was that of a Boyar Knight who complained about the screams of the Turks that Vlad had impaled. In response, Vlad impaled him on a higher stake than anyone else.

Alexei, however, chose to ignore these stories, or at least tried to rationalise them and think of them solely as acts of war. He had been willing to make excuses for Vlad in the past. He had said that the Boyar must have been a traitor and that had to have been the real reason for the impalement. He wanted, no, he needed, to believe in Vlad.

Alexei himself believed he was fighting for the greater good, and that the end justified the means. He wanted to know what sort of man Vlad truly was. He knew he was courageous...he knew he was strong. But were the stories really true? Was he a devil or a warrior? He had to know.

Alexei found himself walking towards Vlad.

When Alexei was just a few steps behind Vlad, he stopped to examine the figure who stood with his back to him. He had never been so close to Vlad before. This was how Alexei would remember him in the future, the picture that would come to mind when he remembered Vlad Dracula.

Vlad's long, dark, tousled hair and scarlet cloak billowed in the night time breeze. Vlad's hand clutched his sword, which was still in its sheath. He gripped the hilt firmly, at a slight incline away from his body, and his head was held high. He had an air of superiority about him, and he made an intimidating yet glorious sight.

This was a leader Alexei could be proud of. He moved in a little closer and attempted to gather the courage to speak to Vlad. But before he could, Vlad started to speak to him.

"I thought you were going to stand there all night. Have you gathered up the courage to speak to me now?"

Alexei was struck dumb. He did not know what to say.

"Or, have you just come to marvel at the sight of the great Prince Dracula?" Vlad turned around to face him.

Alexei could now see Vlad's face. His eyes were dark, almost black. His skin was darkened by the sun. His features were rugged, but not coarse. He looked like a god among mere mortals.

Alexei realised that this was not the sort of man with whom he could just simply talk, so he came straight to the point. "Why do you fight?" he blurted out.

"If you are anything, you are blunt," Vlad said with a slight smile. "Why do *you* fight, my young knight?"

Alexei felt compelled to answer, as if Vlad's every word was a command that he had to obey. "I fight because my father fought before me, and because I believe I am fighting for a good and noble cause. I believe the Muslims to be infidels and the Christians to be worthy of God's absolution."

Vlad smiled at him. "You have answered my question honestly, so I will pay you the same courtesy. My reasons are much the same as yours. Like my father before me, I am a member of the Order of the Dragon, a holy order in which each member has sworn to protect and uphold the beliefs of the Christian church." Vlad paused for a moment as if he heard something in the distance, and then added, "I would leave now, my young Slovak friend. A Boyar Knight is approaching and he may well wonder how you acquired that cloak and sword."

Alexei was startled by the remark. He removed the sword and cloak and ran to hide behind a nearby tree. From there, he watched and listened as a Boyar Knight approached.

The Knight began to speak to Vlad: "Who were you talking to?"

"Just a Slovak soldier who wanted to converse with his leader," replied Vlad.

The Boyar stood in silence for a moment and then continued, "Anyone could lead these peasants. I have found my brother's corpse, but his cloak and sword are missing."

Vlad did not answer him.

"Did you not hear me?" the Knight demanded. "My father's sword is missing. I demand that the thief be found and impaled. I demand justice!"

Alexei listened in terror. He was sure that he would be dead before the morning, impaled as an example to all looters.

Vlad said calmly, "Your brother came to me last night and told me that you had threatened him. He told me that you wanted your father's sword, which he had rightfully inherited. I told him that not even you would kill your own brother—not because you loved or even respected him, but because you lacked the courage to confront him. I was right. You did lack the courage to face him. Instead, you sneaked up behind him and slit his throat. You demand justice? Then you will receive it!"

Vlad unsheathed his sword and swung round, sword in hand. The traitor's disembodied head hit the ground before his body did. His eyes were blinking and his mouth open, as though still trying to gasp for air.

Shaken, Alexei left his hiding place and approached Vlad with the intention of giving back the cloak and sword.

"No, keep them," Vlad said. "You are more deserving than he ever was. Nobility is not something that is in the blood. It is in the soul."

The two Wallachians whom Alexei had seen earlier pushed their cart up to the body. One of them picked it up while the other knelt before Vlad and said, "A message has arrived from the Carpathians, my Lord."

"What is the message?" Vlad asked.

The Wallachian took a nervous breath, "Your wife has killed herself."

Alexei shuddered, and a silence seemed to fall instantly upon the whole camp as they watched.

All of Vlad's men, all of Vlad's enemies watched in disbelief as the warrior—the Devil—swayed. His legs gave way beneath him. His hands clutched at his face, and he fell to the ground in anguish.

DENN DIE TODTEN REITEN SCHNELL
FOR THE DEAD TRAVEL FAST

CHAPTER ONE

The door burst open. Anna did not flinch. She sat still, gazing into the fire. She remained unperturbed by her abrupt intruder.

She had been expecting a visitor in some shape or form. The intruder paused for a moment and stared at her. She could feel his eyes searing into the back of her head. Anna was not a stranger to this man. He had always admired her. She had always been a voice of reason in the village and even amid the chaos that was going on around her, she was calm and completely rational. The intruder began to speak.

"Vlad's dead."

Anna turned her head and glanced up at him, a look of contempt on her face. Yet when their eyes met, her look softened to one of compassion. She started to feel pity for the stranger. He was a young man, but today's events had stolen part of his youth—a part that he would never get back. His clothes and hair were soaked in perspiration, and yet it was cold outside. His hands were trembling. He was frightened and Anna knew why.

Everyone in the village was terrified. Homes were being deserted, possessions abandoned. No one seemed to care about their valuables anymore. Everyone was running away, everyone except Anna. She was the only one who was calm, the only person who was not in a state of panic.

Suddenly a loud, shrill scream came from outside. Anna's visitor turned around quickly to see who had screamed and why. Fortunately, his worst fears had not yet been confirmed. It was just a young girl who had been told that her husband was among the dead.

Anna stood and walked towards the window. As she did so, the floor creaked beneath her feet. The young interloper turned back to look at Anna for a second time.

"That will be the first of many screams you will hear this night," said Anna. "My son?" she inquired.

"Murdered."

"Who killed him?"

"Isabella."

Anna shook her head, "You lie."

"It's the truth!" the soldier said vehemently.

"It is not the truth," Anna replied, firmly but softly. "I'll ask you again. Who killed my son?"

The young man sighed and told Anna the truth: "The English."

Anna nodded in recognition.

"You must leave," he said pleadingly.

"I'll stay. She won't harm me."

"How do you know for certain?"

"I know."

"But how do you know…"

"I know!" Anna retorted. "I know," she said again, calmly. "I know because my father told me…many of my childhood memories have faded now, but this one still remains clear and vivid to me. I was playing on the road to Bistrita. It was a bright day, and the sky overhead was filled with sunshine. As I looked further down the road I could see nothing but dark skies in front of me. It seemed like a warning, as if the heavens were telling me to stay where I was. Of course, I did not heed their warning. I wandered a little too far and I was about to return home, when I noticed a man lying on the edge of the road just in front of me. As I approached him I could see he was obviously sick or injured. I kneeled down beside him. His eyes suddenly opened and he grabbed my dress and pulled me closer to him. He just held me there in front of him, not saying a word, just looking at my face. I could not tell you what colour eyes he had, whether he was fat or thin, young or old. But I will always remember how he looked at me. His eyes were cold and harsh. He looked so afraid that he in turn frightened me. He was completely desperate. He pulled my ear down to his lips and whispered to me, "Leave me…for the dead travel fast." He let go of my dress and I ran all the way home and did not look back once.

"When I got home I told my father what had happened and that he had to go and help the wounded man. My father told me not to worry. He went over to my mother, kissed her on her forehead, and left the safety and security of our home. My mother sat me on her knee and held me tight. She was frightened and I had never seen her so afraid.

"My father came home the next morning unharmed. He told me there was no one there and that I must have imagined the whole thing. I knew I had not but he was so stern and adamant that I did not argue with him. Later that day I heard him whispering to my mother that I was not to be allowed out on my own again.

"Years later my father explained to me what had happened and why the man had said what he did. He told me not to fear them. I was never to be afraid. Our family would always be protected as long as Isabella lived. She had promised one of our ancestors hundreds of years ago that she would always protect us. She has kept her promise…do you think that she will break it now?"

"Did you ever find out what happened to the wounded man?"

Anna turned around to face the stranger, slightly surprised that he was still there. She had half expected her visitor to have left in the middle of her story.

"No, I never wanted to know what happened to him. Would you?"

"This still does not change anything," the soldier continued, "for your son is dead. She did not protect him."

"If my son is dead it is only because she could not protect him. You have to go now and try to save your family."

As the stranger turned to leave Anna called after him, "What is your name?"

"Simon," he answered.

"Hurry away, Simon, for I fear she is already watching us," advised Anna.

Anna returned to her chair and sat down. A single tear rolled down her cheek, the only discernible sign of her grief. A few minutes passed and the door opened again. This time it was someone she knew. It was Catherine, her son's wife, with their children. Catherine was panicking like everyone else, but she tried to compose herself and sat down beside her late husband's mother.

"Everyone says we should leave! My husband's dead! I think we should leave!" Catherine cried out, although Anna could hardly make out what she was saying, for she was rambling and blurting out incoherent sentences.

"If you leave, I cannot protect you. Isabella will kill you, and your children will be brought back to me. Don't you understand? All those people out there, they are all dead! No one is going to survive. She'll kill them all. She won't stop until everyone whom she thinks betrayed Vlad is dead."

"But…"

"Be quiet! I have to tell your children what's happening here. They have to understand."

Anna motioned for her grandchildren to sit in front of her and listen. They all looked so young, and she didn't want to tell them, but she felt she had to. Anna had waited until her son was eighteen before she had told him, but things had changed. Vlad Dracula was dead. Anna began speaking to her grandchildren.

"What I have to tell you is very important. It is part of our heritage. You may not understand, but you do have to listen."

Anna leaned across and took a stone from the wall; a book was hidden behind it. She took the book from its hiding place and opened it. On the first page was a letter from the writer of the book to the reader. Anna sat silently and read the letter to herself, as she had so many times before.

> Dear Reader,
> My name is Isabella Zelonka. I am not the Isabella that you will read about in this book, although my name will be mentioned. My mother's name was Katya. The last thing she asked me to do before she died was to write this book, so that generation after generation of our family could read it and know our family's story.
> I have pieced this book together from stories my mother told me, stories Isabella told me, and rumours and whispers that I have listened to ever since I was a child.
> My advice to any future reader of this book is to read it carefully and pay heed to every passage. For this book was not written as a historical account—it was written as a warning.
>
> Written in the year of our Lord Fifteen Hundred and Fifty.

Anna sighed and began to speak: "This book was written over three hundred years ago." She turned the page and began to read aloud.

※

The chapters of this novel that are written on the succeeding pages are not the passages that were written by Anna's family, but they are the story that was told to the author. What follows is Isabella's story, an account of how she became a Vampire. Anna's family gave testaments to these events, but those were destroyed more than one hundred years earlier.

TRANSYLVANIA
THE LAND BEYOND THE FOREST

CHAPTER TWO

Our story begins in a different time. Anna's ancestral book has not been written and fifty years have passed since Vlad Dracula collapsed on the mountain at the news of his wife's death.

The story of Anna's family begins in a village in the Carpathians. The village is bustling with activity because a young girl is about to be married and this young girl's name is Isabella.

Isabella was beautiful. No, more than that, Isabella was perfect. Her hair was raven. Her lips vermilion. Her eyes were the darkest green, like the forests in the north, and her skin had an ivory glow. She shone like a goddess among mere mortals.

Isabella was aware of her beauty—how could such a creature not be aware of her own elegance? Despite this, she was good-natured. She was proud, not arrogant, precocious, yet respectful and very, very, impetuous.

Isabella had few friends, not because of circumstance nor even because of lack of favour, but by choice. Isabella would not consider anyone she could not trust completely to be her friend. One of the few friends she did have was a young girl named Katya. The two girls had known each other and been friends all their lives.

Katya had been born with a crippled leg and when she was very young she could hardly walk. One day when Katya was only four years old she had lost her footing and fallen. The other children of the village were making fun of her and laughing, but one child came apart from the others, kneeled down beside Katya, wiped Katya's tears away with the hem of her dress, smiled and helped her up. This child was, of course, Isabella. She looked like an angel coming to rescue Katya from the harshness of the other children. On this day their friendship was formed and it would be an enduring friendship, and Isabella's loyalty to Katya would last for longer than either girl could possibly realise.

❈

Katya had recently been married and was on her way to help Isabella prepare for her wedding. When Katya arrived Isabella was ready and waiting for her.

"You're dressed already," Katya began.

"I couldn't sleep," replied Isabella.

"You look beautiful, Isabella. But, then again, you always do."

Isabella gave her the usual obligatory coy smile. "And you get bigger every time I see you!" she said enthusiastically.

"I know," Katya said patting her stomach. "If it is a girl I'll call her Isabella."

Isabella smiled at her friend. "You are so sweetly sentimental, Katya," she said, and then she looked over to where her grandfather's sword stood against the wall and began to speak again. "I wish he could have lived just another year longer."

Katya saw the sadness in Isabella's eyes. "He would have been proud of you today...you and Nicolae," Katya reassured her friend.

"I know. He was a good man and I miss him." A flower gently fell from Isabella's hair.

"Let me fix it," Katya said. Isabella picked it up and stretched out her arm to put the stray flower into Katya's hand. As she did so, the top of her dress fell away and her shoulder was revealed. Katya's expression darkened as she glanced at her friend's shoulder. "It seems..." Katya paused. "It seems...to be healing well." Isabella looked at Katya inquisitively. "Your shoulder," Katya gestured.

"Oh, yes, it does not look as bad now as it did. It will never heal completely. She has left me with a permanent scar."

Katya paused for a moment and then said, "In time you will forgive her."

Isabella's eyes narrowed and dulled, her lips tightened into a scowl. Katya became almost frightened by the look of hatred that came across her friend's face.

"I will never forgive her," Isabella said through clenched teeth. "She had everything I had always wanted and I never said a word. When I had something she wanted she tried maliciously to take it from me."

Katya was now sorry she had mentioned the scar and tried to change the subject.

"Do you remember the day we found Nicolae?" Katya asked. Isabella's smile gradually returned.

"Yes, it must be at least ten years ago now."

"Has Nicolae told you yet?" Katya inquired.

"Told me what?"

"Oh, nothing, he will tell you himself in time...Isabella, you don't still go up there, do you?"

"Oh, no, Katya, don't worry, of course not."

Katya's husband poked his head round the door of the room and said, "Are you planning on missing your own wedding?"

Katya looked at Isabella, caught hold of her hands and smiled. "Forget about the years that have passed," she said. "Look to the future. You have so much happiness ahead of you. You have to allow yourself to at least forget and be happy."

Isabella leaned forward, kissed Katya's cheek and left to go to her wedding.

During the ceremony Katya did not listen to her own advice and thought about the events that had shaped Isabella into the person Katya saw before her.

Isabella had been born nineteen and a half years before her wedding day. Her mother had died in childbirth. Although her father was devastated by his wife's death, he soon remarried and had another child with his second wife, Isabella's half-sister, Natasha.

Isabella did not have the happiest of childhoods. Her father could not bear to look at her because she reminded him of her mother, and he did not pay her much attention. On the other hand, he spoiled Natasha. Isabella's stepmother encouraged this. Her stepmother also encouraged Isabella to visit her grandfather as much as possible.

Isabella did not object to this, for she loved to visit her grandfather. Most of her happiest childhood memories included him. Isabella delighted in listening to the stories he told about fighting during the Crusades. Usually Isabella brought Katya with her to her grandfather's house; he lived about a mile outside Isabella's village and taught both girls how to read. They would walk to his house every day for a lesson.

On one such day, a beautiful day in the middle of summer about ten years before the wedding, the two girls were nine years old and they were at Isabella's grandfather's house as usual. They were agitated and fidgety and could not concentrate because of the heat. Isabella's grandfather was finally forced to tell them to go out and play because they certainly were not getting any reading done. The children went out and started to run about in the sun. Isabella's grandfather always kept a watchful eye on them. He was never too far behind them, especially when they went into the forest.

Katya and Isabella had decided to pick berries, but Isabella soon became weary of this and started to run away from her friend and grandfather. When she was just out of sight she crouched down and hid behind a bush of wild berries, and placed her hand over her mouth to stifle the sound of her own giggles. She could hear her grandfather and Katya calling to her. The calls were getting louder and louder as they approached; she decided to move further from the path. Isabella stood back up and started to run again. Katya spotted her and began to chase after Isabella.

Isabella continued to run for a few seconds more. She was not looking where she was going and she soon tripped and fell. She sat rubbing her leg, which had been slightly hurt by the fall. She looked over and was surprised to see that it was a young boy's leg that had caused her to lose her footing. She moved over to take a closer look.

The boy was lying unconscious on the forest floor. He had a bruise from a bump on his head. He looked a few years older than Isabella. By this time Katya and Isabella's grandfather had caught up.

"Don't ever run off like that again, Isabella!" her grandfather shouted at her. He had been frightened by his granddaughter straying from the path. "Do you hear me?" he continued when Isabella did not answer.

"Yes! Yes!" Isabella shouted back." Come and see what I have found."

Isabella's grandfather bent over to see what Isabella was pointing at through the foliage on the forest floor.

"Is he alive?" Katya asked. Isabella's grandfather gently positioned his hand just over the boy's mouth. He could feel the hot breath of the child on his hand and he answered Katya's question.

"Yes, he's alive." Isabella's grandfather stood erect and examined the ground surrounding the boy. He was looking for something and he soon found it. A small distance from them he could see two other people, a man and a woman, also lying on the forest floor. These two bodies had a more gaunt and deathlike appearance. Not wanting to alert the children to these other two, he said to them, "You wait here. I will go and see what I can find."

Isabella's grandfather walked over to the man and woman. Both were dead. They lay clutching each other. It looked as if they had just fallen asleep in each other's arms, never to wake up. Isabella's grandfather sighed in disgust. This had happened before. He returned quickly to the girls.

"Come on, I will carry him home."

"Did you find anyone?" Isabella asked.

"No...no one. Come on now, it's getting dark." Isabella's grandfather leaned down and checked the boy's neck. He sighed with relief this time. There were no marks on him. This boy had escaped the fate that had befallen his parents.

When they got back to the cottage Isabella's grandfather put the foundling down on his bed.

Isabella was watching her grandfather and asked, "Will he be all right?"

"Yes, I think so. You girls can stay here tonight and look after him. I am going out for a while but I will be back soon."

"Wait a minute, who will look after us?" Katya asked hopefully.

"I'll send Dragen into look after you." Katya smiled in approval and Isabella's grandfather left the house.

Dragen was chopping wood. He was only fifteen but he already helped his father and mother a great deal.

"Where's your father?" Isabella's grandfather called over to Dragen, who stopped what he was doing and approached the older man.

"He's in the house, Alexei," said Dragen.

"All right, I want to talk to him. Could you go and look after the girls for a while? I don't like leaving them alone for too long." Dragen smiled, nodded and walked towards Alexei's home.

Alexei knocked on the door of their house. Dragen's mother opened it. Alexei went in and shut the door behind him. He glanced around the room to check that Dragen's father and mother were the only two there.

"There's no one else here, is there?" Alexei inquired, just to make sure.

"The children are asleep in the other room," answered Sorin, Dragen's father.

"It's happened again," Alexei continued.

"God help us," whispered Dragen's mother, Dacia, under her breath.

"Is it any one from the village?" Sorin asked.

"No, two Gypsies, but this time there is a survivor."

"A survivor?"

"Yes, a small boy."

"Does he know anything? What did he say happened to him!" asked Sorin in desperation.

"Isabella found him. He has been knocked unconscious. He has not said anything yet."

"Did Isabella see anything?" Dacia asked, worried that the little girl might be robbed of her innocence too soon.

"No...we'll see if the boy knows anything when he wakes up." Alexei gestured towards Sorin. "Come on, we have to go and bury them."

Dacia lighted a pair of torches and gave them to the two men. Sorin picked up two shovels and both he and Alexei started to walk towards the woods.

"What do you think is doing this, Alexei?" Sorin asked. "How many bodies have we found this year?"

"This will make ten."

"Why do we bury them?"

"Do you think the murders will stop if we don't bury them? This has been happening for nearly forty years?"

"But we are helping whoever it is to cover their tracks," Alexei sighed.

"We bury the bodies so that the children are not robbed of their childhood. They will learn soon enough about death and despair. Why should they start now?"

"They say it's Vlad," Sorin continued.

"They say it's a lot of things," Alexei answered. "I don't believe it is. How could it be? If he's alive he must be in his seventies by now. Besides, if he lives anywhere I doubt he lives there." Alexei pointed towards the castle. "I have not seen a lighted candle shining down from that place in forty years."

"Then what is it...wolves?"

"If it were wolves there would be signs of a struggle, claw marks, teeth marks, something. I really don't know what it is, but when I was younger and in the army I met many well-travelled men, some from as far away as India and China. They had seen many strange things. Some told me about large birds that would swoop down at night and drink the blood of animals while they slept. Sometimes they even attacked men. Maybe that's the explanation."

The two men soon found the bodies. They buried them and left a small cross and garland of roses to mark the grave. They returned home and would not talk about what they had just done until they had to do it again.

When Alexei entered his home all was quiet. Dragen, Katya and Isabella had fallen asleep waiting for his return. Katya was sleeping on

Isabella's bed. Isabella had fallen asleep watching over the little boy she had found. She was curled up in a chair beside her grandfather's bed.

Isabella's grandfather sat down on the bed beside the boy. This movement caused the boy to stir and open his eyes.

"Ah, so you're awake," Alexei whispered. The boy lay frozen, still, as if he was afraid to move. He lay there motionless just staring up at Alexei. "Do you understand what I am saying?" The boy opened his mouth and tried to speak but he could not make any sound. "Do you remember what happened?" The child shook his head in response. "Do you remember anything from your life before this?" The boy again shook his head and tears welled up in his eyes.

Alexei squeezed the boy's hand to reassure him. "Well you can stay here with me." The boy looked over at the little girl sleeping in the chair beside him. "That's my granddaughter. Do you think she is pretty?" The orphan nodded. "Let me give you some advice, don't ever tell her—she knows it already. Her name is Isabella. You can call her Bella. I think she would like that." Alexei leaned over and pushed the hair out of the boy's eyes so he could look at him. "We shall have to give you a name until you start to remember." Alexei paused for thought. "A long time ago a man taught me to read and his name was Nicolae. I think that is as good a name as any. Now, get some sleep for it will be morning soon."

Alexei waited for the boy to go back to sleep. He then picked up Isabella and placed her on the bed beside Nicolae. Isabella rolled over in her sleep and rested her arm gently on Nicolae's shoulder and then nestled her head into his back. Alexei smiled and sat down in the chair, soon to fall asleep himself.

The next morning Alexei was not the first to awaken. Nicolae and Isabella were already both awake and he could hear his granddaughter chattering away. Alexei kept his eyes shut and remained still, wanting to hear what Isabella was saying but not wanting to let her know he was listening just yet.

"Do you remember how you came to be in the woods?" Isabella asked. Nicolae shook his head. "Never mind, my grandfather said that might happen. He says that sometimes when people get bumps on the head, they forget things. My grandfather knows everything like that; he is very clever. He has taught Katya and me how to read. We can teach you how to read. Would you like that?"

Nicolae made no response to this question. Isabella was talking so quickly that it was taking the boy's entire concentration just to keep up with what she was saying.

"Anyway," Isabella continued babbling, "my grandfather fought in the Crusades. He tells wonderful stories about them, of great battles and mighty warriors and far off places. My favourite stories are about Prince Vlad Dracula—he lives up in that castle at the top of the forest. But we're not allowed to go up there."

At this remark Alexei finally interrupted. "Stop pestering the boy, Isabella," he scolded.

Isabella glanced briefly at her grandfather. Outraged by his remark, she turned

back towards Nicolae defiantly.

"Am I pestering you?" Isabella asked and Nicolae shook his head in response. Isabella looked triumphantly back at her grandfather and said, "See!"

The weeks passed and gradually Nicolae's voice returned to him, but his memory did not. Summer changed to autumn and autumn darkened into winter. The days shortened and the nights grew longer. There had been no more murders since those of Nicolae's parents. But the people of the village waited with uneasy anticipation. They had heard rumours about killings all over the Carpathians but they had chosen to ignore them, putting these rumours in the back of their minds and going about their everyday lives hoping that the most recent murder would be the last, but secretly dreading the unrelenting darkness of the winter months.

No one understood the murders. Wild boars and wolves would occasionally carry people off, but this was different. The only signs of violence were two tiny puncture marks and, sometimes, a few drops of blood.

People surmised that the deaths were caused by the loss of blood, but how the victims were losing this blood and who or what was taking it, no one knew.

Everyone had a theory. Some said it was snakes, others thought wolves but the most prevalent theory was that it was Vlad. People had seen him return to the castle after learning of his wife's death, but they had never seen him leave. There had been rumours that the Hungarian King, Mathias Corvinus, had imprisoned him. There were also stories that he was in the castle when his wife had committed suicide and left the castle with his son after she died, but Alexei knew this not true. Vlad had become a legend during his lifetime and people wanted to believe that even after death he had remained living, killing as he did during his life. Alexei could only believe that the man he had met only once was worthy of the title of nobleman. Alexei would defend Vlad's memory until there was no breath left in his body.

Alexei had returned to his village a month after Vlad heard of his wife's death. He had brought his friend Nicolae with him. They had met once again soon after Alexei's encounter with Vlad. Nicolae soon realised that Alexei was a good man and the two had become close friends.

When Vlad's army had disbanded, Nicolae had planned to join another army but Alexei and Nicolae both knew that Nicolae would become remorseless, cold-blooded, beyond redemption if he joined another army. So Alexei insisted that he come home with him. Nicolae eventually agreed.

Alexei made Nicolae welcome in his home and in exchange for this Nicolae taught Alexei to read. All the books that Isabella had learned from were originally Nicolae's.

The murders had started infrequently at first. One here, one there, but the victims had all been Gypsies. People presumed that they had frozen to death or died of old age. They took little notice of the tiny puncture marks on the necks of the dead bodies.

The sporadic murders of the Gypsies continued for the next two years. The people of the villages paid no attention to them. They did not really care if a gypsy lived or died. Unfortunately for the villagers, they soon paid for their complacency.

A child disappeared from the village, a young, healthy little girl. The people of the village searched night and day in the woods. During their search some of the villagers went missing themselves. After some time passed they found all the bodies, one by one.

The first body they found was that of the child. She was found face down in the ground. When they examined her they found a few drops of blood leading to two tiny lacerations on the child's neck. One of the villagers remarked that he had seen a wound like this on one of the dead Gypsies but had thought nothing of it.

The villagers became angry. They wanted explanations, and they wanted retribution. They needed someone to blame for the tragedy and they chose Vlad. They had heard rumours that he had gone mad, for not only had he lost his wife, he had lost his child as well. Stories flourished about him becoming a recluse, skulking around in the darkened hallways of his castle, completely alone. By the end of a few weeks nearly everyone blamed him for the murders.

Alexei protested this, but Nicolae was not so sure. For Nicolae knew what losing your family could do to a person. He and a few villagers decided to go up to the castle to see for themselves whether Vlad was still there.

They waited for darkness and then started the short trek up to the castle. Their families watched from below. As they got closer to the castle all that the families could see were flickering flames from the torches their husbands and sons carried. The forms of the men were obscured by the darkness and by the dense forest. When the exploration party got within a hundred yards of the castle entrance, a few torches seemed to be suddenly snuffed out and the light from the others darted about as if the carriers were running away from something. Within a few minutes all the torches were out. The families could see and hear nothing of the men who had walked up to the castle, but they feared the worst.

Weeks passed as they slowly recovered the bodies of the men. Nicolae was the last to be found and like all the others his face showed panic and terror. The villagers had no idea what had happened, but the expressions on the faces of the dead convinced them that they did not want to know.

The anger of the people now turned into fear and they refused to talk about what had happened. Forty years drifted past in silence. The murders still continued and the fear remained as strong.

Alexei had been grief-stricken by the death of his friend and had always said if he ever had a son that he would call him Nicolae.

Unfortunately, he had never been blessed with a son. His wife, like his daughter, had died in childbirth. However, unlike his son-in-law, he had loved his own child and enjoyed watching her grow up into a beautiful girl. Isabella was growing more like her mother every day, although even Alexei could see at an early stage that his daughter's beauty would have paled in comparison.

<hr />

The years went by quickly after the day Isabella found Nicolae in the woods. Isabella and Nicolae became inseparable and more often than not, Katya and Dragen accompanied them.

Isabella's pretty girlish looks had now matured into beautiful, delicate, fine features. Although her outward appearance was without flaw, her behaviour was quite different. She had grown into a hot-tempered, mischievous teenager with a strong influence over her group of friends. Her influence was not as strong with Nicolae. He would always be the one to chastise her, the one to tell her she'd gone too far, although, sometimes, even Nicolae could not resist her charms. He, like the others, would often placate Isabella and would also agree to do her bidding.

Whenever the group got into trouble it was always Isabella's fault and she would usually take all the blame. But then again, any time the group got out of trouble it was always due to Nicolae's exertions.

This leads us to another summer's day. This day would change the course of Isabella's life, or should it be said that it would change the course of her death, but she would not realise it at the time.

Katya and Isabella were then both sixteen, walking together along the path that bordered the forest leading to Alexei's house. On this day Isabella was unusually quiet and thoughtful; she could not stop looking up at the wooded hill which led up to Vlad's castle. Isabella's laconic attitude was making Katya nervous.

"What are you thinking about?" Katya asked.

"Do you ever wonder, Katya...if he's still alive?"

"Who?"

Isabella pointed up towards the castle and smiled. "Vlad Dracula," she said. "My grandfather tells us about when he was in the Crusades but he never tells us about what happened afterwards. Do you not wonder about him sometimes?"

"No, absolutely not, and neither should you!" Katya scolded, fearing what Isabella was leading up to.

"Well, I was thinking since we are surprising my grandfather and Nicolae today, they are not expecting us."

Katya looked at Isabella suspiciously.

Isabella smiled. "Why don't we go up and see for ourselves?" she said.

"No, Isabella! We have always been warned never to go near the castle! We're not even supposed to go into the woods on our own!"

"Oh, where's your sense of adventure. We can be back in a few hours and no one will be any the wiser."

Katya knew it was useless to say no to Isabella. She always got her way in the end. "Well, at least let's go and get Nicolae."

"No, Katya! You know he is too good; he would never allow us to go up there and he would probably tell my grandfather what I was thinking of doing. Then I would never get to go! Now, come on!" Isabella had already left the path and was running towards the woods. Katya took a long, drawn-out breath and reluctantly trailed after her.

When Isabella reached the castle she stopped to catch her breath and waited for Katya, who had never quite kept up with her. Sometimes Isabella would forget about Katya's crippled leg and expect her to run just as fast as she could. Katya did not mind this. She liked people to forget about her leg and treat her as if she was just the same as anyone else, but it seemed Isabella was the only one who really did forget. Isabella sat on a large, loose stone that had fallen from one of the broken walls and waited for her friend to catch up. She glanced around the castle that time had ruined.

She was sitting in the middle of a large courtyard. On either side of her were two large, tall brick walls, each with hollow archways that led to what appeared to be passageways. The ground was paved with cobblestones that like the walls were weather-beaten and broken. In front of her was a third large wall with a wooden door in the centre and around the door was a line of smooth stone. Carved on these stones there seemed to be some ancient religious symbols.

When Katya eventually arrived she let out a stifled scream.

"What is it?" asked Isabella who had been startled by the noise. Katya pointed to one of the decaying battlements.

"Look! Someone is watching us." Isabella looked up. The sun was shining in Isabella's eyes and at first it looked as if it was a man but then a large cloud covered the sun, the sky darkened and the vision seemed to mist over and when it became clear again it looked like a wild dog.

"It's just a dog. Calm down, Katya."

"I could have sworn it was a man...it looked like a man," Katya said, baffled. As she watched, the dog disappeared from the battlements.

"Come on, let's see if we can get in," said Isabella.

"Isabella, I think we should leave. You know, by the look of this place it has been abandoned for years."

Isabella was hardly listening to Katya. She was looking at the carvings surrounding the door. Some of them had been broken but the breaks were clean, as if they had been broken them purposely. Isabella pushed on the door.

"It won't budge."

This time Katya was not listening. She had been distracted and started to tug on Isabella's sleeve. "Look," Katya whispered.

Isabella raised her head. The dog that they had seen on the battlements was now in the courtyard watching them. The two girls were now frightened because they now realised that it was a wolf.

"Isabella! We have to leave now!" Katya whispered firmly.

"How can we? He's blocking the entrance," Isabella said, as she kneeled down and pulled Katya down with her. "He is probably more afraid of us than we are of him," Isabella continued.

"Oh, is that right? Isabella, are you mad...?"

"SSSHH!" Isabella stretched out her hand and started to speak softly to the wolf. "We won't hurt you." The wolf approached them slowly and started to lick Isabella's outstretched hand.

Katya sighed with relief and said, "I would have had to see that to believe it. Only you could charm a wolf."

Isabella smiled and began to stroke the wolf. The wolf soon left the pair and went down one of the passageways.

"Let's see where he's going. He must know a way in; how else did he get down from the battlements?" Isabella followed the wolf and Katya reluctantly pursued them. The three walked down one of the passageways leading from the courtyard. Close to the end of it was a door lying open, off its hinges.

Isabella, Katya and the wolf all went through the doorway into the main reception hall. The hall like the rest of the castle had seen better days, but they could tell it was once magnificently opulent. There were several portraits on the spacious walls. The one that caught Isabella's eyes was of a beautiful, sad-looking woman. It had been slashed with a sword and it hung in the centre of the hall over a palatial fireplace. A chair sat opposite and a fur rug lay on the stone floor beside the chair. In the middle of the hall was a venerable stone staircase and around the hall were several other doors.

Isabella ran around the hall trying to open each one, but all of them were either locked or jammed shut. Katya stood just watching her friend.

"Isabella, it's obvious that this place has not been lived in for years. Everything is covered in dust and cobwebs."

Isabella ran upstairs, not paying much attention to her friend. Katya and the wolf followed behind her. Isabella ran around to each door and again none of them could be opened. When she got to the last door she pounded her fists against it and dropped to the floor holding her face in her hands.

"What were you hoping to find here?" Katya asked her friend.

"Oh, nothing I suppose," Isabella said, completely disheartened. "It was just a foolish idea."

"Did you expect to find Vlad? Even if he was up here, he'd be an old man like your grandfather."

"I know that...I knew as soon as I entered the courtyard that he would not be here. But..."

"But what?"

"What I was really hoping for was a library."

"A library?"

"My grandfather has only a few books and I have read them all, but Vlad was the sort of man who would have had a grand library full of books on every subject. I want to teach myself things. I want to learn about other places, I know I will probably never leave the village, but to read about the world is almost as good as seeing it."

"Any books Vlad would have owned would have been in his own language."

"I know a little bit of Wallachian. I am sure I could teach myself the rest."

Katya sighed; Isabella always had an answer to everything.

"Vlad would have taken any books with him when he abandoned this place," Katya answered.

"I suppose you are right."

"It's getting dark, and if anyone found us in the woods at night we really would be in serious trouble."

Isabella started to descend the stairs. The wolf that had always remained close to the two girls started to bark.

"We nearly forgot about him," Isabella said. "Maybe he wants to come with us." Isabella climbed back up the steps and kneeled down beside him, stroking his fur as she did so. The wolf gratefully reciprocated her show of affection by licking her hand.

"Isabella, it's a wolf," Katya said dryly.

"Oh well, we will soon come up and see you again," Isabella said to the wolf as if it could understand her.

"We won't," said Katya.

"Then he's coming with us."

"And who's going to look after him?"

"Nicolae will."

"And where are you going to say you found him?"

"I'll think of something," Isabella said, pulling herself up using a curtain that was beside the wolf. The curtain could not support her weight and fell down to uncover one final door. Isabella looked at Katya, forgetting about their minor argument, and smiled.

"Well, go ahead, try it," Katya urged.

Isabella was filled with fresh excitement as she pushed on the door and this one opened to reveal her sought-after library. It was better than she had hoped for. There were books in her own language, books in Wallachian, Dracula's language, and others in German, Russian, and Hungarian. Some books had several different translations; she would be able to teach herself different languages and learn about the world she thought she would never see.

While Isabella was staring in wonderment at the books Katya was steadily growing more and more anxious.

"We have to go," she said.

"All right," Isabella answered. She grabbed some books from the shelves and the two girls left the castle. The wolf followed them for a short time and then disappeared.

Isabella fell asleep that night reading one of the books she had taken from Vlad's library. The next morning her stepmother woke her up by yelling her name.

"What is it?" Isabella yelled back to her.

"Come here. I want to talk to you." She went into the kitchen where her stepmother was cooking breakfast.

"What's that?" Isabella's stepmother pointed at the book Isabella had fallen asleep reading. Isabella's heart sank, although she did not outwardly show her state of mind. She had not taken the books to her grandfather's cottage because she knew he would realise where she had gotten them and he would be very upset with her. He had always told her never to go up to the castle. He had always been strict and unrelenting on this point. Isabella had always wondered why. She did not know that the last person Alexei had known to go up there had died.

"What does it look like?" Isabella retorted.

"I know it's a book, Isabella. I want to know if you can read it," Her stepmother said.

Isabella was now relieved, for she realised what this was about. Her stepmother did not know she could read. Of course she didn't, for Isabella spent as little time as possible in this house. Her stepmother and sister treated her with little more than contempt and her father ignored her. He could not bear to look at her, let alone show her any affection. Isabella to him was just a perfect picture of painful memories he would rather have soon forgotten. One of Isabella's earliest memories was of her father saying to her, "Your mother died so you could live! You stole your mother from me and I cannot stand the sight of you!"

Isabella's thoughts were broken by her stepmother's shrill voice.

"Can you read?"

"Yes!" Isabella shouted back.

"Who taught you?"

"Alexei!" At this moment Isabella's father entered the room.

"Guy, did you know she could read?"

"Her mother could," Guy answered. Isabella's father did not look at her. He never looked at her.

"Well, I want Natasha to learn. I'm not having her being able to do something that my daughter can't. So you can take her with you to Alexei's from now on."

Isabella's sister entered the room. Isabella watched as her father kissed and hugged his younger daughter. She stood silently as her sister paraded her father's affections in front of her. Natasha took great delight in hurting her sister, a trait she had learned well from both her father and mother. The two sisters had a mutual disliking for each other from as far back as either one could remember, but they had reached an understanding.

Natasha had one day referred to Katya as an ugly cripple. Isabella had caught her sister by the arm and told her if she said anything like that again, Katya would not be the only cripple in the village. Her sister's firmness and the strong almost painful grip she had on her arm made Natasha realise that she meant every word she said. Since then, Natasha would only confront or try to upset her sister when there was someone around to protect her from Isabella's wrath, hence, her ready display and indulgence with her parents.

Isabella hated the idea of Natasha coming with her to her grandfather's. The only time she was really happy was when she was nowhere near her family. Isabella did not protest her stepmother's wish—she knew it was pointless to do that and the more determined her malicious sister would be to go to with her. Isabella would just have to think of some other way of getting out of taking her sister.

The next two years passed more slowly for Isabella. At first she took Natasha with her every day, but after a while she started to get up early and leave the house before anyone else was awake. This would also give her a chance to go up to the castle to get more books, and while Isabella was teaching herself different languages and learning as much as she possibly could, Natasha was making little progress. She really did not have any interest in learning to read. Her main interest seemed to be Nicolae, which made Isabella even more miserable.

During this time Katya had married Dragen and she had stopped coming with Isabella to Alexei's. Isabella missed her friend, but she was happy for her.

Isabella was now nineteen and no one could equal her in beauty. She received quite a bit of attention from the young men of the village, but she was not interested. She only had eyes for Nicolae but he, thus far, had expressed no sign that he returned her affections.

Isabella was still trying to avoid having her sister accompany her on her visits to her grandfather and had planned to get up early and sneak out of the house to avoid Natasha. This would also give her time to get some more books from Dracula's castle. Her plan did not work. Natasha had woken before her and was already waiting outside.

"Hurry up," Isabella shouted when she caught sight of her sister. On the way to Alexei's they met Katya on her way to visit her parents. Natasha hurried on without stopping to talk to Katya, but Isabella stopped.

"What's wrong with your sister? And why is she in such a hurry?" Katya asked.

"She wants to get to Alexei's to see Nicolae."

"Oh."

"She thinks I'm stupid," Isabella rejoined, staring at her sister as she practically ran ahead of them down the path to Nicolae's house.

"Why, what's your sister trying to do to you now?"

"She flirts with Nicolae while I'm there."

"I know lots of girls who flirt with Nicolae and they don't bother you as much."

"But Nicolae's so nice to her."

"Nicolae's nice to everyone. I would not feel threatened by her. Nicolae loves you, surely you know that."

"I don't know anything of the kind."

"Why don't you ask him?"

"And give him the satisfaction of knowing that I cared one way or the other?"

"Isabella," Katya scolded. "You know Nicolae could have been married years ago to anyone he wanted. But..."

"I'll talk to you later," Isabella cut Katya off. She never liked being scolded or told what to do, especially when the other person was right.

She soon caught up with her sister. "It was very rude of you to ignore Katya like that."

"She's not my friend," said Natasha.

"That's not the point. Show some respect."

There was a brief silence. Then Natasha asked, "How long has she been married now?"

Isabella wondered what her sister was working up to but answered her question.

"Her wedding day was a month ago today and she looked beautiful."

"As beautiful as she can look, I suppose," said Natasha.

Isabella bit her tongue. She was determined not to let her sister know she was annoying her.

"I think I'll get married soon," said Natasha.

"Oh, really...and who's the lucky man?"

"I think you can guess," Natasha said.

It took all Isabella's restraint to keep her hands off her sister. She stopped walking beside her and held back a few steps while Natasha carried on. Isabella slipped into the woods without her sister seeing her. She took a shortcut through the forest and arrived at her grandfather's house long before Natasha. When Isabella arrived there she pounded on the door. Nicolae opened it.

"Where's my grandfather?" Isabella shouted.

"He's gone hunting."

Isabella pushed by Nicolae, knocking him against the wall. Nicolae smiled; he knew as soon as he saw Isabella that she was furious about something.

"My sister will be here soon."

"I'll leave the door open for her."

Isabella looked up at Nicolae. "Will you be glad to see her?"

Nicolae shrugged in answer to Isabella's question.

"She seems quite taken with you," Isabella said.

Nicolae started to laugh. "Are you jealous?" he asked in disbelief.

"Jealous! Why would I be jealous? It is no concern of mine what you do. I think you two deserve each other."

"You are...you're jealous," Nicolae said as he continued to laugh at Isabella. This infuriated her even more. She grabbed a cup that was sitting on the table beside her and threw it at Nicolae. The cup just missed his head.

"Are you trying to kill me?" he protested. "Now, just calm down," he said with a sigh and then he went on, "You must know, Isabella, I realise who Natasha is and I know what she has put you through. I love you, Isabella...no one else. I always have and I always will. Even though you are hot tempered and vain."

Isabella tried to make some rebuke to Nicolae's last comment but he pressed his finger to her lips to silence her. "You treat the people you love with kindness and generosity and I have always loved you for that and although you are far from perfect, I love you despite your faults. Whether or not you are more beautiful than Natasha is irrelevant to me. You are the person I love."

Natasha arrived and heard him speaking. She stayed back and started to listen secretly to the couple's conversation.

"As far as your sister is concerned I would not look twice at her. Not when I could look at you," Nicolae said to Isabella.

Hearing this made Natasha almost unbearably envious of her sister, but she remained quiet and kept listening.

"Alexei once told me never to tell you how beautiful you were, but I am telling you now!" Nicolae held Isabella in front of him and stared into her eyes and continued, "You are beautiful Isabella. I could never look at anyone else or think of marrying anyone else." Nicolae took Isabella's face in his hands and kissed her tenderly.

"Why didn't you tell me this before?" Isabella asked. She was completely relieved and overjoyed by this revelation.

"I always assumed you knew. I'm flattered really that you were jealous of Natasha. But she could never compare to you."

Natasha then made them aware that she had arrived. Isabella looked superciliously at her sister and started to speak to her in a disdainful tone: "Wonderful news, Natasha...Nicolae and I are going to be married."

Nicolae would usually object to this sort of behaviour from Isabella, but today he would let her have her little moment.

"I am happy for you," Natasha said, her face twisted in a sneer.

"I can see you are," Isabella responded with irony.

"I think it's time for my lesson," Natasha said.

"Alexei's not here," Isabella answered.

"You usually teach me, anyway."

"I'll leave you to it," said Nicolae as he left the room. Natasha went over to get a book. Isabella just watched her sister. Isabella was enjoying her little triumph. She never got the better of her sister and she was revelling in this moment. Natasha looked up at her.

"What are you smiling at?" Natasha asked her sister. "You're enjoying this."

"Enjoying what?" asked Isabella calmly. Natasha put the book back on the shelf and went over to sit beside the fire. She lifted a poker and started stabbing at the hot embers.

"So, Nicolae does not think I am as beautiful as you."

"I think his words were that you could not be compared to me."

"My parents think I am just as attractive as you are."

"Have they ever said that to you? Have they ever looked at you and said you are just a beautiful as I am?" Isabella asked. She turned around and sat down. "I would not worry about it, Natasha. I am sure your graciousness, charm and wit will see you through. I am sure you will find quite a...decent husband."

Natasha did not know what graciousness meant but she knew her sister was insulting her and at this final remark. Natasha took the now red-hot poker and leaped towards Isabella with it.

"I wonder how attractive Nicolae will think you are with a scar across your beautiful face!" Natasha shouted.

Isabella was not expecting this sudden outburst, but she managed to spring up out of the way so that the poker only hit her shoulder. At first she felt no pain, but as the poker struck her skin a maddening rage swept over her. This rage had built up in Isabella over the years. Natasha had continually tormented Isabella by rubbing her father's affections towards her in Isabella's face; every gift Natasha had received from their father she would parade in front of Isabella. Now, just because of Nicolae's rejection, Natasha wanted to disfigure her sister for life. The hatred that Isabella had suppressed for seventeen years, since Natasha had been born, finally welled up into a raging fury.

Isabella snatched the poker from her sister's hand and was about to strike her back with it when she suddenly stopped, not because she had regained her senses but because Nicolae had put his arms around her waist and pulled her back. Isabella was now wrestling, trying to loosen herself from Nicolae's strong grip.

"Go home and don't ever come back!" Nicolae shouted at Natasha. Natasha just sat there staring at her sister, afraid to move. "Get out of here or I will set her loose on you."

With this, Natasha ran for her life. Isabella struggled to get free but she soon realised that Nicolae would not let her go until she had calmed down. The pain from Isabella's wound started to reach her. Nicolae loosened his grip, sat Isabella down, and started to dress her wound. He sat beside her and waited for Alexei to return. Isabella, who had been silent since her sister had left, started to speak.

"I would have killed her."

"No, you wouldn't have, Isabella; you would have regained your senses in time."

Isabella knew this was not true but she did not argue with him. Nicolae was always sure that Isabella's values were the same as his own and she never wanted to disappoint him.

"What do you think she will tell my father?"

"It doesn't matter. Alexei is your real father. He has been a father to us both." Isabella nestled her head on Nicolae's shoulder and fell asleep. After watching her for a while, Nicolae fell asleep, too. They were both awakened by a knock on the door a few hours later. It was Dragen's father.

"Come with me. Alexei has collapsed," He said.

Isabella ran out the door after Dragen's father. Nicolae grabbed Isabella's coat and followed. When they reached Alexei it was too late…his heart had stopped beating. Isabella fell to the ground and wept and Nicolae placed her coat around her shoulders.

A few months later Isabella and Nicolae were married.

Anna stopped reading. A silence had come over the village. Anna knew by the silence that Isabella had returned. She continued to read…

VROLOK
VAMPIRE

CHAPTER THREE

The ensuing months subsequent to Isabella's wedding were the happiest of her life. She stayed well away from her family, and her family stayed well away from her.

Isabella soon became pregnant and looked forward auspiciously to the birth of her child. Unfortunately for Isabella, her happiness was to be momentarily interrupted by a visit from her stepmother.

Nicolae answered the door that day and was surprised to see Adriana, Isabella's stepmother, but welcomed her into his and Isabella's home. She came in and sat down, not being able to bring her gaze up from the floor. She sat for a few minutes in silence trying to gather up the courage to speak. When Isabella saw her she noticed how tired and pale she looked; this was a woman who had suffered and the harshness of life had broken her, but Isabella was far from sympathetic. Sensing the hostility that Isabella felt towards her, Isabella's stepmother took a deep breath to compose herself and began to speak.

"Your father is asking for you," she said, her voice wavering as she spoke. Every word was hard for her to utter. Isabella was amazed at what her stepmother was starting to say to her.

"My father...I don't understand. Why have you come here? Why are you telling me this?" retorted Isabella.

"I want you to go and see him!" Isabella's stepmother said, her voice seeming more determined.

"Go and see him," Isabella said in disbelief. "Go and see him," she repeated, "I don't...."

"Isabella, he is dying. Your father is dying! Doesn't that mean anything to you?" Adriana said, her voice breaking.

"Why should it? It certainly would mean nothing to—"

"Isabella!" Nicolae silenced his wife. Isabella's stepmother looked at Nicolae with a subtle look of gratitude and continued to talk to her stepdaughter.

"I did not come here to argue with you. If it were up to me I would not be here at all. Your father asked me to come and ask you to go and see him."

"Why?" Isabella asked. "Why now?"

"I don't know. All I can say is that a priest came to see him yesterday and told him he had to make his peace with this world." Isabella's stepmother rose. "Decide for yourself. It's up to you and your own conscience. I have tried...my conscience is clear." Isabella's stepmother left the house without saying another word.

"How dare you talk to me like that in front of her!" Isabella hissed when her stepmother had left.

"Show some compassion, Bella—her husband is dying." Nicolae's words managed to silence Isabella again, which was quite an achievement. Only Nicolae would have been able to silence his wife twice in such a short period of time. Nicolae paused for a moment and then said, "I think you should go and see him." This broke Isabella's momentary silence.

"I can't believe it. I can't believe you want me to go and see him. I can't even believe she dared to come here and ask my forgiveness for him. Of all the people in the world, my father wants my forgiveness."

"Isabella, he is your father," Nicolae admonished.

"My father! How can you say that? He isn't my father! You said it yourself—Alexei was the only father I ever had. I would have been better off if he had died along with my mother."

"Alexei would have wanted you to forgive him."

Isabella threw Nicolae an icy look at this comment. How could he say such a thing to her?

"That's unfair, using Alexei's memory to pressure me into going."

"That is not what I'm doing and you know it," Nicolae scolded.

"I don't know anything of the sort and anyway, how could you possibly know what Alexei would have wanted me to do?"

"You know yourself that Alexei would have wanted you to forgive him, Isabella. Now, answer truthfully, what do you think Alexei would have wanted you to do?"

Isabella made no response.

Nicolae left the room and returned with part of a letter. He handed it to Isabella.

"Alexei left this for me. I want you to read it. He wrote it just before he died. Read it, it's important, Bella."

Isabella began to read.

> Nicolae
> I am writing you this letter because I think my life is coming to an end. I have started to get pains in my chest. They are becoming more and more frequent and every attack is worse than the last.

Isabella looked up from the letter. "He knew he was dying."
"Read the rest," answered Nicolae.
Isabella continued reading:

> I have watched you grow up, Nicolae, and I am proud of you. You have become a fine man and there is not a malicious bone in your body. I know you and Isabella will eventually start to make a life together. I want you to know you have my blessing. I have a few misgivings, though.
> I love Isabella. She is my granddaughter. She is a beautiful, intelligent girl who is kind and gracious to those she loves and who love her in return. Yet she can be malicious and spiteful, and I see darkness within her and it concerns me greatly. Isabella does not begin to hate without just cause, but when she does it's like a poison within her. It fills her with a bitterness and she has no capacity for forgiveness, and this is what concerns me.
> The way she talks about her father has always been foremost in my mind. Her father has treated her shamefully and definitely deserves her enmity. My daughter, Isabella's mother Clara, was different. She in lots of ways was like you, Nicolae. She saw goodness in everyone she knew, including Isabella's father, Guy.
> The first time I noticed him was when they were both children. Guy was watching Clara from

a distance and he continued to do this until they were both adults.

Guy himself was handsome, but he was quiet and I soon realised that it was not gentleness that kept him silent, but harshness. I could have counted the number of times that I saw him smile on my fingers.

My daughter Clara, on the other hand, was a happy child. Her smile would light up a room and I suppose I thought she could smile enough for both of them. One thing worried me about my daughter, though. She was always a weak child, always prone to ill health.

Sometimes it even astonished me how long she held on to her life. Clara was never strong like Isabella. If she even got caught out in the rain she would fall ill for days.

For years Guy watched over her, always keeping his distance, like some sort of guardian angel. If she fell, he would always be there to pick her up and then disappear before she had a chance to thank him. He loved her. He possibly loved her too much, if you can imagine such a thing.

In the winter of Clara's eighteenth year she took it upon herself to care for a sick child in the village. The child's mother was ill also and so could not care for the baby herself. Come rain, hail or storm my daughter would get up early in the morning and go to care for the child and its mother. Every day Guy would come to the house and beg me not to let her go. I told him there was nothing I could do about it. She was doing what she thought was right and I respected her for it. I was also worried about her, for I knew she was not strong to begin with and the exposure to illness could have a serious detrimental effect on her own health. Every day when she returned home she was becoming increasingly more frail. Her eyes had become dark and dull. She had become frighteningly thin, yet she still insisted on going. Isabella's wilfulness and stubbornness she gets from her mother.

When I challenged her about going there she would not shout defiantly at me the way Isabella would. Clara would talk quietly to bring me around to her way of thinking, through gentle persuasion. I don't think I ever had the heart to say no to Clara. She was the best person I have ever known and if she had lived I am sure her gentleness would have been passed on to Isabella.

Clara's health still deteriorated and I continued to worry until eventually one evening on the way home she collapsed and, as always, Guy was there to pick her up. Guy must have carried her for three miles; heaven knows where he found the strength.

Guy arrived at the house. He was soaked to the skin and gasping for breath. He set Clara down on the bed gently and then raced to get the doctor.

Clara lay there on the bed completely motionless. Her skin was deathly pale and her lips were blue with the cold. When the doctor arrived he thought she was already dead. He felt for a heartbeat; then he told Guy and me that she was still alive but just barely and he doubted that she would last the night.

A rage swept over Guy. He wrenched the doctor away from her and flung him out of the house. Guy then started frantically to build up a fire. When he had finished this he sat down on the bed beside Clara and started to rub at her skin, trying desperately to get some heat back into her body.

Clara survived the night and the next day. A week passed and she was still alive. Guy had stayed with her constantly when he wasn't keeping the fire going— he just sat watching her. Praying, hoping, willing her to live. When the news reached us that the child that Clara was caring for had died, I heard Guy whisper under his breath that the child deserved to die. I wanted to chastise him for this, tell him he was being unfair and that it was a noxious thing to say, but I could see how much he cared for my daughter and how distraught he was, so I stayed silent.

In the early hours of that morning Clara opened her eyes. The first thing she saw was Guy and she smiled at him and took hold of his hand and kissed it. Clara's recovery was slow at first. She was too weak to walk. Guy took it upon himself to carry her everywhere. He would have done anything for her.

She eventually did recover and within a few months she was as healthy as she had ever been and it was mostly due to Guy's care and attention. And I think he believed that it was his will alone that had brought her back from the brink of death.

Guy's visits were becoming more and more infrequent as Clara grew healthy. He grew distant again and eventually he stopped coming to see her altogether. My daughter had grown to love Guy. He loved her so much I think she felt compelled to love him back. So when he stopped visiting, she went looking for him. She found him easily and asked him to marry her and they were married soon after.

Clara's health continued to be good until she became pregnant with Isabella. Her health worsened with each day of her pregnancy and the night Isabella was born Clara did not have the strength to hang on to this world any longer; she died in childbirth. The midwife carried the newborn baby to Guy. He looked at the midwife and then looked at the child.

"Take that thing away from me! It killed my wife!" he cried.

At first I thought it was just the grief at losing his wife and that he would eventually come around and grow to love the child that Clara had left him. So I refused to take her and insisted that Isabella stay with him. I was there every day, of course, checking on the baby. I tried to reason with him, telling him every day that the child needed someone to look after her. I told him that it was what my daughter would have wanted. Guy obviously paid some heed to my words, but not in the way I had hoped.

After a year of my pestering him he just suddenly broke down in front of me. "I know my wife would be heartbroken at the way I treat her child," Guy said through his tears. "I try to force myself to care for her but I cannot bring myself to even look at her. Even now she looks like her mother, the same black hair and green eyes. I thought Clara would always be with me. When she got really ill the first time I really believed that it was me and only me who kept her alive and as long as I wanted her to live she would. But I couldn't keep her alive; she died giving her own life to that child. I knew she was ill during the pregnancy but I thought I could keep her alive simply by willing her to live. The night Isabella was born I wished that if only one of them could live it should be Clara. I try not to think like this. I try not to blame her, but when I look at her I can't help thinking that she slowly sucked the life from my wife!" Guy sat silently until he was ready to speak again.

"Anyway..." he began again. "You don't have to worry about the child. I am getting married again. My new wife will take care of it."

This worried me. Guy had just poured out his heart to me telling me how much he loved my daughter and now he was telling me he was getting married again. I felt sure that this would make matters worse for my granddaughter and I was right. The first day I met Isabella's stepmother, Adriana, I noticed how plain she was in comparison to Clara. Also, I noticed the way she looked at her future husband. She obviously adored him. Nevertheless, he looked at her with little more than indifference.

They were married quickly and Adriana soon realised why Guy had married her. It was simply to have someone to look after Isabella. This, she did, but only because she knew that if she didn't her husband would have no need of her. Adriana soon became pregnant and had a daughter of her own.

Natasha was born within a year after they were married and Guy showed great affection towards his second child. He lavished on her the attention he wanted to give Isabella but could not.

So Isabella grew up in a house where everyone in it despised her. Adriana saw her as a constant reminder of the woman who had stolen her husband's heart. Isabella's half-sister Natasha was taught by her father to either be malicious towards Isabella or to ignore her existence completely. Her mother taught her to be jealous of Isabella. So Natasha grew up hating Isabella, also.

After a few years, I went to see if I could take Isabella and bring her up myself. Adriana wanted me to, but Guy said to her that if Isabella was to leave the house then there was no need for her to stay either. Adriana retaliated, asking who would take care of Natasha. Guy shouted back that he would. From then on Adriana made it perfectly clear that I was not welcome in their home. The only time I would see Isabella after that was when she would come and visit me, which happily, was often.

At first, I saw only the good side of Isabella's nature. I was thankful. I thought she had taken after her mother and would be forgiving towards her father when she was old enough to understand.

I used to ask her about her family when she was still a child. At first she would cry and ask me why her father hated her so much. I tried to explain it to the child as best I could, but how could she understand? When she was older and I asked about her father, she refused to talk about him. When I mentioned his name, a dark look would creep over Isabella's face. It was a look I had seen before on the face of her father when the news reached us that the child Clara had cared for was dead.

This worried me. Guy had taught Isabella to hate. He had shown her how to become bitter and it is a lesson she has learned well. Hatred has destroyed Guy's life and if Isabella is not careful she will become just like her father: bitterness and hatred will destroy her life, as well.

Nicolae had only shown Isabella part of the letter. Isabella was hurt by what she had read. How could her grandfather compare her to her father? She was nothing like her father. She put the letter down and looked up at her husband. "It's no excuse for what he did to me," she said.

"I never said it was," Nicolae answered.

"How could my grandfather think I was like him?"

"This is your chance to prove you are not."

Isabella paused for thought, "I will go and see him," she relented.

The next day they went to see Guy; there were several people there already. The doctor was there, Guy's priest, Adriana and Natasha. The mother and daughter were sitting at Guy's bedside. When Natasha saw Isabella her colour faded, she turned ghostly white and she moved into a corner of the room. Isabella scowled at her sister and then took her seat by her father's bed.

Isabella's father wasn't quite lucid. He looked up at his daughter and whispered. "Clara, have you come for me?"

"It's not Clara, it's your...." Isabella could not bring herself to say daughter. "It's Isabella."

"Isabella," her father said, smiling at her. Isabella's father had never smiled at her before and Isabella was not glad to see him smiling at her now. It was too late for that. She was disgusted.

"You look so much like her, Isabella, so beautiful." Guy took Isabella's hand. Although her first impulse was to pull away, she resisted this impulse for the moment. Isabella felt very uneasy with him touching her, but he looked so pathetic that she continued to let him. Nicolae thought this was a good sign. Adriana, who was sitting on the other side of the bed, was trying desperately to stifle her sobs.

"I have treated you unkindly...." Guy continued. "I am sorry. Please forgive me?" At this Isabella snapped back her hand.

"Is that it?" Isabella began. "An insincere apology and then you ask my forgiveness. Is that really all you have to say to me? You thought I would forgive you if you just asked me. Why do you even want my forgiveness? Is it because you fear your own death? Is that why you want my forgiveness? Do you think you'll be condemned if you leave this world without a clear conscience...condemned to hell? What is it, Guy? What is the real reason for your penitence?" Isabella then looked around the room, and then it struck her: she knew why her father was so eager for her forgiveness. "You are afraid you will not see my mother again, aren't you?" Guy did not answer; he just stared at his daughter and the hatred he had created within her. "Forgive you? I am insulted that you asked me to."

"Child!" the priest cut in. "If you don't forgive your father you not only condemn him, you also condemn yourself." Isabella left her father's bedside and went over to face the priest.

"Do you think the threats of your religion frighten me? You may be right, I may be condemning myself. Even if I lose my soul, I will rest easy knowing that he is condemned with me." The priest stepped back from Isabella. He was frightened by the young girl. Isabella turned and walked towards her sister. She leaned in close and whispered in Natasha's ear, "You have no one to protect you from me now, so watch your back, sister."

At this Adriana cried out, "You are damned!"

Isabella turned to face her stepmother. "Yes, I am damned. Everyone in this whole hellish family is damned."

Isabella left the room. Nicolae, who had witnessed everything, followed her, trying to conceal his own disgust at his wife's actions.

Adriana pressed her head down onto the bed beside her husband; she could not stand it anymore. She started violently sobbing. Guy turned towards his broken-hearted wife and rested his hand on her head. He whispered in a frail voice, "What have I done to her? I am the one who showed Isabella how to hate like that."

Isabella's father died before the sun came up the next morning. The funeral was small and Isabella did not attend. Nicolae did.

Isabella had told Katya a lie when she said on her wedding day that she did not go up to the castle. Isabella did go up to the castle and often. It was getting harder and harder for her to get up there. Nicolae was beginning to become a little overprotective because she was coming towards the end of her pregnancy.

One afternoon she had managed to avoid her husband's watchful eye and had sneaked up to the castle without detection. Isabella soon lost track of time and when she eventually left it was getting dark. She hurried down through the woods and when she was nearly home she heard a voice calling her name.

"Bella!" Isabella's heart started to pound. It was Nicolae. "What are you doing in the forest?" he asked her when he saw her. The wolf that Isabella had befriended on her first visit to the castle and which had always accompanied her when she went through the forest had slipped out of sight. Nicolae did not see him.

"I just took a shortcut through the woods," Isabella answered.

"You know you should never go into the forest on your own," Nicolae objected.

Isabella sighed. "You're getting as bad as Alexei," she said to him. "I'm a grown woman and I can take care of myself!" she added, exasperated by her overprotective husband.

Nicolae smiled at his wife. "I know you can, Bella. Let's go home. There's something I want to tell you." When they got home, Nicolae began to relay the story to Isabella.

"A few years before your grandfather died he started to tell me about the murders...." Nicolae went on to tell her about the man he was named after and how the villagers had covered up the murders for years.

Isabella kept quiet, even though she thought it was all nonsense. She wanted to argue with him but held back her reproach, because she knew if she did he would start asking her questions about why she was so sure that the castle was totally safe. So Isabella kept silent all the time, trying to figure out how she was going to get to the castle from then on. She could not risk Nicolae catching her again. If he even suspected that she was up there he would be very disappointed in her.

That was the one thing Isabella could hardly stand about her husband. He judged her. The two of them were very different people. When she did anything that annoyed him he would not get visibly angry with her. He would not shout, or reprimand her. He would just be that little bit colder towards her. He made her feel guilty and she couldn't stand the disappointed looks he would give her. Nicolae knew that shouting at Isabella was pointless. It would just make her more determined and he wasn't the sort of man who would constantly shout at his wife.

If Nicolae found out that Isabella had been lying to him all those times when she said she was going to Katya's, he would never trust her again. He would insist on going everywhere with her. Isabella loved her husband. She never wanted him to think badly of her. And like all wives who love their husbands, she thought that there were some things that he was better off not knowing. So therefore, when Isabella did anything that Nicolae would not approve of, she preferred to keep it from him. When she had not forgiven her father, Nicolae was so disappointed in her. He did not understand why Isabella could not forgive him. The pair in the end had resolved to not talk about it. They did not understand each others reaction to the events and they never would understand each other completely.

Isabella lay in her bed that night thinking about how she could get up to the castle without her husband suspecting. She rolled over and looked at him; Nicolae was sleeping soundly beside her. Many a night Isabella had lain awake watching her husband sleep. He was such a deep sleeper. Then it occurred to her. She could go up at night while Nicolae was asleep and he would never know the difference.

The following night she waited until her husband was asleep and then went up towards the castle. The wolf ran down to join her and walked with her the rest of the way. When she arrived she lighted a fire and read for hours. This pattern continued for weeks. She would return before Nicolae would wake up and then she would sleep late in the morning. She was quite heavily pregnant by this stage and Nicolae would let her sleep as long as she liked.

About two weeks before her baby was due to be born she was up at the castle as usual. The wolf accompanied her most nights and this night was no exception. The wolf appeared to fall asleep at her feet. Isabella was tired herself and before long fell asleep as well. The moment Isabella was asleep the wolf rose and left the room, only to return in another form.

After about an hour, Isabella awoke. She opened her eyes she was startled to see a stranger sitting opposite her. The stranger was a young, very attractive man. He had thick black hair and dark, almost black eyes.

Isabella jumped out of her seat. She was not the type to be frightened easily so her fleeting moment of panic passed as suddenly as it came and was replaced by curiosity. The man stood up and spoke in a different tongue, Wallachian, but this was one of the languages Isabella had taught herself, so she was able to understand him.

"Please sit down. I did not mean to frighten you."

Not wanting to let him know that he had even slightly intimidated her, Isabella answered, "You didn't. I was just surprised to see anyone here, that's all."

The man curled up his mouth into a smile. "So was I," he said. "This is my home. You are the one who is not supposed to be here."

"Your home. You're a Dracul? I thought Vlad was the last of you."

"You have heard of my family."

"My grandfather fought in the Crusades. He was in Vlad Dracula's army," Isabella stated with a certain amount of pride.

"Vlad was my..." he hesitated, "grandfather."

"Your grandfather. I thought Vlad's only son was lost during the wars."

Dracula was used to people blindly accepting everything he said and not questioning him. This girl was different. She would not be fooled by his usual story.

"He was found," he said, sternly enough to silence her for a moment.

She carried on in another vein of questioning. "Have you come back to the castle to stay?" Isabella asked.

"For awhile."

"I suppose I am a trespasser here?"

"I suppose you are."

"I come up here to read the books. I'm from the village below."

"You speak Wallachian very well, but I suspect it is not your native tongue?"

"You are right. I am a Slovak. There is a settlement just at the bottom of the forest. I taught myself Wallachian."

"Using my books?"

Isabella took exception to his condescending tone. "Well, you certainly weren't using them," she said.

"You're quite right," Vlad smiled. "And I don't see why you should stop using them. You are welcome here."

Isabella noticed a glint of light coming in through the window. "I have to go now."

The young prince stood, bowed his head and then escorted Isabella to the door.

Isabella ran through the courtyard and as she did, Dracula called after her.

"Will you be coming back?"

Isabella turned, smiled and shouted back, "I might!"

※

Isabella was not used to this sort of treatment. This man was different from any other man she had ever met in her life. He was a gentleman, a nobleman, a prince and he treated her like a lady. Isabella enjoyed this kind of treatment; she liked feeling superior. She was more than a little bit fascinated by him. He was handsome, but then again so was Nicolae, she kept reminding herself. He was arrogant and that was something you could never accuse Nicolae of being. To be his wife would mean travelling all over the world, not just reading about it in books. Isabella wondered to herself, if he had come along a year ago, would she still have married Nicolae?

Isabella ran the rest of the way home. When she arrived, she watched and waited for her husband to awaken. Lying on their bed beside him she felt ashamed. Nicolae was just as attractive as Vlad and Isabella loved him, no one else. She would always love him —even longer than she could know—and she would never intentionally hurt him. Isabella knew that she could have never married anyone else, even if she had wanted to. She moved her body as close as she could to her husband. She didn't want to let him go.

Nicolae awoke, turned around to face his wife, kissed her on the forehead and then got up and left the room. Isabella lay on the bed alone and thought that just because she loved her husband did not mean she had to stop going up to the castle, and if she happened to see Vlad, how could she help it? Besides, what Nicolae did not know could not hurt him. Isabella turned over onto her side, and went to sleep with a fractious smile upon her face.

On the other side of the village Natasha, Isabella's sister, was talking to a man called Peter.

"Did you follow her?" Natasha asked.

"Yes," Peter answered.

"Where did she go?"

"She went up to the castle."

"The castle. I wonder why she went up there...how long did she stay?"

"I don't know. As soon as I saw she was going up there I turned back."

"You turned back!?!"

"I'm not going anywhere near that place. You've heard the rumours."

"You're not scared, are you Peter? I wonder how long she has been going up there. I am sure Nicolae does not know." Natasha paused. "Anyway, that gives me an idea," she continued. "People go missing in the woods all the time and when they find them they are always dead. Why not Isabella? She shouldn't be going up there anyway. It's the perfect chance to get rid of her once and for all."

"You never told me how beautiful she is," Peter interrupted.

"She's not beautiful," Natasha answered vehemently. "She has a scar on her shoulder. You obviously did not see her too closely!" Natasha leaned her chin coquettishly on Peter's chest and whispered, "I want her dead... you'll kill her for me won't you, Peter?"

Peter smiled, ran his fingers through Natasha's hair and answered, "I will." Natasha kissed her lover and went to sleep. Natasha had so far neglected to mention her feelings for Nicolae to Peter. He'd find out soon enough.

The next day Isabella went to see Katya. Katya was nursing her child.

"It won't be long till your baby is born," Katya began the conversation.

"Hmm." Isabella wasn't really paying much attention to what Katya was saying.

"Just a couple of weeks to go, isn't it?" Katya sighed when Isabella did not respond. "Are you even listening to me? You've hardly said two words since you came in!" Isabella still wasn't listening. "What's wrong with you Isabella? What are you thinking about?"

"Oh, nothing important," Isabella said. She looked quizzically at her friend and asked, "You don't believe all this nonsense about Vampires, do you?"

"Yes, I do, Isabella, and so should you!" Katya said gravely.

"All right, all right, don't shout at me," retorted Isabella.

"Isabella, promise me you won't go up there. They say whatever it is comes from that castle."

Isabella tutted and did not answer her friend. She rose from her seat and walked towards the window to look out at the night. A white mist was pouring down from over the hills and smothering everything it touched. Isabella loved to watch the mist—it seemed beautiful to her.

"Look at the mist, Katya. It looks as if it's pouring down from the sky. I love nights like these. They are so beautiful, the mystery of these nights. I always wonder who goes out on nights like these. People who do not want to be seen, who want to keep their actions hidden, unsuitable romantic attachments, perhaps."

Katya looked at her friend.

"Isabella, you say such strange things sometimes. Sometimes I think you weren't made for this world. It's a horrible night...no one goes out when it is like this." Katya wanted to change the subject. "I saw your sister the other day."

"I am not interested in my sister," Isabella objected, turning away from the window and back towards Katya, her facetious mood now becoming more serious.

"I know you are not interested in your sister. It is the person I saw her with that should interest you or at least concern you."

"Why?"

"She has taken up with a man called Peter. I don't know his second name."

"Katya, I really don't care who she has taken up with," Isabella said, trying to dismiss the conversation one more time.

"You will, Isabella. Everyone in the village is suspicious of him. People suspect him of killing his father. His own father."

"He suits my sister, then."

"Just be careful, Isabella. They may be a dangerous pair."

"I wouldn't worry. I can take care of myself despite my sister. She would be too terrified to even challenge me." With this the conversation ended. Katya's warning was not strong enough for her to be able to make Isabella realise the gravity of the situation.

That night Isabella was restless. She waited till Nicolae was asleep and then once again headed up towards the castle. Peter was watching and waiting for her. Vlad was also watching her approach. He saw Peter and Isabella but stayed concealed from both of them.

Isabella walked past Peter, still totally unaware that he was there. Peter started to follow her. When he got within touching distance of her, he grabbed her from behind and flung her around to face him. Isabella could smell his sour breath; he'd obviously been drinking. Peter pushed her down onto the forest floor and lay on top of her, pinning her down beneath his large frame.

Isabella could feel his rough hand pushing up underneath her dress towards the top of her thigh. His other hand was also occupied by ripping off the shoulder of her dress. "There's the scar just where your sister said it would be. But she was not right about everything. You are very beautiful, even more so up close," Peter leered.

"My sister!" Isabella snapped.

"Yes, she is the one who wants me to kill you, but I think I will keep you alive until morning at least." He pressed his lips over Isabella's.

Isabella became enraged at the mention of her sister. Natasha had arranged this. Not content any more to try and ruin any chance Isabella had of happiness, Natasha wanted to kill her.

Isabella's rage gave her strength and she bit down hard and took off part of Peter's tongue. Then she snatched his hand from under her dress and kicked out and up with both legs to get Peter off her. Isabella was now free from his grasp and he was reeling in agony, holding his bloodied face. She lifted a rock and with all the strength she had left to muster, she bashed in Peter's skull and then spat on him in disgust.

Vlad had watched the whole incident. He had kept quiet and out of sight. He wanted to see if Isabella could look after herself and how strong she was; he was not disappointed in her.

Isabella left the body and slowly walked up towards the castle. She should have gone home but something urged her to continue to her planned destination.

Dracula went over to Peter's body and drained whatever blood was left. He then raced up to the castle so that he would get there before Isabella.

Isabella knocked on the door and Vlad opened it.

"What's wrong?" he asked her, mocking concern.

"I was attacked," Isabella, said, gasping for air, "Attacked, who attacked you?"

"I think his name was Peter."

"Was?"

"He's dead. I killed him." Her words were not laced with any sign of remorse.

"You killed him?"

"Yes."

"You murdered him? You ended the life of a human being?" Dracula said, trying to act self-righteous.

"Yes I have and I will end another human being's life by the end of the day." Isabella said with venom.

"Does this walking corpse have a name?"

"Natasha. She's my half-sister. She told Peter to kill me!" Vlad turned from Isabella and smiled to himself. He liked this woman. Then he faced her again with a look of feigned concern, "I'll walk you back to the village."

"All right."

The pair walked down through the forest together. Vlad brushed past a thorn bush and cut his hand. Isabella lifted his hand to her lips and sucked the excess blood from his fingers. Dracula pulled away.

"You have to get rid of the poison," Isabella said.

Vlad laughed and replied, "Don't worry. I will not die from a prick from a thorn."

"We're getting close to my home. My husband does not know that I go up to the castle. You can't come with me any further."

"What sort of a man have you married, Isabella?"

Isabella hesitated and said, "A good man."

"Oh, I am sure...a good and righteous man. That doesn't suit you, Isabella."

"What would you know about what suits me and what doesn't?"

"I know you better now than your good husband ever will. You may be good on occasion and do the right thing, but it's only because people around you influence you. It is not your natural instinct. No matter how hard you try, you will never be righteous. Think about it, Isabella, you are already lying to him. You would rather keep him in the dark than let him think badly of you. You sometimes even go as far as resenting him for his good nature."

"That is not true," Isabella lied.

"Is it not? Let me ask you this, are you going to tell him about your intention to kill your sister, or that you have just killed Peter? He'll only stop you, won't he?"

Isabella stood silently. She knew he was right.

"Yes, I can picture him now," said Vlad. "He'll be handsome, someone you have known since you were a child and the only reason you married him was because all the other woman of the village wanted him."

Isabella threw out her arms to strike at Vlad. She wanted to silence him, but Vlad quickly restrained her before she had the chance.

"Have I struck a nerve?" Vlad said. "Oh, I see, your sister wanted him for herself. Is that why you hate each other so much? What happens when you get older and you lose your attraction for him? Will you still love him for his good nature?" Isabella tried to lash out with her feet but Vlad tripped her up.

She stood back up immediately and answered him, "Everyone gets old. You, too, will lose your beauty and unlike Nicolae you will have nothing to offer me or any woman when that happens. You know nothing about me. I love my husband and as long as I live we will be together."

"Then you'll never be together again!" Vlad clasped his fingers around Isabella's throat and started to drain the life's blood from her.

Isabella could not feel anything, not even pain, yet she knew enough to know that what was happening to her was not right.

Vlad let go before she was dead—this was something he had never done before.

Isabella dropped to the ground and frantically rubbed her neck and then lifted her hand in front of her face. There was blood on her fingertips.

"Vrolok," she whispered.

Dracula left her there to die.

After he was out of sight Isabella pulled herself up onto her feet and staggered home. She entered her bedroom where her husband was sleeping and fell forward, landing on top of Nicolae, waking him. "Nicolae, the baby," she gasped and then passed out.

Nicolae laid her down on the bed before running to fetch Katya and the midwife. When he returned, Isabella was still unconscious.

Isabella's baby was born soon after. It was a boy. Isabella never regained consciousness.

"I'm glad it's a boy," the midwife said. "It'll break the chain. Her mother and grandmother both died in childbirth."

Nicolae looked up at the midwife. "What do you mean?" he said.

"I'm sorry, Nicolae, your wife is dead," the midwife answered.

Nicolae shook his head. "No. Isabella's strong; she's not like her mother. She's not like her mother," he repeated. "She's strong!" he said again, louder. "She'll never leave me alone!" he shouted as he ran over to his dead wife. He pulled her body close to him and started to rock her back and forth.

Katya, who was as grief stricken as Nicolae, lifted the baby and took him over to his father. "Look what she has left you, Nicolae."

Nicolae looked at the child and cursed. "Take that thing away from me," he said. "It killed my wife."

DRACULA DEVIL

CHAPTER FOUR

Isabella awoke. She was lying in complete darkness, but for reasons that she did not understand she could see perfectly well. From the moment she opened her eyes she realised she was lying in her own coffin. She panicked and pushed up on the lid; it opened and slid off easily.

She sat up and looked around her, disoriented. She realised that she was sitting in her bedroom. There were candles burning and petals scattered all around the room. Isabella did not notice these decorations in her mind's eye. Her attention was immediately drawn to her bedroom mirror. She could see the reflection of the coffin that she was sitting in but she could not see her own reflection.

Isabella got out of the coffin and approached the mirror. She lifted a flower and waved it slowly in front of her. The reflection of the flower in the mirror looked as if it was floating in midair. For the first time in Isabella's existence she was frightened. A growing feeling of bewilderment came over her. Questions raced through her mind. What had happened to her? What was wrong with her? She seized the mirror and smashed it.

Katya who was in the next room heard the clatter and came running into the room to see what had happened. On seeing Isabella was alive she was overjoyed.

"Isabella you're alive, I can't believe it," Katya exclaimed. She rushed over towards Isabella with the intention of embracing her friend. Isabella who was sitting in a heap on the floor pulled back from Katya and warned her.

"Get away from me...there's something wrong with me...I feel different... I am different."

"You've been very ill. Of course you don't feel right. Oh, Isabella," Katya continued, "Nicolae will be home soon, and he will be so happy. He has been devastated."

"You're not to tell Nicolae anything yet!" Isabella commanded. "At least until I know what is wrong with me."

"There's nothing wrong with you," Katya said to comfort her friend, but Isabella lifted up part of the mirror and held it out in front of her face.

"Look! I don't have a reflection!" Katya looked at her friend in astonishment. Then she remembered the coffin.

"Isabella! How did you get out of the coffin?" Katya asked. Isabella glanced up inquisitively at her friend.

"What'd you mean? I just lifted the lid."

"The lid was nailed down," Katya said. "Nicolae did not want to see you. You couldn't have just opened it."

Isabella looked down at the lid. The nails were sticking out through the wood. She had hardly applied any pressure to the coffin lid; it had just smoothly slid open. She managed to control her emotions, even though she was desperately frightened. The only visible sign of her consternation was that she was rubbing her hand up against the side of her forehead slowly, but forcibly. She just sat there trying to figure out what to do.

"Where's Nicolae?" Isabella asked; she was now filled with a sense of urgency.

"I don't know. He went for a walk. He has been acting so strangely since you...since it happened."

"He can't see me like this, not yet. You have to nail me back in," Isabella said, now calmly determined.

"Isabella, you'll suffocate! Your funeral is tomorrow."

"Do what I say, Katya. Then tomorrow after I'm buried come back and dig me up."

"You could really die!" said Katya, making one final attempt to protest, but Isabella was determined.

"I think it is too late for that. I think I'm dead already." Isabella got back into the coffin and Katya nailed down the lid. Isabella began her sleep.

She was awakened once again by whispers in her bedroom.

"Nicolae." It was Natasha.

Isabella wanted to burst out of the casket that was imprisoning her and confront her sister, but she held back and just listened to what her sister was saying.

"I'm so sorry, Nicolae."

Nicolae remained silent. The silence was interrupted by a knock at the door. Isabella heard Nicolae go to the door to see who it was. Isabella could hear a faint whispering emanating from Natasha. She knew she was not speaking aloud but yet Isabella could hear her. Isabella soon realised she was listening to her sister's thoughts.

"If I had known you'd be good enough to die in childbirth, I would not have gone to so much trouble," Natasha thought.

Isabella was furious at her sister's indignity. Whatever happened, she promised herself, she would pay her sister back for her enmity.

Isabella fell asleep again. When she awoke she was underneath the ground. She could not lift the lid so easily this time. She became frightened for the second time in her existence. All she could think of was getting out, getting free of her grave. Isabella closed her eyes, her only thought being that she had to get out. Then a strange feeling came over her. It started as a tingling sensation. Then her whole body felt light and weightless; she felt herself seeping up through the cracks in the coffin and then up through the earth.

Isabella had changed form; she had become a vapour and was seeping up through the ground. When she was above the earth, her body formed itself again. When Katya arrived, Isabella was sitting on the ground above her grave.

Katya had brought a blanket and a shovel with her. She placed the blanket around Isabella's shoulders and dropped the shovel on the ground. Katya sat down beside her friend holding her, but one question was racing through her mind that she had to ask.

"How did you get out?" Katya asked.

"I don't know...all I know is I wanted to get out. I felt myself rising up through the earth and next thing I know, I am sitting here...I don't know what's happening to me. Am I a ghost?" Isabella cried out.

"No you're not a ghost Isabella. You're flesh and blood. I can feel you, touch you...."

Katya, while still sitting with both her arms wrapped around her friend trying to comfort her, noticed something else. "Isabella..." she said.

Isabella looked around.

"The scar on your shoulder—it has gone," Katya continued, as Isabella examined her shoulder. The scar had indeed vanished. There was no trace of it.

"Oh, God, Katya, what am I...something worse than a ghost?"

"There's nothing wrong with you, Isabella. You're alive...it's a blessing." Katya's words were hesitant and lacked conviction. Isabella laughed quietly at her friend and raised her face so that she was looking up at Katya.

"This is no blessing and you know it is not...people who are alive don't rise up from their own graves," Isabella said, nervously laughing as she spoke. "And people who are alive have reflections." Isabella looked at her left hand where her wedding ring used to be. She had left the ring along with her clothes in her coffin. As she was rubbing her ring finger, desperately wishing her ring back on her finger, she noticed that her hands were starting to shake—gently at first and then violently. The shaking then spread up through her arms, her back started to seize, her body fell forward; she was forced to lie down as her whole body started to convulse uncontrollably.

"Isabella! What's wrong with you?" cried Katya.

"I don't know...I'm starving...I need something...to eat."

At that moment Natasha, who had been walking towards Nicolae's house, saw her sister. She was shocked and maddened to see Isabella alive and frantically ran towards her. Natasha grabbed the shovel that Katya had brought and swung around, smashing the back of her sister's head with it. Natasha had used all of her strength to hit her sister, but she might as well have tapped her with a feather. The forceful impact had not even broken her skin.

Isabella found the strength to control her convulsions and stood, slowly and steadily. She turned to face her sister. Natasha was suddenly terrified. She dropped the shovel and turned to run, but Isabella was too quick for her. Isabella reached out and grabbed her sister's arm, pulling it out of its socket. Natasha yelled out in agony just as Isabella reached up and slashed Natasha's throat with her nails, silencing her sister's screams.

Blood poured from the open wound on Natasha's neck. Natasha looked down and saw the blood seeping from her own neck. She put up her hands to her throat, trying desperately to hold in the blood in a futile attempt to hang on to her young life. Isabella pulled away her sister's hands and she drank. Natasha feebly struck Isabella, trying to beat her back, but it was useless. Natasha's arms finally fell limply to her sides, her eyes flickered one final time and then her eyes shut, never to open again.

"Isabella!" Katya screamed out, staring at her childhood friend, unable to lift her eyes from the abhorrent scene she had witnessed. "What are you doing?"

Isabella turned towards Katya, blood dripping from her mouth. She looked at her friend malignantly. She licked the blood slowly from her hand and wrist. "I feel better now," she whispered.

Katya was repulsed by Isabella's actions. She ran from her friend. For not only did she find what she had witnessed repugnant, she was frightened of Isabella and what she had become.

When Isabella saw Katya run from her it forced her to return to reason. The blood lust that she had experienced left her. She looked down at the body of her dead sister. Isabella did not care that she had killed her. The fact that Natasha was dead did not bother her. It was the way in which she had killed her sister that frightened Isabella. When she had seen the blood she could not control her desire. It had felt as if her very existence depended on her drinking it. And when she had drunk her sister's blood, a rush of energy surged through her; she felt revitalised. She could feel her own blood starting to pump through her veins. She felt as if she could do anything, see anything, hear anything. She felt alive, and a feeling of total satisfaction was upon her. It was the greatest sensation she had ever experienced. It was something she had never even come close to feeling before and she knew from that moment that she could not live without experiencing it again.

Then Isabella dropped to the ground and wept, for the euphoric feeling that she had received from her sister's blood had left completely. She held her face in her hands. Tears trickled down through her fingers. She wiped her eyes and then wiped her hands on the blanket that Katya had brought for her. Isabella noticed a red stain where she had wiped her hands. She wondered where it had come from.

She held her hands in front of her face: they were covered in blood. At first she thought it was her sister's blood but then a single red tear fell on to her pale white leg. Isabella realised that the blood was coming from her eyes. She began sobbing uncontrollably and started violently rubbing her eyes. The more she cried, the more blood poured from her eyes. Her eyes weren't bleeding. She was weeping tears of blood. Isabella could not stand this any more; it was just another sign of her malignancy. She looked up to the skies and called out in despair.

"Who has done this to me?" Her gaze dropped down and there in her line of sight was the castle. "Vlad," she whispered.

Isabella leaped to her feet and sprinted towards the castle. She did not notice how fast she was running, that every step was a leap. She made it up to the castle gate in seconds. She threw open the inner door to the castle. Vlad was sitting in the chair beside the fire when he heard the door burst open. He jumped out of his seat. He looked absolutely amazed to see her.

"What did you do to me?" she screamed.

Vlad could not believe his own eyes. "I don't know...I thought I had killed you."

"You did something worse than kill me...look at my eyes!"

Vlad looked at the bloody tears. "You're a Vampire," he whispered in amazement.

This stunned Isabella.

"Vrolok? I couldn't be! I'm human...you did this to me!" Isabella pointed at Vlad stabbing the air with her fingers. "You did this to me!" she repeated. Isabella turned and ran back out through the castle door.

Vlad chased after her. "Isabella," he called after her. "You can't go back to the village. You're not one of them anymore. They will despise you for what you have become. They're better off thinking you are dead."

Isabella tried to ignore Vlad's words but she remembered how Katya had looked at her when she killed her sister. She knew he was right and yet her feet still carried her home. She would try to explain to Katya, at least. She would try to explain that she could not have helped what had happened to her.

Isabella stopped running when she came to Katya's house. She crept up and looked in the window; she could see Katya sleeping inside. Isabella gently tapped the window trying to awaken Katya but she did not stir. Isabella closed her eyes and whispered.

"Come out, Katya, please come out." Katya's eyes opened. She had not heard Isabella's words, but something she did not understand made her get up and leave the safety of her own home. When Katya saw Isabella, she hid her face, afraid to look at her former friend.

"I won't hurt you," said Isabella. Katya did not respond. "Katya, please listen to me...." Isabella begged. "I have to tell you what happened the night...the night I died."

Katya looked at her friend. Even though she was frightened of her, she was filled with pity and answered, "Tell me."

"There were two attempts on my life that night. My sister planned the first; she sent Peter to kill me. You were right to warn me about him. He attacked me and then I killed him, but it was only in self-defence, for he would have killed me. I will not lie to you. I planned to kill my sister as well. You saw for yourself even last night, Katya, she tried to kill me again. I killed her and I am not sorry that I did. I wanted her dead and she deserved to die. Vlad made the second attempt on my life. The rumours are true; he lives in the castle and is a Vrolok."

Katya listened and as she did she saw something of her old friend in Isabella's eyes. She was no longer afraid of her. Katya tried to stifle her tears as she looked at Isabella. "Isabella, what will you do?" she asked.

Isabella laughed nervously. "I have no idea…What can I do?"

Katya tried to embrace her friend but Isabella would not let her. "I don't want your pity. I don't deserve it. I don't want anyone else to know about me, especially not Nicolae. He's better off thinking I'm dead."

"I'm not so sure about that, Isabella," Katya responded. "There's something I have to tell you…about Nicolae." She continued trying to find the words. "I'm looking after your child."

"My child…my child's alive?!" Isabella said in a state of happy disbelief.

"Yes, Isabella, it's a baby boy," said Katya. "We all assumed you died in childbirth, like your mother and grandmother."

"Why are you looking after him?"

"Nicolae doesn't want the baby near him. He said the baby killed you."

"Let me see him."

Katya went into her home and brought the child to its mother. Isabella glanced lovingly at the tiny infant and said, "I'm going to take him home to his father."

"Isabella, he won't take care of him. Do you want him to have the same life you did?"

"No, he's not like my father. Nicolae could never be so cruel. It's not in his nature. Go and see him tomorrow if you are worried. Everything will be all right, I promise."

Katya believed Isabella. Isabella took the child in her arms and ran from Katya's to Nicolae's.

After Isabella left, Katya was filled with anxiety about the child. She had just given a baby to a Vampire, a Vampire that only a few hours ago she had witnessed slaughtering her own sister. She wanted to follow her but something held her back. It seemed as though Katya was bound to do anything Isabella asked of her.

Isabella stood over her sleeping husband. She placed the baby on the bed beside him and then kneeled down. She laid her head down beside his and started to whisper in his ear.

"Nicolae." Nicolae did not wake up or even open his eyes but he answered his wife.

"Bella."

"Yes, Nicolae it's me, I'm here," Isabella continued whispering. "I've come to remind you of something. Listen to me, Nicolae. Do you remember how my father treated me? How his rejection hurt me? Do you want to do that to our child? Do you want our child to feel that pain?" Nicolae still didn't open his eyes and yet tears were streaming down his cheeks. "I want you to look after the child. I want you to love him as you would have done if I had still been alive. You do not want him coming to your deathbed and cursing your name. Will you do this for me? It's my final wish. I don't want our child to turn out like me. I want him to be like you. Please, Nicolae, will you do this for me?" Isabella pleaded.

"Of course I will, Bella." answered Nicolae.

"Thank you, sleep well." Isabella ran her fingers through his hair. She watched him sleeping for hours. She didn't want to leave him. She had this awful feeling that it would be the last time she would ever see him. He was always so beautiful in Isabella's eyes, but never more so than tonight. She had seen other attractive men, but none compared to him.

Nicolae's skin was slightly browned from the sun. He took the sun so well. The slightest rays would colour his appearance. His nose was narrow but not overlong. His cheeks were chiselled but not sharp. He had dimples in his chin and in his cheeks when he smiled. And he smiled often. His eyes were light green, not dark like Isabella's. They were bright and clear. His hair was dark brown with streaks of red that shone in the sunlight. He had always had a proud but welcoming look about him.

Isabella, close to tears, sat staring at her beautiful husband. Maybe she could stay with him, she thought. She could keep what had happened from him. She had kept things from him before. A single tear trickled down her cheek. This blood red tear fell from her face and splashed on the white sheet of Nicolae's bed. Isabella knew then that she could not hide this from him and she leaned forward again and whispered one last thing into Nicolae's ear.

"I will always love you." Isabella leaned over and kissed her husband on the lips. This woke Nicolae with a start and he looked around the room, but Isabella was already gone.

※

When Isabella left her old home she again started to convulse. She was hungry for the second time that night. She went back into the woods to try and find something to eat. She eventually found someone and killed him to feed her desire.

Dracula appeared in front of her as she was feeding. Isabella looked up at him.

"You've made me a murderess!" she said.

"You had already killed...I had nothing to do with it. You murdered Peter, remember."

"That's not the same! He was trying to kill me."

Dracula pointed down to the corpse that Isabella had just recently slain. "Do you not think he would have tried to kill you if he had known what you were? Do you not think even your husband would try to kill you if he knew what you are now?"

"And what am I?"

"In their eyes you're a devil. You're a Dracula. You don't belong with those people any more."

"Where do I belong?"

"You belong with me. Where else is there for you to go?" The words issued out of Vlad's lips like a death sentence, but Isabella knew he was right.

"I'll stay with you only until I decide where else I can go," she answered.

The next day Katya went to see Nicolae. When she entered his room he was cradling his son.

"Hello, Katya."

Katya smiled and responded, "Well, hello to you. You look well."

"I feel well."

"What brought on this sudden change?"

"I think you are partly responsible for it."

"Me."

"Yes it must have been you who brought the baby here." Katya nodded nervously. "I had a dream last night that seemed so real," Nicolae continued. "I dreamt that Bella came down from the heavens and told me to look after our child. It was so real, Katya," Nicolae rubbed his lips with the tips of his fingers, remembering Isabella's kiss. "It was as if she was actually here with me."

Nicolae's thoughts wandered for a second. The baby let out a soft cry. Nicolae's eyes were drawn back to his son and he smiled at him. "Anyway," he continued, "it made me realise how selfish I was being. How could I blame our child for Isabella's death? What sort of person would do such a thing? I will never forget her and I'm going to make sure our son knows everything about her. How beautiful she was, what a good person she was and how much she was loved."

Katya looked at the baby in his father's arms and she was thankful, not only to see Nicolae caring for his son, but also because she realised that Isabella had made this happen, that she was not beyond hope. There were still some remnants of the friend Katya had loved and trusted, despite what had happened.

SEMPER AVIVA
ALWAYS LIVING

CHAPTER FIVE

Isabella reluctantly returned with Vlad to the castle. She walked beside him but she didn't speak to him; she didn't even look at him. Vlad tried to talk to her but she refused to answer. Isabella held her head up high and looked straight ahead of her at all times, not acknowledging the former Prince's existence.

Vlad entered the castle with Isabella and showed her to a room. It was a room she had never been in before; she hadn't been in any of the other rooms. All the doors had always been wedged shut, and all she had seen of the castle before then had been the front hall and library. The room that Vlad gave her was lavishly decorated. She could see that the room at least at one time had belonged to a woman. A large four-poster wooden bed was in the centre. A polished jewellery box sat on a dressing table beside a mirror that was obviously imported from Italy, not like the crude piece of glass she had in the room she had shared with Nicolae. But of course this ornate trinket was no good to Isabella anymore. The box lay open, packed with necklaces and bracelets that were encrusted with diamonds and rubies. They were exquisite, but Isabella did not want them.

Aside from the jewellery, other exquisite trinkets were littered throughout her new room. There was a candelabra, although there was no need for any more light in this room. There was only one window, but it filled up the wall on the left side of the room and moonlight flooded through it. It was really quite beautiful and in other circumstances Isabella would have been overjoyed to live in a room like this, but all it was to her now was a pretty prison cell for her to occupy.

"There are clothes in the chest over there." Vlad pointed to a large wooden chest, Isabella was still wearing nothing but the blanket Katya had given her, having left her own clothes in the coffin along with her wedding ring. "This room is yours now," Vlad continued, but Isabella ignored him. Vlad nodded his head in courtesy and left her alone. He knew it was useless to stay with her. He would speak to her tomorrow when she had calmed down and resigned herself to her new situation.

When he left, Isabella went over to chest and opened it. She found a nightgown for herself, put it on and got into bed. She lay awake staring at the ceiling; she could not sleep and yet longed to. She tried to block out the recent events in her mind. It was too bright to fall asleep in this room. The strong moonlight was irritating. Her eyes could not really focus properly. Isabella pulled the silken quilt over her head and yet it was still too bright for her. She got out of the bed and lay underneath it. This still didn't help, she rolled over in frustration and the chest caught her eye. She walked over to it and opened the lid. Isabella threw out the contents and climbed inside. She shut the lid so that she was in complete darkness. Finally she could sleep and gain the sweet vacuity that it offered her.

Isabella was awakened the following night by Vlad entering her room. She opened the lid to reveal to Vlad her resting place. Vlad looked shocked when he saw Isabella climbing out of chest. However, he soon smiled at her.

"I should have guessed you'd learn quickly," he said. Isabella did not respond. Vlad's smile hardened into a glare. "You'll have to talk to me eventually; who else do you have to talk to?"

These words hurt Isabella because she knew they were true, but her facial expression remained cold and emotionless. She simply walked towards him, staring him straight in the eyes, almost beginning to smile. Vlad smiled at her thinking she had finally come around. When she could almost touch him, when they were nearly face to face, she turned her head from his gaze and walked around him. Acting as if he was just an obstacle in her path, Isabella left the room in silence.

Weeks became months and the months drifted slowly into years. Isabella continued to ignore Vlad; she took every chance she could get to slight him. Isabella had learned from her father that it was not insults that hurt most. The worst thing you could possibly do to someone was to completely ignore them. Acting as if they did not exist could drive a person mad. She did not shout at him; she never yelled angry recriminations at him; she simply acted as if he was not there, never even looking at him.

Isabella wanted to do the cruellest thing she could think of and this, ignoring him, pretending he was not there, was the worst thing she could imagine. She wanted him to suffer as she was suffering. This tactic of hers was working. She could feel Vlad's enmity towards her growing daily.

Isabella at first was ignoring Vlad because she hated him, but there was soon another reason. Isabella was miserable; she had never been this alone before. During her life even when things were at their worst she had always had someone to rely on. Her grandfather, Katya, Nicolae—but now there was no one. She wanted this to end. Over the years since Isabella's death people had tried to kill her and she had let them try but the most anyone had managed to do was break her skin. Isabella knew Vlad was strong because her own strength had increased since she had died and if anyone could end this misery for her, he could. She could sense his intense anger towards her when she ignored him, and over the years she felt it building. He'd lash out at her soon and hopefully he would kill her and end her miserable existence completely.

While she waited for her final days, she spent her time discovering the extent of her newfound powers. Isabella had been a strong woman in life but now her strength had increased tenfold.

She had other abilities as well. She could not disappear but she could change form and shape. She discovered that she could also influence the weather; Isabella could stir up the winds and start a thunderstorm. She could make a cloud come from nowhere and block out the sun. Her senses were incredibly heightened. She could hear and see things that were happening miles away. She could hear certain people's thoughts, but she would have to touch others to be able to listen to what they were thinking. She had tried to read Vlad's mind but could not. She often wondered if he could read hers. She presumed he could not but was not sure.

Isabella's skin was still quite vulnerable to scratches and cuts but they healed almost instantly. She did not feel very much pain at all any more. She certainly did not feel pain from any wound she received. The only time she came even close to feeling pain was when she did not feed and was hungry, but Isabella did not let herself get hungry too often. The only pleasure she received was from the sensation she felt when she fed. Although she was killing people, she could not resist it, and so she blocked out any thoughts of remorse. It was an addiction and she had come to enjoy the kill. She no longer saw her victims as humans. They were just a source of nourishment to satisfy her inexhaustible appetite.

Her abilities were at their strongest when it was dark, but unfortunately with each of her strengths came a weakness. In life she could see perfectly well during the day and her vision was impaired at night, by the dark, like everyone else. Now, she could see perfectly well during the night. Her vision was impaired by the daylight. She could see things close to her during the day, but things that were far away from her just seemed like shadows basked in the brightest of light. Pungent smells annoyed her like onions, garlic, rot and decay. Isabella sometimes could smell death all around her and through this ability she could tell if someone was going to die, if death was close. Death had its own unique smell.

Her hearing was so much increased that shrill sounds annoyed her. Isabella had grown to hate screamers. If she were killing a woman she would prefer to break or slash her neck to immediately silence her. Sunlight also irritated her. When she was out during the day it felt as if the sun was constantly shining directly into her eyes. If she closed her eyes or hid her face it would make no difference. So therefore Isabella grew accustomed to sleeping during the day. Sometimes even bright moonlight irritated her. In fact, any light at all would irritate her and even suppress her powers, but the most effective light that lessened her abilities was sunlight.

Five years had drifted slowly by since Isabella had died. She had not been down to see Katya since the night she took her baby home. Isabella missed her friend and she had to talk to someone or she felt she would go mad. She made up her mind to visit Katya. She fed well before she went near her friend that night. She felt she could control her feeding but did not want to take that risk where Katya was concerned.

Katya greeted her with a smile. Isabella was reassured by Katya's smile and returned it warmly. Katya's husband and children were sleeping. Although Isabella desperately wanted to see her friend there was someone else she longed to see.

"How's Nicolae?" she asked Katya, immediately.

"He's fine and your son has just turned five."

"Five? Has it only been five years? Nicolae must be twenty-six by now."

"He is."

"What did Nicolae name our son?"

"Alexei." A single red droplet trickled down Isabella's ivory cheek. This shocked Katya but she tried to hide it. "He's a good boy," Katya continued. "You'd be proud of him," Katya said, smiling. "He's the image of his father, but he acts like you used to—"

Isabella held up her hand to stop her friend from continuing.

"Stop, I don't want to know," Isabella sighed. "It's too hard."

VROLOK

Katya was silenced only for a moment as she continued to try and comfort her friend. "I know it must be torture for you to hear about them. It's something you won't have to worry about for much longer." Isabella gave Katya an inquisitive glance. "Seeing and hearing about them, I mean."

"Why? What are you talking about?" Isabella retorted impatiently.

"Nicolae is taking his son and leaving the village."

"Leaving to go where?" Isabella cried out, now panicking.

"It's too much for him here. He goes and lays flowers on your grave every Sunday. He has nightmares and screams out for you in his sleep. He can't stand to be without you, and he is so desperately lonely. He has to go somewhere away from here, a place where he can forget."

"Forget!" said Isabella.

"Yes, forget! Your son needs a mother."

"A mother! I'm his mother. Do you think I can forget? What about me? Do you think it is easy for me? To go through every day without my husband and son. If anything, it's worse for me!" Isabella grimaced and ran from her friend.

"Where are you going?" Katya shouted after her.

"I'm going home."

"You can't, it will destroy him to know the thing you have become." The words left Katya's lips before she could think about what she was saying. On hearing this remark Isabella stopped running and slowly turned to face Katya. She looked back at Katya; her glance was piercing and hellish. It chilled Katya to her core as she was thrown back against the wall of her house by Isabella's look. Katya again was frightened by her friend and for the first time she realised how powerful Isabella had become. A mere glimpse from her was enough to hurl a grown woman backwards.

Despite Katya's fear, she was sorry for what she had said and almost immediately regretted it. She never intentionally wanted to hurt Isabella. Isabella knew this to be so and it was the only reason she did not kill Katya there and then. For like it or not, Isabella was now a cold-blooded, remorseless killer.

Isabella turned her back on Katya and ran home. She was just about to turn the handle on the door of her old house when she hesitated. Images of how Nicolae would react when he realised she was a Vampire stopped her from entering. She slunk back into the forest and watched and waited for morning. The night brightened into day and Isabella still sat there waiting and watching for just a glimpse of her husband and her child.

After a few hours of daylight, a small boy opened the door. Isabella crawled forward to see him more closely. The boy was playing with his dog. He picked up a stick and threw it for the dog to chase after. A little time later the boy threw the stick a little too far and the stick landed at Isabella's feet. The child unknowingly ran to his mother.

"Hello," the boy said. Isabella was on her knees and handed Alexei the stick.

"Thank you."

"You're a very polite boy."

"I know."

Isabella smiled, "Oh, you do, do you?"

Alexei looked at his mother's face, "You're very pretty."

Isabella leaned over and tucked a loose strand of hair behind the boy's ear and said, "So are you."

"Boys are not pretty! They are handsome. I am handsome."

Isabella laughed softly and answered, "Yes, you certainly are."

"You don't need to tell me I'm handsome. I know that I am, just like you know you are pretty."

"I know, but it is nice to be told once in the while."

"My father says my mother always liked to be told she was pretty, as well."

"Oh, was she pretty?"

"Yes, she was even more beautiful than you. My father says that she was so beautiful and good that this world could not hold onto her and the angels came down from heaven to take her."

"It's good that your father remembers your mother that way. Nothing should ever happen to tarnish his memory of her."

"What would?" Alexei asked.

"Nothing," Isabella replied, "absolutely nothing." Isabella heard a far-off cry.

"Alexei! Alexei!" It was Nicolae calling for his son.

"That's my father; would you like to meet him?"

"No, not today," Isabella answered.

"It'll have to be today; we are going away soon."

"I know. Be a good boy for Nicolae," she said.

Nicolae called to his son again. The boy leaned forward and kissed Isabella's cheek, then ran back to his father.

Isabella pressed her hand against her cheek where her son had kissed her. She knew now that she could never go back there.

※

Isabella wandered through the woods aimlessly until night fell. Then she headed back towards the castle. She slammed the heavy door of the castle behind her when she entered. Vlad was sitting with his back to the door. The back of the armchair he was sitting on obscured his body. All Isabella could see of him was his hand, which was draped over the side of the chair holding a goblet of wine and when the door slammed shut it must have startled him as some of the wine spilt over the floor.

"Where have you been?" Vlad said, his tone angry. Isabella let out a sigh and walked towards the staircase. "Answer me!" Vlad roared, hurling the goblet of wine against the wall.

It was Isabella's turn to be startled. Despite this she continued to climb calmly up the stairs. Vlad rose from his seat, lifted the armchair he had been sitting on above his head and hurled it at Isabella. It struck her and knocked her to the floor. Isabella jumped immediately back to her feet and faced Vlad. They glared at each other, malevolence distorting each of their faces. Isabella spoke to Vlad for the first time in five years.

"What do you want me to say to you?" she asked. "Do you want me to tell you how much I hate you? Do you want me to tell you that the smell of you makes me nauseous? That I can't stand to be this close to you?"

"How dare you say such things to me? You are not my equal."

"That is exactly what I am. I may be the only creature on this earth that is your equal."

"You are nothing but a peasant! I am of noble birth...."

"You were! There's nothing noble about you anymore! You are a malignancy, an infestation! And you have infected me with the poison that you are cursed with."

"Be quiet! I am a descended from the highest of men. Attila is at the head of my ancestry. You're just a Slovakian barbarian's daughter."

Isabella's lip curled into a triumphant grin.

"Attila was nothing more than a Germanic Barbarian," she said calmly, "who destroyed a nation that was already crumbling."

Vlad rushed towards her and clasped his hand around her neck, lifting her off the ground.

Isabella spat in his face. "Go on, kill me," Isabella whispered.

Vlad was amazed at this comment and he dropped her to the ground and laughed contemptuously at her. "Kill you. I can't kill you. No one can kill you."

"You tried to kill me before! Finish what you started!" Isabella raged.

"You can't die. Don't you understand? You're immortal."

"Immortal," she whispered and she looked up at Vlad. "Immortal," she repeated in anguish, realising for the first time that her agony was never going to end. "Could you have done anything worse to me?" Isabella threw her arms against Vlad's chest and he pushed her back away from him and she fell to the floor, weeping.

"It's much worse than you even realise," Vlad answered. "You're going to live to watch everyone you care about deteriorate and die. Your husband and your child will rot in their graves while you continue to live," Vlad said with malice.

Isabella leaped up and threw her hand out towards Vlad's face. She struck him across the cheek. A cut appeared and then disappeared immediately afterwards. He retaliated with his fist and sliced open Isabella's cheek with his ring. Isabella hit him again with more force this time and knocked him down to the floor. These exchanges continued until both Vampires were exhausted.

Isabella turned away from him and began to ascend the stairs. All the wounds from the fight had healed by the time she got to the top of the staircase. Vlad watched her ascension. Even though they had fought, and showed nothing but contempt for each other, Vlad knew that this woman was his only possible companion. And he wanted Isabella to share his life with him. He wanted to comfort her, he wanted to reach out to her and tell her that they could find some form of happiness together, but he knew she would not allow him to do so. He turned his back on Isabella, walked over to the fire and stood watching the flames.

"I'm leaving," Isabella called out.

"You'll be back," Vlad answered, whilst spitting out one of his back teeth, which had been irreparably damaged by the fight.

When Isabella got to her room she closed the door and stood with her back up against it. She started to panic and held her face in her hands. *She was immortal—she couldn't be.* She ran over to her bed and broke one of her bedposts in half, slashing her wrists with the splintered wood. The wounds healed within seconds. This was the final confirmation: she was doomed to wander this world for eternity. Isabella was devastated. The priest had been right. She was damned for not forgiving her father. Had she issued this sentence upon herself, then, she wondered?

She waited quietly to hear Vlad leave for the night. Then she searched the castle for money; she soon found enough to sustain her existence for years.

Vlad watched as she left for the forest. He let her go, hoping that she would return to him.

RENAISSANCE
A REBIRTH; A REVIVAL

CHAPTER SIX

Isabella had one thing left to do before she left the place she had always known. She went down to her grave, dug up her empty coffin and retrieved her wedding ring; she would wear it on a chain around her neck from that day on.

All Isabella took with her from the castle were the clothes she was wearing, her empty wooden chest and the money she had found. It was quite a sum, enough to last years. She had felt fortunate to find such an amount, for Isabella had searched many times before and had not found anything of any real value to her.

Isabella walked aimlessly through the night, dragging the chest behind her, wandering in any direction as long as it was away from Vlad. After a few days she arrived at Bistrita. It was early in the morning and darkness still shrouded the town. She wandered through the empty and silent streets with only the sound of her own footsteps to keep her company. There was not a light in any of the houses; with the coming of night the people of Bistrita had retreated first into their homes and then to their beds. Isabella had not seen anyone for miles and her hands were starting to tremble. She was hungry but she would not disturb the sanctity of any person's home. It was the one principal she held onto: she would not steal into a person's home and murder them while they slept. For although Isabella was a killer who had lost all her remorse and conscience, she would never disturb the safety that a person's home offered to that individual. She considered this action beneath her. Thus, before she would enter anyone's home she would have to be invited.

Isabella remained silent. She turned to face each of the four corners of the town in turn; she was listening for the silence to be interrupted by some unfortunate who had foolishly left their home before daylight had broken. Isabella soon heard the noise she was listening for, footsteps. In the distance on the edge of the town a man was watering his horse. Isabella ran swiftly towards the sound. She ran until she was a few steps behind him; the man felt only a gentle whisper of a breeze at his neck. He shivered, unaware of the true danger he was in, and before he could realise the gravity of the situation, he was dead.

After her hunger was satisfied, Isabella decided to take the horse with her. A woman carrying a heavy wooden chest was attracting too much attention and for the first time in her existence she did not want any attention; she longed to disappear. She continued to travel with no sense of an eventual destination.

Isabella continued this pattern of behaviour for months and then years. She didn't know how long; she didn't care. One day melted into the next with only the daylight and the night that followed to tell her that another interminable day was over. When she found people she killed as many of them as she could to satisfy her insatiable thirst. Isabella had become addicted to that sensation. It was the only pleasure she got from her melancholy existence. She killed without discrimination or even a glimmer of remorse. If she stayed in one vicinity too long, she would start to hear mutterings about outbreaks of plague to explain away the sudden increase in mortality that came and left with Isabella. She must have killed hundreds, thousands; she was completely merciless. All she did was sleep and feed. This feral subsistence eventually led her to a town in central Italy.

Isabella had walked for miles the night she arrived in Tuscany. She walked through the Porta Romana, followed the meandering path of the Arno River, and walked over the Ponte Vecchio, which led her into the heart of the city. Dawn was breaking and the streets were starting to fill with people. The streets were narrow and the buildings tall; they had constricting chasms for windows and each one seemed to be competing with the last to see how elaborate the carvings could be. Merchants of silver, silks and everything imaginable were starting to set up their individual stalls and parade their wares. Isabella walked along the paved dusty street beside them, paying them no heed.

She walked through an immense archway into a prodigious courtyard. Statues lined all sides of the courtyard. They were all perfect. The sculptors had paid the utmost attention to every detail. Isabella's journey for the time being had come to an end. She chose to stand beside the best of them all. It was a large white marble statue of a naked man that stood nearly ten feet above her head, and the word "David" was inscribed on the plaque below. The intricacy of the carving and the magnificence of the statue were lost on Isabella. She was not in the least bit impressed by her lavish surroundings in the Piazza della Signoria. She leaned against the plinth and stared blankly at the ground as the world passed her by.

Isabella did not feel any compulsion to lift her eyes from the ground but she had become slightly interested in the bustling activity that surrounded her. She started to listen as she heard people talking about her, trying to conceal what they were saying by whispering, but of course Isabella could hear every word. She understood certain words of this language, for she had been travelling through Italy for at least a year and had picked up quite a bit. She recognised words like gypsy, vagrant, beggar. One man threw a few gold coins at her. This was the ultimate indignity for Isabella. She looked at her dress; it was tattered, torn and filthy. Her legs and feet were covered in mud, and dirt was embedded in her fingernails and toenails. For the first time since her death she had gotten what she had aspired to. She felt totally anonymous, completely insignificant, and to her surprise she did not like this feeling. No one was staring at her, admiring her beauty. She wasn't the centre of attention. If she was attracting any recognition it was for very different reasons than any notice she had ever received before. Isabella resolved to change her ways and become beautiful again. She would stay in this city for awhile; it was as good a place as any for her own private renaissance.

Isabella drew up her gaze and watched the faces of the people that surrounded her. It was a dark winter's day and she could see quite clearly. She descried a man walking across the open courtyard, his head was held high. He looked arrogant. This reminded her of Vlad and unfortunately for this man, this reminiscence sealed his fate.

Isabella knew she needed somewhere to stay. This man was quite extravagantly dressed and because of this Isabella surmised wherever he lived would be quite suitable. She stayed a few steps behind him, as she didn't want too draw his or anyone else's attention. She followed him for about an hour and then watched him enter a house. She wanted to make sure it was his home, so she watched and waited outside. Soon after, he emerged in different clothes. It was settled. This was her new home, but still remembering her principles, she would not enter until she had been invited.

A few moments later a woman came out of door below the stairs of the house. She started to pelt a rug with a brush to get rid of the dust. Isabella approached her. When the woman saw her she felt pity for Isabella, and it was this feeling of pity that saved this woman's life.

"Come in child and get some food, you look half-starved." Isabella walked through the door knowing she had received her sought-after invitation, that now she could kill him in good conscience.

The woman laid food down in front of her. "My master would not approve of me giving you food; you have to eat up before he returns."

Isabella sat in silence. A noise echoed into the kitchen from outside. The woman jumped fearing it was her oppressive master returning home. The servant then bent over to pick up a glass and fill it with water for Isabella to drink, but before she could set it down. Isabella grasped her hand and held it tight. Isabella did not utter a word but thoughts that were not her own entered the woman's head.

"You have no master any more. Leave this place; if you stay you will not live." The woman's sallow skin turned pale. She would not stay here another minute. She ran from the house, never to return.

Isabella left the kitchen and went back through the servant's entrance to the exterior of the house. Isabella would never have to gain admittance to the house through the servant's entrance again.

Beside the house was a darkened alleyway leading to a few other cobbled streets, Isabella considered this to be quite convenient for her purposes; just in case she ever needed to leave in a hurry. The exterior of the house was quite weather-beaten, but it had once been the home of a rich family, for the decoration outside in the stone was quite ornate and detailed. Someone at one point had spent a lot of time on this house. Isabella liked the house. It was perfect; it was just opulent enough to please her and yet not to extravagant that it would attract too much of the wrong sort of attention.

Inside the house there were several unfinished portraits. Isabella did not know very much about art but she knew enough to tell these were not very good. He was obviously not earning enough through his painting to live here. His income must come from another source.

Isabella climbed the stairs that led to the top of the house. His bedroom occupied the top floor of the house. Inside his room was a chest of clothes. Isabella opened it. It was filled with fine garments made from assortment of delicate expensive fabrics. These clothes were a bit too grand for this man, Isabella thought. The man himself was handsome and young, and she could tell by the way he carried himself that he was proud and confident.

He obviously thought a lot of himself. Isabella rummaged through the chest to see if she could find anything of any value.

A box was wedged in the bottom. She took it out and looked at the contents inside. It was filled with jewellery, expensive trinkets and gold pieces. Some of the jewellery was inscribed with phrases like *always yours, forever mine* and they were not all from the same woman.

There was some water and a wash basin on a bedside table. Isabella decided to clean herself. She wanted to wash away the grime that covered her true beauty. She was a little nervous; she wondered if she had changed, had aged. She could see that her long hair was still the same raven colour it had always been. After she had washed she felt the skin on her face to check that it was still smooth and supple. She was relieved to feel that nothing had changed; she could not feel any lines around her eyes, no indentations that were not there before. As far as she could tell by touch she was still as beautiful as she ever was.

Isabella, during her life, had never been too concerned with her outward appearance, but now that she was a Vampire it had become increasingly important to her. It was the only thing that had not been marred by the experiences of the previous years and it was the one thing that she still possessed and that she now valued above all others.

The sun was starting to stream in through the open window where Isabella was sitting. She was tired so she opened her own chest, climbed in, and went to sleep. She was awakened that night by the heavy, scattered footsteps of an inebriated man climbing up the stairs to the door of the outside entrance. It was the young man returning to what he thought was still his home.

Isabella opened her resting place and stepped out of it quietly. She waited for the arrogant youth to make his way up to his bedroom.

He entered the room and staggered towards his bed and threw himself on top of it face down. He turned his face to the side and caught his first glimpse of Isabella. She was sitting on her chest in the corner of the room, smiling. Needless to say he did not return her smile; instead he leaped off the bed and started shouting at her. Isabella did not catch all of what he was saying, for his speech was slurred and broken, but she knew he was angry at seeing her in his home. A woman, although beautiful, who was dressed in rags was not to his taste.

Isabella, using the Italian she knew, looked him straight in the eyes. "You are going to die. You can make your death the most pleasurable experience of your life or the most painful; you choose."

He became enraged; Isabella knew he was screaming profanities at her, but she did not appreciate such vulgarity. Isabella drew out her approach, languorously lingering on every step. When her advance was complete Isabella lashed out with her arm and clasped his neck with her hand. She pushed his body down so that he was on his knees; she pulled him in close to her so that she could feel his heart beating.

Isabella began to whisper in his ear. "You didn't make the right choice."

She saw that the young man now was very nervous; his heartbeat had quickened. His nervousness was turning rapidly into fear. He could now feel how strong this woman was. Isabella let go of him and he just managed to remain standing. He threw out his fist to defend himself, but Isabella quickly grabbed his clenched fist with her own hand before he could strike her face. She twisted back his arm until it snapped and her latest victim fell to the floor writhing in agony. The fractured bone of his arm had forced its way through his skin. Isabella noticed he had another wound which she had not inflicted but thought nothing of it at the time. He started to scream for help; it was a loud shrill scream that painfully resonated through Isabella's head. She placed her foot on his broken arm and softly said, "Be quiet!"

He continued to scream.

Isabella now shouted at the top of her voice and the whole room shook, "Be quiet!"

This terrified him and his screams quickly softened to muffled whimpers.

"That's better!" said Isabella. "Does anyone live here with you?" she asked.

"My servant."

"Oh, yes, I have a message from her. She says with great regret she has left your employ."

"My wife," he answered, trying to think quickly.

"Don't lie to me. Where are her clothes?"

The man panicked. "If I tell you the truth, will you let me go?"

Isabella smiled and shook her head. "I am not going to mislead you. My grandfather taught me never to lie. You will die tonight, but if you tell me the truth I will take away your pain."

The man spat at Isabella and cursed her. Isabella slammed her foot down on his leg, breaking that limb as well.

"You'll be damned for what you have done to me!" he said, struggling to get free.

Isabella leaned in and whispered to him, "Too late, I already am...." She lifted the man off the ground by his clothes and held him in front of her. He dangled in her grasp, scratching at the floor with the tips of his toes trying frantically to find his footing. "Apart from your servant, does anyone else live here?" she asked again.

"No!" screamed the man.

"I told you to lower your voice," Isabella uttered through clenched teeth. The young man now understood he was going to die and burst out with one last attempt to save his own life.

"You are a beautiful woman. I can introduce you into Florentine society. With my help you could accrue great wealth."

"I have no desire to have great wealth; at this moment all I want is this house, but I am happy to know that I am still beautiful. Thank you for that." And with this she hurled the young man up against the wall. This action bashed his skull open and he fell to the floor, never to awaken.

Isabella opened the window and looked outside; she wanted to look at her new view. It was dark so Isabella could see perfectly. She heard a noise and her attention was drawn to the steps leading up to the door of Isabella's new home.

A woman was climbing these steps. She was trying to be quiet and hide in the shadows, and her actions would have been hidden from everyone but Isabella. The woman opened the door and entered the house. She crept towards the young man's bedroom; clearly she was concealing something in between the pleats of her skirt. This young woman intrigued Isabella and she stayed silent and let her come in.

The young man's bed was unmade and, to a human eye in this darkness it looked as if someone was still sleeping in it. The woman uncovered the object that she was concealing, a knife. She started to stab at the bed with every inch of her might. She soon realised that there was nothing on the bed but scattered sheets. She dropped the knife to her side and slumped on to the bed banging down her hand and sighing in exasperation.

"If you wanted him dead, I have done it for you," Isabella said making her presence known. The woman was startled by the voice from the darkness and jumped up onto her feet. She started to blindly look around for Isabella, holding the knife in front of her, trying frantically to make an attempt at defending herself.

Isabella stepped into the moonlight that was streaming in through the window so that she could be seen by the girl.

"Who are you?" the anxious girl asked.

"Who are you?" retorted Isabella.

"This is my sister's home."

"You are mistaken. This is my home." Isabella said firmly.

"Your home,"

"Yes."

"Can I light a candle so that I can see you more clearly?"

Isabella nodded. She wanted to see her reaction to the dead body.

When she lit the candle and saw him lying bloodied on the floor she did not flinch. "Did he suffer?" she asked.

Isabella smiled and said, "He did."

"Good," replied the woman.

Isabella smiled again. She liked this girl.

"What did he do to you?" she asked Isabella.

"He overstayed his welcome," Isabella answered.

"I can't believe this is your house," the girl swore and spat on the corpse.

"Why did you want him dead? What did he do to you?" Isabella inquired.

"It is not only what he did to me. He shamed my sister and drove her to suicide." There was a loud noise that came from outside. The girl jumped in fright. "We have to get rid of the body."

Isabella too wanted to get rid of it. The two women wrapped up the body and started to carry him down the stairs. Isabella only helped a little. If truth be known she could have easily carried the body herself, but she did not want to give all her secrets away to her fellow conspirator; at least not yet.

They walked to the river. No one was on the streets this early in the morning so no one saw them. Isabella was imperturbable, for she had killed many times before, but the girl she was helping was frightened for her life. Isabella would have simply killed any one who came across the two women. But the slightest sound was making the girl jump in fright. They reached the river after a little while and pushed the body under the water.

"He'll rise in a few days but it will give us time to get out of here," said the girl nervously.

"I have no intention of leaving," said Isabella. "I'll weigh him down with something." Isabella dived in after the body and dragged it two the middle of the river. In the darkness of the river Isabella's sight was nearly perfect. She could see that the riverbed was like quicksand. She slit his stomach open with her nails so that the body would fill with water and could not easily float back up to the surface. She pushed the body down with her feet and the riverbed encapsulated him. It would be months before he surfaced, if he ever did.

Isabella emerged from the water to see the girl smile at her. Still a nervous sort of a smile, but a smile nevertheless.

"I'm glad to see you are all right."

"You are?" Isabella answered.

"Of course!"

Isabella was quite touched that this stranger was glad to see her alive. No one had felt any compassion towards her in such a long time, but then she reminded herself that this young woman did not know the sort of creature Isabella really was.

"We have to leave Florence," said Isabella's companion, still nervous and agitated.

"Why?" Isabella asked.

"Because we have killed a Medici."

"A Medici?"

"Yes, and we have to go."

"Not yet," said Isabella. "Come back with me to the house." The girl did not want to go but Isabella's will was her bidding and she didn't know or realise why.

The two women entered the house as the dawn of the next day was breaking and sunlight started to stream in through the windows. Isabella closed the shutters and sat down on the bed. She was curious about this woman. Isabella wanted to know more about the man who was dead and why he had inspired so much enmity.

"Sit down," Isabella said. The girl reluctantly sat. "You said he was a Medici, What did you mean?"

"The Medici family rules Florence. He was Alessandro de Medici's bastard son."

"Surely they would not care anything for him," Isabella said.

"Heaven knows who or what they would care for. Alessandro, like his worthless son, was a tyrant. Alessandro was killed before he was thirty, but he was duke at the time. The man who killed Alessandro, even though he was praised for his actions and was a Medici himself, was eventually hunted down and slaughtered like an animal."

"I don't think anyone cared for this man, not really," Isabella interrupted her.

"You obviously are not from Florence; you know nothing of what you speak...." The woman looked into the distance; she was remembering something. Isabella was curious as to what. Isabella gave her a drink to steady her nerves and as she did so she brushed her hand to see the memory that was running through her mind.

It was a story her grandfather used to tell her when she younger. He was a child when it happened. He was playing, not bothering anyone, just a child whiling the hours in playful innocence. His activities were suddenly interrupted by shouts and cries about murder and conspiracy. He heard the names Pazzi and Medici ringing through the air. His mother grabbed his hand and held it tight. People rushed into the Piazza from all sides. He was now completely surrounded by the suffocating crowd. When he looked up all he could see where the heads of the people that surrounded him. The sky was now completely hidden from the child; it had been totally obscured by the crushing crowd that engulfed him. He was getting jostled and he tried to pull away from his mother, but her hand remained tightly clasped around his own as if to let to go was to lose him forever.

The child began to cry. He wanted away from all these people. He wanted to be out into the open air; he could hardly breathe in this tiny claustrophobic space that he had been pushed into. He let go of his mother's hand and without his assistance she could not hold onto him any longer.

The boy headed through the crowd towards the front. His mother tried to frantically grab him back stretching out her hand, grasping for him, but he was too far away. The child made it out of the crowd; he was relieved he could breathe the fresh air again. He took a deep breath. The cool fresh air caressed his face. A cool droplet of liquid struck his forehead. The child thought it was starting to rain. He closed his eyes and looked up, his mouth open, waiting for the rain to cover and refresh him. But whatever was raining down on him, tasted strange and it was not cool and refreshing as rain was.

The child opened his eyes and realised to his horror that it was blood that was pouring into his open mouth. He looked up to see dead eyes staring down at him. This was a memory that he would never forget. He ran back to his mother, who carried him away.

These men had been tortured and killed and their only crime was they had witnessed the assassination of Giovanni Medici and their last name was Pazzi. The crowd was cheering as these men were dying. They were enjoying watching these men in their death throes. They killed hundreds that day in retribution for just one man's death.

✦

"I think that they would care that Giulio had been killed. He is still one of them," the woman answered.

"If you know this, why did you take such a risk?" Isabella now understood why this woman was so afraid because she had been involved in the death of a Medici. It seemed in this city that this was the worst crime anyone could commit.

"It's a long story."

"We have time," Isabella answered.

"No, we don't."

"You're too tired to go anywhere; I guarantee you will be safe with me," Isabella answered.

For some reason that was not yet apparent to the girl, she believed that she would be safe with Isabella. She settled down into a chair and started to recite her story.

"I haven't even told you my name," she began. "It's Lia Filarete. I met Guilio a year ago; my sister introduced him to me. He was introduced as my sister's fiancé. I knew from the start that he was not the man she thought him to be. Everyone in our family did but my sister. She looked at him with nothing but love and adoration. In her eyes he could do no wrong. We tried to convince her that she should not esteem him so highly, but she did not listen, she would not listen.

"We came from a family of painters. My father had no sons and he wanted to pass on his legacy to his daughters, so he taught us to paint. We both were quite good and had inherited my father's talent. He, as you can see by his efforts, was not good at all. I always wondered why he was so attracted, or at least pretended to be attracted, to my sister. She had no money and I suspected he was the type to only like insecure woman with money. My sister was neither of these. My sister used to give him presents of portraits we both had done. One day I saw him in the market; he was passing our sketches off as his own. I went straight home and told my sister and our father. My father told my sister never to see him again, that he was taking us all for fools. My sister said she wouldn't, but I knew she would. She loved him too much to just end the relationship at my father's request. However, my father's health was declining rapidly and this extra worry was making him worse.

"I knew I had to do something because if my father found out that his daughter had not only lied to him but was continually deceiving him every day, the shock would kill him. I thought I could give Guilio money to leave my sister alone or promise to paint him a picture every once in awhile for him to sell. So I made up my mind to visit him. I banged on the door but no one answered. I heard voices inside and the door was open so I went in and climbed the stairs.

"He must have heard me. He opened the door to his bedroom and leered at me. I started to get nervous. Something wasn't right; this man was worse than I had even realised. There was another man in his bedroom with him, a bigger, stronger-looking man. He was drunk. Guilio was completely sober, completely lucid. He knew what he was doing. He called to his friend that the entertainment had arrived. I tried to turn and run but it was too late.

"Both men started to chase after me. I tripped at the bottom of the stairs and the pair dragged me back up to the bedroom. My sister arrived ten minutes later but her fiancé had already raped me. She had thankfully arrived in just enough time before the other man had a chance to." As Lia spoke the words, a single tear rolled down her cheek. She stopped a moment and then continued.

"My sister had heard a ruckus from outside and had grabbed a knife from the kitchen on her way up to the bedroom. Not in her worst imaginings could she have envisioned what was going on upstairs. When she came into the bedroom she was horrified by what she saw. Not only had her sister been attacked, but also the man she loved and trusted had been responsible for it.

"She was still holding the knife when she entered the room. She yelled at the pair at the top of her voice to get away from me. They both laughed at her and she approached her lover and lashed out at him, slicing open the skin on his arm. He screamed in pain like the pig that he was. The other one tried to grab at the knife my sister was holding. She then lashed out at his hand and sliced his hand open as well. She called out to me to get up and go with her. I got up as best I could, and made my way over to her. I stood behind her and clung to her dress for support and the two of us backed out of the room.

"We ran from the house as fast as we could. When we arrived home my father opened the door. He saw the state I was in and shouted angry recriminations, asking who had done this to me.

"My sister told him what had happened. My father looked at her in disgust. He told her she had been deceiving him by seeing this man behind his back, and he threw his fists at her in a rage. She moved out of the way and he stumbled and fell to the ground. We tried to pull him up back onto his feet but he was clutching his head. Blood was seeping out from between his fingers. Our father was dead within moments.

"Over the ensuing weeks we pulled ourselves together and arranged his funeral. My sister and I became very close. We had never really liked each other before but we had been brought together by what had happened."

"You never loved your sister before this happened?" interrupted Isabella.

"Oh, no, I always loved my sister. We were sisters. Of course we loved each other. We just did not like each other very much sometimes. Anyway we were closer then, than we had ever been. The day after my father's funeral my sister was told about her inheritance, she looked at me and told me that she didn't deserve this money. 'Don't be foolish, of course you do,' I told her.

"I don't," she said back to me, "because I am the one who killed him. I should not profit from his death."

"I tried to reassure her and tell her that she did not kill him, that it was just an accident. She answered that our father certainly thought she was responsible for my rape. The last time she had ever seen him, he had tried to strike her. If she had only let him, he would still be alive. And with that she left me. I called after her but she did not listen. That was the last time I ever saw her alive.

"Yesterday morning I got up before my sister. She had been very quiet in her room for hours. I felt that she wanted or needed to be on her own, to come to terms with her own guilt. I waited until the mid afternoon and then I went up to her bedroom. I knocked on the door. She didn't answer, but I entered anyway. I could not see her. I heard a creaking coming from behind the door. I shut the door to see what was behind it. At my eye level all I could see was my sister's waist swinging back and forth. I was afraid to look up. I slowly drew up my eyes and I saw my sister's once beautiful face contorted into an agonising grimace. She had hanged herself.

"In the previous weeks I had put out of my mind all thoughts of revenge but now I wanted his blood and I grabbed a knife and ran here. My only regret is that I was not here to see him suffer."

"Don't worry, I drew out his death and when he died he was begging for his life," answered Isabella.

"Thank you for telling me that, but again, I must say we have to leave here."

Isabella felt that she could trust this woman completely and if she found out that she could not trust her, Isabella could easily kill Lia. So Isabella decided to take a risk.

"Lia, my name is Isabella; you have told me your secrets and in return I shall tell you mine. That man I killed never did anything to me. I killed him because I liked the look of his house and I was hungry."

Isabella was using her influence on Lia to make her listen to her words and not be afraid. Although this was true, Lia's will was her own. Isabella had learned to use her powers wisely.

"I am not like you," Isabella continued "I used to be but not any more. I am immortal, a Vampire." Isabella held out her wrist towards Lia and with her nail made a gash across it. Lia watched in disbelief as the blood seeped from the wound and then trickled away to reveal a wrist, which was unmarked.

Isabella relinquished any influence she had used on Lia so that Lia was completely free to feel and react as her own will dictated.

"Are you not frightened?" Isabella asked.

Lia looked at Isabella and said, "If you, being such a creature, wanted me dead you would have done it by now."

Isabella nodded in reply and said, "You can stay in Florence. I can protect you."

"I am not sure I should stay," Lia answered.

"Well you at least should stay until you have settled the score." Lia looked at her with curiosity. "The other man," Isabella continued, "the one who held you down."

※

Isabella stood in the ale house watching him. He was a large man; he looked strong. However, there was nothing in his appearance or his demeanour to recommend him to a woman. He was eating his dinner in the most grotesque fashion. A good amount of the food was embedded in his beard and the food that actually reached his mouth was spat out again. The thought of him coming near a woman, never mind attacking her, was enough to make anyone wretch. A dog came over to where he was sitting and whimpered, begging for a scrap of meat. This man answered his whimpers by kicking the dog. He resumed eating his dinner, throwing the scraps into the fire beside him to spite the animal.

Isabella approached the man and sat in the chair opposite him. He looked up at her and spat out a piece of fatty skin that was wedged in the corner of his mouth. As a consequence of this action saliva came shooting out of his mouth in all directions. Isabella hid her disgust, but disgusted she was. She curled up the side of her lip into a smile. She leaned over towards him, setting her elbows on the table. Isabella rested her chin gently on her hands and waited. She did not have to wait very long. The insidious creature sitting opposite Isabella started to speak.

"What do you want?" he said, and he quickly followed this phrase with. "I haven't got any money." Isabella was slightly offended. She might no longer have human blood in her veins but she still had a modicum of self-respect. This man assumed she was a prostitute. In spite of this, Isabella retained her smile. He was starting to get unnerved by her. This beautiful creature had chosen to sit in front of him rather than with anyone else in the room. This made him curious and suspicious and yet he was fascinated by her. He asked again.

"What do you want?"

"I don't want anything," Isabella said softly.

"Then why did you sit here?"

"Why would I not sit here?" He sat silently still eating, looking at Isabella curiously. "Maybe I liked the look of you," Isabella continued, and the man grunted in response.

"You want something," he said. "A woman like you always wants something." Isabella smiled. Maybe he was not as stupid as she thought. She would have to try a different approach.

"All right, I need a room for the night." Isabella said.

"A room."

"Yes."

"And what will you give me in exchange?" Isabella leaned coquettishly back in the chair, her arm draped over one side, her back pressed against the other, and answered.

"Whatever you want."

In response, the man fumbled about in his pockets hurriedly and pulled out a few coins, slinging them onto the table. He was excited in anticipation. He leaped up out of his chair. "Hurry up," he growled to Isabella.

But she was not as quick to get up as the man would have liked and he lost his patience with her and pulled at her arm. Isabella used all the restraint she had. She had killed people for much less than this, but this was not going to be her kill. That pleasure was reserved for someone else. They left the inn together. A woman was watching them from the shadows outside. She followed them, keeping herself hidden from the pair, but Isabella knew she was there. The man was dragging Isabella by the wrist. Isabella was not used to being treated like this and she would not put up with it for long. Thankfully, she did not have to.

They soon arrived at the man's apartment. It was at the top flight of a dilapidated house. They went up the stairs and he shut the door behind Isabella. He turned and pushed her up against the wall and then pressed his lips on hers. Isabella gently pushed him back. He seemed slightly disgruntled at this, but his frown turned back into a lecherous smile when Isabella lay invitingly on top of his bed. Isabella pulled up the bottom of her dress slightly to reveal part of her leg. He ran and clambered over to the bed and quickly removed Isabella's shoes and then clumsily started to kiss her feet. Isabella had had more than enough of this man's company, so she decided to hurry up the proceedings. She leaned down and placed her finger under his chin so he was looking up into her eyes.

"I'd like to ask you a question," Isabella began.

"Anything," he spluttered. Isabella's hypnotic voice filled the room and when she asked a question in this manner very few people could have resisted answering her.

"What is your worst fear?" The man sat back on the floor relinquishing any grip he had on her. His mind filled with dreadful memories that he would have rather never thought upon again. He looked up at Isabella; he was totally within her thrall. He looked gentle, as if he was only to be pitied when he started to speak. But Isabella would hold no pity for him.

"When I was young, just a child, I became very ill and was declared dead. They put me in a coffin and lowered into me into a grave. When they were piling on the dirt, burying me I was awakened by the sound of the earth thudding against the coffin lid. The crowd outside heard a faint scratching, followed by screams of a child who was petrified of the dark. My mother demanded that the coffin be pulled up and opened. I rolled out gasping for air. I have always remembered how I felt when I was trapped in that constricting box. I have had nightmares ever since. I dream that I wake up in the dark unable to move, not knowing where I am at first. I struggle and try push up on the lid but dirt pours in through the cracks and then I realise that I am underneath the ground. I stop struggling, afraid that the dirt will suffocate me, but the air then starts to get sour and it becomes more difficult for me to breathe. I am shouting out for my mother but this time she doesn't come, and I know no one else will hear me before I die."

Isabella leaned down and the man thought she was going to kiss him to comfort him, but she had no comfort to offer him. Isabella bit down hard into his neck. He squealed out in agony and blood gushed from his open wound. The girl he had helped to rape finally entered the room. Isabella grabbed his face and forcibly turned it around so that he could see Lia.

"Do you remember her?" Isabella asked. The man now knew that his life was in the hands of the two women. Blood was still pouring from his open wound. He ran for the door in a last attempt to save his own life and the two women grabbed both his arms and pulled him back.

"What are you going to do to me?" he whimpered.

"You are going to go to sleep," Lia answered. "When you awake you will be in your own grave." The man started to tremble and after a few minutes he fainted.

He awoke the next day; he couldn't move. He was imprisoned in his final resting place. He started to struggle but the earth started to pour in on him from between the cracks in the lid. The air around him quickly started to turn sour. He yelled out for help but he knew no one could possibly hear him.

The two women woke the following morning. Isabella looked at the girl she had helped kill her attacker. She looked sad. Isabella was afraid was she feeling remorse

"Are you feeling guilty?" she asked.

Lia looked up at her inquisitively.

"You look remorseful." Isabella continued.

"No, I am not remorseful. Far from it. I am sad because I think I am pregnant and the gratification I felt while killing that man was nothing compared to the happiness I once shared with the family he helped destroy. I will always miss them, but I do not feel anything for him; he was beyond my pity. I hope he rots slowly in his grave."

Isabella recognised the dark look that came across Lia's face. For, like Isabella, she had been touched by malevolence and it had poisoned her.

Lia and Isabella never spoke again of the events that had happened the previous night.

※

The following months were spent in the house Isabella had acquired. Lia stayed with her. Isabella was happy during this time, as happy as she could be. Lia was a woman who did not pass judgement on Isabella. She knew the cruel things Isabella was capable of and did not think badly of her. Lia understood Isabella and Isabella understood her. The two women were now bound to each other.

Isabella wished she could keep this woman with her forever as a constant companion. She often tried to discuss this with Lia, but all Lia ever told her was that she did not want to hang on to this life any longer than she had to. Life had brought her nothing but pain and she did not want to prolong it.

The pair spent their nights together wandering through the streets hunting for Isabella's next victim. Isabella had also started stealing from her victims. She was running out of money and she wanted to live in the manner that she had become accustomed too. They were becoming quite skilled at picking the right sort of victim and they were both acquiring quite a fortune. During the day Isabella slept. Lia would sometimes visit the graves of her father and sister, or visit the more distant members of her family.

One day in the autumn she invited Isabella to a family party. Isabella laughed at the very idea but she went anyway out of respect for her friend.

From the moment she entered the house Isabella felt out of place. Love and warmth filled this place. Lia was going round all her family in turn, laughing and enjoying herself. In the time she had known Lia she had never seen her so happy. Isabella had never seen anything like this. She had only been close to her grandfather and had never had or even seen a family party before. For the second time in her life Isabella felt totally anonymous until an elderly gentleman came over and sat beside her.

"My name is Matteo Bandello. I am a distant cousin of Lia's," the elderly man introduced himself.

Isabella smiled at the man. She had promised her friend that she would be polite and also most importantly that she would not kill any one, unless Lia said she could. So she tried to remember the manners her grandfather had taught her so many years ago and answered the friendly-looking old gentleman.

"I'm Lia's friend."

"I know...I thank you for looking after Lia. She has been so melancholy since her father and sister died. Her happiness has been forever marred by that tragedy."

"I know. It is good to see her smile again," Isabella answered.

"Yes, it is. Maybe there is hope for her yet," Matteo answered. "You look sad as well. You are a melancholy pair," he said.

Isabella smiled slightly.

"What makes you so sad? Why should such a beautiful young girl not be happy?"

"Beauty doesn't automatically bring you happiness. If anything, quite the opposite," Isabella responded.

"You are quite correct but with such a beautiful girl surely the odds of being happy are definitely in your favour."

"I thought so once. I thought my beauty could bring me happiness and it did, it got me everything I wanted, but later, it also took everything from me."

"You speak so maturely for one so young," Matteo commented.

"I am older than you think," Isabella answered.

"You cannot be any more than eighteen," Matteo said, laughingly.

"I am considerably older than that," Isabella said. Isabella thought she had ended the conversation, but Matteo was very persistent.

"You say you were happy once?"

Isabella looked at the man. He was being too inquisitive for her liking.

"I am sorry; I am a writer—I like to hear people's stories," Matteo explained, sensing Isabella's slight reluctance to his persistent probing.

"A writer. I should have guessed. No one in this city is anything else but a writer or an artist, and yet I see you are all selling your wares during the day, but none of you seem to admit to being merchants."

Matteo laughed. "You are being quite churlish. Maybe I should not have sat beside you!"

"I know, and I promised your cousin Lia I would be good," Isabella commented sharply.

"You don't have to be good on my account," Matteo replied. "People who do not speak their mind hold no interest for me. So you are not impressed by Florence, then?"

"Not really," Isabella answered.

"Have you ever looked around you?" Matteo asked with a look of confusion.

"Not really," said Isabella.

Matteo then in a matter-of-factly way replied, "Well, you should. There are many beautiful sights to be seen."

"I take it you like it here," said Isabella.

"This is the place where dreams come true," Matteo responded.

"I don't have any dreams and certainly not anything that can come true here," said Isabella.

"You are a cynic. You need a little romance in your life, a little love," Matteo laughingly replied.

"No, thank you. That is one thing I do not need any more of…I have had my fill of it," Isabella replied.

"Don't be so hasty. I promise you will want to love again," Matteo said.

"I am afraid you are very wrong, I do not ever want to love again."

"Ah, but that does not mean you won't."

Isabella could not help but smile at this man. He was an old romantic, an optimist in a cynical world.

"Love is what keeps us alive and what brings us together," he continued. "I'm writing a story now about two young lovers from warring families. The love that the two people share brings their families together. Love unites them."

Isabella laughed out loud. "Love doesn't solve anything. It certainly doesn't heal any old wounds; it makes them fester. It brings nothing but jealousy, bitterness and reproach. I have never heard of anyone who has been made completely happy by love alone."

"Something or someone must have hurt you very deeply," Matteo observed.

"No, it is just simply observation. Can you honestly tell me that you have known anyone who was made happy by love? I mean real love...the type that when it happens to you, you can't stand to be away from that person? Then when you are torn away from him you can't stand to be without him? The only thing that can end your misery is your own death! Believe me, your two lovers in your story would be better off if they both died."

"Which is better? Being alive and miserable, or to die without knowing misery?" asked Matteo, with much confusion.

"Death is better. The sweet oblivion that it offers is always better," Isabella answered.

Matteo replied in sympathy, "You say that as if you know it to be true."

"It is true," said Isabella. "Let your two lovers end their family feuds if you want to, but it won't happen because of their love. That wouldn't be true. Let them end it by their deaths," said Isabella. She then got up and left the old gentleman sitting by himself, pondering. He was baffled by the young, beautiful woman who was so obviously miserable.

A few months later Lia came home to Isabella's with a short story written by her distant cousin and gave it to Isabella.

"Matteo insisted that I gave this to you. He said you inspired it. It's quite a tragic story. He has named one of the characters after you. Did you tell him your name was Juliet?" Lia asked curiously.

"I did, for it seemed as good a name as any," Isabella said with a smile. She liked the story and decades later she took it to England with her.

The next several months passed pleasantly for Isabella, more pleasantly than any time she could remember since her death. She believed herself to be close to sixty years old, but she was not sure.

Isabella sometimes would go down to the alleyway beside the house where the two women lived. Once there, she would wait in the darkness for unwilling victims to pass by. The alley was getting quite a reputation among the residents of the city. People used to run through it, daring what lurked in the shadows to grab them as they ran by. Some got out alive; some didn't. At first, when the killings began, the authorities would send men to investigate, but somehow they never seemed to return home. So Isabella was left alone to kill as the mood struck her.

Isabella when she was happier regained some of her human compassion and sometimes even considered who she was to strike before she did. On a night in midwinter she was waiting in the alley for sustenance to find her; it came in the guise of a woman. This woman was crying, begging quietly for her death. Isabella wondered why such a young girl should be so unhappy and want to give up her life quite so willingly. Isabella resolved to ask her.

"Why does someone so young ask for death?"

The girl was frightened by the voice but answered. "Are you a ghost or are you death itself?"

Isabella smiled but she made no obvious sign of her mirth.

"What would you prefer?" Isabella asked.

"Death itself," said the woman.

Isabella replied, "I suppose I could be called a sort of ghost."

The woman in desperation asked, "Then you can kill me?"

"What sort of a ghost can kill the living?" asked Isabella.

The woman again in desperation replied, "I want to die." The girl begged Isabella to kill her.

Isabella, now very curious, replied, "If you tell me why maybe I will grant your request."

"I want to die because this morning I had a child and it died in my arms," the woman said through her tears.

"You can have another child," Isabella said. She rarely had the patience or the inclination to comfort any one.

The woman responded with "I can't—this was my only chance."

This peaked Isabella's curiosity and she asked, "What about the father?"

"He is too grief-stricken," the woman sadly replied.

"Do you love him?" Isabella asked.

The woman without thought and very lovingly stated, "Yes with all my heart."

"Does he love you?"

"He tells me he does," the woman replied with some uncertainty.

"And you think the day after he loses his child he wants to lose his wife as well?" Isabella scolded.

"No, but I can't face him, I feel responsible," the sad woman said.

"You are not responsible," Isabella stated firmly. "I had a family once and my father would rather have lost me than his wife. You have lost your child and that is a tragedy, but you have to keep living. You and your husband must comfort each other. Go back to your husband and be with him. Death will not find you here."

The woman left; still sobbing. Isabella had an odd compulsion to follow her. She felt sorry for the woman. She wanted to make sure her husband was worthy of her and something in this girl's story reminded her of her own loss.

The woman wandered slowly home ahead of Isabella. She paused before she went inside; there was a candle burning in the window. Isabella crept forward and stared in at the couple. When her husband saw her coming in through the front door he ran towards her and embraced her. He held her face in his hands and kissed her tears away. The pair sat down together in the darkness holding each other and comforting each other. The scene made Isabella pine for Nicolae and a single blood-red tear hit the dusty street below her feet.

Isabella returned back to her home and as she approached the stairs of her house she could hear screams coming from inside. It was Lia! She was having her child. Isabella ran upstairs to find Lia in agony. Blood had soaked through all the sheets. Isabella could immediately see something was wrong. Lia was bleeding far too much.

"Make the pain stop," Lia cried out.

Isabella looked at the midwife. "What can be done for her?" Isabella asked.

"Nothing," the midwife replied.

Lia grabbed Isabella's arm. "Isabella, you know you are the only one who can take the pain away."

"I can't," Isabella cried.

"You can...please." At this point the baby's head appeared and then the body. "Please, Isabella, make the pain stop." The midwife picked up the wailing child and placed him down gently, away from his mother. Isabella looked at the child and then looked up at the midwife.

"Leave," Isabella said looking at the midwife.

"But—"

"Leave now," Isabella reaffirmed. The midwife ran out the door. Isabella had frightened her.

"The baby is born now, Lia, the pain will stop soon." Isabella again tried to convince Lia to hold onto her life. Lia shook her head.

"The pain will never stop as long as my life persists...." Lia tightened her grip on Isabella's arm and uttered one final time, "Please, Isabella."

Isabella realised this had always been Lia's plan, to wait until her child was born and then end her own life. Isabella kissed Lia on the forehead and then bit her neck and drained her of just enough blood so that she would fall peacefully asleep forever. Isabella made sure she did not feel another thing.

"Thank you," Lia whispered

Isabella placed the child on his mother's lap and Lia lived just long enough too see the baby open his eyes and look once upon his mother's face.

❦

Isabella arranged a quiet funeral for Lia and as she stood by her graveside she held Lia's baby in her arms. She stared at the child. She knew she could not possibly look after him, but she had an obligation to see that the child was properly taken care of. She wasn't too concerned that the child be brought up by a rich family; she just wanted the child to be loved. She wondered who she could give him to. Then she remembered the couple who had just lost their own child. Lia's child would be safe and happy with them. Isabella took the baby boy to the only two people on this earth that she knew would look after him. She laid the baby down on their doorstep and knocked on the door. She waited and watched from a distance as the mother came to the door and saw the baby. The mother could not believe her eyes. She picked up the child and went inside to show her husband. Isabella was relieved she had paid her last debt to Lia.

Isabella returned to her now empty house only to see Medici soldiers banging on her front door. She shouted up to them from the ground below.

"Can I help you?" Isabella asked knowing it would take more than two soldiers to make her give up her home.

"Do you live here?" one of the soldiers asked her.

"I do," Isabella answered.

"Not anymore," said the other soldier. The two soldiers descended the steps and each one grabbed Isabella by the arm. "You are coming with us to see Cosimo Di Medici you can explain how you came to live in this house that belongs to him."

Isabella was a little curious as to what the Medici would be like. She wanted to meet this man, who was known as the King of Florence in everything but name. Isabella decided to let the soldiers march her to the Palazzo Pitti.

Isabella entered the grand hall of the palace with a smile on her face. She looked up at Cosimo; he was still a young man. Isabella was quite disappointed on first seeing him. She had expected to see an elderly, imposing man whose every command would quickly be obeyed. She had wanted to see a man worthy of Lia's fear, but this man seemed to be quiet and unassuming. He was tall enough, but thin; he had chestnut hair and a good face, but the sight of him would not intimidate anyone. Not at all worthy of the Medici's reputation.

"Who is this?" Cosimo asked. When he began to speak, even though his voice was little more than a whisper, the people in the room were immediately silenced.

"She is the woman who occupies Giulio's house," the soldier answered.

"Oh, yes, but where is Giulio? Do you know?" Cosimo asked Isabella.

"I have no idea," Isabella answered.

"I think you do. What is your name?"

Isabella decided not to lie and answered. "Isabella."

Cosimo now clicked his fingers and a woman entered the room from a side door. It was Giulio's servant.

"Do you recognise this woman?" Cosimo asked the servant.

For the second time, thoughts that were not her own entered this woman's head. *"Be careful what you say, these soldiers cannot hold me for long."*

"I am not sure, sir, I cannot remember," the woman said, trembling as she spoke.

"You have frightened this woman with just a look," Cosimo said, and he walked over to the window of his palace. "Do you know what we found yesterday morning floating in the Arno?"

Isabella smiled. "I have no real interest in what you found in the Arno."

Cosimo turned back to face Isabella. This woman was not afraid of him. He had never met anyone who was not the slightest bit scared; she was not even slightly intimidated. There she stood, her head held high, keeping her smile fixed on her face.

"Why are you not frightened?" Cosimo asked.

"I have no reason to be frightened," Isabella answered. Cosimo was impressed by Isabella's refusal to be intimidated. He realised there must be a reason for her complete lack of fear.

"You are a woman with secrets," Cosimo stated. Isabella's slight disappointment on first seeing Cosimo was now overshadowed by the command and presence that she now felt he possessed. This man had gained Isabella's respect; he was worthy of the Medici name. She liked him.

Their conversation was interrupted by shouts from outside in the courtyard. Cosimo was still standing by the window. The soldiers' grip on Isabella tightened and by this time Isabella had had enough of them. She shook herself free. The two soldiers fell back on to the floor. The people occupying the room heard more shouts, but only Isabella could discern the sound of an arrow ripping through the air and heading towards Cosimo's back. She swiftly ran in front of him and the arrow penetrated her heart instead of Cosimo's back. Isabella fell back against Cosimo. He fell to the floor under her weight and Isabella's body fell partly on to his lap. Cosimo held her head in hands, pushing back stray strands of hair that had fallen out of place by the violence of her fall.

"Call for the physician," he shouted. "This woman has saved my life."

The Doctor arrived promptly but had no good news to tell Cosimo. "The arrow has pierced her heart and even if it had not, it's laced with poison. No one could survive such an attack."

Cosimo looked at Isabella and took her hand in his. "Do you know, no one has ever saved my life. I have avoided assassinations before, but never because someone actually risked their safety to ensure mine." The doctor had called for a mortician to remove the body. When Cosimo saw the mortician, he said. "Take her and bury her well—I owe her a debt that I can never repay."

The mortician carried Isabella's cold and still body out of the palace. He left her alone to run an errand. When he returned to his place of work to prepare her for burial, the body was gone. The mortician was too afraid to tell Cosimo he had lost the body so he buried another woman in her place. Cosimo attended the funeral.

A few years went by. Isabella remained in Florence but she had not returned to her house since the day she had met Cosimo. She was walking through the streets on a day the city was having one of its many festivals. Isabella stood at the edge of the crowd that had gathered and watched to see what was attracting so many people. It was the same as all the rest of these occasions; someone was marrying someone else or, someone had had a great honour bestowed upon them. There were jesters and dancers running about the streets in bright costumes. Musicians playing various instruments accompanied them, playing tunes that excited their audience, filling them with merriment. The onlookers clapped their hands in time with the music, children giggled and adults grinned. These sights never held Isabella's attention for very long. She turned her back and walked away from the lavish celebrations.

"You are not impressed, then?" Isabella turned to see who was talking to her; she was sure she recognised the voice. She was shocked to see it was Cosimo. She tried to hide her face but it was too late. "I know you," he said.

Isabella sighed. She wondered whether after saving his life she would now have to kill him.

"No, you don't," Isabella answered, using her influence, but this man had a strong will and resisted her.

"I do. You are the woman who died...saving my life,"

"You are mistaken; I have never seen you before," Isabella lied.

"Yes, you have, I knew you had secrets," Cosimo said.

Isabella turned around to face him. "Cosimo," she said, "believe me, you don't want to know my secret." Isabella ran from him; she didn't want to kill him.

That night Isabella decided to visit her old house. She had stayed away for many months, trying to keep up the pretence that she had died that day in Cosimo's court. She had missed it. It felt like home to her.

Isabella entered the house. It was unchanged, slightly dustier than she remembered but it was filled with happy echoes from her past. She went up the stairs to her bedroom and was shocked to see Cosimo sitting waiting for her.

"I knew you would come here."

Isabella laughed. "You did?" There was an uneasy silence between the pair and then Cosimo restarted the conversation.

"I named my daughter after you."

Isabella laughed. "Why ever did you do that?"

"The woman who gave up her own life to save mine. Why ever would I not?"

"But I didn't."

"Well, I realise that now." Cosimo smiled and Isabella returned his smile. Cosimo looked around him. "You like this house,"

"I did."

"Well, the least I can do is give it to you; after all, you did save my life,"

"Thank you," Isabella said. "I have missed this place."

"Tell me one more thing...did you kill Guilio?"

Isabella smiled. "I did. He was not a good man,"

"I know, he had too much of his father in him."

"Let me finish...I didn't know what sort of a man he was before I killed him. I only came upon that knowledge afterwards. I killed him because I wanted this house and that is the only reason I had to take his life."

"If you are that sort of a person, then why did you save me?"

"It was a sudden impulse, nothing more than that, just a whim." At this point the festival started to proceed down the street beside Isabella's house. Isabella went over to the window and looked out. Cosimo came over to look with her; Isabella turned away.

"Still not impressed?" Cosimo asked Isabella.

"Still not impressed," Isabella said.

"Have you ever been impressed by anything?"

Isabella thought for a moment. "I have, when I was just a child."

"What was it?"

"My grandfather had taught me to read, but I had very few books. There was a castle near our village and in that castle there was a library. The library had hundreds of books in it. I used to steal up to the castle from the village and take a few every couple of weeks. I loved that place, before...." Isabella stopped herself. She had told this man enough.

"Did you get through them all?" Cosimo asked, sensing Isabella was remembering something that she would have sooner forgotten.

"Almost," Isabella answered.

"I want to show you something that will impress you." Cosimo led Isabella back through the streets of Florence and to the old Medici palace. He led her down several corridors into the heart of the building. They approached a pair of huge doors. Cosimo pushed them open and motioned for Isabella to enter. She entered, not prepared to be impressed. Her eyes were immediately drawn up to the highest point of the room. A resplendent fresco spanned the length of the curved ceiling. Cherubs carved from gold were trumpeting in every corner and beneath it, laid before her, was Cosimo De Medici's famous library. There were thousands of books, two floors filled with a myriad of manuscripts. Isabella was impressed.

"Well, have I managed to impress you now?" Cosimo asked.

"Slightly," Isabella replied.

"It would take you several lifetimes to get through these books."

"I may have that much time," Isabella said.

"You have my permission to use this library," Cosimo said. There was a faraway look in Isabella's eye. "I suspect even if I visit here often I will not see you again." Cosimo added.

"You won't," Isabella agreed.

"I suspect that not seeing you again may be a good thing. I think you are a very dangerous woman." Isabella smiled at Cosimo. He bowed and left her in his ancestor's library.

Another fifteen years went by. Isabella visited the library often. She never did see Cosimo again, but had heard recently of his passing. Isabella was sitting in the library a few days after his death when a young girl approached her.

"Isabella," she said. Isabella was taken aback that someone had called her by name. No one had spoken her name since Cosimo. She got up to leave. She did not want to talk to this girl. Unfortunately for Isabella the girl was not so easily discouraged and she chased after her. "Please listen to me," the girl pleaded.

Isabella turned towards her. "How do you know my name?"

"If you sit down and talk to me for a few minutes I will tell you."

Isabella wanted to know how this girl knew her name, so she sat and listened.

"My father told me I would find you here."

"Your father?"

"Cosimo, the Grand Duke."

"You must be my namesake."

"I am,"

"I was sorry to hear about your father's death. He was a tolerant man."

"Thank you."

"What did your father tell you about me?"

"Many things."

"What, specifically?" Isabella said, suspecting that she was going to have to kill Cosimo's daughter.

"He told me that you saved his life."

Isabella sighed. "If I had of known it would have come back to continually haunt me I would not have bothered." Cosimo's daughter looked at Isabella. She was a good woman and would never be able to understand the creature that sat in front of her, but she was determined to ask her something.

"Only moments before he died told me of you. He was very ill but something made him struggle to his feet and walk to the window to see the festival that was going by. He asked me was I impressed by the festival. I said that I always was and he said he once knew someone who wasn't. Then he looked at me and smiled. He was remembering you. He said that he knew he could impress you and he told me that he did. He held my face in his hands and said that if I was ever in danger I should come here to his library and look for you. He described you as a woman with dark hair and dark green eyes and he said that even now you would probably be the most beautiful woman in the room."

"You are not getting to the point," Isabella rejoined.

"I am in danger. My husband is going to kill me," the girl cried.

"And what has that got to do with me?" Isabella asked.

"My father told me that you would help me."

"That was very presumptuous of your father. I never said or even gave him the impression that I would do any such thing."

"You can't mean that! My father was wrong about many things but he was always a good judge of character. I know you will help me."

"You and your father are wrong. I won't help you. I am a woman without compassion. I never deceived your father he knew the creature I was." Isabella got up to leave, but before she did Cosimo's daughter called out one last thing to her.

"My father told me that you believed you had no goodness in your heart but he knew you did. He saw it in you."

Isabella did not look back again at Cosimo's daughter and if she had, she would have seen the tears running down her face. She was desperate, and this Vampire was her last hope. Isabella arrived back at the home that Cosimo had given her. As she went through the door, the Medici coat of arms that was carved into the wall beside her caught her eye. She looked at the three feathers. They represented temperance, prudence, and fortitude. Cosimo, she thought, had all these qualities. He was a decent man and she had no doubt that his daughter possessed them as well. Isabella sighed and leaned her forehead against the door. She would help Cosimo's daughter if she could.

Isabella went straight to the Cereti Guido. Cosimo's daughter lived there with her husband, but by the time she got there it was too late.

※

Isabella Orsini had returned from her meeting with the Vampire completely disheartened. Her husband had arrived home before her. He came over to her and kissed her on the cheek, Isabella flinched back from his touch.

"That's understandable," Paolo Orsini said to his wife, "but can we not make amends?"

"Like you made amends with Vittoria's husband."

"I had nothing to do with his death," Paolo protested.

"I don't believe you," Isabella exclaimed. Paolo stepped back from his wife and spoke with as much sincerity as he could muster.

"Isabella, you are totally safe. I am not so stupid as to kill a Medici. Sit down and let us have a pleasant dinner together." Isabella sat reluctantly and the next hour did pass quite pleasantly. Paolo was being uncharacteristically charming and at the end of the dinner he leaned over to kiss his wife. Isabella let him but it was the last thing she ever did. When Paolo was close to her, almost touching her, he signalled to the balcony where four men lowered down a rope and he strangled his wife.

Isabella entered the house and saw her namesake lying on the floor. For the first time in a long time Isabella actually felt grief. She would personally avenge this young girl's death. Isabella's thoughts were interrupted by a young man running into the room in search of Isabella Orsini.

"My god, no," the young man cried out, "I am too late!"

"It appears we were both too late," Isabella answered.

"Who are you?" the young man asked.

"I am acquaintance of her father's. Who are you?"

"Troilo Orsini. I loved her," Troilo blurted out.

"It appears her husband didn't."

"No, he never did. He has fallen for another woman. All Florence is talking about his conspicuous affair with Vittoria Accoramboni. I only received the news yesterday that she had her husband killed and I immediately rushed here, I knew it was only a matter of time before Isabella would be killed."

"Do you know where they are now?"

"I suspect getting married. Paolo did not know about us. He still kept me in his confidence to a certain extent. I can't believe he did this! He will regret it."

"He will, don't concern yourself. I will avenge Cosimo's daughter," Isabella said. "Do you know where they will go?"

"Probably Venice. He has friends there."

"He'll be first and then I will settle the score with Vittoria," Isabella stated.

"You won't have to. Paolo changed his will. He has left Vittoria everything. His brother, who would have inherited, will not let her live long." Isabella got up to leave and Troilo grabbed her hand before she could.

"Promise you will kill him," Troilo asked.

"Don't worry, listen to the town crier. He will speak of his death soon enough." Troilo did not know this woman but he knew that she was telling him the truth.

Isabella went straight to Venice. Paolo was in hiding when Isabella found him, waiting for his new love to come to him, but she never would. Paolo thought that Isabella was a prostitute sent to amuse him while he was waiting for his new wife. He approached Isabella with lascivious intent. However, when he got close to her, something in her eyes unnerved him, a coldness, a determination. He knew then that she was there to kill him. He turned to run but Isabella grabbed his arm before he could escape and struck at him until he was on the point of death. Then she leaned towards him and whispered. "Did you think you could get away with killing a Medici? You should have known better." In one last stroke she killed Paolo Orsini.

Troilo, as he had been told, listened for the town crier to announce Paolo's death. He did not have to wait very long. By the time Isabella returned to Florence, she had heard of Vittoria's death also. She had been stabbed by her dead husband's brother.

Isabella never went back to Cosimo's library. She had felt by letting his daughter die that she had lost the right to visit it.

※

Isabella still resided in Florence for the next five years. She slowly returned to her former remorseless self. She soon lost any compassion that she had gained from Lia's company and influence or from the distraction that Cosimo's library offered her.

Isabella was wandering through the streets as she often did; she decided to sit down on the edge of the steps leading up to the Duomo. Behind her the Campinile towered over her head. She remembered the words of Matteo Bandello. He had told her to look around at the city and the wonderful sights it had to offer. For the first time she wanted to see what had inspired so many artists. Isabella looked up at the elegant building in front of her. She stood and ascended the steps to the grand doors of the church. Gold carvings camouflaged the wood. She had been in this city so many years and she had never really looked at them. She rubbed her fingers over smooth figures that were carved into the gold; each picture represented a Bible story. She tried to remember some of them, but could not.

"It's beautiful isn't it?" A voice came from beside her.

"Is it?" Isabella answered.

"Of course, it is almost as beautiful as you."

Isabella sighed; she was no mood for compliments this evening. Isabella made it clear that she would not be receptive to his advances but the man continued his chattering, unperturbed by Isabella's stoic responses.

"It took Ghiberti twenty-eight years to complete," he said. "When Michelangelo saw it he stood back and said these gates are fit to be the gates of paradise."

Isabella, growing weary of his garrulous manner, turned around to face him with the intention of striking him to keep him quiet. She held back her fists when she saw his smile. There was something in his eyes she recognised. He looked like Lia.

"What's your name?" Isabella said and returned his smile, suspecting she knew the answer to her own question.

"Vincent de'Bardi." It was Lia's son, she thought.

"What are you holding in your hand?" Isabella asked.

"A drawing of the Duomo by moonlight." Isabella smiled again. He was a painter, just like his mother.

"Another painter—that's what this city needs."

"I am not just another painter; I am a greatest painter in Florence! I have a perfect eye and my sense of dimensions and perspective is brilliant."

Isabella laughed out loud. "Your enthusiasm for yourself is overwhelming."

"Well, look at my drawing and see for yourself."

The light was fading fast so Isabella's eyesight was starting to become very clear. She could see that the painting was brilliant, the perfect reflection of the exquisite building that stood before them. She was not one, however, to flatter those who flattered themselves.

"It's passable, I suppose," Isabella said with little enthusiasm.

"Passable? It's perfect!"

Isabella smiled. He had his father's arrogance but his mother's charm and they were a good combination. Isabella liked him and she was sure Lia would have as well. Isabella could not fault anyone for being conceited; his conceit would only be exceeded by her own.

"Now," he began, "do you know what a beautiful woman should have on her arm?"

"No, what should a beautiful woman have on her arm?"

"A handsome man." Isabella laughed again. Vincente stood and pushed out his arm for Isabella to take.

"May I escort you home? It's getting dark." Isabella without hesitation interlocked her arm with his and answered him.

"You may." She was quite taken with him. It had been a long time since she had met someone as charming, and flattery always pleased her.

The pair arrived back at her house, and Isabella invited him in. As they sat talking, just enjoying each other's company, Isabella for a brief moment almost felt human again, and she liked that feeling.

"I notice there are no mirrors in this house," Vincent said. "I always thought a woman like you would look at herself often."

"Am I still as beautiful as I was?" Isabella asked.

"You are the most beautiful creature I have ever seen," Vincente answered.

"I like to be told that; it's nice to hear."

"You have not even one portrait of yourself in this house."

"A portrait?" It was such a simple idea but it was something she had never thought of before. "A portrait. Yes. I could see my own likeness again."

"What do you mean?"

"Nothing! Would you do it?"

"I would, gladly."

"Could you right now?" Isabella was excited and she had not been excited by anything in over fifty years.

"I didn't mean now," he called after Isabella, who was impetuous as ever and was already running to her room to change.

"Would you miss the chance to demonstrate your skill?" Isabella shouted back, bursting with enthusiasm. She tore off her clothes and put on a midnight blue velvet dress that she had taken from one of her many victims. She had always wanted to know what she looked like in it, but of course was unable to see it. She desperately wanted to feel beautiful again. She ran to let him see her in the dress. "I want you to paint me like this!"

Vincente looked at her. She was stunning. Her long black hair was pinned up and her dark green eyes shone from across the room. The velvet dress clung to her voluptuous figure. She was a vision, an excellent muse for any artist.

He started to work. He worked all through the night and the next day. Isabella left him intermittently to feed and get some rest. Vincente wanted to prove to her what a good artist he really was and he painted a dozen pictures in the following week. When he had finished. Isabella asked him to blow out the candles.

"You will not be able to see them," he remarked.

"Don't worry, I will see them," Isabella affirmed.

As Vincente started to put out the candles around the room the portraits started to become clear to her. She had almost forgotten what she looked like: her black hair, her dark green eyes, and her smooth white skin. For the first time in forty years she once again saw her beautiful face. She was captivated looking at herself. He had captured her beauty perfectly.

She ran to him, grabbed his face and kissed him. She had not kissed anyone since Nicolae. The young artist returned her kiss and Isabella felt a tingling sensation run through her. She pulled back and looked at him. Could she love him, she wondered? Could she love a mortal? Isabella held him close to her. She knew in her heart that she could not have a relationship with any man but she was enjoying the touch of another for just a brief moment. Then a strange familiar smell touched Isabella; it was a scent she recognised immediately.

"Vlad," she whispered. A fear came over her she looked at her new young companion and said to him. "You have to leave now." He looked bemused. "I have to go away for a few weeks I have business to take care of." Vincente protested but Isabella touched his lips with her finger to silence him and said. "Don't worry. I will be back."

She left that night with one painting, her wooden chest, some money and several changes of clothing. After a few weeks of travelling, Isabella arrived back at the ancient castle. It was even more dilapidated than when she had left.

Vlad was sitting on a chair beside the fire. At first she did not recognise him at all. He had grown old. Isabella's first reaction was to feel her own face but her skin still felt smooth and young.

"Why have you aged?" she asked.

"I haven't rested in weeks," he responded.

"Is this what happens if we don't sleep?"

"If we don't sleep and or feed."

"Why are you not feeding?"

"Why do you care?"

"I don't."

"Why did you come back then?"

"You told me I'd be back. Surely you are not surprised?"

"I did not think it would take this long."

"I'm not going to stay long," Isabella quickly responded. She then left him and went up to her old room. The next evening after she had slept she went down to see Katya. She was shocked when she saw her. Katya was so old; she had still been a young girl when Isabella had left.

"Isabella," Katya greeted her warmly. "You still look the same as when you left, still so beautiful!" Katya whispered.

"I'm glad to see you," answered Isabella.

"I am glad to see you, too."

"Did you ever hear from Nicolae and my son after they left?"

"Isabella...he never left."

"He never left, why? I thought he was determined to go."

"His son told him about meeting a beautiful lady. The way Alexei described her she sounded just like you. I tried to make him dismiss it as nonsense but he was sure it was a sign that he should not leave and that he would be closer to you here."

"You mean he is still here? Where is he, Katya? I need to see him," Isabella begged.

"He's dying. He is an old man; he has not got much time left."

Isabella grabbed Katya and nearly shook the life out of her. "Please, Katya, where is he?"

"He's inside!"

Isabella let go of her friend and Katya fell to the ground. Isabella ran inside. She slowed her pace as she entered the room. There he was lying, slowly dying on the bed in Katya's room. A handsome, middle-aged man strikingly similar to Isabella's dying husband sat beside him in the chair. It was Isabella's son, asleep.

She sat quietly on the bed beside Nicolae, not wanting to wake her son. She looked at her husband. His swarthy skin had paled through the years. It had lost its smoothness. The red traces in his hair had been replaced by grey. He opened eyes briefly but it was too quick and he was in too much pain to register anything that was in the room. It was enough time, however, for Isabella to see that his eyes had lost their brightness. He was only a semblance of the man she had once known and adored. Isabella closed her eyes and imagined him as he once was. She leaned into kiss him and Nicolae was awakened by her touch. He opened his eyes to see his wife just as beautiful as she ever was.

"Is my life over?" Nicolae asked, thinking he was delirious.

"Not yet. Are you in any pain?" Isabella answered.

"Yes," he answered.

"Would you like me to end your life in a way that will not cause you any more pain?"

"Yes," he answered again.

The tears flowed from Isabella's eyes as she leaned over and kissed her husband on the neck, draining the last of his energy. Isabella's tears fell on her dying husband's lips and into his mouth. Nicolae lay silent. He looked peaceful as he was slowly slipping away. Isabella could not contain her grief the tears flowed and continued to fall into her husband's open mouth.

Nicolae's eyes suddenly opened. He looked as if he was regaining his strength. Isabella was awestruck. She did not understand, and then she remembered events of the day that she had become a Vampire. The reason why she was different and had become what she became instead of dying like all the rest. She had drunk Vlad's blood! When he had pierced his finger on the thorn she had tried to drain the poison by sucking the blood from his finger. Isabella slit open her own lips with her fingernail and leaned into kiss her husband.

Nicolae's skin became smoother and his eyes started to brighten. The grey hair began to disappear, replaced by the thick red hair he had once had. Nicolae's hunger for Isabella's blood was great, so much so that Isabella started to feel herself weakening and pulled back from him. In the few seconds that Nicolae was drinking from her she had aged ten years. Her husband was now fully restored to his former self. He stood up and looked at Isabella.

"Is this heaven?" he asked his wife.

"Not quite," Isabella answered. Katya now entered the room she looked at the two unholy creatures and crossed herself.

"Isabella," she murmured, "what have you done?" At this point Nicolae began to convulse with pain and he called out for Isabella to comfort him. His anguished cries woke their son.

"Why am I in pain?" Nicolae said to Isabella.

"You have to feed," she answered.

"Feed on what?"

"Blood."

Their son, now fully awake, jumped up and ran to embrace his father. He didn't understand what was going on, but he was glad to see his father alive. Nicolae was confused and disoriented and was still in torturous pain. All he could see was the bulging vain on his own son's neck. He grabbed his son and driven by his blood lust, drank until his son was dead.

Katya was horrified as she tried to pull Nicolae away from his son, but she was not strong enough. Isabella was stunned. She could not move.

Everything seemed so surreal to Nicolae, but as his blood lust diminished the harshness of reality was slowly starting to return. He looked down and saw his dead son on the ground at his feet.

Isabella looked at the body and then looked up at her husband.

"You have killed your own son!" Katya said, looking at Isabella as she spoke. She considered Nicolae almost blameless for the death of their child.

"I can save him," countered Isabella.

"You can't save anyone!" Katya said, reviling her. "You've condemned your husband. Are you going to condemn your son as well?"

"What's wrong with me?" Nicolae shouted, interrupting the women. Blood was flowing from his eyes and staining the shirt of his dead son. "What's wrong with Alexei?" he asked nervously, his voice quivering with fear.

"He's dead," Katya answered. "You killed him."

"How can that be true?" Nicolae said in disbelief.

"It is true, Nicolae, you have killed your own son," Katya responded, without compassion.

"Why would I do such a thing?" he said as tears began to flow from his eyes. "And why are my eyes bleeding?" Nicolae asked frantically.

"Ask your wife," Katya solemnly answered. Nicolae looked up at his wife. A single crimson tear was trickling down her ivory cheek.

"Why are your eyes bleeding?" Memories came suddenly flooding back into Nicolae's mind, memories he had blocked out since he was a child. He looked up at Isabella. "I remember what happened to my parents," he said.

Isabella shuddered and took a step back from her husband. She knew what he was about to say.

"It was dark," Nicolae continued. "My parents were lying next to each other. I saw a man leaning over them. He was biting at their flesh. The colour was slowly draining from their faces. I yelled out to them and the creature looked over towards me. His mouth was covered in blood. I ran as fast as I could from this abomination and then I fell and bumped my head and the next thing I saw was you, lying asleep in a chair beside me. I thought you were the most beautiful thing in the world, but now when I look at you, you seem repugnant to me. You've turned me into the creature that killed my parents. You've made me kill my own son. Your father was right—it would have been better if your mother had lived and you had died. Everything you have touched in your life you have poisoned! I am amazed I ever loved you."

Isabella stood there stunned by his words. She could not move. She would have loved this man forever, but what she had become disgusted him and Isabella did not understand this.

"I want this to end now," Nicolae said to Katya.

"It can't end. You're immortal," Isabella said. She stretched out her hand. "Come with me, Nicolae. You couldn't mean the words you speak."

"I do! It can end now and it will. Katya, fetch Alexei's sword." Katya did as Nicolae asked. Nicolae kneeled down and Katya swung the sword at his neck. It sliced straight through. His head fell to the floor. Katya was oblivious to it but Isabella sensed an aura of peace emanating from Nicolae's body. It was a feeling that ran through her and it comforted her slightly. She felt that Nicolae was at peace and it was a peace she longed for.

Isabella cried her last tear that night. She would not cry again for anyone, not for three hundred years. She became the creature that Katya thought her to be. She would be merciless from this moment on. Her last human instinct would die with Nicolae, she resolved.

AUTO-DA-FE
ACT OF FAITH

CHAPTER SEVEN

Isabella returned home. The night's events had made her understand that the castle was her only true home, the only place where she belonged. Any thoughts she had about going back to her house in the village were stricken from her mind forever. Unfortunately for Isabella, through it all she had always thought some miracle would happen and she would be happy with Nicolae again in this world or the next, but now she knew that wasn't true and never would be.

Isabella passed through the doorway into her home. Vlad was sitting where he always sat, in the armchair beside the fire. Isabella found some comfort in this familiar scene. It was as if, after all these years, she finally realised that he would always be here and she could depend on him to always be with her. Isabella had hated him for so long, but now she had lost the will to hate him. And she desperately needed to talk to someone who knew to some degree what she was going through and who didn't feel the slightest bit ashamed at what she had become. She knew now he was not wholly to blame for what had happened to her. She had brought this on herself through her constant lies and deception. By lying to Nicolae she had kept him out of a large part of her life and as a consequence Nicolae had never really completely known the person Isabella was. Nicolae had never loved her; he had loved *his* idea of her.

She went over and sat on the stone floor beside Vlad and gazed into the fire. The flames licked further and further up the chimney. She leaned forward and placed her hand just above the flames. As they licked higher

her hand caught fire. Isabella did not feel any pain but she pulled her hand out of the fire, nevertheless. Isabella watched her hand burn.

"My grandfather used to say that fire could kill anything," she began as she turned around and looked up at Vlad, seeing his face for the first time since she had come home. He had become young again. "You've fed," Isabella continued.

"And slept. I didn't want my appearance to make itself even more repugnant to you than usual," he answered.

"Your appearance was never repugnant to me." She looked back towards her hand again and blew out the flame. There was not a trace of evidence to show that Isabella's hand had been on fire. "Fire can't kill us, can it? No. It can't even mar our flesh."

"Nothing can kill you, nothing can harm you. Some people would think of that as a blessing," Vlad answered.

"This life is certainly not a blessing," Isabella said as she turned her head slightly towards him. "And you know it's not...but also, you're wrong. We can be harmed. I found out tonight we can even die." Isabella sat up to face Vlad. She placed her hands and arms on his lap and with enthusiasm in her voice she said, "I want you to kill me. I know you can."

"I can't and I won't," Vlad said firmly.

"You tried killing me once, surely you bring can bring yourself to do it again." Isabella berated.

Vlad pushed Isabella off his lap and out of the way. He stood and walked towards the fire.

"I didn't mean to kill..." Vlad said softly, almost whispering. "I've told you we will live for eternity. We could share that life...together, Isabella... comfort each other...find some sort of solace." Isabella turned away from Vlad; she was oblivious to his words. Like so many other times in their life together she was only partly listening and the true meaning of his words was not penetrating her mind. If she had listened to or thought about what he was saying to her, she would have understood how much he cared for her. But at this moment Isabella had only one thing on her mind, her final repose.

"Tonight I watched my husband die," Isabella said, interrupting Vlad.

"He must be an old man by now. You should have expected it. It is inevitable that everyone you once knew will die and you will be there to see it, if you choose to be."

"He was an old man...so old...so frail," Isabella continued, her voice wavering as she spoke. "I hardly recognised him and I wept when I saw him. I couldn't control my tears; they fell onto his lips. When he tasted them he opened his eyes, for they had begun to brighten slightly. Then it struck me, I suddenly remembered back to what had happened the day I died. I drank from your blood, remember?" Vlad nodded. "I let him drink from me and his desire for more blood overcame him."

Isabella stopped. She was finding it difficult to relay the tragic events of the night before but she forced herself to continue. "Our son rushed to his father, overjoyed to see him well…and Nicolae…Nicolae killed him without a moment's hesitation. He could not control his desire."

Vlad sat down again and Isabella leaned in beside him. She turned her head back towards the fire, resting her head on Vlad's knee. "He killed our son," Isabella continued. "I tried to save Nicolae from death but he did not want to be saved. He would rather have died than become like us. When he regained his senses he realised what he had done and asked Katya to kill him. He was loathe even to look at me."

Isabella drew out her grandfather's sword, which had been hidden in the folds of her skirt. Nicolae's blood was still fresh on the blade. She turned towards Vlad with the sword and said "I want you to kill me as Katya killed Nicolae."

"No…! Isabella I cannot…." Vlad said to her, his voice betraying his feelings. "I don't want to be alone again," he said softly. "As always, Isabella, you only think of yourself!" he said harshly.

Isabella was getting impatient now. She turned back towards the fire and then quickly turned towards him again with fresh enthusiasm. "We can do it together. We can both strike each other at the exact same time." Vlad did not move or make any sound. "We will be free from this life. I want this to end, I want to be free of this world; it has held onto us both for too long," Isabella said, still hoping to convince him.

"Yes. But where will it end? You talk of being free of this world, but what awaits us in the next? We could be free, only to go to hell," Vlad answered.

"We are in hell…and even hell would be better than this." Isabella paused. "But I don't think we would. I can't explain it, but when Nicolae died a peace came over him. It was as if he had been able to make his peace with God. It was a feeling of total contentment. It emanated from Nicolae's body and it surged through me. It comforted me. It made me realise that there is an end to this and it is nothing to be afraid of."

"But Nicolae was different from us—you have said so many times that Nicolae was a good man."

"He was in life but tonight he killed his own son! Our son! What greater crime and torment can there be than that?" Isabella paused before she made one final plea. "Please. I have never asked you for anything. Please grant me this."

Vlad finally relented and nodded his consent to Isabella's request. She smiled and handed Vlad Alexei's sword and then ran to get another sword for herself. Vlad wiped the blood stain from the sword so that it was clean; it glinted in the light from the fire. They both stood facing each other, swords in hand; a cautious smile crept over Isabella's face, Vlad returned the smile only slightly. There was a clatter as both swords struck each Vampire's neck at the exact same moment. The blades hit the two creatures with such a force that they knocked each other unconscious but the blades didn't even break the skin.

Isabella was first to awaken, for Vlad had held back the full force of his swing, but Isabella had not. She crept over to Vlad and pulled his hair away from his neck. There wasn't even a mark. She was glad to see he was alive as well. She found some comfort in the fact that she had not been left alone. He opened his eyes and looked at Isabella's beautiful face. "It didn't work?" Vlad inquired.

"How do you know? This could be heaven," Isabella said smiling.

"If this was heaven you would be with your husband."

Isabella smiled reassuringly at Vlad.

"I'm not so sure...I believe now that my husband would have ended up hating me no matter what had happened."

"I don't believe that."

"I do. I would have always loved him no matter what he did, but I cannot forget the look of hate he threw me when he discovered what sort of creature I had become, or maybe, it was when he realised what sort of creature I have always been."

"Why do you think we didn't die?" Vlad asked.

"Who knows? Maybe there is no salvation for us. Maybe we are both completely beyond redemption...maybe atonement is only granted to those who have led good lives for the most part, and that is why Nicolae was allowed to die."

Isabella got up and curled up into Vlad's chair by the fire. "What happened to you? How did we end up like this? Surely if you owe me anything you owe me some sort of an explanation"

"It's so long ago I can hardly remember," Vlad lied.

"You can remember every instant," Isabella scolded. "My life, the memories I have, these are very clear. I remember everything as if it was yesterday."

Vlad smiled, "So can I."

"So answer my question, how did you become a Vrolok? You must know something, at least more than I," said Isabella.

"I remember I was fighting the Turks. It seemed as if the whole world was following me. I was a King, a Ruler, and a God among men. Men followed me willingly to their deaths and didn't ask why. I could have married any woman I wanted and I chose Markéta. She was so beautiful I was enraptured from the start and I thought that she felt the same way about me. She was the sort of woman who, if you looked at her and caught her glance, would not look away like most women would; she would smile at you, instead. No matter who you were—the lowest of subjects, or the highest of Kings."

When Vlad spoke of his wife, Isabella's pride was slightly hurt, but for once she let him continue uninterrupted.

"Her mother did not approve of the match," Vlad continued. "I was never sure why. I was from the best families; if anything, I was marrying beneath me. Markéta's father realised this, silenced his wife's protests and Markéta was betrothed willingly to me.

I soon learned that Markéta returned my affection; perhaps she even loved me too much. Every time I would go into battle she would beg me not to go, for she never wanted to be alone in the castle. She was petrified of the Turks attacking and that I would not be there to protect her. She had witnessed firsthand the brutality of the Turks and their treatment of those they took prisoner. They had captured her and her sister when Markéta was just a child. She had heard her sister's screams as they were torturing her. However, Markéta was not touched. She was just left to hear and witness her sister's agony. But she held onto the memory, and when she saw her sister again she was not dead but her back was covered in scars and they had branded her. Her sister was shamed; she was due to marry, but her future husband changed his mind when he heard what had happened, and her sister died.

Left mad and alone, Markéta had an irrational fear of the same fate befalling her. I tried to tell her that I would never abandon her as her sister's future husband had, but she didn't believe me, not completely, at least. Despite my constant reassurances, she was still petrified that if I was killed by the Turks the same fate would await her and she would end up alone, locked away, out of anyone's sight, crying out in the night for her lost husband and lost life. I presumed at the time that when she saw the Turks coming through the forest towards the castle, it was too much for her to bear. She had not had any correspondence from me in months and feared I was dead. The Turks riding towards the castle confirmed her fears. I was told she threw herself off the battlements.

I remember the night I got word that she had killed herself. I even remember your grandfather." Isabella looked at him inquisitively. "I recognise the sword. I met him again when he was much older; he was burying one of my victims when I came across him. He was startled to see me. His first reaction was to kneel before me and then when he lifted up his head to look at my face he realised that I was still a young man. I didn't recognise him at first. I just grabbed him and held him in front of my face. Then I saw something familiar in his eyes and I remembered who he was. I let him go, I am not sure why— maybe it was something still left within me, a part of my old self."

"I think that must have been the night he died. He died of a heart attack."

"I didn't know. I didn't mean to frighten him to such an extent."

"You didn't. He knew it was only a matter of time before he died. If he hadn't met you it probably wouldn't have made a difference." They both sat in silence for a few moments. "My grandfather told me that you fell to your knees when you heard the news that your wife was dead. He always would say that is what love is. Only love could have reduced such a man to his knees."

"I did. I fell to my knees and wept like a child. I was not interested in leading men to their deaths anymore. I came home as soon as I could. When I came through the door, my wife's corpse was lying on the table. Her pretty face was now contorted and white. A priest came into the room with my son. The priest brought the screaming child over to his mother and held the boy's face in his hands, making him look at the body of his dead mother. The priest said to the child that that is what happens when we defy God's laws.

I lifted up my sword and without a moment's hesitation I plunged it into the priest's chest. He fell to the ground. The people around me stared aghast. I had killed a priest. I was condemned in the world's eyes. I didn't care. I took my son and left with my servants, leaving my wife's body in the castle. I let one of them look after the boy and we travelled west away from danger. The servant disappeared with the child along the way and my other servants were too petrified to tell me immediately; it was hours before I was told he had dropped back out of the party. I went back to hunt for them but I could not find him. I never saw my son again.

I found myself eventually back at the castle. I had always considered myself a religious man. And God had now rewarded me by taking my family from me. I ran through the house breaking every religious symbol I could find. The stone carvings around the doors, the crosses, the crucifixes, everything and finally I slashed my sword through my wife's portrait, for even, like God, she had abandoned me. I knelt down before my wife and next thing I remember was waking up in a Hungarian prison.

Someone had struck me and knocked me unconscious.

I woke up with a large lump on the back of my head. The gate of my prison cell was being opened and I recognised the person who entered—it was my brother. I was glad to see him, but not for long. I was still lying on the ground. My brother Radu came towards me and leaned down in front of me."

"Brother," he said to me.

"It's good to see you," I replied back.

"Is it?" he answered.

"Of course it is," I replied. "Where am I?" I asked him.

"In a Hungarian prison," he answered. "Matthias Corvinus has imprisoned you at my request."

"I don't understand, at your request."

"Yes."

"But why?"

"How can you ask me that? You left me there in Constantinople. You left me without a second thought."

"That is not true, Radu, I tried to get you back many times, and I tried to negotiate your release."

"Lies!" Radu shouted at me.

"It is not, it is the truth, I promise you."

"I don't believe you!"

"You can believe what you like, it is the truth. I will not argue with you any further."

"Well, I have gotten my revenge on you."

"Revenge, what do you mean?" I asked him.

"Let me show you," Radu said, loosened his clothing to reveal a back that was covered in scars from whips and branding irons. I was appalled by the treatment he had gone through.

"I am sorry," I told him. "But you can't blame me for this,"

"I can and I have! These are only the visible scars of the Sultan's abuse."

"I can only say I am sorry so many times. You have suffered greatly, but how would showing me this enable you to get your revenge?"

"Because I wanted you to see the last thing your wife saw. I showed them to her as the Turks were approaching. It was all just too much for her. She tossed herself off the battlements. But before she did that, not wanting your son to suffer as I had, she gave him poison and I paid a servant, one of your servants, to bring his body back to me."

"I leaped up and tried to grab him, I wanted to kill him. But he was too quick for me and he got out of my prison cell before I could reach him.

"Your line ends with you," he said.

"I reached out my hand through the bars of my prison, but Radu just walked away—that was the last time I saw him.

I was there for fourteen years. I grew old in that prison and when I was released I returned to the castle once more and ruled for several months until my death. I was a broken man without my wife and child. Ruling again meant nothing to me.

The next time I was conscious in this world was at Snagov. I was in my own tomb and I was awakened by the stone lid being slid off. I felt disoriented at first and I looked up; I thought I saw my wife but she looked older. When my eyes focused I recognised the woman standing over me was my late wife's mother.

Elisabetha, my wife's mother, had lighted a fire in the chapel where I had been entombed. She was stoking the fire as I clambered out of my stone coffin. She told me that we didn't have much time and that the Sultan's men were coming for my body to take it back to Constantinople. I asked her if I was dead. She told me not quite. I didn't know what she meant. She asked me to help her place another body in the coffin so that the Sultan's men would have a body to take back with them. It was my brother's body. I told her that they would never fall for it and they would try to seek me out but she said that no one had seen me in fourteen years—they would be satisfied with my brother's body. I heard later that his head was stuck on a spike and paraded through the city streets; it was left by the city gates for the entire world to see. Vlad Dracula was dead.

Elisabetha told me to go back to the castle and she would meet me there, but first I had to feed. I was overcome with hunger and I started to feel the strongest hunger pains I had ever experienced in my life. Elisabetha handed me a goblet. I examined the contents. It was a goblet of blood. I was appalled, but something within me was compelled to drink it. It didn't satisfy me; on the contrary, it made me feel weaker, but I was spurred on by my blood lust and I drank every last drop.

I travelled back to the castle and Markéta's mother followed soon after. She asked me to come and sit with her when she arrived."

"Do you remember anything?" she asked me.

"No," I answered.

"I have been feeding you for the past few nights. You have a blood lust; you always did."

"A blood lust?"

"Yes, it has been lying dormant within you. You got it from your father and he got it from his. Your grandfather Mircea the Great was a Vampire."

"Nonsense."

"It isn't, you know it is not. In your mind as I speak to you it is all becoming clear—there have been signs. All your life you have known that there was something different about your father and grandfather."

"There were no signs!" I protested.

"You know you are different, just as they were."

"Even if that is true, what do you know of my family?"

"I am Mircea's daughter."

"His daughter?" I said in disbelief.

"Yes...my mother is not your grandmother. I am the last of my kind, just as you are the last of yours...you are the last Vampire and I am the last Dhampir. Mircea and your grandmother made a promise to each other never to create another Dhampir or Vampire ever again. As a consequence both our kinds have nearly become extinct. Your grandmother was the same as me; she was a Dhampir and a Szekely."

"A Szekely."

"When she said this I knew she was speaking the truth. My father had always teased us that we were of the Szekely race and therefore descendants of Attila.

"Let me finish," Marketa's mother censured. "She was sent to kill your grandfather, but instead she fell in love with him. And it was the beginning of the end for us all. But something in his dark Vampire's blood was passed on and lay dormant in his descendants; it would survive until there were nearly no Dhampirs left to fight you. It would have died with you, as you are the last of your line, but I could not let it."

"Why not?" I asked her.

"I should have. I promised Mircea that I would not interfere. Only my Dhampir blood could awaken the latent Vampire within you. I had every intention of keeping my promise until you let my daughter die!"

"But I didn't," I said, trying to protest.

"Yes, you did. From the moment you saw her you slowly destroyed her, you and your whole poisonous family. When word reached me of my daughter's death, I knew what I had to do. I had to devise a punishment for you that you would never be able to escape from. That is why I awakened you. You are a Vampire now! That is my punishment for you. You will live the long, stagnant years in complete solitude, with only the memory of my daughter to keep you company."

"I told her it was my brother who was to blame for my wife's death. She told me she knew he had dealt the final blow that had coerced Markéta to suicide. She had hunted him down and killed him, but in her eyes I was primarily to blame. She left me after that and I never saw her again." Vlad turned away from Isabella. This last statement was a lie. Elisabetha did not leave him, but he was not ready to tell Isabella this yet.

"She must have so many answers," Isabella said.

"Whatever they are she took them with her...I, like you, tried killing myself many times," Vlad continued. "I stabbed myself with a knife in the heart and it just stunned my senses; it had no more effect than that. I tried again to kill myself the next time by slitting my wrists and again it did nothing, for the wounds healed quickly. I tried again and again, but nothing left so much as a permanent scar. Then all I could think about was blood—I had to kill. I started to kill Gypsies and still it wasn't enough. Then I started to kill my own people.

And that's when rumours and whispers started about the murders. I think the first person I killed from the village below was just a child. Your guilt only lasts awhile. Then I began to wonder, what would happen if I didn't feed? Would I starve to death? I resolved to stop feeding. I noticed my skin was not as smooth as it used to be. But when I went back to sleep it seemed to become smooth again. So I started to go without sleep as well. I thought I would eventually die of old age but I didn't; it just got more and more painful. Then something happened that made me feel like I wanted to live and grow young again."

"And what was that?" Isabella asked.

"A young girl wandered up into the castle. I first saw her from the rooftop. She was with a friend but all I could see was her. She was the most beautiful creature I had ever encountered. She made me wish I were young again. I used to watch you every time you would come to the castle. I disguised myself as a wolf just to be near you. I didn't want to make myself known to you until I was sure what kind of woman you were."

"You waited long enough to talk to me," Isabella interrupted.

"It was when you started to come up at night that I realised you were hiding something from someone, probably the man you were married to. When I first saw your wedding ring I wanted to kill you, but I couldn't imagine any man down in that village being worthy of you. So I waited to see if you loved your husband. The night I killed you I was totally in love with you. When you talked about how you loved your husband I couldn't stand it. I struck out at you. But when I thought I had killed you I was devastated. Then, two nights later when I saw you alive, I was the happiest I had been in any lifetime. I thought you would forgive me eventually. But you didn't. You hated me, and how could I blame you. I had done to you exactly what had happened to me. But it was making me insane, watching you, having you so near."

Isabella turned up the corner of her mouth into a wry smile, "It was meant to."

"I didn't know what to do to change my feelings towards you. I tried to despise you but I couldn't. I thought if I left you alone you would eventually realise that I was your only companion in this world. The only one that understood you. So the night we had the argument I left some money out and watched you leave. I knew you had to get away from here to come to terms with what had happened, but I didn't expect you to be gone for fifty years. Then I took it upon myself to find you, but you knew I was watching you, didn't you?"

"I could feel you near me and a familiar scent made me aware that you were close."

"I let you know I was there. I wanted you home. Who was the man you were with?" Vlad asked.

"No one of any consequence. I killed him before I came home." Isabella paused and changed the subject. "Do you know this land is ruled by the Turks now?"

"Yes...I don't care, really."

"I don't believe that. You, who fought so hard during your lifetime. You would have given up your life willingly to stop them invading this land." Vlad made no response to her statement and they both sat in silent for a few moments before Isabella began to speak again.

"Thank you for telling me this. If you had of told me this from the start I probably wouldn't have hated you as much."

"If you had let me, I would have told you sooner," Vlad said, and he took Isabella's face in his hands. "When I saw you alive," he said, "I felt I could find some form of happiness again. I felt you could be my companion, some one to share eternity with. Do you still hate me?"

Isabella looked at Vlad; he was amazing to look at, not just an attractive man, but a confident, proud man. His black eyes stared straight at her and he was just like her. He wasn't under any illusions about Isabella; he had known her true character from the very start and had loved everything about her. He would never look at her in disgust as Nicolae had done. From the very first moment she had seen him she had been attracted to him as well, in spite of herself. She answered Vlad.

"I don't think I ever really hated you. I blamed you for taking away something which was never really mine to begin with. It never occurred to me that the same thing had happened to you."

"Will you stay here with me then?"

"I will." As soon as these words had left Isabella's lips she felt a slight sense of uneasiness. She felt as if he owned her. But at that moment she did not mind his ownership too much. All thoughts of her Italian friend had left her. Maybe she could find some measure of happiness with Vlad. She embraced him. When she did her eyes were drawn to the slashed portrait of the woman above the fireplace. She pulled back from Vlad. "If your wife had lived...do you think you would have ever been happy with her?" she asked.

"I think so. Yes, she was the perfect wife. She loved me unconditionally and she was easy to love." This, to Isabella, was the wrong answer.

"The perfect wife! You mean she did what she was told?" Vlad smiled at Isabella.

"No, I mean she was perfect. She was a beautiful and dutiful wife. She didn't argue with me, she respected my wishes and would have agreed with everything I said."

"She killed your child. Is that the act of a dutiful wife?" Isabella asked.

"She was coerced into doing that. She thought she was doing the right thing."

"It sounds to me like she had no will of her own."

"She was not like you. You have too much will. To love a woman like you takes effort, Isabella. It doesn't come easily."

"Well then...maybe I should leave you with the memories of your... perfect wife."

Vlad took Isabella in his grip. "I loved my wife and you loved your husband. What does it matter?"

"It matters...I will never be anyone's second choice."

"No one could even pretend to be settling for you and you know that, Isabella. You have not made it very easy for me to love you. Surely, you have to believe that I truly do love you after all these years. If I didn't love you I would have given up on you long ago."

"If that is the case, let me take down the picture."

Vlad looked shocked at her request and quizzically replied, "You want me to take Markéta's picture down?"

"Yes," Isabella quickly blurted out.

Still unable to believe what Isabella was requesting, Vlad questioned her, "And what do you want me to put in its place?"

"A picture of me," Isabella firmly replied.

"You haven't got one," said Vlad, not quite sure what Isabella was alluding to.

"I have," stated Isabella, impatiently waiting for Vlad's response.

"Where?" questioned Vlad.

"Back in Italy," Isabella rebutted.

"Who painted it?" asked Vlad, still unsure of whether Isabella was telling him the truth.

"A man," answered Isabella.

"The man I saw you with?" Vlad asked.

"Yes."

Vlad then replied with a cynical tone in his voice, "You don't want to be second choice...why should I settle for being yours?"

"I will get the picture and we can start all over again," Isabella suggested.

"I don't want you to go back there. I cannot bear to spend another fifty years alone without you," Vlad said with passionate determination.

Isabella, testing Vlad's trust, replied, "You won't. I will be back within a month."

Vlad reluctantly stated, "You'd better be."

Isabella, knowing her own will and questioning Vlad's last response, then replied "I'd better do as I please."

"You are so wilful, Isabella! It can be exhausting!" Vlad said, exasperated.

"I am what I am—I will never change, and neither will you." Isabella replied with a wry smile.

"I can't change you?" Vlad asked implying that he could.

Isabella, still smiling, said, "Men have tried before and failed."

"I could make you change." Vlad pulled Isabella's hair back so that she had to look at him. She pulled away from him.

"No you couldn't. I would just leave. Or worse still, I could stay here and ignore you, like before."

"Isabella...."

Isabella knew this was going to develop into another argument. So she pressed her finger to Vlad's lips and said.

"If you let me go I will stay loyal to you forever. I promise, and you know when I make a promise I keep it." Isabella somehow, in ways she could not fully grasp, that she would keep this promise, that she would always stay loyal to Vlad in her own unique way.

"I will let you go, but be back within the month."

"I will be back soon but because I want to be, not because you told me to do so."

Isabella left without another word. She had lied when she told Vlad her pictures were back in Italy. She had brought one back with her, but she wanted to return to Tuscany. Ever since she had left Vincente, she had felt that he was in danger. At first she assumed it was because she knew Vlad was watching them, but now she wondered if it was something else. She wanted to make sure he was well taken care of. She at least owed this to his mother.

Isabella had every intention of her keeping her promise to Vlad. She would be back within the month and this time she be would be happy to return. She arrived back at her Italian house after nightfall. She looked out the window and saw lights in the distant piazza—they were burning fires there. She could hear loud shrill sounds and whispers about inquisitions and acts of faith. She was not so sure what this meant. A strange smell was filling the streets. It was a smell that made Isabella want to wretch. It was the smell of burning flesh.

Isabella was hungry, so she began walking towards the crowds. The stench was getting stronger but she was ravenous, she needed to feed. She followed the sounds of the crowd.

When she reached the piazza she saw what she thought looked like some sort of celebration. There were people cheering and music was playing. She overheard a man talking to a woman, telling her to make sure the straw was dry so that that the heretics would not be made unconscious by the smoke fumes. The man said that it was imperative that they felt themselves burn to purge their souls. Isabella was repelled by these people. She was supposedly the demon amongst this crowd, and yet she had never thought of anything so abhorrent. She looked up at one of the victims. The flesh was slowly burning off his legs. She felt pity for him she looked up towards his face. It was contorted in agony and yet she still recognised him. It was Vincente.

Without thinking Isabella leapt into the fire and slashed the ropes that were binding him. She carried him off away from the crowd. The people around her were so stunned at this woman leaping into the burning flames that they did nothing to stop her, but even had they tried it would have been a futile task. Isabella took him home, but it was nearly too late. She laid him down on her bed. Then she ran and got water and poured it on his legs. He was drifting in and out of consciousness. He looked up at her and grabbed her dress.

"You," he whispered. "Isabella...take the pain away." It was same plea his mother had made. Isabella was faced with a dilemma. Not only could she take the pain away, she had the power to let him live. Would he thank her for saving him? Isabella was reminded of Nicolae and how he had reacted. Vincente screamed again in pain. She was running out of time—she had to decide what to do. She leaned in towards him.

"I can take your pain away," Isabella said.

"Hurry!" he screamed in anguish.

"I can also make sure that you live?" she said, her tone indicating a question.

"Hurry!" he screamed again.

"Do you want to live?" She asked.

Vincente, not knowing the full gravity of his situation, agreed in a tortured voice. "Yes, Isabella I am too young to die."

Isabella wanted to make sure that Vincente knew exactly what he was asking her. She replied, "No matter what the cost?"

"Yes, Isabella, hurry!" he screamed again.

Isabella leaned in and bit his neck, and then she slit her own wrist and let him drink from her. The burned flesh on his wrist started to heal and then his legs gradually healed. He wanted more blood but Isabella could not spare him anymore. She ran out and brought back the man who had said to keep the straw dry. Vincente drank from him and was soon fully recovered.

Vincente was somewhat disoriented. He looked at Isabella. "What happened? How did you save my life?"

"You may not think that I have. You may have preferred to die." Isabella answered. Vincente sat up to examine his burned flesh.

"I'm not burned."

"No, you're not." Isabella answered.

"What did you do?" he said calmly. Isabella was hesitant to tell him. "Whatever it was, I am grateful," he said.

"When you asked me why I had no mirrors around the house, I never answered you. I'll answer your question now. The reason I have no mirrors is because they are useless to me...I have no reflection."

Vincente opened his mouth to speak. But Isabella pressed her finger to his lips to silence him.

"Listen," she continued softly, "have you ever heard of Vampires?"

Vincente sat before her stunned by her revelation, for he understood her, finally. He nodded.

"I am a Vampire," Isabella told him, "and to save you I turned you into one. You'll never grow old and you will never die; but you have to kill."

Vincente thought for a moment and then looked at Isabella and said, "Who can I kill first?"

"I take it this means that you are not repulsed by the creature you have become." Isabella replied.

"I get to spend eternity with you. How could this make me unhappy?" Isabella was worried by this comment, for although she held great affection for Vincente she had no intention of spending eternity with him, but she would not tell him this yet.

"You have to understand Vincente, killing is not as easy you think and if you do not kill you will be in constant pain."

"You saw what has been done to me? How can I have any feelings towards humans when they are beset on killing me and the only one who stood up against them was a Vampire?"

"You have other weaknesses as well. Have you realised yet how well you can see at night...that there are no lights in this room?"

"I wasn't really thinking about that. It means that I will be able to paint at night just as well as I paint during the day. I have perfect eyesight at night. This is not a weakness," Vincente said.

"You have perfect eyesight, yes; but now only at night. During the day you see nothing clearly. It's just a blur. It's as if you are staring into the sun, all you see are shadows enshrined in light," she said.

Vincente's face dropped. This was the first piece of news that seemed to upset him, but he shook off his disappointment.

"It doesn't matter." He smiled and embraced Isabella, but when his face was buried in her shoulder his features darkened again. He had lost his perfect eye for painting. Painting was the only talent he possessed and to not be able to paint during the day was devastating for him.

They sat together in the dark. Vincente held Isabella's hand tightly; he was adjusting to the implications of his new circumstances. In the early hours of the morning they heard people gathering below Isabella's window. She approached to watch them; they were carrying torches and planning more murders—they were a mob. "What is happening here?" she asked Vincente.

"It's the same thing that is happening everywhere. Acts of faith, they are called. They started in Spain. The Queen declared that Jews were to be burnt as heretics and then it spread to include anyone who was not practising the Catholic religion. It has gotten steadily worse. Now it seems that anyone who was different at all is in danger of being burned. I have heard in the country villages members of the Inquisition have come through and tortured every woman until she confessed to being a witch and her reward for her confession was to be burned at the stake. I have heard of villages where not a woman has been left alive after the Inquisition has left."

"There is evil in this world and I am only a small part of it," Isabella said. There was a pause in the conversation and then Vincente said.

"Where did you go when you left Florence?"

"Home...well the only home I have and I have to go back there soon."

"Good, I will go with you."

"I wish you could." Isabella relayed her story, about Vlad, her sister, all there was to tell him.

"You see, you can't come with me. You must stay here and I will get away as often as I can."

"You have to stay here with me. Please don't go back."

"I promised Vlad I would stay loyal to him and I will keep my promise...for now."

"Then let me go with you."

"No, Vlad would kill you."

"But you said it yourself he can't, you have made me immortal."

"I don't know that for sure yet. I still can't explain why Nicolae could die and I could not. Even if Vlad couldn't kill you, he could do other things that would cause you pain. If he knew about you he would find ways to torture you. No, he can never know you are still alive."

"When will you leave?"

"I promised him I would be home as quickly as possible...I am going to leave tomorrow."

"So soon?"

"Yes."

"I pretended that I just came back for my portrait. I want him to take down a portrait of his wife and put mine in its place."

"Why would you be concerned about the portrait of Vlad's wife?"

"I'm not."

"You are."

"Maybe I just don't want a picture of another woman in my home."

"No it's more than that..." Vincente paused and then it struck him. "You love him."

"Don't be ridiculous...I have just recently stopped hating him."

"My mother used to tell me, that to truly hate someone you must have at one time truly loved them."

"Nonsense...as I told you, I just don't another woman's picture in my home."

Another realisation seized Vincente. "You don't have any feelings for me, not really."

"Now you really are being ridiculous. If I felt nothing for you I would have left you to the religious zealots."

Vincente smiled, "No, you wouldn't have let me burn. You do feel something for me, but it almost feels like a sense of obligation—is that it?"

"Don't be a fool, Why would I have any sense of obligation towards you?"

"Maybe some day you'll tell me."

Isabella ignored his last comment and as day was approaching, she felt tired. She had a long journey home ahead of her.

Isabella soon arrived back at the castle. Vlad looked indifferent to see her but he really wasn't. He was overjoyed to see her return so swiftly. But he hid his feelings. He felt he poured his heart out to her before she left and she ran from him. Isabella returned his indifference, but she too was overjoyed to see him. She sat down opposite Vlad and looked up at the portrait of his dead wife.

"Where is your portrait?" Vlad asked.

"It's behind you." Vlad stood to look at the portrait. It was beautiful, he thought. It was more beautiful than the picture of his wife. But Vlad had loved his wife and although he loved Isabella even more, he knew that Isabella would never look at him with the complete adoration his wife had. He also knew that he would never be completely sure of Isabella's feelings for him. But Isabella was the most beautiful creature he had ever seen and he was besotted by her, though he feared his love of her would make him more miserable than he had been without her.

Isabella looked at Vlad surveying the painting. She was not sure until this moment that she loved him. Vincente was right; he had inherited his mother's perspicacity. Isabella believed Vlad was still totally enamoured of his dead wife and she was only a distraction for him. She would never be sure that he loved her completely. And eternity with this man was sure to make her miserable, but she could not imagine eternity without him. A knock at the door interrupted the thoughts of the two Vampires.

Isabella looked at Vlad and he returned her gaze, both of them bewildered—who could it possibly be? They were both prepared to kill whoever it was. Isabella put her finger to her lips to keep him silent. She crept towards the door and he opened it slightly. A woman was standing outside; she was in her late fifties. Isabella saw the girl's mother in her eyes. It was Katya's daughter.

"Isabella?" the Vampire asked.

"Yes," her human namesake answered. "How did you know it was me?"

"You have your mother's eyes."

"I want to talk to you."

"Evidently…" Isabella answered. "I will come outside." Isabella slipped outside and shut the door behind her. "Why did you come up here? You certainly took a risk," the Vampire said.

"My mother asked me to come up and fetch you."

"Why?"

"She is dying. She wanted to speak to you and see you before she left this world."

Isabella's outward appearance was cold and emotionless. She did not know what to expect but she consented to travel down to the village with Katya's daughter.

"Are you not afraid of me?" she asked.

"My mother told me you would not harm me," Katya's daughter answered.

"She did." Isabella smiled. After all that had happened, Katya still had faith in her childhood friend and Isabella knew she didn't deserve this trust.

The pair arrived at the cottage. Isabella sat down on the bed beside her dying friend. Katya opened her eyes and glanced one last time at Isabella.

"Still so beautiful, Bella." Isabella made no response. "You're still angry with me."

"I'm not angry with you, Katya," Isabella began. "Your actions have always demonstrated a caring for the others around you. You were right to kill Nicolae; he would have never accepted what I had changed him into."

"You look the same, but yet you are different," Katya said.

"I am different. I am not the woman you once knew. I can't even remember what that woman was like."

"Oh, yes you can, Isabella, or you would not be here and you would have killed my daughter." Isabella remained silent and Katya winced in pain. "My time is running out and I have something to ask you."

"What is it?"

"Will you grant me a wish?"

"It depends on what it is."

Katya used all her might to sit up and then grabbed Isabella's arm.

"Don't play games, Isabella. Will you grant your dying friend a final wish?" Isabella was moved by Katya's determined emotion.

"I will," Isabella responded. "What do you want me to do?"

"I want you to promise me that from now on no member of my family will ever be harmed by your hand." Isabella looked at her friend; Katya was making her promise to look after her children and their descendants. Her final thoughts were of her family. Katya was a good woman.

Isabella answered her request. "I promise you, Katya, that as long as I am living and your family is loyal to me, no member of your line will ever be harmed by a Vampire. In fact, I will keep watch over them for you and if it is in my power to protect them from any other danger, I will."

Katya brought Isabella's hand to her lips and kissed it. She then dropped Isabella's hand as her strength gave out and she gasped her last breath.

Anna was still reading her story when she was silenced by a woman bursting through the door of her cottage. This woman was beautiful, but her face was cold and expressionless. It was Isabella, the Vrolok.

CHEVALIER SANS PEUR ET SANS REPROACHE
FEARLESS AND BLAMELESS KNIGHT

CHAPTER EIGHT

Catherine was terror-stricken at the sight of Isabella. Anna's grandchildren still did not really understand what was happening but when they saw their mother struck still with fright, they began to become frightened themselves. And within a few brief moments all Anna's grandchildren erupted into tears. Isabella immediately threw a harsh glance towards the children, which managed to silence them instantly. She spoke to Anna.

"Come with me." Anna obeyed the command immediately. She shut the door behind her so that the children and their mother could not hear the conversation that was to go on between the old woman and the Vampire. Once the two women were alone outside, Isabella continued to speak.

"I could not save your son," Isabella began.

"I know that...you do not need to tell me."

"I do not need to do anything. I am telling you because I wanted you to hear it from me, no matter what these people say," Isabella remarked superciliously.

"You were once one of these people yourself," Anna replied. Isabella had killed people for being less familiar with her but she liked Anna, she always had. Anna had never been afraid of Isabella, as so many others of her family had been, and she had never shied away from speaking her mind where Isabella was concerned. So Isabella just smiled at her temerity.

"You are right, I was, but I would not remind me of that too often if I were you."

"I am too old to hold my tongue, and you are no threat to me."

"I'm not?" There was a pause in the conversation. Isabella wanted to frighten Anna, but Anna would not be frightened and Isabella understood this.

"You're not."

Isabella sighed and said, "I have cursed Katya many times for making me promise never to hurt your family."

"I had heard you made that promise willingly and often did more than you were asked," Anna replied.

"Your family for the most part deserved my respect and protection. I did whatever I could, which was usually too little too late."

Anna began to think about her own future. "What will happen now... what will become of us? Will we go to a new village and start again?"

"Do you want to do that?" Isabella replied. "I will never come back here. All ties with this place have been severed now. No member of your family will ever have to teach their children to be guardians of Vampires ever again."

"I have already started to tell my grandchildren," Anna replied

"Tell them it was just a story that you had once heard and that there is no truth in it. In time they will forget, as children always do. I don't want your family to be under any further obligation to me."

"Thank you," Anna replied.

Isabella did not want to leave Anna like this. She wanted to give her something. She looked up and saw the castle on the edge of the forest and smiled.

"There...that will be your new home and you can have Vlad's fortune. He has it buried all over the Carpathians." Isabella laughed. "As if anyone would dare steal from him. Do you know when he was alive he left a golden goblet in the middle of the village square for people to drink from, and no one ever tried to steal it? He was so feared even then."

"What about you, do you not need money?" Anna interrupted Isabella.

"I don't want his money. I don't deserve to have it." Isabella looked over towards Anna and smiled. Isabella was touched because Anna actually looked concerned about Isabella's well-being. "Don't worry I will survive; that is one thing I can guarantee. Take the money for your family. Consider it payment for centuries of loyalty."

"Thank you again."

"Don't thank me just yet. I do want one final thing from you." Isabella responded.

"Anything," Anna replied.

"I want you from now on to deny my existence and the existence of Vampires. I want us just to be a story in this land, dismissed as a figment of frightened children's overactive imagination. In time we will become a myth, not even a distant memory. Will you do this last thing for me?"

"I will, of course I will," Anna replied. "But what about the other people in the village, they will tell people of you and Vlad and the others."

"I would not worry about them; they won't be getting a chance to tell anything to anyone."

"But people will come to the castle and ask where we came from and what we are doing there." Isabella considered her answer before she spoke; then an idea struck her.

"Tell them you are descendants of the Dracul family. Yes, that's it, tell them of his family. Deny all rumours of Vampires. Condemn any people who spout such nonsense as fools. Tell them Dracula's family history. Make it up. Tell them of other princes after Dracula who continued his line, that his son was not poisoned, that he didn't die, but ruled Transylvania after Vlad Dracula had died and you are his direct descendants. Write a history and make people believe it. As far as the whole world will be concerned, Vlad died four hundred years ago. People who visit Snagov can even see his tomb. I have even seen it. There is another tomb near a monastery where Vlad's brother was supposed to have been laid to rest. His body was stolen but his tomb still exists. Tell people it is Dracula's son's grave. Anna you can make a good life for you and your family if you do as I ask."

"I will never be able to convince people of this. They will not believe such stories," Anna protested.

"People will believe anything you tell them as long as you have the confidence to do it. Vlad told me a story once. It was about a French knight. His fellow knights had deserted him. He stood on a bridge alone where two hundred men were marching towards him. He stood there facing his own death, determined to fight off as many as he could before they overcame him. Vlad was watching from afar. He was overawed by the knight's pugnacity and decided to help him. Together they fought, and when they were finished not one single man had made it across the bridge. The only request Vlad made of this knight was that he never told anyone that Vlad had helped him. The knight protested, saying people would not believe he had done it alone. Vlad simply said that people will believe anything as long as you have enough conviction when you tell them. Later I read of a fearless and blameless knight who fought off two hundred men singlehandedly and I knew it was him," Isabella said, smiling. She was remembering.

"You really loved him, didn't you?" Anna asked. Isabella laughed.

"I hated him, but someone once told me that to truly hate someone, you have to have truly loved them. Vlad was the only man who never judged me. He never tried to make me different from what I was." Isabella fell silent; memories were filling her mind.

"You will miss him, won't you?" Anna asked.

"More than I even realise. Unfortunately, I always believed he would be there if I needed him. I always thought he was dependable. I could always rely on him to be skulking about in that castle whenever I needed company. I came as close to loving him as I have done to any man. There were times when we hated each other. There were times when we made each other miserable, but there were also times when he truly made me as happy as I ever have been and took me as close to perfection, as love can ever take you. I was never completely happy with him but we could have been and that is my greatest regret."

Anna watched as a red tear fell down Isabella's cheek. She tried to change the subject, not wanting to cause Isabella anymore distress.

"Thank you for giving us this. It's a second chance for us all," Anna said.

"It is no less than your family deserves," Isabella answered.

"Can I ask you for another favour?"

Isabella smiled. She had just given this woman everything she had and still Anna was asking for something more. Only Anna would have dared.

"What else do you want?" Isabella asked.

"I want to know what happened to you. I want you to tell me about the things you have seen."

"You are the third member of your family to ask me that. I'll grant you this last request."

"I actually have another." Anna stated.

Isabella laughed and said, "I have nothing left to give you."

"You can give me this…." Anna gathered up her courage to ask Isabella for this last thing. "A man called Simon came to visit me today. He tried to save me. He thought I was in danger. I believe him to be good man and guilty of nothing more than just being there when Vlad was killed. I would like you to spare him and his family."

"No," Isabella said, resolute. "I will not and cannot grant you this," Isabella said firmly. "These men let Vlad die. They are all guilty of nothing more than just being there when he died. They watched him die and they must suffer as he did. They watched as he was slaughtered and did nothing to stop it. For that they will follow him to the grave. All of them."

"And what about the men who killed my son?" Anna asked, remembering her own loss.

"Rest easy, Anna, my punishment for the English that pursued Vlad and hunted him down like an animal will be greater still. They will suffer the worst of all fates. I will not stop until their worst fears have been realised. That is a promise."

Anna was stunned into silence; she almost pitied the men who had killed Vlad. Isabella realised she had slightly frightened Anna when she had spoken so vehemently. She wanted to give her comfort but she didn't know how.

"I have to leave soon but before I do I will give you my memories," Isabella said, and she placed her hands on Anna's head. Thoughts and memories flowed into Anna's mind. She saw and remembered Isabella's life as if she had been there observing it all along. Some things were horrible, some beautiful and some sad. She understood Isabella that little bit better and she knew that no one would be spared. For the first time in her life she felt pity for Isabella and Isabella sensed her pity.

"Do not try to rationalise my actions," Isabella began, "because have no doubt—I am a cold-blooded killer. I have killed children while they slept in their beds and not felt a moment's remorse. Your pity is wasted on me, but I thank you for feeling it. Take your grandchildren and their mother up to the castle and you will eventually forget these memories that I have given you. Live the rest of your life in peace and forget about Vampires, for you will not hear from me again."

Anna felt sad as she watched Isabella depart. She knew what Isabella was, but she could not help but feel the loss of a friend as she saw her walking away.

The night Katya had died Isabella was distraught. She left her friend's house and walked back up through the forest to the castle. She went to her bedroom and lay on her bed staring out the window. Emptiness filled her. She felt Katya's death had severed the last link to her old life. She was now truly a Vampire and nothing else. She did not know what to do now. The best thing she could think to do was to take comfort in Vlad's company and live here with him. Any thoughts of her painter in Italy left her. She would stay here for the foreseeable future and see if she could finally forget her old life. It would also give her time to grieve for her old friend.

Vlad was pleased that Isabella stayed. They actually seemed to be enjoying each other's company. They slept together and they fed together. This was the closest thing to happiness either one had ever experienced in their afterlife, but it was not to last long.

One night as the dawn was just about to break, Isabella crept downstairs and sat on the floor beside Vlad's feet and leaned her head on his lap. He was pleased if not surprised by this show of affection, but he knew her too well and realised she wanted something. The pair shared everything but neither one was that intimate with the other. They didn't completely trust each other; perhaps they never would—each one knew the other's character too well.

Vlad rested his hand on her head and waited for her to ask him whatever it was that she wanted. The pause was not long before she started to speak, for Isabella was impatient and impetuous.

"I have grown tired of this place," she began. Vlad thought this meant that she wanted to leave him. He lifted up his hand from her head and got up, ousting Isabella's head off his knee.

"You want to leave so you can go back to Italy!" Vlad snapped.

"No, I have seen enough of Italy, too—quite the contrary, in fact. I thought I would quite like to fight in a battle." Vlad looked at Isabella, bemused as she continued to speak. "A German army prepares to fight the Turks in Hungary. Why don't we go and lend a hand? Since my promise to Katya we have been going further and further afield for food. If we got into a war there would be plenty of blood at our disposal. A King, Maximilian I think, is rallying troops against the Turks.

"I could not fight for Christianity," Vlad answered.

"Then you could fight for the Turks."

"I don't think I could fight for them, either."

"The point is not that we are fighting for any side, the point is we could feed to our hearts' content, and not get noticed by anyone."

"We are not noticed here," Vlad said.

"You know that is not true. The villagers whisper about us daily. Even I heard stories when I was alive about the Vampire that lived in this castle. And since I have promised not to kill any more of Katya's people…."

"Whatever inspired you to make such a foolish promise?"

"An old friend. Don't tell me you have not had a moment of compassion because I know you have."

"Maybe I have, but I do want you to forget this promise you made to Katya. It is better to be feared than loved. Isn't that what you keep telling me?"

"Don't worry—no human will ever love us." Isabella answered.

"So you want to fight a war?"

"I want food. I am hungry and so are you."

"When do you want to leave?"

Isabella smiled. He was going to go with her. "I must go down and see Katya's daughter first before we leave. I will go tonight and then we can leave tomorrow."

※

When Isabella arrived down in the village she went straight to Katya's old cottage.

"It has been a long time," Katya's child, Isabella's namesake, began.

"It has," Isabella responded.

"Why have you chosen tonight to visit me?"

"I have come to tell you that I am leaving. I will not be back for a while." As Isabella spoke a girl entered the house. Her face was bruised and she was trying to hide it. The human Isabella looked at the girl with pity and turned back to the Vampire.

"I am glad you came to see me. I wanted to ask you a favour. That girl is my granddaughter."

"What's wrong with her face?" Isabella asked.

"Her husband beats her."

"What has this got to do with me?"

"You promised my mother you would protect our family. I want you to use…gentle persuasion to make sure he does not beat her anymore."

"Why doesn't she just leave him?"

"She loves him."

"She's a fool; I cannot help people who won't help themselves."

"Is she a fool? My mother told me stories of a woman, a girl who lives with someone who tried to kill her." Katya's daughter was so like her mother. Isabella couldn't help liking her. The Vampire would comply with her namesake's wishes and use gentle persuasion, as she put it, to stop the young girl's husband from beating her to death some day.

Isabella sighed and began to speak again, "Tell your granddaughter not to go home tonight. I will go and wait for her husband."

"Thank you…and Isabella…don't kill him," the young Isabella shouted after the Vampire.

Isabella looked back at her, smiled wryly, and nodded.

"He'll live," she replied.

Katya's daughter coughed. The Vampire knew that her friend's daughter was nearing the end of her life.

※

Isabella sat in the dark waiting for the girl's abusive husband to come home. When he eventually entered the house, he reeked of wine. On seeing Isabella, he started to shout at her.

"Where is my wife?" he barked.

"She's not here," answered Isabella.

"I can see that!" he shouted back. Isabella stood. The husband staggered over to where she was standing. "What have you done with my wife?"

"Do you care?" At this the man lashed out at Isabella. His blow knocked Isabella off balance and she fell to the floor. Before she could get up the man struck out again with his foot. The side of his shoe caught her cheek and split it open. He kicked out again but this time Isabella caught his foot in her hand and squeezed hard, breaking his bones in several places. He screamed out in pain and stumbled back away from Isabella.

Isabella looked up at the husband of Katya's grandchild and he began to fear for his life when his eyes met hers. He fell back into the corner of the room. It was as if Isabella's stare had thrust him backwards. She lifted her hand and rubbed her fingers against her cheek, wiping off the blood to reveal a completely healed wound. He ran for the door, his fear overcoming his pain. Isabella got to the door before he did and slammed it shut. The man, now terrified, backed again into the corner of the room. Isabella pushed him back further so that he was pinned up against the wall.

"You would hit a woman…?" Isabella asked; her voice full of disdain. The abusive husband said nothing. "Always be careful when you do; some woman hit back," Isabella continued.

At this she grabbed him round his neck and lifted him off the ground. The man now gasped for air and struggled to get his words out.

"Who are you?" he whispered.

"I am…a dark angel. More importantly I am your wife's guardian angel. If you are not the epitome of kindness towards her from now on I will come back and rip the flesh from your throat." Isabella pressed her finger nails into his neck, and a few drops of blood started to spill onto her fingers. "Be warned I only make a threat once," Isabella said, and then she let go and he dropped to the ground. He curled his body up into a ball and lay there not moving…too scared to move. Isabella leaned down and with her finger nail slashed his cheek exactly where he had wounded her.

"Just a scar so that you never forget my warning," Isabella stated.

This man never hit his wife again. In fact, he turned into a kind husband that his wife could love without reproach.

Isabella returned to the castle and when she entered a man was sitting with Vlad. Isabella was horrified when she realised it was Vincente.

Vlad could see that Isabella was extremely agitated at Vincente being there and he knew why. Vlad walked up to her and kissed her on the cheek.

"My love...we have a guest," Vlad said sarcastically.

"I can see we have a guest," Isabella reaffirmed.

"Say hello to our guest. You are being quite vulgar. It must be your upbringing." Isabella threw Vlad a supercilious look. She had become as much of a snob as Vlad was and had put her underprivileged childhood behind her. Vlad liked to remind her of it every chance he got. He knew how to antagonise her just as she knew how to antagonise him.

Isabella by now had regained her senses and went over to their guest. Vincente, being totally ignorant of the danger he was in, took Isabella's hand and kissed it. Dracula did not outwardly show any reaction but Vincente had just signed his own death warrant, simply by having the audacity to touch Isabella in his presence.

"Hello, Vincente," she said, her words stilted and sharp.

"That's more like it, Isabella. This man has travelled from Italy to visit you; you should show him some courtesy. He must hold you in great admiration to travel such a distance just to see you." Isabella now knew that Vincente was dead. She would try to protect him, but he had killed himself by coming here. "I have invited him to come with us," Vlad continued.

"I am sure he has better things to do than come with us," Isabella answered.

"Yes, he may. He has brought paintings with him; they are mostly of you, Isabella," Vlad said. "Isabella, do you know what else he is? He is one of us. I wonder how he became a Vampire." Vlad left the pair in the room after this remark, but he would never actually leave them completely alone.

Isabella's heart fell. How could Vincente have been so stupid, she wondered? As soon as Vlad left the room Vincente ran to Isabella to embrace her. Isabella stepped back from him. She would not let him touch her.

"Don't touch me. Do not show me any affection. Don't you realise what you have done...you have just killed yourself!" Isabella said.

"But you told me I couldn't die."

"There is a way we can die, we just do not know how yet. But I guarantee Vlad will figure out the way and I will not be able help you."

"You are overreacting Isabella; he could not have been more pleasant towards me."

"He is furious. I told him you were dead."

"He is no match for us Isabella. We can kill him."

"Do not say such things—you are a fool. Don't you realise I would never kill him? What makes you think I would join with you against him?" answered Isabella. "Your mother would have never been this stupid,"

"My mother—what do you know about my mother?" Vincente asked.

"Never mind."

"You knew my mother?" Vincente asked again.

"Yes, but that doesn't matter now. I need to think what to do. You'll have to leave, but not yet. If you leave now he will only follow you."

Vincente did not believe Isabella's words. He thought she was overreacting. He did not know that she meant everything she said.

Isabella would always love Vlad, even when she tried to convince herself that she did not. She would never conspire against him with anyone. Isabella had liked Vincente, but she did not and would not ever love him. If it had been anyone else she would have just let Vlad kill him, but she could not let Lia's child die. So she would try to save him, but she felt it would be impossible. Isabella fell asleep contemplating what to do.

The following evening, the three of them left the castle together. The three Vampires set off on their journey. Isabella was filled with a sense of foreboding. She had lost all the affection she had once had for Vincente. She could not tolerate fools and that was what she thought he was. Any affection she had felt for him was just merely a short and slight infatuation. She had longed for company when she met him. Even though this was true, she knew she owed it to his mother to keep him safe and she would protect him as much as she could.

They arrived on the battlefield late in the evening; the three were ravenous and were not picky about whose soldiers they were killing. There was a camp set up near the battlefield where the soldiers were to fight the following morning. Isabella, Vlad and Vincente went through their tents until their hunger was satisfied. The next day when the remaining soldiers awakened they blamed influenza for the deaths that had occurred during the night. There had been a small outbreak recently of the virus and they had no reason to suspect foul play, yet. So the three remained until the battle started. They killed dozens of soldiers that day. Isabella was trying to keep a close eye on Vincente but the brightness of the day was obscuring her vision. Her hunger by this time had taken over and she was feeding, forgetting about him for the moment.

This went on for weeks and the soldiers from the camp believed that they would have to return home because the influenza outbreak was getting so bad. But they were going to make one final stand. This was the night Vincente was to die.

※

When Isabella awoke that evening she had decided to finally confront Vlad about Vincente. She was going to tell him about her obligation to Vincente's mother and that this was the only reason she wanted him to live. She would not go as far as begging Vlad, but she would tell him the truth in the hope that it would save Vincente from Vlad's wrath.

The three had been resting in one of the abandoned tents of the people they had killed. Vlad had already left his resting place and was standing on the edge of the forest. Isabella approached cautiously.

"Why are you standing here on your own?" Isabella began.

"I thought you would want this time to spend with Vincente," said Vlad.

"I am sorry he came here. I didn't want him to," Isabella answered.

"I'm glad he did. It reminded me that we are not under any obligation to each other."

"I feel I have an obligation to you," Isabella answered. There was a gentle sincerity in her voice that Vlad had never heard before.

"You shouldn't."

Isabella sighed. "Let me explain. I knew his mother. I promised her when she died that I would protect him, and when I went back to Italy he was being burned alive. I had to save him, I owed his mother that much!"

"That is no concern of mine," Vlad said harshly.

"This woman, I thought of her as a sister. I cannot stand idly by and let you kill her child. Do you understand nothing of family loyalty? How could you? A man who left his brother to be tortured and sodomized by the Turks."

"Do not lecture me about family loyalty, and certainly do not mention my brother to me. You who know nothing about the things you speak."

"I know more than you think," retorted Isabella.

"Quiet, Isabella. That is always your mistake. You are always talking when you should listen. Do you remember ever hearing about a man called János Hunyadi?"

"I am in no mood for one of your stories," Isabella answered.

"Be quiet, Isabella and listen to me for once. Do you know who he was?"

"Yes, he was the man who killed your father and brother. He supposedly tortured them and then you joined forces with him to regain the throne. Are you trying to tell me that Vincente is dead and that you don't care about my obligation?"

"Isabella, listen to me please, how did he die?"

"There are conflicting reports. Some say he died of plague, and others say he died in battle."

"He did not die in battle. He had pledged to help me regain the throne, which I was about to do. I didn't need him any more. So I knew that it was time that János paid for my brother's and father's deaths. I knew where he was about to attack because he had taken me into his confidence. It was cold the night the he died. I crept into his tent; no one knew I was there. I was supposed to be fighting with him. He was asleep. He had the look of an old man about him. I couldn't just kill him. I wanted him to suffer. I put a little hemlock poison in his wine. Every night I continued until he was on the brink of death; then it was time to confront him.

"He was in so much pain by this point that he could hardly stand when he saw me. I wanted him to know who was killing him and why. I whispered in his ear...did he remember the looks on my father's and brother's faces when he tortured and killed them? This startled János—he got up from his bed and looked at me. He looked at me with affection, not even suspecting I had been slowly poisoning him. I asked him again. Did he remember what my father and brother looked like when he tortured and killed them? He asked me what I was taking about; I asked him...did he honestly think that I would forget what he did to my family? I had dug up their coffins and had seen his brutality. His men had burned out their eyes and buried them alive.

"János protested and said they were his enemies. He screamed out in pain; it was getting painful for him to even breathe. I told him I had done this to him. I had caused him this pain. I approached his deathbed and said that I would not rest until every one of his line was dead. He screamed out once more and then he died. I had slowly tortured him to death, just as he had tortured my father and younger brother. As a tribute to him, his soldiers whispered that he died in battle. They thought it was the plague that had actually taken him. The soldiers were too loyal to what they thought was a great military leader and they spread a rumour that he died fighting and not in his bed.

"Later on Matthias, his son, was ruler. He had kept me in prison at my older brother's request and I never forgot my promise, even though I had lost the will to do it. The last thing I did before I died was go to Vienna and kill him. I slowly poisoned him with hemlock poison just as I had done with his father. As he was nearing death, I appeared to him and told him what I had done to his family. You see, I know all about family obligation."

"That is not the same and you know it. You paid that family back for revenge. Vincente's mother was my only friend and I cannot let the boy die; he is simply foolish and impetuous. I promise you…I feel nothing for him but I have a strong obligation to his mother. Please let him live and I will send him away, I promise you. I will never see him again," Isabella made her last plea to save Vincente's life.

"Vincente is safe from me, rest easy," Vlad stated.

Isabella believed Vlad would keep his word and the sense of foreboding that had accompanied all throughout this journey soon dissipated. She was wrong to let it do so.

❈

Isabella went to wake Vincente; he looked like a child to her now, just an impetuous fool who thought he was in love. She woke him and started to tell him what had happened.

"You are safe Vincente, but after today you must leave this place," Isabella warned.

"When will I see you again?"

"You won't," Isabella said gently.

"But…."

"But nothing. I have saved you twice from death. My debt to you and your family is paid in full."

Vincente was angry. If Isabella had abandoned him, he would have nothing in his life. "Your debt is far from paid in full…for you stole my vision from me," Vincente shouted. "I can't paint anymore! All I see are blurred visions shrouded in light. I don't want to paint only at night!"

Isabella was startled by this revelation. He was a child, just a spoiled child.

"Your vision? You can't paint anymore? Is that what you are upset about?" Isabella scolded. "Would you rather I had let you burn? Do you remember how that felt, do you remember the pain?"

"Do you think I would have wanted to live if I had been told the truth? Told about what an abomination I was to become? Someone that skulks around in darkened alleyways looking for food? How dare you cast me aside after all that you have done to me!"

"All that I have done to you? I saved your life! You have no idea of the gift I have bestowed upon you and the power that you have and what I risked to give it to you. I wanted your mother to live forever; I never really wanted you to live more than your time. As I watched you dying I thought your mother would have wanted to me to save your life and that is the only reason that I did."

"How did you know my mother?" Vincente demanded. "Tell me!"

"I helped your mother kill your father. He was a Medici and he raped your mother."

"A Medici?" Vincente said in astonishment. "I could have been rich." Vincente didn't seem to care that his father had raped his mother.

"Didn't you hear what I said? He raped your mother. You could have been brought up in his world and have been shown no love whatsoever."

"That was not your choice to make," Vincente said. "You have taken so much from me."

"I ensured that you were loved, Vincente. Believe me, that is a precious thing."

"It means nothing to me."

Isabella by now had grown exhausted with this conversation. "I can't talk to you anymore. I have given you a lot more than I have given anyone else. I may have taken earthly power from you, but you should realise the power you now have."

"If I could throw your great gift back in your face I would."

At this Isabella left the tent in fury. She knew Vincente would have to leave soon but she would let him calm down before she would speak to him again. And of course Vlad had heard their discourse.

The troops were starting to take their places on the battlefield. Isabella, Vincente and Vlad were waiting for them to begin as they all had insatiable appetites. The fighting started and Isabella rushed into the battle, killing as many as she could to quell her thirst. Vincente did likewise but Vlad remained behind them. The army fought long and hard into the night. Isabella had not been paying attention because she believed that Vincente was safe from harm, but she should have known better. Vlad picked out a soldier from the crowd and stood beside him and started to whisper in his ear.

"Look in front of you. Do you see a man killing your troops? All your other enemies mean nothing. He is killing everyone. Do you see him?"

The man answered *"Yes!"* Everything apart from Vincente was a blur to him, and all he could see was Vincente under Vlad's influence.

"He is killing everyone in your army; you have to stop him. You will be a hero if you do."

"He is strong, how do I kill him?" the soldier asked.

Vlad poured a red liquid on the soldier's sword and said, "You cut off his head with your sword. Now go!"

The man ran towards Vincente, his sword in hand. A sudden panic came over Isabella; she sensed something was going to happen. She looked around and saw Vlad smiling at something. She turned to see what he was looking at and saw the man running towards Vincente, wielding the sword.

She ran towards Vincente, screaming for the soldier to stop. Isabella got close enough to reach out for Vincente's hand. He looked at her for a second and smiled as if to say all was forgiven. In the next moment the smile was stricken from his face as the soldier's sword struck him from behind, his face now contorted in pain, his head fell to the ground. Isabella screamed out for her friend's dead son. She sat on the ground weeping for him. She touched his hand and a familiar feeling swept over her; it was a peaceful feeling. It was just as she remembered it. Vincente had joined Nicolae and she was glad.

Isabella's scene of bereavement did not go unnoticed by the rest of the fighting armies. She was sitting on the ground staring at Vincente's bloodstained clothes. The men started to whisper to each other that they had not seen a woman on the field until this moment. Isabella had camouflaged herself using her power but now she was so overcome with grief she let her power slip and she appeared to the soldiers. It seemed to the soldiers that this woman had appeared out of thin air and they were scared; they thought she was a ghost. Isabella was too distraught to notice the rumblings of the soldiers. The army started to panic. There had been so many deaths within the camp that they thought they were cursed. One of the soldiers approached Isabella.

"She looks to be flesh," he shouted.

"She must be killed to free us from the curse," Vincente's killer shouted.

Vlad was watching from close by and just before Vincente's murderer struck Isabella, Vlad had her in his arms and whisked her away from danger. He carried Isabella deep into the nearby forest.

When Isabella regained her senses she pounded her fists on his chest and shouted, "You lied to me!"

"Did you honestly believe I would let him live?" Vlad answered, "You know me well enough."

"I believed you would not lie to me," Isabella said, and her voice shuddered as she spoke. Vlad tried to hold Isabella but she flinched from his touch. She had had enough of him. She started to walk away.

"Come back, Isabella, where are you going?" Vlad called out after her, but Isabella did not answer him and disappeared into the forest. Vlad would not see her again for another ten years.

SANQUIS EST VIA
THE BLOOD IS THE LIFE

CHAPTER NINE

Isabella had left Vlad. She was resolved never to see him again. She may not have been cognisant of it yet but something would always bring her back to him—no matter how determined she was to stay away. However, not for the first time, Isabella was determined to get as far away from him as she could.

Isabella went home briefly to see Katya's family before she left. Katya's daughter, Isabella, had died and when she entered Katya's old house she found Isabella's granddaughter, Gizella. Isabella's granddaughter looked happy now. There were no signs of abuse, no more bruises on her skin. Isabella was glad, not for the girl, for if the truth be told she thought Gizella was an idiot, but she was pleased that she was keeping her promise to Katya.

"Are you well?" Isabella asked, feigning concern.

"I am," Gizella answered. Both women seemed to have a mutual contempt for the other, which neither of them could completely disguise, but these women were bound to each other and Gizella would be part of Isabella's life until she died and was replaced by another member of her family.

"Does your family need anything?" Isabella continued.

"Nothing you can give us."

Isabella was amazed at this woman's abrupt reply but said nothing. The two women were distracted as a young child wandered into the room and ran to tug at her mother's skirts. "This is Katalin," said Gizella.

"How old is Katalin?" Isabella asked.

"She's eight." Isabella bent down to greet the child, she perceived a foreboding aberrancy in this child; it was as if a darkness enshrined her, a strange maliciousness, a sense of some wickedness that this child would be responsible for. Gizella then leaned down and picked up her daughter. She had been unnerved by the Vampire's attentions.

"Don't worry, I won't hurt her," Isabella said.

Gizella instantly replied, "I know you won't. I am just afraid of your influence," with a sharpness in her voice.

"My influence. Be careful Gizella, I will only tolerate so much acrimony."

"I just mean the child is easily led astray; she has a viciousness within her," Gizella said dismissively. The door now opened for second time and the child's father entered the room. When he saw Isabella he dropped the wood he was carrying and fell back against the wall. The man cried out at the top of his voice.

"I never touched her!" he said frantically.

"I know you haven't. That is why you are still alive," answered Isabella with a smile. Isabella's granddaughter looked at the Vampire standing in front of her. She had not known until this moment why her husband's attitude towards her had changed. Gizella's heart softened slightly towards her grandmother's namesake.

Isabella walked towards Gizella's husband, who was shaking all over. She ran her finger over the scar that she had left him.

"It has healed well," Isabella stated. The man batted Isabella's hand from his face, a nervous almost involuntary reaction to Isabella's touch. Katalin's father was standing in front of the door. Isabella pressed her finger gently on the top of his left arm and pushed him out of the way. When she was outside the door she turned back towards him and said.

"Be good."

"I will...I will," he called to her fervently. As he did so, he tripped over the wood he had dropped and fell to the floor.

Isabella wanted nothing more from Vlad; she was intent on leaving the province without returning to the castle. She was not even tempted to retrieve her portraits. However, she could not resist one last look up at the castle before she left. There was no sign of life, not a candle in a window or even a glimpse of smoke coming from the chimney.

As before, Isabella travelled through Europe and as before whispers about plagues and the Black Death followed her, for Isabella was not one to curb her appetite. She now was starting to hear a new sort of rumour about witches and reformation. A fresh plague was crossing Europe, but this one was completely abhorrent and completely synthetic.

After a few months she found herself in France. She was walking through the streets on a dark, misty, near silent night with only the church bells echoing through the air. Isabella as always was looking for food. She was suddenly struck by the stench of death. Someone in one of these silent houses was dying, and where there was death there were always people. She heard whispers coming from the top of the house beside her. Isabella listened and waited outside. A priest was talking to a dying man.

"Until tomorrow," the priest said.

"You will not find me alive at sunrise," the man responded. This man would not be the only one who would be dead at sunrise, Isabella thought. She waited for the priest by the door. The priest came downstairs and saw Isabella with his failing eyesight and in the failing light the priest thought she was a nurse coming to look after the man inside.

"Thank goodness," the priest said "for he is in a lot of pain." The priest opened the door and invited the Vampire to enter the house. He did not know it but with this action he had saved his own life. Isabella went inside and climbed the stairs leading up to the dying man. The man was already asleep when she entered the room. Isabella crept towards him but he sensed her presence and awoke. He lit the candle beside his bed and peered around the room. His eyesight was declining but he still managed to see Isabella standing there in the shadows. He was terror-stricken by the sight of her

"The black angel has come for me!"

Isabella was intrigued by this response. "What do you mean?" Isabella inquired.

"I have seen you!" he gasped.

"Seen me?" asked Isabella.

"Visions of you, ever since I was a child," he said, wanting her to stay and listen to him.

"Visions?" Isabella replied. The man was slowly starting to calm down. He had not expected the black angel as he called her to be so rational and articulate.

"If you tell me what you mean, I will spare your family," Isabella continued.

The man settled down and motioned for Isabella to sit on the chair beside him. He believed her and he also was aware that if she wanted to kill him, nothing would stop her. Isabella sat down and listened to the dying man's revelations.

"I have been a man of medicine for most of my life. When I was about eighteen I saw my first plague victim. They blamed the Black Death outbreak for the deaths in the village, but this outbreak was different. There were no visible signs of the plague but people were still dying before their time. I examined several of the victims. There were no signs of disease or decay on the skin. The other doctors I was with dismissed it as the Black Death. When physicians can't explain what has happened to someone they blame the most prevalent disease of the time.

"After the tenth man of the village had died, I was left with the body and I went over to examine it. I saw no visible signs of disease, no sign of violence, either. I felt for a pulse on his neck, thinking maybe he was still alive, fearing that the other doctor I was with was completely incompetent. But there was no pulse.

"When I pulled my fingers away from his neck I noticed a couple of spots of blood on my fingers. I examined his neck more closely and suddenly a myriad of pictures fused together in my mind, coalescing into a vision. It was of you in that vision! I saw you creep into this man's room, kiss him on his neck and then suck the life from his body. I knew at that instant that you would kill my future wife and children like this and that one day you would sneak into my room.

"People have said for years that I am a good physician, for if any outbreak like this occurred, I could usually stop it. But it had nothing to do with my medical knowledge on this occasion—in the vision I saw something. I saw you step away from roses that were by the dead man's bed. From then on, in every potion I made, I crushed rose petals into it, to ward you off. Just in case it was not plague that people were dying of, but the touch of a Vampire."

Isabella was amazed by this story. She had premonitions and could read people's minds but she had never heard of a human being able to do the same thing. It scared her slightly; it reminded her not to underestimate anyone. Here was an old man who had held a clue to what could keep Isabella away from humans. Some roses were pungent enough to make her feel nauseous, and if one of her intended victims had consumed such flowers, she could smell it of them, she could taste it their blood. This man had probably saved dozens of lives.

"I won't kill you," she said to the dying man. "You will be dead soon enough. The stench of death fills this room. I would kill you if I thought you were going to survive the night, but as promised I will leave your family in peace." As Isabella got up to leave the room the man grabbed her arm. Isabella drew back from him but could not quite relinquish his grip. A faraway look came over his face as if he was seeing something off in the distance, something harrowing. He began to speak.

"The one that will obtain government from the great seized, will be induced by some to execute ruin: The Twelve Reds will agree to soil the cloth, under murder, murder will perpetrate itself," the old man said.

"What are you saying?" Isabella asked, for he was not making much sense.

"You will be there; you will see the reign of terror."

"I don't understand," Isabella replied.

"You will be there," he repeated.

"Be where?" Isabella asked, trying to make some sense of what this man had said.

"You will know when it happens," the old man pleaded.

"When what happens?" asked Isabella, desperately wanting to know more.

"You have to stop it! Promise me you will?" His grip was tightening on Isabella's arm and he pulled her in close to him. Isabella felt that this man believed that the whole world hinged on her agreeing to do what he asked. She was compelled to appease him.

"I will do what I can," Isabella said. "But how can I stop anything if you do not tell me what it is?" The last breath left his body and he did not say another word.

Isabella remained for another few days; she watched and waited for the man to be buried. The funeral was quite large; this man would be missed. Isabella decided to ask one of the attendees who he was. She wanted some clue as to what the man had asked of her.

"Whose funeral is this?" Isabella asked.

"Michel, Michel De Nostredame." This was no help; Isabella left not knowing what his words meant; perhaps she never would.

※

A few years later Isabella found herself back in the woods near Vlad's castle. She felt it her duty to check in with Katya's family. Or rather, she told herself that this is what brought her back to her home country.

When she opened the door she was surprised to see no children in the house. This house had always been filled with the echoes of children's laughter. The only person who now occupied this lonely and abandoned place was Gizella. Isabella's entrance woke Gizella and she started to talk to the Vampire.

"It has been a long time," she said. Isabella turned to face her. She could see that the woman standing before her had visibly aged.

Isabella answered her ward. "Has it been?" Isabella asked.

Gizella replied sadly, "Eleven years."

"Eleven years? Time makes such visible changes to you humans," Isabella remarked.

"Time is precious," Gizella answered.

"Not to me. When you have so much of it, it seems less precious," Isabella replied poignantly.

"I am sure it used to be precious to you as well," Gizella inquired.

Isabella reflected on her life and said, "I am not sure any more what was precious to me…I can't remember."

Gizella looked at Isabella and replied thoughtfully, "You can remember. You'll never be able to block it out; that is your curse, to be completely alone with your memories."

"That's enough!" Isabella declared. Obviously Gizella had not lost her contempt for her.

"Why are you alone? Where is your family?"

"My husband is dead; he had a bad heart," Gizella said.

Isabella laughed. "I wonder what gave him a bad heart! Your daughter Katalin, where is she?"

"She married and left the village," Gizella answered.

"To go where?" Isabella asked.

Gizella replied, "I don't know."

"You're not in contact with her?" continued Isabella.

"No, not since she left," replied Gizella.

"Do you need for anything?" Isabella asked.

"Nothing," said Gizella.

"I will return before your life ends." Isabella left the woman to her solitude.

✦

One of Isabella's favourite hobbies had become participating in court celebrations. She had started to hunt in more "noble" society; the rich could be such willing victims. They would invite anyone to their parties as long as they looked as if they belonged. She had gotten into a pattern of killing them and then stealing their possessions. After all, a woman with no independent means had to make a living somehow.

Isabella hid her tracks under the guise of a plague. There had been many outbreaks and disease was no discriminator of class. So with the added advantage of money she slipped back and forth, in and out, of elegant society, using different names and speaking in different languages. Nobody asked too many questions. In court they gossiped constantly, of course, but open accusations were never the norm. Isabella paid no heed to the gossip unless she wanted to influence them in her favour.

The few months succeeding Isabella's last visit to Katya's family home were spent in a Hungarian court. A fifteen-year-old girl was preparing to marry. The court was filled with the hustle and bustle that usually accompanied such occasions. The night before the wedding when most of the guests had gone to bed and the castle hallways were deserted, Isabella found herself walking through the great hall to look at the paintings. She was interested in the histories of such prestigious families. She heard footsteps coming down the corridor and the door swung open.

"Who are you?" asked the young girl who had just entered the room.

"A member of the wedding party, my lady," Isabella said, making a small curtsey.

"I don't think I have noticed you before."

"I am not that noticeable," Isabella answered.

"Oh, yes, you are. In fact, I would prefer my future husband not to see you."

"You pay me too much heed, my lady; I pale in comparison to you."

"You know that is not true."

"Whether it is true or not, never let your insecurity show. That in itself is not very attractive," Isabella stated.

"I am not jealous of you."

"That's good for there is no reason to be."

"I am getting married tomorrow."

"I know...you are very young to be getting married."

"I am fifteen."

"My apologies. You are so old," Isabella said sarcastically.

"Oh, no, I am not old. I will never be old."

"Age catches up with us all," Isabella answered.

"Not with me, I will not allow myself to become old."

"Why are you so afraid of becoming old?"

"I remember my mother. She was the toast of Hungary, the most beautiful of women, noticed everywhere she went, and then suddenly it stopped. Her hair had turned gray and her skin was not as smooth as it had once been. Men did not look at her any more. My mother, who had once been so generous and kind, became malicious; she scolded and beat me at every given occasion. That will never happen to me."

"It does not have to happen to you. With age comes wisdom and that in itself is an attractive quality—your mother obviously did not acquire any." These were just the prattlings of an inexperienced child. Isabella was growing tired of the discourse and decided to take it in another direction.

"So tell me about your husband, the Count Nádasdy?"

"In a few days I will be Countess Nádasdy."

"Why not Countess Báthory? It is such an illustrious name in Hungary—why do you want to exchange it for a lesser name?"

"It is tradition that the wife takes her husband's name."

"It seems an archaic tradition. Do people of fashion not break these traditions? Why should a wife take the name of a husband?" The girl thought about what Isabella had said for a few seconds.

"Yes I think you right."

"Erzsébet! Erzsébet!"

The young girl could hear her mother calling her. She turned to see her mother coming up the corridor towards the open door and when she turned back Isabella was gone.

Isabella went downstairs to the servant's quarters looking for food. She had considered killing the girl but decided that it would be very impolite to ruin the wedding that someone had so kindly invited her too. Only one servant was awake, washing clothes, and when Isabella came close she could see it was Katalin.

"What are you doing here?" she asked the laundry woman.

"I am catching up on my chores, madam." This girl does not know me, Isabella thought; after all, she had only met her once when she was a child.

"Do you not know me, child?" Isabella inquired.

"No madam, should I?" Katalin obediently answered with her head bowed.

"I suppose not. You were only a child when you saw me last. You are Isabella Zelonka's great grandchild. You are Katalin Kocur, are you not?

"My married name is Benecká," stated Katalin.

"Your mother told me you had married," Isabella replied.

Katalin, intrigued now, asked, "How do you know my mother?"

"Your grandmother was named after me." Katalin was shocked by this revelation, dropped the sheet she was washing, and looked at Isabella.

"You're the Vrolok?" she replied, stunned.

Isabella smiled. "I am," she said.

Katalin just stared at Isabella for a moment and then replied in awe, "I thought it was just a story."

"It is the truth. Why did you leave your mother alone?"

"I had to go with my husband."

"I suspect that you are your own woman and go where you wish to go."

"I wanted to get out of that house; three generations of our family have lived and died in that place."

"I suppose no one can blame you for that. Are you safe here?"

"I am."

"Do you think you will stay?"

"I do."

"Well, I will tell your mother you are safe."

"Thank you for your concern," Katalin answered.

"Oh, make no mistake, it is not concern, it is obligation. I will return again to check on you." The malevolence that Isabella had seen in the child was still there. It was a malevolence that covered her like a shroud. Isabella was now coming to the conclusion that this latent malevolence would someday cause great harm.

※

Another few years passed and Isabella returned to see Gizella had aged another few years and was obviously very lonely. Isabella was lonely as well but it was not in her nature to be sympathetic.

"I am glad you are here," said Gizella.

Isabella was suspicious of this remark. No one in a long time had said that they were glad to see Isabella and this was the last person she expected to say it.

"Why?"

"No reason, just that I am glad to have company, even yours."

Isabella laughed. As much as she hated to admit it, she was beginning to like Gizella.

"I am sorry to hear that you are lonely enough even to appreciate my company. How have you been?"

"Fine. I have something I should tell you though."

"What?"

"It is about Vlad."

"I do not want to hear."

"I know; however, I think you should listen."

"There are rumours that he has taken some Hungarian Countess away from her husband."

"A Countess." Isabella was upset by this, even jealous, but she had learned not to show her emotion. "He always did have expensive taste," she quipped.

"Countess Báthory."

"Countess Báthory!" Isabella remembered the young fifteen-year-old girl she had met a few years earlier. She had obviously taken Isabella's advice about keeping her own name. "I have met her," Isabella continued. "She is just a child, a pretty one at that, but just a child, nevertheless."

"She is not a child any more."

"I sometimes forget that people age while I stay the same. Her husband wants her back, I take it."

"The rumours are that he is searching for her," Katalin's mother answered. "Hungarian troops are searching the land and they do not care about any devastation they may leave behind."

"He will get her back," Isabella stated. "We can't have Vlad enjoying a companion when I have none," she added, thinking aloud, "and certainly not the company of an easily influenced child," Isabella continued.

Isabella took Gizella's horse and rode swiftly to the castle. When she arrived she crept silently up to the door. As she approached, she saw smoke rising from the chimney. Isabella looked through the window at the people inside. Vlad was sitting in his armchair and the Countess was sitting on his lap and in a very coquettish fashion. Isabella waited until dawn broke and then crept in through the door. The fire was now just smouldering embers, the young woman lay sleeping on the ground in front of it. Vlad had left her there to sleep. Isabella looked at her neck for any signs or marks and examined her teeth for bloodstains or sharpened incisors. There was nothing; Isabella was pleased to find no sign of vampirism. For although Vlad had taken this woman he had not made her immortal and now he would not have a chance to.

Isabella lifted the girl into her arms and crept out of the castle. Vlad was watching her every move. He was happy at seeing Isabella for he presumed by her actions that she would return to him soon, if only to chastise him for his dalliance.

Isabella threw the girl over the horse and started to ride with her. This understandably awakened the girl. She did not know what was happening and was frightened. She started to scream and kick. The journey back to Count Nádasdy's castle would take several days. Isabella took her down to the village first. She could not listen to a screaming woman for days on end.

She opened the door to Katya's old house and entered with the girl slung over her shoulder. Isabella threw her to the floor and slapped her face hard. This immediately silenced her; no one apart from her mother had ever dared to strike her.

"Be quiet," Isabella demanded. The Countess sat there rubbing her face and whimpering slightly. "Be quiet!" Isabella repeated. "Do you realise how close you are to death?" Isabella said. The girl was shaking and Katya's great-grandchild Gizella entered the room.

"She is terrified," said Gizella.

"She should be...I am not going to be able to take her home. I think I would kill her before I got there." The Countess was looking at the pair totally bewildered confused and most of all frightened.

"Can you get her home?" Isabella asked.

"I know where there are Hungarian troops; they will take her home to her husband."

"That will do. I will watch them from a distance to make sure she comes to no harm."

"Why are you concerned?" Gizella asked.

"Because I want her to live."

"Why?"

"I want to see if Vlad chases her."

"He will," said the young Countess, finally joining the conversation.

"I think you flatter yourself too much. He will not give you a second thought," said Isabella.

"He will come after me, and I will run back to him. He promised to give me something."

"What did he promise to give you?" Isabella grabbed the girl's arm and shook her.

"Youth, he promised to give me youth."

"That is the one thing you shall never be given," retorted Isabella. "If you go anywhere near Vlad I will hunt you down and kill you and I will prolong your death so you can feel every agonising minute."

Isabella approached the young Countess and placed her hands on her head. She showed the girl how she could torture and kill when she wanted to. The girl saw pictures in her mind of people Isabella had seen die and people Isabella herself had killed. The Countess knew Isabella's threat was real. She would never willingly pursue Vlad in her lifetime again.

"I will never come back here, but I want to stay young," she said. "I know you know the secret. Tell me what it is?" she begged.

"There is no secret; he was telling you stories to seduce you."

"No he wasn't, he never touched me,"

Isabella smiled. To her surprise she was glad at hearing this. She still loved him.

Isabella took the Countess to the Hungarian troops and followed for a few days while they took her home. Erzsébet's husband took her back willingly. Isabella decided to visit Katalin while she was there.

"When did Vlad come here?" she asked Katalin.

"He came at night about a month ago."

"Did any one else see him apart from the Countess?"

"I did. He almost killed me, but then he realised I was a Slovak. He asked me who my mother was and who my grandmother was. I think he knew or at least suspected who I was."

"He knew I would find out about the Countess," Isabella thought aloud. "Did he plan to take the Countess after you told him who your ancestors were?"

"I think so, yes."

"He was testing me. He wanted me to find out to see what my reaction would be. He still cares for me," Isabella smiled. She was willing to forgive, or at least forget Vlad's earlier betrayal.

"What's wrong?" said Katalin.

"Nothing."

"You look almost happy."

"I am...I am going home, I will come back to see you soon."

Isabella returned home that night but what she did not realise was that the Countess had heard all of Isabella and Katalin's conversation. The Countess approached Katalin after Isabella had left.

"You know that woman?" asked the countess.

"I do," said Katalin.

"What is the secret?" the Countess begged.

Katalin looked at the young countess and sensed an opportunity staring her in the face. Katalin answered, "Blood, my lady, Sanquis est Via, the Blood is the Life."

MAKE ME IMMORTAL WITH A KISS

CHAPTER TEN

Isabella travelled quickly back to the castle; she could not wait to see Vlad again. She still loved him; she knew she always had. Isabella had looked for years for the slightest excuse to return to him. However, she was not so naive that she believed this love of hers would ever make her happy. It would make her miserable and she knew it, but being in this world without him was agonizing. She had to be near him and she hoped that Vlad wanted her back as well. He had made no attempt to chase after Erzsébet and she hoped that Vlad had only taken up with this child to make her come home to him.

Vlad himself was eagerly awaiting her return. He knew she would return after she had so quickly whisked the girl away from his company. He too longed to see her for he loved her completely. Vlad also realised that a lifetime spent with this woman could be heartbreaking, but life without her was unbearable and insignificant.

Isabella entered the castle and searched for Vlad. He was not to be found. She waited for him and when it was nearly morning Vlad returned to her. An hour before his return Isabella had become tired and crawled into her chest to fall asleep. When Vlad saw the chest in the corner of the room he was overjoyed, but he would not visibly display his rapture. For each partner in this relationship would not show their true feelings to the other. For that would mean showing a need or a dependence on the other and they believed that this would show a vulnerability that each one of them would be able to use against the other.

Isabella awoke and climbed out of the wooden chest. She sat down beside him demonstrating little more than indifference. He returned this with only a slight smile of greeting crossing his lips. Vlad made no vocal acknowledgement of her return and after a few moments of silence, Isabella began to speak.

"We should leave here for awhile," she said.

"We?" Vlad asked.

"Yes, we should leave this place; it is filled with nothing but sour memories for both of us. We should find somewhere different to live, see if we can try to live together…without being tempted to kill each other," Isabella said with a wry smile.

"Have you got somewhere in mind?" Vlad asked.

"Anywhere, it doesn't matter, as long as it is far away from here."

"We are safe here," Vlad stated.

"I have realised that we can be safe anywhere. The world is riddled with war, disease and famine. We can hide ourselves amongst the humans anywhere. Death is not such a strange event that it cannot be explained by some reason other than us."

"Is this what you have been doing for the past century, living among the humans?"

Isabella smiled. "Any humans I have lived among have not lived long."

Vlad smiled at her. "All right, we will go travelling together to see if we can live with each other, as you say."

After a few weeks the pair left and started to travel throughout Europe for the first time together. Before long they arrived in England and decided to settle near London. Isabella saw England as just another place to see. She had never been impressed by progress or the beauty that she witnessed in the world, but Vlad on the other hand loved the place. He loved the history of the country; it was so like his own land—there had been the crusades to defeat the Turkish moors and the history of the royal courts was filled with intrigue and plots against the kings and queens of the time. But the reason he loved it most of all was that as well as its history of plots and conspiracies, it had managed to modernise itself and become a huge power in the world. This is what Vlad had wanted for his own land and because of this he admired this country greatly. Vlad would have been happy to stay there forever, with Isabella's company, of course.

Isabella, on the other hand, was different; she was a maverick and had a naturally nomadic nature. She never wanted to stay in one place for any length of time; she was restless, eager to travel, and any country she occupied was merely a stepping stone to the next destination. Things around her would, to a certain extent, impress her, but she did not think that any country held enough allure for her to remain there long.

Vlad for the moment was staying in England and had no intention of leaving. So to appease himself and Isabella they both decided to have Isabella travel around the country, thinking that she would eventually get her restless spirit out of her system. This was enough to placate her at least for the time being and she began to explore some of the country alone. Although Isabella loved to travel, she would not wander far or for very long on her own, however; she left Vlad for only a week at a time, as she could not stand any more time apart from him than that.

Isabella's exploration of England consisted of travelling from inn to inn in the guise of an English noblewoman named Helen Hawthorne. On a dark winter's evening her coach driver had been forced to stop because of a storm, and Isabella found herself in an Auberge that was a little less reputable than she was used to. While she was waiting for her room to be prepared, she sat down beside the fire to warm her cold hands.

A man had been watching her from the instant she entered the room. He was a young and bright-eyed man, who was observant of everything that surrounded him. By his demeanour he was obviously intelligent and well-educated and looked out of place in this establishment. He had caught Isabella's eye for no other reason than the fact that she had caught his. He was drinking very heavily and talking and laughing with his friends but he hardly ever lifted his eyes from Isabella. He gazed over at her with a constant smile upon his face.

Isabella smiled back at him. She liked gazes like these. Vlad would never look at her like this, at least never when she could see him. This young man was looking at her with eyes full of admiration. Isabella's admirers were repaid with their lives; she didn't like to kill anyone who paid her a compliment.

One of the young man's friends shouted at him, "Recite us a poem, entertain us!"

"I think I will," he said. He climbed up onto the table with his pitcher of ale still in his hand and his voice carried into the crowd, "A poem translated by myself, called "The Seduction of Corinna" and dedicated to the woman sitting beside the fire."

There were lascivious roars from his friends and the rest of the people in the tavern. Isabella was silent; maybe she would kill him, she thought. Crassness and exhibitionism never impressed her. The young man began his verse.

"Stark naked..."

He paused to receive more lascivious roars from his audience.

"As she stood before mine eye,
Not one wen on her body did I spy
What arms and shoulders did I touch and see;
How apt her breasts were to be pressed by me!"

He paused again to take a swig of his ale and again to receive a rapturous and gleeful applause from his audience.

"How smooth a belly under her waist saw I!
How large a leg, what a lusty thigh!
To leave the rest, all liked me passing well.
I clinged to her naked body, down she fell
Judge you the rest, being tired she bade me kiss...Jove,
send me such afternoons as this."

Everyone in the tavern was clapping for the young man and begging for another brazen verse.

"No, friends, I have said enough this evening." He bowed. "Till next time." The man jumped off the table and walked over to Isabella, who was the only one in the tavern who had not been impressed by his performance. He sat beside her, which she thought was quite presumptuous, but she let him sit down opposite her because she was growing hungry.

"Can I get you a drink of something?" the young man asked.

"No," Isabella replied firmly.

"Can I get you anything?" he asked her.

"What have you to offer me?" Isabella inquired with disdain. "What I mean to say is you have the look of a man who does not have anything, apart from a wicked tongue. I wouldn't offer gifts that you cannot deliver."

"I would rob and steal for such a beautiful lady," he said, in a mocking tone.

Isabella, growing impatient with the man's impertinence, replied "Such talk can get you killed,"

"A small price to pay for such a vision," the young man said, and he laughed. He was spewing out these eloquent phrases with a licentious smile. He was sincere in what he was saying, but he was drunk, and trying to seduce the Vampire with his own wicked sense of charm.

Isabella's icy countenance was beginning to soften a little and she sat with him for awhile talking. He was consuming jug after jug of ale, and getting steadily more and more inebriated. After a few hours he eventually passed out. Isabella was slightly flattered by him and she would not leave him in such a condition with the thieves and cutthroats that frequented that establishment. Isabella helped him to a room and waited for him to awaken.

He awoke very late the next afternoon; rubbed his eyes cautiously and sat up on the bed that Isabella had procured for him. He looked around the room and spied Isabella. He smiled over at her, but as he did so the previous night's drinking hit him, and his smile turned to a grimace and he rubbed his throbbing, clammy head.

"I am surprised you can sit up at all," said Isabella. The young man sighed.

"You are not going to lecture me on the evils of drink and tobacco are you?"

"You are feeling the evils of them well enough with out me saying a word," Isabella replied.

"Oh, no, even worse than a lecture, you are being self-righteous."

Isabella had been accused of many things but never of being self-righteous. She smiled and said, "Were you trying to impress me?"

"That depends," he said, attempting to smile.

"Depends on what?" Isabella asked.

Still trying to focus on Isabella, he smartly remarked "On whether I succeeded."

"I cannot say I am ever impressed with men of your kind," she replied.

"And what do you know of my kind?" he asked.

"Nothing, but your countenance and manner suggests I would not like to know."

The young man, very sure of himself, replied, "I, on the other hand, would enjoy getting to know you."

"I am sure you would," Isabella sighed. This was just another young fool with no visible depth of character. He could make her smile and she was flattered by him, but that was all the charm he held for her.

"Well, I will leave you now, I am sure you have other women to impress." Isabella got up to leave.

"Wait, what is your name?" the young man asked.

Isabella replied without giving the young man a second glance. "Helen," she answered as she walked out his door. She would meet this man again quite soon under very different circumstances.

※

Isabella was walking through the streets of Canterbury a month later when she heard a raucous sound coming from a nearby alleyway. Keeping herself hidden, she crept up to where the noise was coming from. Two men were attacking a much younger one. The young man was getting badly beaten. He kept getting up to face his attackers again and again, even though they were obviously too strong for him to ever gain the upper hand. Isabella recognised the younger man; it was the salacious poet she had met the previous month. She took it upon herself to intervene on his behalf.

"I don't think this is completely fair," Isabella said. One of the attackers, who was holding the young man up by his shirt, was distracted at the sound of a woman's voice. He relinquished his grip and dropped his victim into the dirt of the ground below. Again the young man struggled back onto his feet to face more punishment. Isabella still could not be seen. One of the men walked a few steps in her direction, hoping to see the woman that belonged to this voice.

"This is none of your affair," the other attacker said blindly into the darkness.

"I am a good citizen. That makes it my affair," Isabella said contemptuously. "I am wondering why you are beating up a defenceless boy."

"I am not a defenceless boy," the young man shouted, spitting blood over his would-be murderers. "Excuse me sirs, I am sorry if my blood has marred your clothing." The young man started to laugh as he mockingly tried to wipe away the blood that was now all over his attacker's clothes. He is drunk again, Isabella thought. "As I was saying, I am not a defenceless boy."

One of the attackers shoved him back down to the ground. The battered young man wiped more blood out of his own eyes and continued speaking. "I realise all evidence points to the contrary." He was still trying to struggle up on to his feet and when he finally regained his footing he wiped a spot of blood off one of his attacker's cheeks. "Now let us resume sirs, as you may have guessed I have been holding back." In response to this, he was again kicked back on to the ground. This young man would not be satisfied until these two men had killed him.

"I think you should stop," Isabella stated.

"I think they should stop, too, before I really lose my temper," the young man stated, half laughing, half drunk.

"I think you should be silent," Isabella warned. He was only angering these two men and his beating was getting more and more severe.

"What has it got to do with you?" one attacker asked.

"Absolutely nothing. I am just making a request. What could he have possibly done to deserve this?" Isabella asked.

"He is an Atheist," a different attacker responded.

"And who are you to punish him, if he is an Atheist? God will punish him." Isabella lifted her hand to recoil the fog and made herself visible to the assemblage.

The attacker continued, "What is a woman like you doing wandering the streets, alone at this time of night?"

"Would you like to find out?" Isabella learned forward and grabbed the man closest to her by the hair, pulling his neck to her mouth. She slowly drained the man's life's blood. He writhed around trying to pry himself free, but Isabella's grip was too strong. Isabella made sure this deathly sight was obscured from the other two men. She summoned up a shroud of fog to engulf her.

"What is happening?" the remaining attacker yelled out. Isabella now moved beside him so swiftly that all he could feel was a rush of air whispering through his hair.

"Let him go," Isabella whispered in his ear. The man was terrified. This ungodly creature was now so close to him.

"Who are you?"

"An angel of death, and I have come for you," Isabella said, and she grabbed his neck and drank the life from him.

The young man who was so badly beaten was somewhat disoriented and totally oblivious to the events going on around him, until Isabella helped him up.

"What happened?" he asked.

"You fought them off," Isabella answered.

"I knew I would, when I found my stride," the young man quipped. Isabella could not help herself. She smiled even though her smile was accompanied by a sigh of exasperation.

"Come on," she said. "Since you have found your stride, surely you are able to walk."

The man struggled to his feet again. "Alas, I think my stride has left me again, but with your help I could try to walk home." He couldn't even manage a step before he swiftly passed out. Isabella caught him before he fell and dragged him to the nearest inn. She again procured a room for him. He woke up the next morning and Isabella was still sitting opposite him.

"This is beginning to become a habit," Isabella began.

The young man smiled and replied, "It is becoming a habit, a good habit I would like to continue."

"I'm sure. How do you get yourself into such messes? They could have killed you last night," Isabella lectured.

"Ah, but they didn't, and that is what really matters," the young man replied.

"Why did you deserve such enmity?" Isabella inquired.

He adamantly replied, "Because I refused to take holy orders. They think I am guilty of treason against the Queen."

"And why did you refuse to take holy orders?" The young man became uncharacteristically serious for a moment and said.

"I can't swear allegiance to something that I do not believe in."

"And why do you not believe?" asked Isabella.

The young man matter-of-factly replied, "Show me evidence of God's existence and I will believe in him,"

"Show me evidence to the contrary...?" Isabella quipped. "Why is it so important for you to take holy orders anyway?"

"They won't grant me my degree otherwise,"

"If your degree is that important to you, why don't you just take the holy orders?" she continued.

"It's the principle," he firmly stated.

"Obstinate principles get men killed. You are being foolish. I think I was right in my original assessment of your character; you are just a spoiled child," Isabella said as she stood to leave.

"Don't leave without promising me that I will see you again."

"You might," Isabella said.

"Sweet Helen..." The young man called out, trying to stop Isabella from leaving.

"No, just Helen," interrupted Isabella, turning back to look at him.

"My name is Kit," he volunteered.

Isabella answered "I don't believe I asked you for your name."

"You are quite right, you didn't, but I knew you wanted to know what it was," Isabella sighed and said, "Kit, you have to grow up some day go and do something to make yourself into a man. Your flippant attitude to life will get you nowhere, or worse, it will get you killed."

Isabella left. She liked this man. He was charming, but not unique enough to keep her interest for long. The following evening she overheard a conversation discussing the young man in a nearby alehouse.

"But we cannot award him a degree. He refuses to take holy orders."

"But he is genuinely gifted. He will be famous some day and we will be the ones that will be criticised for not giving him his degree."

"I think, personally, I will be famous on my own merit."

The other man laughed at this man's absurdity.

"No sir. If we are famous, it will only be because of our association with him," said another.

"We'll see." The man who spoke these words got up and left.

Isabella decided to follow him. She stirred up the wind and fog so that the street this man was walking down was filled with it. The fog was making it difficult for the man to see and the rustling wind was making it hard for the man to hear. He became frightened and began to run. He sensed he was in danger. Isabella tripped him. He fell, trying desperately to see who had caused him to fall, but he could see nothing. He had begun to think he was about meet his maker, and then Isabella started to speak to him.

"Let the boy have his degree."

"What?" the man whispered, looking frantically around him to see where the voice was coming from.

She repeated herself, "I said let the boy have his degree."

"Who are you?" the man asked.

"That's not important—you must let the boy have his degree," Isabella repeated more slowly.

"Who are you?"

Isabella was losing patience with him. She stepped on the man's leg and pushed on it to the point of breaking.

"Let the boy have his degree!" Isabella said through clenched teeth. "I will not say it again,"

"I will...I will!" The man eventually complied.

"Good," she said.

"But please tell me who you are," he pleaded.

"I am..." Isabella thought for a moment, "Sweet Helen," she replied.

The next day the man visited Kit.

"We have decided to award you your degree, whether you take orders or not."

"That is very kind of you," Kit said ironically. "What made you change your mind?" he enquired.

"It was always our intention to grant you your degree."

Kit knew this to be a lie.

The man got up to leave and just before he walked out the door he turned back to Kit and asked, "Do you know of anyone who calls herself sweet Helen?"

Kit looked at the man and smiled, but made no reply.

Three years passed and Vlad and Isabella were still in England. In fact Vlad hinted about permanently moving there. Isabella hated the idea but she went along with it for the moment. She had never seen Vlad so content.

She enjoyed seeing him this way. They were fairly happy together, although Isabella was obviously bored with England. She hated being stuck in one place for so long.

They still occupied the same house near London and Isabella would amuse herself by going into London often. The two had even managed to be accepted into Elizabeth's court at Richmond Palace. They would often go there to see the plays that were performed for the Queen. On a day in June, Isabella and Vlad were at the Palace. Isabella was unexcited by the play that was being performed; she crept out to look around the impressive building she was in.

When Elizabeth took over the reign from her sister, she had put it upon herself to add to the depleted treasury, and restore England to its former greatness. This was evident in every palace she occupied. Palaces by their very nature were opulent, but Richmond far surpassed any that Isabella had ever seen.

It could only be approached by boat on the river Thames. Anyone entering would cross the threshold into the grand hall, which was spectacular. The ceiling of this room was as high as the roof of most people's homes. A majestic fireplace was the centre point of the hall and it stood well above Isabella's head. There were great works of art on every wall. Everything from Hilliard's miniatures to Holbein's portraits of Henry VIII. Golden candelabras stood on every mantelpiece and every table. The ladies-in-waiting that glided through the hall wore dresses that were made with only the finest of silks and satins, and the diamonds, sapphires, and emeralds woven into the cloth sparkled from their bodices. Everyone looked so exquisite. Isabella had given into temptation and stolen a few for herself. She told herself she had done this only to ensure that she fitted into this society.

On the next floor, in the bedroom chambers that used to contain hard wooden beds in the days of Mary, the Queen's sister, there were now beds covered with mattresses filled with feathers. The world was changing, becoming more and more luxuriant, and even Isabella had to admit that England was the place where these changes were most evident. After all, Elizabeth had enabled this time to be thought of as the golden age.

Isabella's exploration of the palace was interrupted by someone whispering in her ear.

"Ah, Sweet Helen." Isabella was struck by a familiar voice. She turned around to see Kit. She could not help but notice his clothes; he made her Juliet gown look dull and unremarkable. His tunic was a midnight blue with gold threads intertwined all the way through it. It glistened even in the dim lighting of the room. His silken ivory chemise was visible at the collar, and lace ran all around the outer edge. He looked terribly extravagant; she almost laughed at the sight of him.

"Kit," Isabella said, "have you grown up yet? By your dress I am not sure you have."

"Why should only the women have the elegant attire?" Kit answered.

"Yes, you are definitely still a child," Isabella replied.

"Why are you always so critical of me?" Kit asked.

"I suppose you are right; I don't have the right to criticise anyone. So why are you here? I didn't think a conspirator like you would be allowed in the Queen's palace."

"I have acquired friends in high places."

"You have"

"I have. You told me to grow up, didn't you, and I have become a spy."

Isabella roared with laughter. "A spy! Who would make you a spy? You are hardly discreet."

"That does seem to be a problem."

Isabella laughed again, not believing a word Kit was telling her.

"Why are you really here, Kit?"

He hesitated and then renewed his smile and answered her, "I am here to see Edward Alleyn. I am going to write for his Admiral's Men."

"More comedies, I suppose."

"Would you prefer something more tragic?"

"I certainly would. At least it would be a change. You should write about some of these great leaders that are in these pictures; surely they have better stories to tell an audience?"

"You may be right," Kit answered.

"You should know Kit, I am always right," Isabella answered.

"You certainly are, or at least you have been so far." The pair heard the sound of applause coming from the other room. The play was obviously over.

"Well, I think this brings our conversation to an end," Isabella stated.

"Why should it? Don't tell me you have an old oppressive husband who would not like you talking to a younger, more handsome man."

"Sorry to disappoint you, I have a young gloriously handsome husband who would never be jealous of anyone who had such a meagre standing as yourself." Vlad now appeared at Isabella's arm.

"Helen," Vlad interrupted, summoning Isabella to come with him.

"I will take my leave of you," Kit said, completely ignoring Vlad. Kit lifted up Isabella's hand and kissed it, never taking his eyes away from Isabella's face. This angered Vlad but as always he kept his feelings hidden, knowing that Isabella would take any visible sign of his jealousy as a compliment. But Isabella was much cleverer than that. She knew this had annoyed him, but she said nothing.

Isabella lifted up the side of her skirt so she could turn to face Vlad and stretched out her hand for Vlad to take it. He did so and Isabella walked to the front hall and down the steps.

"Who was that?" Vlad asked.

"No one of any importance," said Isabella, smiling to herself. Vlad noticed her self-indulgent smile and turned to see the man that had been so insolent, and so familiar with his Isabella. Kit was watching Isabella still. Vlad was furious. This man's face was etched on Vlad's memory—he would come to regret his familiarity.

As Isabella stepped up into the carriage that was to take the pair home, she turned to see Kit, and now she too noticed that he was still smiling at her. Vlad and Isabella did not speak about these events, but Vlad knew that this sort of attention flattered Isabella and she loved to be flattered. Isabella knew that Vlad was angry so she would stay close to home for awhile to make sure that Kit was safe from harm.

Isabella became very attentive to Vlad over the next few months and all thoughts of Kit left her mind. The pair hunted, slept and ate together. The ensuing months, were actually quite happy for the two Vampires, but like all other happy times that the pair had shared, it was fleeting. This time their happiness was to be interrupted by an invitation to a play.

It came in the morning when both Vampires had just gone to sleep. Unfortunately for Isabella, Vlad was the first to awaken and he saw the invitation. Vlad opened it and read the contents; he then resealed it with hot wax. He placed it where it would look as if he had not seen it.

Isabella awoke an hour later just as Vlad knew she would. She tried to conceal it from him and acted as if nothing had arrived for her. Vlad thought she was concealing it because she favoured, even loved Kit. He was right to some degree, but he was in no danger of losing Isabella to Kit. By concealing the letter she thought that she was ensuring Kit's safety from Vlad's jealousy.

Isabella went into the other room to take a better look at the invitation. It said, "You are formally invited to a showing of the play, a tragedy, *Tamburlaine the Great*." Isabella was quite flattered by the invitation and would try to get to see Kit's play.

Isabella attended the play and although she was unaware of it, Vlad also attended. Kit observed Isabella in the crowd and after the play was over he went to find her.

"Did you like the play?" Kit began.

"It was different," Isabella answered.

"Is that a good thing?"

"Maybe."

"I have the feeling that is about the greatest compliment I will ever get from you."

"My grandfather always taught me never to praise those who praise themselves."

"He was very wise," Kit remarked.

"He was," Isabella answered.

"What other things did your grandfather teach you?" Kit's tone of voice now changed; all of a sudden he was trying to be sincere. "What I mean to say is, I want to get to know you, Helen."

Vlad, who was standing out of sight of the pair, decided to break into their conversation.

"Helen, I didn't expect to see you here," Vlad said. Obviously lying, he motioned to Kit and asked, "Helen, are you not going to introduce me to your friend?"

Isabella was now obviously anxious but she should have known Vlad would follow her.

"This is Edward Hawthorne, my husband—this is Kit, the writer of the play and an acquaintance of mine," Isabella said politely.

"An acquaintance...I am sorry, Kit was it? I always wonder where my wife finds time to make her acquaintances."

"Your wife is an independent woman, sir," replied Kit. His previous sincerity had now completely dissipated and was now replaced with disdain. "I am sure you have many acquaintances that she does not know about."

Isabella knew that Vlad saw this as insolence and thought it would be better to take Vlad and leave. "I think on that note we will leave; it was nice to see you again Kit and I enjoyed your play very much. Let us go, Edward."

Vlad was staring maliciously at Kit and Isabella tugged him on his arm. He turned his head swiftly towards Isabella and threw her a venomous look. It was a look that would have scared or at least silenced most people, but not Isabella.

"Our carriage is waiting for us outside," Isabella said sternly. Vlad reluctantly started to move to the door of the crucible-shaped theatre, but as they were just about to step outside, he turned back.

"The next time you want to send an invitation to my wife make sure it is addressed to both of us," he said.

Kit made a bow of mocking respect and said, "I certainly will not."

At this Vlad was enraged. He swept swiftly towards Kit and grabbed his throat. The people who were still in the theatre were stunned at this man's outburst and whispers and shrieks resonated throughout the crowd.

Isabella crept up beside Vlad, took his hand from around Kit's throat, and whispered in his ear, "You are the one who wants to stay here. Do you want people to know what we are?" At this Vlad let go of Kit's throat and he dropped him back onto his feet. "I would suggest, sir, you do not contact me again," Isabella said to Kit.

Vlad then proceeded to lean towards him and said, "You have been saved, but just for a moment."

The two Vampires left the theatre. Isabella looked back around at Kit just before he was out of sight. He was rubbing his neck but when she caught his gaze he smiled and winked at her. Isabella thought at that instant this was a man who would not live long.

Isabella and Vlad returned to their home nearby without saying a word to each other. They were both furious with each other. Vlad was the first to speak when they entered the house.

"Why did you go there this evening without telling me?"

"Because I knew the way you would react," Isabella stated.

"I would not have reacted that way if you had been honest with me and not deceitful."

"Oh, yes, you would! Only you would have covered your tracks better and not nearly killed him in the middle of a crowded theatre."

"You persist in trying to torment me like this."

"Is this what our life together is going to be like? We are happy and then someone invites me to a play and you fly into a jealous fit?"

"You know that is not the way things happen. I wish you were more like my wife!"

Isabella walked up to face Vlad and whispered slowly to him, "I wish you were more like my husband."

Vlad lashed out at Isabella, knocking her to the floor. She jumped to her feet again and struck Vlad, knocking him to the floor. She walked towards the door.

"I will come back when I think you can control your tantrums," she shot back at him. Vlad just lay there rubbing his face where Isabella had hit him. He wanted to run after her and stop her, but he couldn't and he wouldn't.

Isabella picked up her wooden chest and a few dresses and left Vlad again. She secretly wanted him to chase her. She was travelling down the cobblestone street in the carriage willing him to be behind, calling out her name. She looked back, but he was not there.

Isabella left England soon after her argument with Vlad. The two Vampires had now spent a few years apart, and although Isabella was still annoyed with Vlad, she missed her life with him. He was company for her and without him she was completely alone. She pined for him. So Isabella made her way back to England.

There was one other reason for her going back to England. She had found some writing that she wanted to give to Kit. She thought he might like it. She missed him as well, and missed his childish wickedness. The article was called *The History of Doctor Johann Faust, the Infamous Magician and Necromancer.* She knew Kit would appreciate it, so she was determined to return with it.

In England, everything was the same as she had left it. There was no emotional greeting between the two Vampires, but they were both happy to be close to each other again.

Vlad enthusiastically told Isabella that he had not injured Kit in anyway, as a favour to her. Isabella was pleased, if somewhat surprised.

"Good. I intend going to see him," Isabella began.

"Fine." Isabella was slightly uneasy by Vlad's eagerness to demonstrate how much he did not care, but she would hope for the best, and the next day she went to see Kit with his present.

She looked for him at the theatre but didn't find him. She then started searching the taverns. Isabella eventually found him sitting in a dark corner of a nearby tavern. He was by himself and he looked dreadful. Isabella smiled and approached him, intent on giving him the story she had brought with her.

"You are looking rather melancholy," Isabella began.

"Leave me alone," Kit said.

"You could at least look at me before you tell me to leave you alone." Kit looked up and smiled when he saw Isabella.

"Ah, sweet Helen, have you come to torment me?"

"You manage to torment yourself well enough."

"The wisdom of a woman," Kit said sarcastically.

"Do you want me to leave?" Isabella asked.

"No, quite the contrary,"

"Still a child, I see,"

"Only in your eyes. You are the only one I know who thinks of me as I child. How is your oppressive husband?"

"He is well, and a better man than you," Isabella quipped.

"Then why are you here?"

Isabella found herself asking the same question.

"I brought you something," she said. "It's a book I found it in Frankfurt. It is about a man who made a pact with the devil. He sold his soul for pleasure and power. It might interest you."

"It might," Kit said, completely uninterested.

"I will leave it with you, then." Kit made no response and Isabella threw the book at him and left. After a few more drinks Kit picked up the publication and started to read it. He became immersed in the story.

Kit's behaviour had made it easy for Isabella to resolve never to go and see him again. She returned to her home and promised Vlad that she would never see Kit again.

However, after a few months another invitation to a play arrived. It was an invitation from Kit to see the tragedy of *"Doctor Faustus."* It came through the door and again Vlad was the first one to see it. This time he did not open it. Isabella, unaware that Vlad was watching her, lifted the invitation and ripped it up.

Another few months went by and another invitation arrived, *"The Famous Tragedy of the Jew Malta"* and again Isabella ripped it up, for she was stubborn. Vlad was now content and so was Isabella; they stayed together fairly happily for the next few years.

※

Isabella had not seen Kit since he had been so rude to her and she no intention of seeking him out. But, one night in November, 1593, he decided to seek her out. Isabella was out alone looking for food. She was getting irritated. She could usually rely on beggars and thieves to be out at night, but tonight the streets were empty. A few hours passed and she heard a coach travelling quite fast a few streets from where she stood. She waited for the coach to approach her. Isabella threw herself out in front of it to stop it. This was a trick she had used before.

Kit had been following Isabella. She had not seen him and unfortunately for Kit he cared whether Isabella lived or died. The horses reared and then plummeted back onto to their four hooves, trampling Isabella. The violent impact broke her skin. Blood seeped out from wounds all over her body. She was lying there motionless and covered in blood; the coach driver pulled back the horses from Isabella. Any mere mortal would have been killed by such an accident.

Kit ran to her and fell to his knees beside her. He lifted up the upper part of her body and turned her around so he could look at her face. He wanted to see if she could have possibly lived through such a horrific accident. He held her just watching her desperately hoping for some sign of life. A wound which Isabella had received was gushing blood but as Kit watched, the wound completely healed before his eyes.

Isabella eyes fluttered and then she opened them. Kit was stunned. Tears that had welled up started to flow down his face. Isabella looked up at him. She realised immediately who it was. *Could she kill him?* She thought she would probably have to, but she could not bring herself to do it. Her body was starting to convulse with hunger pangs; she had left it too long between feedings. Isabella did not think as she pushed Kit aside with such force that he bumped his head off the cobbled street. He sat back up immediately and watched in horror, as Isabella satisfied her hunger.

She was swiftly moving through all the onlookers in turn. Some of them tried to run and some tried to fight back, but she was too strong and too fast. None of them would live. First the coachman, then the people in the coach. She bit into their flesh, sucking the life's blood from each of their bodies and they fell to the ground in lifeless heaps. Their blood spilled over her, mingling with her own.

Isabella stopped when she was totally satisfied and every one apart from Kit was dead. She rubbed the blood from around her mouth and looked over at him. He was terrified at such a sight and he crawled on his hands and knees, backing away from Isabella, afraid to move too quickly.

She stood contemplating whether she would kill him or not. She stared at him. He was trying to edge away from her. What should she do? Would he tell other people? Even if he did, who would believe him? But when they saw the bodies, they would believe; however, they would never believe that a mere woman had overpowered six people all by herself. They would notice the blood loss, which would go towards backing up his story.

Kit now stood up and ran from Isabella. Isabella let him go for now; she needed time to decide what to do; Isabella would hide any evidence of her attack and find him tomorrow to see what sort of a threat to her he actually was.

She piled the bodies into the coach and drove it away from the city. She waited for the break of day so that the people in the town could not see the fire flickering through the darkness. She searched the coach for anything of use to her, but found nothing. She unbridled the horses and then set fire to the coach with the bodies inside. She mounted one horse and led the other one home.

When she arrived home, Vlad was curious to see the beautiful dress she had worn on the night before drenched in blood.

"You look to have had an eventful evening," Vlad stated.

"I have just came back to change my dress and wash."

"Why, you are the one who always says we should not go out in the daylight when we are more vulnerable."

"There was a witness,"

"That has never bothered you before. I am sure you were the last thing they ever witnessed."

"No, they got away."

"That has never happened before," Vlad said, a note of suspicion evident in his voice.

"No, it hasn't," Isabella answered sharply. She had no time for Vlad's suspicions.

"So why last night?" Vlad asked.

"I guess I must be slipping."

"You must," Vlad answered, his suspicion never waning. He watched as Isabella changed and left the house. He knew that she was either lying to him or not telling him the whole truth. She had never let a witness escape from her; she was always so careful.

Vlad got dressed himself and followed Isabella. She saddled a horse and rode towards the centre of London. Vlad kept a safe distance on foot behind her. She arrived near Kit's apartment, went up the stairs and knocked on the door. A man answered it. Isabella had met him before.

"Thomas, is he in?" Isabella asked.

"He is, Lady Hawthorne," Thomas Kyd answered.

"Can I see him?"

"I don't know if he wants to see anyone?"

"Why?"

"He has been acting strangely; he seems frightened of something."

"Frightened? Thomas I want to see him." Isabella pushed on the door slightly.

"But...." Thomas protested.

"Now." This man was always quite weak-willed and he let Isabella in quite quickly. Kit was sitting beside the fire, shivering. He was in shock. His clothes were still covered in Isabella's blood from the night before. She walked over and sat in front of him. She used all the power she could sum up during the day to get Thomas to leave them alone and coerce Kit into listening to her.

"Kit," she said softly, Kit slowly lifted his head and looked into her eyes.

"I expected you to come for me," Kit answered.

"I haven't come for you."

"Are you going to let me live?"

"If I was going to kill you I would have done so last night and not risk you letting people know what you saw."

"I haven't told anyone."

"I know."

"Why did you come here?"

"I came to see you."

"You have seen me," Kit said.

"Kit, I could have killed you. You should ask yourself why I didn't." Isabella got up to leave and Kit grabbed her arm to stop Isabella.

"When did you make your pact with the Devil?"

Isabella turned and said. "I didn't choose to." She sat down and began her story. "I was born over one hundred and fifty years ago...."

❊

When Isabella was finished telling him her story, Kit asked. "What is your real name?"

"Isabella," she answered.

"Why do you stay with him? He destroyed your life. How can you forgive him for that?"

"I would have destroyed my own life, given enough time."

"Do you honestly believe that?"

"It is not just a belief; I know it to be true."

"But you have showed me nothing but compassion."

"You amused and flattered me; that is the only reason you are still alive."

"I don't believe you."

"Believe it...I am a killer...never forget it. If you get in my way I will not think twice about slashing your throat. I have no desire to stop killing, I have not the resolve to give it up. It gives me too much pleasure."

"Who would give it up, having been through what you have?"

"Vlad would and he did. He suffered the pain and endured it for as long as it took for him to grow old. He thought he would starve to death. He has done this twice. Vlad let himself grow old and my vanity could never let me suffer the indignity of growing old. I like killing people. I enjoy the sensation I get from it."

"I don't believe you like killing people."

"I do. You just have a higher opinion of me than you should. I don't deserve anyone's high opinion. You believe me to be a just a tortured soul. That I am just a victim of circumstance who would have been a good person had she not had a hard life beset by tragedy and filled with hatred. A lovely idea, but I am not one to mislead anyone. I know what I am. I am worse than Vlad. I am probably the most malevolent and malicious creature that God has ever put on this earth."

"You are not malicious. You must have great compassion, since you let me live."

"Compassion is a human emotion; people without souls cannot have compassion."

"But did you not say that when your husband died you felt his soul lift up to heaven?"

"My husband had never done anything wrong during his life. Maybe God forgave him and blamed the death of our son on me. Who knows?"

"So what are you going to do to me?"

"I don't think you will tell anyone my secret. I will let you go."

"Are you going to make me a Vampire?"

"No, never again will I condemn anyone to my fate. It is not worth it. You would end up hating me."

"I can't imagine I could ever hate you. Even last night I was terrified of you but I didn't hate you. I want to experience what you have experienced to live a life of eternal youth."

"You think that now, but with every power I have comes a weakness. Who knows how this curse would affect you, and I certainly do not want to find out. Anyway, I have stayed long enough. I have to go home. I am tired and Vlad will be missing me."

"You can stay here."

"No. Vlad would look for me and you should be careful, for I am amazed he has not killed you yet."

"I am not afraid of him."

"You should be!" With this Isabella left.

Vlad, who was watching from the street corner, saw who was bidding her farewell. He raced home and was there before Isabella arrived.

"Did you find him?" Vlad asked when Isabella arrived home.

"What makes you think it was a he?"

"Was it not?"

"No, it was a woman," Isabella lied.

"Did you find her?"

"I did."

"So nothing to worry about."

"Nothing at all," Isabella confirmed.

Vlad was hurt by Isabella's lies but he knew that if he had let her know that he was hurt, she would become overprotective of Kit to save him from any danger. Vlad feared that Isabella would turn him. He knew that Kit was not a Vampire yet. Vampires had a certain smell or way of moving, a look about them that is the only distinguishable to other Vampires. Kit was still human and if he was human he would be easy to kill. But he had to be careful. He could not kill Kit openly. He would have to be discreet or

Isabella would leave again. He would form a plan to kill Kit without letting anyone know that he wanted him dead.

Vlad would have to be as manipulative and cunning as Isabella could be in order to get rid of Kit, and he was more than capable. He started to ask around about him. Kit frequented the most disreputable of places. He was outspoken and had annoyed a great deal of people, including Francis Walsingham, one of the queen's advisors whose death a few years ago had probably saved Kit from harm. He had friends in the government who sometimes had been accused of treachery against the Queen. He had also annoyed his own peers, writers and actors. His extravagance and self-professed talent irritated and annoyed his fellow artists, especially since they could not say he was not talented. He was a member of the "School of Night," a secret society that was already accused of treason.

Vlad thought it would be easy to trick Isabella into believing someone else killed Kit, given that he had so many enemies. In fact, Vlad was amazed that Kit had lived this long. His greatest crime was refusing to take holy orders during his degree—all rumours of Kit's heresy and treason sparked from this. Religion was such an emotive topic; this was what Vlad decided he would use to kill him.

Vlad started to frequent some of the establishments that soldiers would use. He used his influence and discussed Kit at great length in these places, putting thoughts into the soldiers' heads of heresy and corruption, even treason. Kit's decadent lifestyle served only to confirm these rumours and he had also publicly described the inconsistencies in the Bible. Soon everyone was talking of his heresy. It had been easy for Vlad; Isabella soon got word of the growing enmity towards Kit. Fearing for his safety, she went to see Kit at the theatre.

"I have heard gossip, Kit," Isabella began.

"You don't strike me as one to listen to gossip," Kit answered her.

"I'm not...but this gossip I believe has a foundation in truth. You are accused of heresy as you have been before. And, this time Richard Baines has made accusations about you to the Privy Council, in writing."

"Richard Baines, if anyone, is an Atheist. He is. The council will not listen to him."

"You are very calm about this."

"They have been accusing me of heresy since I was seventeen."

"Maybe you should be more discreet about what you say."

"I say what I say; I am not going to hide the person that I am."

"They are planning to arrest you."

"They haven't yet."

"Your frivolous attitude will get you killed, Kit," Isabella appealed to him

"Well...you can stop that." Isabella looked at Kit inquisitively "You can make me immortal with a kiss," Kit told her.

"I will never do that."

"I will keep asking."

"And I will keep saying no."

"Then let's not talk of it again. Come out with me tonight."

"Why?"

"I am going out with a pack of tricksters and thieves and you will love them,"

Isabella smiled. "Maybe, but promise one thing."

"Anything."

"Be careful," Isabella pleaded with a smile and turned to leave him.

"You know me...I am never careful," Kit called out after Isabella.

Isabella went home and slept. She was tempted to meet Kit that night and she had made up her mind to do so when she awoke, if only to make sure he was safe from harm. After nightfall she went to Kit's apartment to meet him, not knowing that Vlad was close by and had arranged Kit's death for that evening. Vlad knew if Kit was arrested Isabella would save him and he had planned this evening with precision.

Isabella arrived at Kit's apartment an hour after nightfall. The door was open and a trail of blood led her upstairs. Isabella became frightened—she feared the worst. She ran upstairs and broke open the lock of the door. Isabella found Thomas Kyd inside sitting alone in the dark. He was shivering beside the fire; he had been severely beaten. A blanket was wrapped around his shoulders. Isabella had never had any respect for him. She thought he acted like a whining, weak-willed child at times. She grabbed his chin with her hand so that his face was forced up to look at hers.

"What have you done to get yourself in such a state?" Isabella asked.

"What have I done? What have I done?" he asked again in disbelief. "Ask Kit why I have been tortured!"

"I am asking you!" Isabella said, her voice a warning. "Who did this to you? You're of no importance to anyone. Where is Kit?"

"I don't care about Kit anymore. My life is the only thing that is important to me now," Thomas shouted back. "Thomas Walsingham arranged this," he continued.

"Arranged what?"

"My torture. They arrested me a few days ago and have whipped, beaten, and burned my skin. Until I finally admitted that...."

"Until you admitted what?" Isabella said firmly.

"That Kit is a heretic and a traitor."

"You did what!" Isabella grabbed Kyd and shook him.

"I would like to see what you would do under such circumstances."

"I would not betray a friend," Isabella reviled

"You know that is a lie. You do not strike me as the honourable type." At this Isabella did strike him and he fell from his seat onto the floor.

"I may not have any honour but mark my words, if anything happens to Kit you will die in misery and poverty out in the streets, and that is no lie." Isabella left and Thomas understood that his fate was assured.

She ran to the tavern where she knew Kit would be. When she got there everything was fine. Kit was laughing and enjoying the company of his friends. Isabella was relieved and went over to sit beside him.

"Where have you been? I have been waiting for you," Kit greeted Isabella.

"Nowhere. I think you should go home. I have to tell you something."

"Go home...no I wouldn't think of it. I am having a grand time here. I will not leave. Sit down and rest awhile. Besides, Ingram here has promised to pay for the festivities. I have to witness that. Don't worry, I will go home with you soon."

Isabella leaned over and whispered in Kit's ear, "They are going to arrest you tonight for heresy."

"Nonsense, they are always going to arrest me, but they haven't yet."

"It's true," she said. Kit silenced Isabella by pressing his finger on her lips. This was something Nicolae used to do and it worked; she remained quiet.

"You know for an immortal you worry too much about death when you have no cause."

Isabella looked around her. There was no sign of any danger. She started to calm down. The lights were bright and the tavern was noisy. She could not hear much beyond this noise. Still there seemed to be no apparent danger. She settled down and the evening drifted on without incident.

The group Isabella was sitting with had just finished eating. She was still watching the crowd and not paying much attention to the conversation of her companions. She was completely oblivious to who they were. Then she heard Kit shouting about something beside her.

"Kit, what is wrong with you?" Isabella asked.

"He is refusing to the pay the bill," Kit answered.

"It doesn't matter," Isabella scolded.

"Of course it does. This is the only reason I came out with him, on the prerequisite that he would be paying. Isn't that right Walsingham?"

"Walsingham. Thomas Walsingham?" Isabella enquired.

"The very same," Kit answered. Isabella stood up with the attention of walking over to Walsingham but she did not reach him. She heard screams coming from behind her. Terrified to see what had happened, she slowly turned around only to see Kit lying on the floor, stabbed through the eye. He was dead.

Isabella ran from the tavern, overwhelmed and devastated by Kit's death.

※

Vlad's vision of events was slightly different. A few days before Kit died, Vlad was waiting outside his apartment. He watched until Kit left. A few minutes later another man came out of the rooms. Unlike Kit, who walked with his head held high, this man walked with his head down; he was bound for the nearest hostelry. Vlad followed him in. Thomas Kyd sat down in the corner, not paying attention to anyone. Vlad sat watching him. He was looking pitiful, a pathetic individual, Vlad thought.

Another man came in and sat beside him. Vlad recognised this man. He had seen him in the Queen's court. He knew his name was Thomas Walsingham, who, like his cousin Francis, was one of the Queen's chief advisors. Vlad wondered why such an important man would bother with Thomas Kyd. So he listened to the pair's conversation.

"How goes it with you, Thomas?" Walsingham asked.

"Not well," Kyd answered.

"Why, what has happened?"

"They refused to publish my play."

"Why?"

"They said it was not good enough."

"The next one will be good enough, do not lose heart," Walsingham reassured tapping Kyd on the shoulder.

"No as long as I am associated with Kit Marlowe. I don't think any of my plays will be good enough."

"You are being foolish,"

"Am I? Every other week they threaten to arrest him. They are always talking about it at court, you know that."

"They say a lot of things in court, and a lot of it has no real meaning. Everyone there has been accused of conspiring against the Queen."

"Even you?" Vlad watched as a dark look crept over Walsingham's face—he was remembering something.

"No, not me, never me," Walsingham answered firmly.

"Maybe you should choose your friends more wisely then; your friendship with Kit will endanger you, too," Kyd remarked.

"Be quiet or I will make sure you will regret those words." Thomas Kyd drank his wine and left. Walsingham went to the front of the tavern to get himself another drink. He sat down and Vlad approached him.

"Can I join you?" Vlad asked.

"You can," said Walsingham. "Have I seen you somewhere before?"

"Probably around court," Vlad answered.

"Yes, that must be it."

"Who was that you were talking to you?"

"A friend of mine, or so I thought."

"We must keep our friends close in these ominous times," Vlad said, and his voice adopted a hypnotic influence.

"What do you mean?"

"I mean there are rumours, Thomas."

"There have always been rumours about Kit."

"These are not about Kit. They are about you." The colour drained from Thomas Walsingham's face as he was again reminded of a painful memory.

"About me?" Thomas said in disbelief.

"Yes."

"That is absurd. Everyone knows I would never go against my Queen," Walsingham said nervously. Vlad was surprised but pleased at how well this was working, but he still was curious as to know what this man was remembering. He looked into his thoughts. A dark memory was troubling Walsingham.

Vlad saw a dark passageway and a child he knew. Thomas Walsingham was chasing a toy that was rolling along the ground. He was chasing it further and further, deeper into the belly of the dungeons below the castle. The toy stopped rolling at the opening of a doorway into another dungeon that the child had never seen before. The child was now distracted from the toy by the noises that were coming from the corridor. He wandered slowly into the darkness of the narrow and damp passageway.

The boy walked down the lengthy dark hall until he saw a glimmer of light. He walked towards it. The noises that he had heard could now be recognised as screams. He walked into the open doorway and he saw his cousin taking a branding iron and whipping the man who was screaming with it. The iron seared his skin. His face was contorted in pain. His blood-curdling screams were unlike any sound the child had heard before. The tortured man looked at the child and held out his hand begging for mercy. He was squealing every time the iron came near him. The child was sickened by the smell of burning flesh. All he could say under his breath was to ask his cousin to stop hurting him. It was loud enough for Francis to be alerted to his presence and he walked over to his young cousin, picked him up and left with him in his arms.

"Why were you doing that Francis?" the child asked.

"The man is a suspected traitor."

"Only a suspected traitor?"

"Yes—only a suspected traitor, I am actually starting to believe he may be innocent. Traitors are to be punished, even suspected ones. He should have chosen his friends more carefully." The boy said nothing more. He had hidden away this memory, until today.

✵

Vlad's influence was making him remember this all too clearly. Thomas understood what it meant to be called a traitor; even a suspected traitor. He had forgotten and now he was frightened. Vlad's plan was working and he resumed talking.

"You must prove that you are faithful."

"How?"

"Prove you are not a traitor—turn your friend Kit into the government."

"How? There has never been any proof."

"I am sure you will think of something. That man who left?"

"You mean Thomas Kyd?"

"Use him."

Walsingham went straight to the Privy Council and got a petition for the arrest of Thomas Kyd on suspicion of treason.

✵

The soldiers arrived at Kit's apartment when Thomas Kyd was there by himself. Thomas Walsingham had planned it that way. He wanted to torture a confession out of Thomas Kyd so that he had proof before arresting Kit.

On the third day after Kyd's arrest he finally accused Kit of treason. This was longer than Walsingham thought he would last.

When Vlad heard of Kyd's accusation, he paid a visit to the prison where Kyd was being tortured. He wanted to talk to both Kyd and Walsingham, one final time.

"He told us that Kit was a traitor," Walsingham told Vlad.

"He confessed then," said Vlad. Walsingham hesitated before he agreed. He knew that the information he had gathered could never be called a confession, certainly as far as his own conscience was concerned.

"Yes," Walsingham reluctantly agreed.

"Fine."

"We are going to arrest him tonight," Walsingham said.

"Why rush? Wait awhile. I suspect now the woman you told me about is involved. We want to observe Kit for awhile. I want you to invite Kit out this evening and ask Kit to bring the woman."

"Have I not yet absolved myself from guilt?" Walsingham asked.

"Do this one last thing and you will have proved your loyalty. Let Thomas Kyd go home just before nightfall. I want you to make sure Ingram Frizer is there."

"What do you suspect him of?"

"Nothing, I just want him there."

"Kit hates him; he is a money lender and as immoral as Kit is, he does have some principles."

"I want you to tell him that he is going to pay for dinner."

Walsingham nodded. Vlad went further into the prison to talk to Thomas Kyd.

"Thomas," Vlad whispered. "Thomas." Thomas who was lying on the floor bleeding opened his eyes and looked up at Vlad. "Do you want the pain to stop, Thomas?" Vlad asked.

"Yes," he sobbed.

"I can make the pain stop."

"Thank you."

"Don't thank me yet. I want you to do something for me."

"Anything."

"Do you know Helen?"

"Helen?"

"Yes, you know her don't you?"

"I do."

"I want you to tell her you confessed to Kit being a traitor and that Thomas Walsingham was behind it."

"He was behind it."

"That's right. You will simply be telling her the truth."

Vlad left. He had a few other things to do before this evening. He wanted to ensure that at worst Kit was arrested and at best he was dead. He wanted Isabella to be there so that she would believe he had nothing to do with it.

He had to go and see one other man to make sure his plan would work. He had to go and see Ingram Frizer himself. Vlad stopped on the way to buy a dagger; it cost him twelve pence. He mused about how little it cost to buy a weapon that was to cause such great harm, weapons being something that a Vampire never needed.

Ingram was walking along the path in the Common Grounds when Vlad caught up with him.

"Walsingham wants you to go out with him tonight. He sent me to tell you," Vlad started.

"All right."

"Who is that?" Vlad asked. Ingram looked around. He was pointing to a man standing at the corner.

"That is Paul Nesbitt; he owes me money," Ingram said.

"He does? He has been following us for the last half hour."

"Has he?"

"Isn't he a friend of Kit Marlowe?" Vlad asked, sowing the seeds of paranoia in Ingram's mind.

"I don't know," Ingram replied.

"I think he is."

"He's going to be evicted." said Ingram.

"If I had a man like that following me, I would carry weapon."

"I have no need for weapons," Ingram said.

"I would think differently. Just think, if he kills you he doesn't have to pay your debt. A man who is to be evicted may be desperate."

"He wouldn't kill me."

"You are probably right. Kit Marlowe would stop him from harming you," Vlad said. He drew out the dagger and handed it to Ingram.

"Carry this. It will keep you safe." Ingram took the knife and Vlad left him.

Vlad arrived in the disreputable establishment where they were all to meet before anyone else. He sat waiting for the first of his guests arrive. The first was Paul Nesbitt, who approached Vlad.

"Are you going to give me my money?" Vlad had promised Nesbitt that he would pay his debts.

"Soon. Stand over there so that Ingram can see you when he comes in. I want you at some point in the evening to go over to Kit Marlowe and say something to him."

"What should I say?" Paul asked.

"Anything, it doesn't matter. Do this for me and I promise you, I will repay all your debt." Nesbitt went over and sat near the door so anyone who came in could see him.

Next to arrive was Ingram Frizer; he had two others with him—Nicholas Skeres, and Robert Poley. Ingram noticed Paul right away as he walked in. He shuddered when he saw him; Vlad had made him nervous of Nesbitt. Vlad observed that Ingram placed his hand on his dagger. He smiled. It was working. The last to arrive was Kit with Thomas Walsingham. Paul nodded to Kit as he came in and Kit instinctively returned the nod. Vlad quickly looked at Ingram again. He was getting more and more nervous. His hand was white, for he was clutching the dagger so tightly.

An hour later, Isabella arrived. She ran into the room and dashed from table to table looking frantically around for Kit. She soon caught sight of him and ran to his side; after speaking to him, she seemed slightly less agitated and sat down beside him. Vlad could hear her conversation. Isabella could not see Vlad, for it was too bright. The room was mostly a blur to her; she could only see movement immediately around her. The bright lights reduced her senses to such an extent that she could not even smell the other Vampire in the room.

Vlad watched Isabella, the bright light making no difference to him, for his power was greater than hers. Isabella looked nervous for the sake of her companion, but as time went by, her nerves started to calm and she sat slightly more easily in her seat. By this time, even Ingram was beginning to calm.

Kit got up to get another drink and as he did he stopped to say a few words to Paul Nesbitt. Ingram Frizer's nervousness returned to him and was now rapidly turning to fear.

Vlad needed to control his conspirators and he started to speak to them in a voice that only they could hear. The speech that was issuing from his lips was less than a whisper but a little more than just thoughts.

Eleanor, bring them the bill. Vlad directed.

Kit, having managed a fresh drink, was again sitting next to Isabella.

Eleanor, who was the proprietor of this establishment, immediately stopped what she was doing and arrived at Kit's table with the bill they had run up.

"You are paying," Kit stated in Ingram's direction.

"I am not," Ingram replied, for even though he was nervous with Kit and felt threatened by him, he still was as cheap as ever and reluctant to pay the bill.

Kit, introduce Thomas Walsingham into the conversation. Kit, too, was not free from Vlad's influence.

"Thomas, didn't you tell me Frizer was paying?" said Kit.

"He certainly told me he was," said Walsingham.

"Walsingham, Thomas Walsingham," Isabella cut in. She got up, turning her back to Vlad and moving swiftly over Thomas Walsingham. The following happened in a matter of seconds.

Paul Nesbitt, shout Ingram's name.

"Ingram!" Nesbit shouted. Ingram turned around to look at Paul Nesbit with his back towards Vlad.

Kit, see the dagger. You hate Ingram don't you, you wish he was dead. The world would be a better place, wouldn't it?"

Kit grabbed the dagger and lashed out at Frizer. Vlad approached the group; Isabella still had her back towards Vlad and could not see his approach.

Kit, don't see me.

Vlad took the dagger from Kit's hand so that he missed Ingram; he then placed the dagger in Ingram's hand.

He was trying to kill you Ingram! Kill him before he kills you. Kill him before he kills you!

Ingram took the dagger and stabbed Kit through the eye. *"All of you forget me."* Vlad whispered his last instruction. Kit fell to the floor and Isabella turned round to see him bleeding to death. Vlad had already left.

<hr>

Frizer was arrested but Thomas Walsingham got him a pardon from the Queen, on the condition that no one mention he was ever there. And no one ever did. This was possible, as Kit and Ingram were the only two of the evening's party who knew him. Thomas Kyd appealed to the Privy Council and other members of the Queen's Council to try and vindicate himself, but Isabella made sure his pleas fell on deaf ears. He ended up destitute and on the streets and died within the year, just as Isabella had promised.

A few days after Kit died, a woman approached two writers, George Chapman and Thomas Nashe. She gave them several unfinished manuscripts by Kit Marlowe. They finished them and made sure they were published. The woman was never seen by these two men again.

ACERCA DE LA CONDESA SANGRIENTA
CONCERNING THE BLOODY COUNTESS

CHAPTER ELEVEN

After Kit died, Isabella fell into a melancholy. Nothing could console her, not even Vlad's company. Kit was the second mortal she had cared for since she had died and the second she had watched die. Isabella, despite her great strength and power, had not been able to save either Kit or Lia. She had never loved Kit, not like she loved Vlad, but she had felt great affection towards him and she felt once again that she had lost her only friend. Friends for Isabella were precious, never sought, and rarely found.

Isabella by this time was totally disenchanted with England. She had seen more than enough of the intrigue at court and wanted to go home. It took Isabella some years, but she eventually convinced Vlad to return with her. She would not even contemplate going anywhere without him. He would always be there whenever she needed him and she thought that she would never have to watch him die.

When Isabella returned to the Carpathians, the first thing she felt she must do was visit Gizella. She found Katya's house in the same state that she had left it in—empty. Katalin's mother was still left alone, abandoned by her kin.

"Katalin never came home to you?" Isabella began.

"She visits very occasionally but never stays long. As soon as she arrives, you can tell she can't wait to get back to her mistress," replied Gizella.

"Erzsébet." An inner voice told Isabella to fear an alliance between these two women. "I might pay her a visit," Isabella stated.

"I would be grateful if you did," Gizella answered.

"Then I definitely will. You should have family around you."

"Thank you, Isabella!" Isabella nodded. She travelled that night to visit Katalin.

Her journey was swift and when she came within walking distance of Count Nádasdy's castle, she was bombarded by a strong malodour. The smell of death filled the air surrounding the castle, the stench thick and suffocating. Isabella was made ill by it. She had never came across its like before. She could hardly approach the castle without retching but she was determined to see Katalin, especially now. Isabella was afraid for her and for what she may have done.

Isabella slipped into the castle unseen. Considering she had no intention of killing anyone inside, she felt she did not need to be invited. She searched the servants' quarters for Katalin. Isabella did not find her or anyone else there, so she widened her search. She heard screams coming from the lower chambers of the castle. Descending the spiral staircase, she noticed that the stench was getting considerably worse, which hardly seemed possible. Isabella hurried down the stairs and followed the sound of the screaming. Lavender lamps lined the corridor and every one of them was burning. Isabella was nauseous; the strong smell of lavender mixed in with the smell of decay was attacking her acute senses.

She reached the last door at the end of the corridor. Isabella paused before she opened it, fearing what she would find inside. The door was locked, but Isabella tore it from its hinges. She stood at the opening to the room watching the execrable scene inside.

Her glance was immediately drawn to Katalin, who was thankfully unharmed. Katalin was hoisting up some sort of contraption to the ceiling. It looked strange to Isabella, something she had never seen before and never wanted to see again. It was a wrought iron cage containing a young girl who cowered behind the bars of this harrowing and pernicious prison. There were spikes on the inside of the cage and as Katalin hoisted it up the spikes were closing in on the girl. The young girl was now screaming in pain as the spikes penetrated her skin and blood started to pour from her. Erzsébet was standing underneath the cage waiting for blood to cascade down on her.

"Katalin!" Isabella shouted. Katalin was shocked at seeing Isabella and dropped her iniquitous implement to the ground. The girl who was in it did not stir. The fall had finished off what was left of her life.

"What are you doing?" Isabella demanded. There were several other women in the room and they stared at Isabella with disdain, wondering who this woman was, and how dare she interrupt them. Isabella recognised

Erzsébet but no one else. Katalin was so frightened she was unable to answer.

"Katalin, what are you doing?" Isabella asked again, hoping against hope that her eyes were deceiving her and that a descendant of Katya's could not be involved in such malefic acts.

"Grab her!" Erzsébet shouted at Katalin. Katalin turned to Erzsébet and shook her head. Katalin was terrified of defying Erzsébet but Katalin knew enough to know that she should be even more afraid of Isabella. "Do as I say," Erzsébet hissed.

"Do as your mistress asks," said one of the other women.

"Who is she?" Isabella asked casting a glance at the third woman.

"Anna Darvulia. She is one of Erzsébet's servants," Katalin finally answered.

"Katalin, I am not going to tell you again," Erzsébet scolded.

"You don't understand, my lady, she is too strong." At that precise moment Anna came apart from the rest and lunged at Isabella. In response Isabella jabbed out her hand, grabbed Anna's neck and swiftly broke it in two. Anna Darvulia fell to the floor dead. Erzsébet along with every other mortal in the room was now frightened.

"Ficzkó!" Erzsébet yelled. In response to this a man considerably small in stature came running into the room with a sword in his hand.

Isabella looked over at Erzsébet and said, "You think he can save you?" Isabella lifted up Ficzkó by his clothes. His limbs were flailing in midair as Isabella hurled him against the opposite wall. Ficzkó fell to the floor, but he was still moving. He had survived Isabella's attack. Isabella turned back towards Katalin.

"Explain this," Isabella demanded, looking at Katalin and pointing to Erzsébet.

"I can't," answered Katalin.

"You had better," Isabella answered firmly. She stepped into to the light to reveal a flawless and youthful face.

"You are still so young," Erzsébet exclaimed She ran to Isabella and threw herself at her feet. She reached up her arms and clung to the skirt of Isabella's dress. Begging Isabella, she said, "Tell me the secret, please tell me."

Isabella threw her off. "You are humiliating yourself, Erzsébet," commented Isabella.

Erzsébet, insulted by Isabella's remarks, stood up defiantly and stepped back. She was not used to being talked to like this.

"Katalin, I need to speak to you outside," Isabella said, returning her glance to Katalin.

Katalin was frozen; she was so frightened of Isabella she just stood gazing at her, unable to move.

"Now!" Isabella bellowed.

Katalin jumped at the sound of Isabella's harsh voice and scurried over to her. She obediently followed Isabella out into the corridor. Isabella picked up the door she had unhinged and pulled it back towards the wall with a thud, jamming the door into the stone wall so no one could get out and she would be left in peace to talk to Katalin.

"What is happening here?" Isabella asked. Katalin did not know what to say, so she began by telling the truth.

"Erzsébet wanted to know how you still looked twenty years old...."

Isabella held her hand up to her forehead, dreading the answer to the next question. "What did you tell her?"

Katalin hesitated and Isabella grabbed her, shook her and threw her back against the wall. "What did you tell her!?!" Isabella shouted again.

"I told her, I knew it was something to do with blood," Katalin sobbed. Isabella started pacing up and down the corridor, rubbing her temples. After a few moments she turned back towards Katalin.

"Katalin, how many people have you killed?" Isabella asked.

"Not many."

"Tell me the truth," Isabella demanded.

"Not many," Katalin shouted again, desperately trying to make Isabella believe her. Isabella lifted Katalin off the ground by the neck and asked again.

"How many people have you killed? The truth is the only thing that will save you."

"Perhaps a hundred." Isabella knew that if she was admitting to a hundred it was much more that. She let Katalin go and the girl fell to the floor again in a heap.

"How could you be involved in this? Where did this malignancy come from? Your family consists of the most kind-hearted and generous people I have ever known."

Katalin grabbed hold of whatever courage she had left to answer, "I don't think you should be lecturing me on malevolence."

Isabella grabbed Katalin again and said as she lifted her off the floor, "What I do is no concern of yours." Then she relinquished her grip on Katalin and turned away from her, adding "But unfortunately, what you do is of great concern to me."

Isabella paused and walked up the corridor, trying to think. She could not believe what Katalin had become involved in. Another thought struck her and Isabella asked, "Have you killed Slovak girls?"

Katalin became nervous again and answered slowly. She knew it was useless to lie. "I believe so," she said.

Isabella ran over to Katalin and slapped her across the face. The force of the impact flung her back and she fell down hard against the stone floor, rubbing her bruised cheek. Isabella was furious; no one apart from Vlad had ever made her this angry before.

"This has to stop," Isabella said, quietly determined.

"How?" Katalin cried out.

"Do not speak to me." Isabella was disgusted by Katalin. Not only had this woman killed Slovaks, but worst of all Isabella knew she had to save her from the wrath of the murdered girls' families. "It has to stop and it will," Isabella repeated. "I will make sure of it," she said, with grim determination.

"But Erzsébet is obsessed," Katalin said nervously. "And if anyone found out, they would slaughter us all, burn us all to death."

"You're right, we can't just tell people, because you would be ripped apart."

Katalin shuddered as Isabella tried to think of a way out of this situation.

"We have to ensure that she gets reported to the king," said Isabella. "Matthias cannot openly tolerate such behaviour, whether she is a relative of his or not. He will not allow her to be killed by the mob. She will have a fair trial and it will buy me time to save your sorry life."

"Matthias will ensure that Erzsébet is tried fairly, but what about me?"

"You are worrying about yourself now; I think it is too late for that."

"You have to save me, Isabella."

"Save you...? I shouldn't! I should abandon you here! Those girl's families deserve their retribution. But...I will save you," Isabella sighed. Katalin was sobbing piteously in the corner of the corridor. "You are lucky you are Katya's descendent, for I would gladly let you die for betraying your own people. Katalin began to cry more violently. "Not one more tear, Katalin. Save your tears for when they can be of use to you. How do you dispose of the bodies?"

"We burn them mostly. Hungary has been hit so hard by the Inquisitors that a few more bodies are not noticed when added to the burnt corpses of the others."

"And the rest?"

"We bury them."

"Are there any bodies within the castle that have not been disposed of yet?"

"Yes, a few."

"Those bodies are going to be found. I want you to show me where they are." Katalin did as she was instructed. Isabella tossed the bodies over the side of the battlements. Isabella waited and watched from the nearby forest until the mutilated bodies were found by a single man.

※

Csaba was concerned for his youngest sister. She had disappeared and he had gone to the Hungarian Palatine, George Thurzó. He had been Csaba's mentor and he would know what to do.

"My sister has gone missing," Csaba said.

"When?" Thurzó asked.

"A few nights ago."

"Have you any idea where she is?"

"None."

"I think I may know where she may be."

"Where?" Csaba asked hopefully.

"Go to Erzsébet's castle at Čachtice. I hope to God that your sister is not there." Csaba bowed, left the castle and quickly made his way to Čachtice.

※

Isabella walked over to the man who had found the body. She would use her influence to stop him questioning her presence; she needed his cooperation to use him in her plan. She was surprised to see that the man had fallen to his knees and was weeping for his dead sister.

"Who was she?" Isabella asked.

"My sister," Csaba answered.

"I am sorry," Isabella said and she was not lying. She was very sorry; she felt responsible. She should have stayed close to Katalin. She had known from the first moment she saw her what this woman could be capable of doing.

"These girls have been tortured and killed," Isabella said. "And they are not the only ones. Can't you smell the stench of death around this place?"

"I can," Csaba answered.

"You know the Countess is to blame? You must tell King Matthias about this," Isabella continued.

"I will."

Csaba left Isabella and on his way to King Matthias' stopped to speak to the Palatine.

"My sister is dead."

"I am sorry," Thurzó answered.

"Tell me one thing…"

"Anything."

"You did not hesitate; you knew exactly where my sister might be as soon as I told you she was missing."

"I had a strong suspicion."

"I know there have been many, many others and so do you, don't you?"

"I do."

"And you did nothing?"

"I was waiting for the right time."

"Right time for what?"

"To expose her and bring down the whole Báthory family."

"Why?"

"I have ambition. The Báthorys stand in my way,"

"So you let girls die…innocent girls…for this reason only?"

"I did. With all due respect, they are peasants; they mean nothing and are expendable, as you will one day come to learn. You could go far, Csaba."

"If becoming like you is the only way I will go far, I want none of it." Csaba turned and left the presence of George Thurzó, never to return.

A few days later Isabella watched as Matthias' troops arrived. Isabella knew they wouldn't try Erzsébet as a murderess in a proper court. The fact that she was a relative of the King's would save her, and in addition the nobles of the land would not stand for it. They never wanted one of their own tried as a common criminal, no matter what they had done. The courts, they believed, were for the proletariat. Despite this, Isabella knew Erzsébet would be punished for her crimes. Even the nobles of the land would consider them abhorrent. Worst of all, Erzsébet had actually dared to kill some of the nobility; this last fact would seal her fate in the eyes of her own kind.

Isabella had two concerns. She was obligated to save Katalin and she wanted to make sure that no one ever found out about her own involvement, limited though it would be. To achieve this she needed help; she couldn't do it alone. She needed Vlad, she concluded. Isabella once more made the trip home.

She had never asked for Vlad's help before. He was flattered and would have done anything she wanted. For the first time he felt that Isabella needed him and this was a good feeling to him. Erzsébet and her conspirators were being held at Bytča. The pair travelled to the makeshift prison in grand style. They planned to pose as Hungarian nobility. They could gain access to the trial disguised this way.

The night before the trial Isabella sneaked into see Katalin, who had been imprisoned in the lower chamber of the castle at Bytča. Two guards were playing cards by the entrance to Katalin's cell. Isabella approached them and they immediately spotted her. "*Ignore me*," she whispered. The two guards continued their game as if they had never seen her.

Isabella entered the room where Katalin was being held. Katalin was sitting on the floor in the corner weeping like a child who had just been caught doing something she shouldn't.

"Stop your tears. They are of no use to you." Despite Isabella's unsympathetic remarks, Katalin was glad to see the Vampire.

"Thank God, you have come to help me escape... Isabella, I am so sorry," Katalin continued.

"Quiet! You are not sorry for what you have done, you are only sorry that you got caught," snapped Isabella. "I have not come to help you escape. You must stand trial."

"I will be executed!" cried Katalin. "You will be in violation of your promise to my family. You promised Katya," Katalin said hysterically.

"I am well aware of my promise to Katya and I will not have you sully her family name. If you escape, Matthias' soldiers will hunt you down and kill you and it will only confirm your guilt. If you get home to your mother's she would inevitably take you in and she would be shown no mercy when you were both caught. Trust me, this is the best way. Now you must tell me everything and I will see that you live through this. You have to confide in me. We can possibly even paint you as another victim of Erzsébet's. Tell me everything." Isabella sat down while Katalin recited her story.

"Erzsébet first saw you over thirty years ago when I too was just a young girl. She was fascinated by you even then and the allure you held over the people that surrounded you. Even before her youth had started to fade she was obsessed with her appearance. Her mother had slowly gone insane as she had aged and this same madness was inherent in Erzsébet. I was just a servant then. She didn't notice me at all, but when she saw me talking to you years later, then she noticed me. She remarked how your appearance had remained as perfect as it was before. She quizzed me about it and at first I resisted telling her."

Isabella knew this to be a lie but she let Katalin continue.

"I told her that you bathed in blood."

"That was a ridiculous thing to have told her."

"Would you rather I had told her that you were a Vampire?" Katalin answered back.

"I would rather you had come and told me what was happening."

"Yes, I should have done that because you have always been so approachable." Katalin was gathering courage as the conversation progressed.

"Just tell me the rest," Isabella interrupted. She didn't have any time for insolence.

"I then realised that this was too vague and that I could have been endangering my own life. So I reiterated that it was the blood of young girls, maids. By saying it was young girls I was ensuring that my own family would be safe, as I have only sons. I told her that adolescence was the key. I suggested that their youthful blood contained an invigorator, an *elixir vitae* that only they possessed and to bathe in their blood was to replenish the body with its youth."

"And she believed you?"

"Not at first. But she wanted to believe me. She considered it for awhile and then one night when her maid was combing her hair she stared at her reflection in the mirror. She was only thirty-five but her eyes had dulled slightly, her skin was losing its glow and her face was developing tiny lines at her temples. She was desperate; she looked at her servant's smooth, flawless skin and decided to test my theory. She slashed the girl's arm with a knife and squeezed blood out of the wound. She let the blood drip on to her skin.

"The maid screamed out in pain trying to get away from her but Erzsébet was too strong for her. Erzsébet rubbed the blood into her skin. Erzsébet, tainted by her mother's madness, believed that it had worked, such was her desperation. The servant who had managed to free herself was now shaking uncontrollably in the corner, wondering what was to be her fate. Erzsébet killed her without a moment's hesitation and drained as much blood from the body as she possibly could. The girl struggled and kicked as she died. Erzsébet realised that the next time that she had to have help. She needed people to help her kill and that is when we were all recruited.

"I was the obvious choice. She presumed I had killed for you. Dorottya, Ficzkó Ilona and Anna were her trusted servants. It was just a few girls at first. Erzsébet was happy with that. She was convinced that she wasn't aging, but as the years passed she grew older and her blood lust grew more and more consuming. She and the others devised a cage made with sharp spikes, which closed in on the girls, piercing their skin where the most blood would flow. The blood would fall on Erzsébet's skin like a shower, completely covering her. The girls were dead in minutes; they didn't suffer." Katalin added, trying in some small way to rationalise her actions.

"How would you know what they felt? The girl I caught you with certainly seemed to be suffering!" Isabella retorted. Isabella was repulsed by these revelations. "Tell me the rest," Isabella demanded, for Katalin had stopped telling her story.

"Erzsébet again saw herself aging," Katalin continued. "She now resolved that it might be the quality of the blood that she was using and so she set upon getting a higher calibre of victim. Erzsébet started to kill the daughters of nobility. If you had not have found us, I am sure the killings would have ended soon."

"And yet you did not leave or try to stop her?" Isabella asked.

"How could I? She would have killed me."

"I suspect you enjoyed it too much to leave?"

"That's not true. It is as you said; I am a victim in this too."

"Don't believe your lie. I will save you but I will not tolerate hypocrisy. What have you told them about me?"

"Nothing."

"You're sure?" Isabella knew she was telling the truth. Katalin would not implicate the only person who was capable of saving her. "You have to look like the victim in this," Isabella continued. "You have to look pale and half-starved. You also have to be seen to be suffering from blood loss yourself."

"How can I do that?" asked Katalin.

Isabella answered Katalin's question without making a sound. Isabella caught Katalin's arm and pulled her close into her. Isabella bit down hard into Katalin's neck and drained as much blood as she possibly could without killing her. When she let go Katalin fell back exhausted, hardly capable of moving without assistance. Katalin for the first time in her life looked like a victim.

On the first day of the trial everything was in place, Katalin looked as close to death as Isabella could safely take her. Dorottya and the others would be the last victims in this sorry tale. Isabella was unsure what would happen to Erzsébet. She knew she would not be executed, but Isabella would ensure that she had a just punishment for what she had done, no matter what the outcome of the trial was.

As Vlad and Isabella approached the castle on the day of the trial, Isabella looked outside at the crowds of people who had gathered along the road to Bytča. Peasants and nobles alike lined the paths that lead to the castle. Isabella could not help but notice the mothers weeping for their lost daughters. There were hundreds of distraught families and a lot of them were Slovak.

Isabella was sickened but her righteous indignation was to be short-lived. When she got out of the coach in front of the castle she recognised one of the weeping women. She was a German woman who Isabella couldn't help but remember; she had killed her daughter, not Erzsébet. As Isabella went inside she wondered how many others she had been responsible for. How many had Vlad been responsible for? She didn't know and couldn't remember. She didn't want to remember and somehow it made the task ahead of her a little bit easier. She could easily save Katalin now, because she realised that she was indeed just as guilty.

Vlad and Isabella entered the makeshift court. Katalin, Erzsébet Ilona, Ficzkó and Dorottya were all lined up together. Isabella had decided to wear a veil just in case she was recognised by any of them. The highest judge in the land presided over the trial. This was to ensure that King Matthias knew exactly what was going on. Vlad placed himself at one side of the court and Isabella was at the other.

Vlad and Isabella stared at each other from across the room and smiled. They were about to put their plan into action. The first person to testify was Csaba. He brushed passed Vlad as he went to the stand. Vlad whispered in his ear, *"Forget the woman who talked to you when you found your sister."* Csaba nodded and went to the stand. He made his testimony without any mention of Isabella.

The next important testimony was Ficzkó; he pushed his way through the crowd in the courtroom. Isabella caught hold of his coat and said, *"You have never seen me before and Katalin did nothing to hurt these girls. It was the others only."* Ficzkó as directed did not mention Isabella and told the crowd that Katalin was innocent of any of the crimes.

The next witnesses who were called were family members of the girls who had disappeared. They related stories about their grief and the abhorrent crimes to which they suspected their daughters had fallen foul. There were so many of them.

While these testimonies were being given, Vlad and Isabella moved among the crowd, whispering randomly into the ears of the onlookers, *"Look at Katalin, how ill she looks,"* Isabella was repeating. *"Dorottya, Ilona and Ficzkó, they are the guilty ones. They should be punished; Katalin is just a victim in this."* The pair spent all day whispering similar sentiments to each person with whom they came in contact and by the end of the first day it was working. Sympathy was growing for Katalin, but

Isabella had one final trick up her sleeve for that day. Katalin was called up to the stand and as she slowly climbed the stairs to take her place. Isabella whispered.

"Faint, Katalin, faint."

Katalin was compelled to act. She fell against the front of the crowd that filled the room, and the crowd gasped. Several gentlemen rushed to help her to her feet. Vlad and Isabella held back as they heard the crowd whispering among themselves. Voices murmured "poor Katalin" and similar sentiments echoed throughout the crowd. The Vampires' plan was working. Weeks later Dorottya, Ilona and Erzsébet were to testify.

※

Dorottya and Erzsébet had stronger wills than the others. A whisper of influence would not ensure their compliance. The night before they were to testify, Isabella visited Dorottya's and Ilona's prison cell, while Vlad visited Erzsébet's. Isabella entered their cell and found Dorottya sitting in the corner petrified. Ilona was too naive to be terrified and was sleeping soundly. Ilona was not much more than a child herself. Isabella decided not to wake her; she sensed that the young girl would do anything Dorottya told her to do. Dorottya, on seeing Isabella, pleaded for her life.

"You are both going to die," Isabella replied to her pleading.

"No," shouted Dorottya, rocking back and forth in a nervous state. "We were coerced, we are the victims here," Dorottya said "Erzsébet and Katalin forced us to do these things."

Isabella actually believed Dorottya. There was sincerity in her voice that was missing from Katalin's. Isabella had heard all these people blame the rest, but not themselves. Dorottya, however, was the first one she had heard that she was even tempted to believe, and she was not just speaking for herself, she was speaking for Ilona. None of the others had shown any compassion for anyone else. But Isabella knew that they both could not be spared.

"Dorottya, you witnessed terrible acts. Why did you not do anything?" Isabella asked.

"I couldn't do anything about it! I was being held against my will." This Isabella did not believe. She knew that Dorottya's crimes were at their worst playing a full part in the torture of the girls and at their best she had been guilty of nothing more than standing idly by and letting them die. Dorottya, unlike Katalin, would have to pay her debt to the victims. The mob needed blood and retribution. And she and Ilona were the women who probably had the least role in these events, but they too would have to pay the ultimate price.

"I cannot save you, Dorottya, nor Ilona," Isabella continued.

"Oh, please," Dorottya pleaded.

"I can't," Isabella confirmed. "But what I can do is ensure that you and Ilona do not suffer. You have seen the mob outside. You know you are both going to die. I can ensure that your deaths are as painless as possible. That is all I can possibly offer you."

"No, help us!" wept Dorottya in anguish.

"You have to have courage, because that is what is going to happen," Isabella said. She was losing patience. "You know that you will be burned if no one interferes on your behalf. You couldn't imagine what that pain feels like," she said. One of Isabella's many aptitudes was borrowing pain. She remembered Vincente's pain. She touched Dorottya's head and Dorottya felt her skin burning for just a few seconds, but it was enough. Isabella let her go and she reeled back in pain.

"I cannot go through that!" Dorottya exclaimed.

"If you do not do exactly as I say, you and Ilona will feel every moment of it. I will make sure you do," Isabella warned.

Dorottya was still shaking; she looked up at Isabella, tears streaming down her face, still trembling from the pain she had felt. "What do you want me to do?" she said.

"Firstly, you must never admit to having ever seen me, and you must convince Ilona of the same. If you betray me, you will be burned."

Dorottya nodded in compliance and asked, "What else?"

"You must confess to everything; you must state that you Ilona and Erzsébet are solely responsible and that you kept Katalin as your prisoner. You continually tortured her... Katalin is blameless."

"Why are you saving Katalin?" Dorottya asked.

"That is not your concern. Will you do as I ask?" Dorottya hesitated. So Isabella let her feel Vicente's pain one more time. Isabella held the back of Dorottya's hair so that she was pulling her head upwards. "Will you do what I ask?" Isabella reaffirmed.

"Yes!" shouted Dorottya in anguish.

"Good... I promise that if you follow my instructions you will feel no more pain."

Isabella left Dorottya's cell and could not resist going to Erzsébet's to see how Vlad was convincing her to confess. She crept down the hall and looked in. Isabella listened to what Vlad was saying.

※

Vlad had entered Erzsébet's cell and at first she did not recognise him but when he spoke she instantly remembered.

"Erzsébet," Vlad began.

"My love," Erzsébet began she was as dramatic as ever. "Why didn't you follow me all those years ago? You have left me alone for twenty years, why?"

"It is the hardest thing I ever had to do," Vlad lied, telling Erzsébet exactly what she wanted to hear.

"It was?"

Vlad by this time realised Isabella was listening.

"Yes, Erzsébet."

"Then why do it? I would have left my husband for you in an instant."

"I know, but I could not condemn you to live as I do."

"I wanted to! I loved you."

"I know you did, but I didn't want condemn you to a life of living off the blood of others... but now I see it may not have been such a hardship," Vlad said dryly. "I am going to tell you the secret. You don't bathe in blood. You must feed on blood, but first you have to drink the blood of a Vampire."

"Are you a Vampire?"

"I am." Erzsébet leaped forward and tried to break Vlad's skin with her teeth. Vlad caught her before she could touch him. Vlad and Isabella both realised that this woman was completely insane.

"Not yet, be patient. I want you to do something for me first and then I will give you your youth, and when I give someone youth they never lose it again."

"What do you want me to do? I will do anything; I just want to be young and beautiful again."

"You will be, but first you have to confess to the killings of the girls. I want you to say Katalin is innocent."

"Why?"

"Because Katalin is my brother's descendant, I have an obligation to her and my family, and it is my wish. After the trial I will make you young again, but you must do this for me."

"I will do anything you say." Erzsébet crawled over to Vlad and rested her head on his chest. Vlad lifted up his hand and started to stroke her hair. Isabella who was still watching was struck by pangs of jealousy. Erzsébet looked up into Vlad's eyes and moved herself up to kiss him. Vlad leaned down to greet her lips but Isabella was sickened; she had seen enough of this tainted love scene. She ran back to the guards and whispered to them.

"I think there is an intruder in Erzsébet's cell."

"Who are you?" shouted one of the guards.

"Never mind who I am, go arrest the intruder," Isabella demanded. Erzsébet and Vlad were disturbed by the sound of the guards running up the corridor.

Vlad kissed Erzsébet on the forehead and said, "I have to go." He transformed himself into a mist and seeped out through the window of the room. When the guards came in, he was gone.

"Who is with you?" the guards shouted.

"No one," replied Erzsébet. "Why would you think anyone was here?" The guards looked at each other. They had no idea why they expected to see someone with Erzsébet. They walked back up the corridor scratching their heads, completely bemused.

Isabella was waiting for Vlad when she saw the mist floating down towards where she was standing below. Vlad re-emerged and Isabella threw him a cloak.

"How did it go?" she asked.

"I think you know—I heard you scratching at the door." Isabella smiled; he knew her so well. "How did it go with your charges?"

"I am not sure. I think we may have trouble with Dorottya."

"Well, we will both attend the trial tomorrow to make sure all goes according to our plan," Vlad answered.

The next day Erzsébet's testimony was delivered as directed. After speaking, she sat and caught sight of Vlad in the crowd. She smiled on seeing him and he returned her smile, nodding to acknowledge her. This ensured her compliance.

Ilona walked up to the stand she looked back at Isabella and Isabella whispered, *"Do everything that Dorottya told you to do."* Ilona was compliant.

Dorottya approached the stand very nervously. Isabella was watching her every move and so was Vlad. Dorottya started off well but she was not as confident in her statement as Erzsébet or Ilona. Her answers were clumsy and disjointed, but she was relaying the story as planned. Isabella still had her veil on to keep from being recognised.

There was growing tension in the room because the crowd that had been gathering outside for days were by this time baying for blood. They had started to throw things at the windows of the castle. Every time one of rocks thudded against the wall, Dorottya would jump in fear and her eyes would dart about the room. The nobles in the court room were also getting more and more agitated. The crowd outside had now reached over a thousand people and they were all seeking retribution.

A rock suddenly broke the glass window. It flew past Isabella's head, knocking her hat off, and consequently, her veil fell to the floor. The rock ricocheted off Isabella and struck Dorottya on the head. Dorottya fell. She rubbed her forehead where she had been struck and looked at the blood on her hand. She pulled herself up on to her feet only to see Isabella staring at her.

Dorottya now felt that Isabella could not ensure that she was not going to be given to the mob. She stretched out her arm and pointed towards Isabella. "It was her," Dorottya shouted, but her voice was not heard over the din of a panicking crowd. Ilona, seeing Dorottya accuse Isabella, also began to shout accusations at the Vampire.

Isabella and Vlad had both predicted the betrayal of the two women only moments before it began. The two Vampires shouted into to the crowd simultaneously, "Burn them!"

The crowd joined in. They wanted people to blame and they wanted a sacrifice to placate to the mob outside.

"She is the one!" Dorottya shouted, still protesting her innocence as several of the crowd pulled her from the stand. Dorottya and Ilona were frantically trying to implicate Isabella.

"She is responsible," Ilona cried out. The crowd carried Dorottya and Ilona over their heads. There was a small gap in the crowd and they dropped Dorottya to the floor. Isabella rushed over to Dorottya and lifted up her chin so that she staring into Isabella's face.

"I warned you," Isabella said. Dorottya burst into tears and Isabella relinquished her grasp. She was then lifted up again and dragged outside. By the time she got there, Ilona was already burning. The mob outside had already erected Dorottya's stake and she was being pushed and pulled towards it. Isabella watched from the broken window above. The flames were licking higher and higher. Dorottya and Ilona were screaming in agony. Isabella, as she looked down on the women's faces, was surprised to realise she felt guilt. She turned towards Vlad and said.

"No one deserves to die like this. Make the pain stop for them. They are guilty of no more than we are."

"You are not supposed to have a conscience. You are a Vampire, remember?" Vlad answered.

"Sometimes I remember my humanity. There is still some human blood in these veins." Vlad walked towards Isabella and gently pressed his finger under her chin and lifted up her face. They looked at each other. Vlad raised his other hand and rubbed his fingers gently over her eyes and face. He then pressed his lips to hers and they kissed. In all their years together this was as intimate as the pair had ever been. They loved each other; they always had. The pair heard another scream from outside.

"Go, hurry, stop their pain," Isabella said.

"You will have to get rid of that human blood of yours," Vlad said.

"I cannot—it is my grandfather's blood."

Vlad held Isabella's hand and pulled it towards him as he left so that Isabella's arm was outstretched. They did not let go of each other until they absolutely had to. Vlad ran down the stairs and out into the crowd. Isabella and Vlad both projected their thoughts into the crowd. *Don't see him.* Isabella thought. The crowd obeyed and did not see him, but Dorottya and Ilona did. He quickly killed Ilona to stop her misery and then Vlad walked through the flames and climbed up so that he was face to face with Dorottya.

"I can make the pain stop," Vlad stated.

"Please, please make it stop," whimpered Dorottya.

Vlad said "close your eyes." Dorottya complied. Vlad bit into her neck and projected his elation at draining her blood into her mind. Dorottya's pain was over, and so was her life.

***

Ficzkó, who had done as he was asked, was mercifully beheaded. Katalin as planned was found innocent and returned to her home and her mother. She was the only one who had escaped with not only her life, but she had escaped prison as well.

***

Erzsébet had smiled during her sentencing. She kept her smile even through the journey back to her castle, which was to become her prison. Nothing could wipe the smirk from her face. Her smile seemed to even grow wider as every entrance to her castle was bricked up. She was unsettling the guards as each brick was put in place. She watched from inside as her tomb was being sealed, unafraid of her fate.

Erzsébet should have been afraid, for both Vlad and Isabella were following her back to the castle at Čachtice. Both of them agreed that imprisonment was not a befitting punishment for this maleficent woman.

***

When Isabella had returned to the castle a few months before asking for Vlad's help, Vlad had shared with her a few more of his secrets.

"My powers did not come to me instantly as yours did," Vlad began. "I am going to tell you a secret. Vampires can be controlled, and their powers can be suppressed. My wife's mother wanted to punish me for my wife's death…she still blamed me. Through the centuries Dhampirs had learned how to torture Vampires. They were the only creatures who possibly could. When I awoke from my sleep I was not strong like you were; I certainly could not have risen from my own grave. You drank from me a pure Vampire's blood, but I had been fed on a Dhampir's blood only. She had revived me because she wanted to keep me alive, to watch me suffer. I was in constant pain, and I was growing old rapidly, but yet my thirst for blood forced me to drink from her.

This went on for almost a year. She would let me drink from her intermittently and she was enjoying watching me suffer, until one day I had managed to crawl out into the courtyard. I espied a Gypsy walking along the path beside the castle. All I saw was blood. I couldn't chase after her. I was not strong enough. I called over to her and she came over to me willingly. She had flowers with her. She was obviously on her way down to the village to see if she could sell some of her wares. She was old and frail like me. I said for her to come closer and I would buy all her flowers. She believed and trusted me. I asked her to come closer again so that I could see what she had, closer. I kept on repeating, until she was within reach. I grabbed her neck and threw my body on top of hers, pinning her down. I bit down hard, the more I drank the stronger I became. She struggled at first and cried out but as my strength increased, so too did my grip. When she was dead I let go and I felt powerful for the first time. I must have killed ten people that day and by nightfall I was strong and young again. I could see in the dark and I waited for the Dhampir to arrive.

She did not realise at first that anything had changed. I knew she didn't have the abilities I had. She couldn't see me clearly and she didn't realise that I was young again. I immediately knew I had the advantage. She came in, sat down and put out her wrist for me to drink from. I crawled over to her as if I was still weak and was about to drink. When I looked up at her she saw my young face smiling at her. I then grabbed her arm and wrenched her collar bone from its socket. She squealed in pain; she was no longer stronger than me.

I lifted her up and threw her against the wall. As she hit the wall she broke several ribs. She was nearly at the end of her life anyway and I was determined to finish her off. 'Your blood is poison to me,' I shouted, and she shouted back that she knew it was and she had taken great pleasure in watching me in pain. I put my hand around her neck and was slowly squeezing the last breath from her body. She just managed to say that my pain may have ended but my eternal suffering had just begun. Her corpse lay on the floor and blood was still pouring from it. The blood trickled on to my skin and burned slightly. I realised this was a valuable commodity and filled as many wine jugs as I could with it."

"Have you ever come across another Dhampir?" Isabella asked.

"No, she told me she was the last one of her kind. I think she was; I think if our powers are at their full capacity we may be able to sense them, but I have never killed anyone whose blood was poison to me. Have you?"

"No, never."

"We may be able to use this blood."

"How?" Isabella asked.

"When I was drinking only the Dhampir's blood and nothing else, I felt as close to death as I have ever felt. It may be able to kill us."

※

Erzsébet was waiting for Vlad and he did not want to keep her waiting long. Erzsébet had lit a candle and she was excited to hear a banging on the brick wall that had just been so recently erected. The first brick fell to the ground. Erzsébet was overcome with excitement when she saw Dracula's face looking in at her from outside her bricked tomb.

"Erzsébet, come with me," Vlad said. Erzsébet ran to Vlad and embraced him.

"Anywhere," she said. "Make me young again?" she continued, as this thought was never far from her mind.

"Soon," Vlad answered. "Come with me."

"Of course, I will follow you anywhere. Please make me young again," Erzsébet repeated.

"I told you, soon," Vlad reaffirmed. He led Erzsébet by the hand out of the castle and onto the grounds. Vlad took her quite a distance from the castle. All Erzsébet could talk about was being young again. Vlad was getting quite irritated by her virtual and constant chatter about having her youth returned to her. Vlad thought that eternity with this woman would be unbearable.

They stopped in a clearing in the woods a few miles from the castle. Vlad turned to Erzsébet and said.

"It's time," Vlad was appalled by the happy look in Erzsébet's eyes. She clapped her hands in glee, like a child who had been given a present. She was completely insane. Vlad leaned in and bit her neck he let her feel his bite. She let out a small whimper and then she said.

"I knew it would hurt," she said, "but continue, please, I don't care if it is painful." Vlad bit down harder. He drained her blood until she was very weak. He then slit his wrist and let her drink from his blood. Vlad let her drink just enough from him so that she started to regain her youthful looks.

"You are young again, you are a Vampire." Vlad stated.

"I am!" She looked at her hands. The skin on her hands had smoothed and the ivory colour of her youthful skin had returned. She felt her face; it felt smooth and supple again. "Thank you, thank you!" she cried out in joy. She kissed Vlad but Vlad pushed her away. He was disgusted by her, but he did not show his disgust, not yet.

"We have to go back."

"Why?"

"Because people are still angry with you. They have to hear you moving around in that castle—just for awhile."

"But why?"

"They will come after us and hunt us down, if you do not do as I say."

"You are right and we cannot take that risk," she said.

The pair travelled quickly back to the castle. Vlad enlisted the help of two Slovaks to brick Erzsébet back into the room. Just before the last brick was put in place Vlad reached through the gap in the wall and handed Erzsébet a bottle full of blood.

"You will need this," Vlad stated, "for when you get hungry." What Erzsébet did not realise yet was that Isabella was now in the room with her. Erzsébet was examining herself, dancing round the room in excitement. Isabella, like Vlad, was sickened by the Countess's foolishness.

After a few hours, Erzsébet began to cry out and convulse. She was in agony, and she was hungry. Isabella watched her suffering and then when she could not stand the sound of Erzsébet's shrieks any longer, she made her presence known.

"Are you in pain?" Isabella asked. Erzsébet was astonished to see anyone with her. However, she was in too much pain to be worried about Isabella. But she needed to be. Isabella held a lighted candle in front of her face so that Erzsébet could not see her.

"Who are you?" Erzsébet asked.

"Isabella. I am Vlad's ..."

"Servant, of course. He sent you to look after me," Erzsébet interrupted. Isabella was amazed at the woman's arrogance. "Do you know how to stop this pain?" Erzsébet asked.

"You are hungry; you need blood," Isabella answered.

"Did Vlad leave you for me to feed from you?" Erzsébet pounced forwards towards Isabella and tried to grab her. Isabella easily avoided Erzsébet's grasp and said.

"Did Vlad not leave you blood?" Erzsébet remembered the bottle that Vlad had left.

"Yes he did, I will drink it to regain my strength and you will not escape me then," she threatened. Erzsébet bent over in agony and looked for the bottle; she clambered over to the bottle and started to drink. She drank all of it but she did not feel any better. The pain did not leave her and she felt no satisfaction from the blood. She felt weak and she collapsed. It was the Dhampir's blood that Vlad had left. Isabella watched as Erzsébet began to age, and she aged rapidly.

"Look at your hands," Isabella whispered venomously. Erzsébet looked at them. The ravages of age had returned to her as quickly as they had left her.

"No!" screamed out Erzsébet.

"Did you honestly think you would not have to pay for your sin?" Isabella blew out the candle so that Erzsébet could see her face. Erzsébet looked up at Isabella and now she recognised her. It was the woman she had seen so many times before. It was the woman who had started all of this and now was going to end it. "You will stay in this room for the rest of your existence. The pain you are feeling will continue and will get worse. And you will age and age rapidly. You will become old and decrepit and abhorrent to anyone who looks upon you. By drinking that blood you have poisoned yourself. You have no vampiric power; you will never be able to leave this stone tomb. I don't honestly know if you will die, but you may starve to death. Be thankful you have been given a gift that a Vampire is rarely afforded, the possibility of death." Erzsébet was crying out in agony and anguish, sobbing uncontrollably. It was how she would spend the rest of her existence.

Isabella transformed herself into a mist and seeped out though the wall. When she was on the other side Vlad was there, waiting to greet her. He gave her clothes and when she was dressed she punched out a brick of the wall. A ray of light fell into the room and Erzsébet was still there, sobbing for the moment of youth that Isabella had stolen back from her. Isabella called out to her.

"Erzsébet?" Erzsébet ran to the wall and stared out in amazement. When she saw Vlad she called out.

"My love," she cried out to him. She stretched out her hand and tried to stroke Vlad's handsome face. He pulled away from her touch. "My love, make me young again," Erzsébet beseeched him.

"Never," Vlad retorted. Isabella took Vlad's face in her hands and kissed him in front of Erzsébet.

"No!" Erzsébet cried out. Isabella looked at her and said.

"I am leaving you with a view to the outside world to let the families of the people you killed see you in such distress. Perhaps this will give them some comfort and also let the world see the hag you will become. And believe me when I tell you, when anyone talks of the Báthorys they will not mention your name. Your portrait will not hang with the rest of your illustrious family on the walls of the palaces in Hungary. It will be hidden away from sight like a shameful secret." Isabella turned away from the door and Vlad went with her. They left Erzsébet to face her misery and the slow torturous starvation of a Vampire alone.

THE LAST VROLOK
THE LAST VAMPIRE

CHAPTER TWELVE

Simon and his family had fled after speaking to Anna; they had now survived just over a week. Simon's wife was heavily pregnant and needed to rest for at least one night or she would not be able to travel. So despite Simon's better judgement, they stayed a night in an inn near the German border. Simon stayed awake, keeping watch while his family slept in the bed beside him.

In the early hours of the morning while he was struggling to keep his eyes open, he caught sight of a coach which was approaching the inn at quite a rapid speed. He wondered, or at least hoped as it approached, that it was another Slovak family fleeing from Isabella. He had recognised several faces at the inn from the village but did not acknowledge them, as he feared that it might endanger their lives or his own family if any of them were caught. The coach was now only a few hundred yards away and Simon's blood chilled as he noticed that a woman was holding the reins of the horses, a beautiful woman with white, glowing skin and long black hair. The coach drew up outside the inn and Simon, who had been transfixed by this pernicious beauty, was unable to take his eyes from her.

Isabella jumped off the coach and looked up at the window, sensing she was being watched. Simon, who was still staring down at her, was startled as their eyes met. Simon's fear was now confirmed. He knew that she knew exactly who he was and she had come for him. He let the curtain drop to block out her gaze and quickly tried to roust his family.

"Get up!" he shouted frantically. "We have to leave right now! She is here," Simon's wife looked up at him from her resting place and said through the tears that had suddenly started welling up in her eyes.

"Simon, it's useless, we cannot escape from her." Simon's children, seeing their mother's tears, started to cry themselves.

"We have to at least try, Tereza," Simon said to his wife, "for the children's sake," he whispered.

"We will all die anyway if we carry on living like this." Tereza's conversation was interrupted by shouts and cries coming from downstairs. The family could hear pleas for mercy which were silenced as suddenly as they had begun. Simon slumped down onto the bed and placed his face in his hands. He knew his wife was right; their running was finally over. His wife crept over to the side of the bed where her husband was sitting and placed her arms tightly around his waist. She pulled her body in close to his back, and she laid her head against his shoulders.

"Come over here, children," Tereza summoned. Simon's two children climbed over the bed to where their mother and father sat. They too pulled themselves in close, hugging their parents in desperation, hiding their faces in their parents' arms. Simon gently held his wife's hand and looked up at the door and waited for Isabella.

A few moments went by and Isabella threw open the door and even though Simon had expected her, he still quaked at her entrance. Isabella stood, bloody sword in hand, and stared at the family that was clutching each other. Simon used Isabella's hesitation to his advantage and threw himself at her feet.

"Please, Isabella...please I beg of you. Kill me, but spare my wife and children...they had nothing to do with the death of Vlad. They are innocent."

In response to Simon's words, Tereza threw herself at Isabella's feet and also began to beg, "I want to die with my husband, but my children, spare them! They did nothing," Tereza pleaded.

"You all did nothing; that is the reason you all must die," Isabella responded venomously. Isabella had killed perhaps a hundred Slovaks in the past week, but none of them had begged for the lives of their children in such a heart-rending fashion. She admired the courage of this couple and their disregard for their own safety. Their only thought was for the lives of their children. Isabella was touched, but still her resolve was strengthened—all the Slovaks must die. "Not one of you will live," Isabella said.

Simon's wife turned to her husband, held his face in her hands, and whispered, "I will always love you, Simon...always."

"Simon," Isabella enquired. "Is that your name?" Simon nodded. "Did you try to save Anna?" Isabella asked. Simon nodded again.

"He is a good man," Tereza affirmed.

"That information it is of no relevance to me. What sort of man he is does not matter, but Anna felt that it was important. You will all die, but not tonight. I promise you will be the last to die. You will have more time than anyone else."

"Thank you, thank you!" cried out Tereza.

"Do not thank me nor believe that I will forget about you. I have not spared you; I have just delayed the inevitable."

"Thank you, all the same," Simon added.

"You might as well stay here and have time with your children. Running is useless. Live well, as I will be back for you, I promise."

Isabella left the room and the children ran to their parents. The family was grateful for this reprieve, even if they knew it was only temporary.

※

Isabella slaughtered the rest of the Slovaks, giving no one else the slight consideration she had shown Simon and Tereza. She returned to the inn six months later. The land was at the full brightness of day when she eventually arrived there. Isabella watched the family from a distance; the children were playing outside and their parents were watching them. Tereza was sitting with her new child in her lap and laughing while she was watching the rest of her family play. Simon soon saw Isabella but he did not alert the rest of his family. He let them enjoy what he thought was to be their last day on this earth. Isabella waited for nightfall and then crept into the family's room. Simon had let them fall asleep in an unsuspecting peace. Simon himself did not sleep, but waited for Isabella, fully awake.

"Thank you, Isabella, these last months have been the happiest for us. If I could just ask one thing?" Simon asked, when Isabella silently entered the room.

"I have been more generous to you than anyone else. I gave you more life than you deserve," Isabella answered.

"I know and I accept my fate willingly, but I will just ask one last time for you to spare the lives of my family."

"I cannot," Isabella replied.

"Then I would ask you, if you could make their deaths as painless as possible?" Isabella nodded in response. She approached the bed silently and looked at the mother with her children sleeping around her, unaware of the danger they all were in. Isabella turned back to Simon and said.

"Anna was right, you are a good man."

"I am no better than the next," Simon responded.

"You are wrong if you think that you know very little about the other men that occupy this world. There are very few men like you." Isabella stood in silence for a moment and smiled and said, "I will not kill your family; I think I would come to consider such an act beneath me." Simon threw himself at Isabella's feet and kissed the hem of her skirt. "Get up," Isabella demanded, "or I will change my mind," she added sharply.

"You are as merciful as you are beautiful," Simon whispered.

"Do not grovel at me," Isabella commanded. "Stand up." Simon stood. "You will give me your life freely?" Isabella asked.

"I will," Simon responded and he pulled his shirt from around his shoulder to reveal a bare neck.

"Oh, don't be so dramatic, I am not going to take your life. However, you must be punished. I want five years of loyal service from you. Your family will stay here, but you will come with me. I will give you a day to say your goodbyes. Meet me a mile down the road tomorrow night and I guarantee no harm will ever come to your family by my hand."

※

Isabella watched as Simon approached her. He walked with a spring in his step; he looked almost enthusiastic. When he caught sight Isabella he started to run and kneeled before her.

"Stop that, I will not have you kneeling to me every time you see me," Isabella commented, Simon stood. "Your wife, is she amenable with this arrangement?"

"I would not use the word amenable but consider the alternative, she realises it is a reprieve and a chance for our children."

"Very well."

"If I may ask, Isabella?"

"You may ask but be careful…I did not let you live because I felt pity for you."

"What do you want from me?"

"Your loyalty."

"You have it."

"We'll see," Isabella said.

"What else?" Simon enquired.

"I need another pair of eyes. My revenge is only half complete. The English who hunted Vlad across Europe will suffer their worst fears to be realised."

"How can I help you with that?"

"You can't."

"Then why do you need me"

"You will be home with your family long before my revenge even starts. I want the English to believe that it is over. I want their nightmares to stop and them to be sleeping easy in their beds before a Vampire enters their lives again. We will have to leave soon."

"Where are we going?"

"To the new world… You will be travelling as my husband."

"Your husband?"

"If I have learned anything it is that it is better to travel with a man posing as your husband. A woman alone with money attracts too much attention and I need to attract as little as possible."

"You need me for this?"

"I need you to help me find someone."

"Who?"

"Someone who will help me with my revenge."

"What is so special about this person? How can he help you?"

"He is the last Vrolok."

ALEXANDRU THE DEFENDER OF MANKIND

CHAPTER THIRTEEN

After they had both conspired to punish Erzsébet, Isabella and Vlad travelled back to the castle together. Vlad was totally at ease with the recent events. As far as he was concerned he had protected his own and Isabella's anonymity, and he had ensured that Erzsébet would not talk, and even if she did, people would presume it was the lunatic ravings of a deranged and aging woman. The pair had also ensured that Katalin was perceived to be without blame. Vlad, of course, did not care at all for Katalin, but he knew Isabella took her promise of loyalty very seriously and so he was vicariously pleased.

Isabella, however, was far from at ease with recent events. When she was awake she was haunted by the face of the mother of one of her own victims. When she slept the image of the mother's face awakened her. She had to do something to rid herself of this new feeling, guilt.

"We succeeded...." Vlad said a few days after they returned.

"Yes I suppose we did," Isabella answered.

"You don't seem pleased."

"I am... but..."

"But?"

"I saw a woman in the crowd at Bytča; she was there because she thought Erzsébet had killed her daughter, but it wasn't Erzsébet: I killed her."

"That is only one you recognised, I am sure there were more," Vlad answered.

"I didn't ask you," Isabella responded. She hated to be told the brutal truth.

"I think you did." Isabella stood and walked to the fire. Vlad had just confirmed what she had feared.

"How many do you think you have killed?" Isabella asked, looking for reassurance, but she would not find it here.

"I couldn't possibly even begin to count," Vlad answered. "Hundreds, maybe even thousands, and that is just when I was alive."

"Be serious," Isabella scolded.

"I am being serious...Isabella, you are a killer. You know that. You have known that for over a century. What you are has never disturbed you before."

"Did you not find Erzsébet's actions abhorrent?"

"I found her methods and her reasons abhorrent but not her actions. The sooner you realise that you are a creature similar to Erzsébet, the happier you will be."

"I am nothing like her!" Isabella declared defiantly.

"Well if it is more palatable for you to believe that we are higher beings and humans are lower than us, then so be it. After all, does a human regret killing an animal for food? They don't, not for an instant. Consider also how they killed Dorottya—those upstanding members of society, those humans. They gave her to the mob and watched and cheered as she burned at the stake. Isabella, have you even come close to inflicting that sort of pain on anyone?"

"We both have inflicted our share of pain," Isabella answered.

"Not anything like that," Vlad responded.

"Perhaps not."

"Then rest easy, your conscience can be clear."

"It's not clear. It is far from clear!" Isabella said, still in the throws of this new torment. "It will never be clear." Isabella started to pace the room, her arms folded. "There must be a way to ease it?" she said.

"You could stop killing, become old, suffer the pain that comes with age and starvation. Could you do that Isabella?"

Isabella threw Vlad a virulent look. Vlad and Isabella both knew she couldn't. "I am not going to stop killing," Isabella said. "I couldn't stop. You know I get too much delectation from it," she stated honestly.

"I'm glad to hear it," Vlad responded. Isabella was trying to think of some way to ease her conscience. Then she had an idea. As far as she was concerned, it was perfect.

"I can kill only those who deserve to die."

"Isabella, you can't do it. How are you going decide who gets punished and who doesn't?" Vlad questioned, trying to warn her not to start down a path that would never lead to any Vampire's salvation.

"People who are guilty of brutal and malicious acts will be punished," Isabella continued, ignoring Vlad's warning.

"You won't be able to do it... you will drive yourself mad." Vlad rested his hand on Isabella's shoulder, and she batted it away. The intimate moment they had shared in the Erzsébet's castle was obviously long forgotten by Isabella.

"It will work, I will make it work. I will kill no one unless they deserve to die."

"Did you deserve to die?" Vlad asked.

"What are you talking about?"

"You killed a man brutally and maliciously before you died. Was death a fitting punishment for you?"

"I had a right to kill, Peter."

"You know that. But how could you have proved it to anyone else."

"You are making this far more complicated than it needs to be," Isabella responded, getting impatient with Vlad's constant questioning of her perfect idea.

"No. I am trying to show you how complicated it is and will be. It is a foolish notion, Isabella."

Isabella started to walk quickly towards the door.

"Where are you going?" Vlad asked.

"Down to the village," Isabella said, without looking back.

"To see Katalin, I presume, if ever a person deserved to die!" Vlad shouted after her. Vlad knew Isabella was an impetuous creature, going from one scheme to the next, not able to sit still for a moment. He would placate her in her new purpose. Perhaps even help her, but he knew it was impossible. After all, he had tried it as well.

※

Katalin was sitting with her mother crying like a baby, relaying the story with a few very notable exceptions. Isabella interrupted her alerting the pair to her presence.

"I hope you are telling your mother the whole truth," said Isabella.

Katalin was struck silent and stopped telling her version of the story immediately. She did not want to be caught in another lie, not in front of her mother. She could have convinced anyone else, even her husband, that she was an innocent victim in anything, but not Isabella. "I will finish telling you later, mother," Katalin spluttered nervously and left the room.

"I will finish it for you," Isabella interrupted. Katalin's mother looked up at Isabella. The old woman looked so frail she was near her death. Isabella softened. What good would it do to tell Gizella what her daughter had done?

"What did she do?" Katalin's mother asked.

"Nothing that she wasn't tricked into doing," Isabella answered.

"Thank you for bringing her home," Gizella answered.

"This is the second time she has come home to you but I believe this time she will stay," Isabella answered.

"I hope so; she is my daughter, no matter what she has done." Katalin's mother knew there was more to the story than what she was being told.

"Well, I hope you enjoy her being home with you." Isabella left Katalin's mother and went into the other room to see Katalin.

"Tell your mother what you like, for I will not interfere," Isabella began.

"Thank you."

"Keep your thanks, I do not do it for you…I want to talk to you."

"What about?"

"Dorottya's punishment. I have seen it before. But I thought it was just a sporadic act used by men of religion. Is this usual way to execute people?"

"It has been for some time now."

"I have never seen anything so nefarious."

"Coming from you I think that is saying something," Katalin quipped.

"Don't be impudent. I will not tolerate it, especially from you. What is it a punishment for?"

"Anything. Mostly they accuse people of necromancy, but that is usually not the real reason, I have heard that there have been whole villages in which all the women have been killed in this way."

"Someone else told me that before. Is it only women?"

"Mostly women."

"What about the surrounding villages in Walachia, Moldavia?"

"It has not spread that far as of yet."

"It won't; I will make sure of it," Isabella said firmly. Katalin who was always primarily concerned with her own well-being, asked, "What will happen to me?"

"Nothing. But I am going to give you a chance to atone."

"Atone?"

"Don't worry. I am not asking you to do much. I just want you to listen and watch out for me."

"Listen and watch out for what?"

"The wickedness in this world."

"Wickedness?"

"Yes, I will not tolerate the wicked anymore, especially these burnings. I will not rest until I have rid my land of this maleficent punishment." Katalin was bewildered by the Vampire that stood before her.

"Why are you doing this Isabella?" Katalin said now curious.

"I want to atone. Those villagers who burned Dorottya and Ilona—if they knew what I am guilty of—they would have burned me, not that it would have done any good." Isabella sat silently for a moment and then Katalin began to speak again.

"I know where you might start."

"Where?" Isabella enquired and there was excitement in her voice.

"Gábor Báthory, Erzsébet's nephew."

"Go on."

"He is the Prince of Transylvania now and his brutality is renowned. They say in Hungary he is most brutal prince since…"

"Since?"

"Since Prince Vlad,"

Isabella laughed, "Vlad was never very popular with the Hungarians." Her voice now adopted a more serious tone. "In life he was a great man. He did not become the vicious prince of legend until after he lost his family. The twenty thousand Boyars he was supposed to have impaled was a number more like twenty. Every one of them had conspired to kill his brother and father. When Vlad dug up his brother's grave he realised how much his brother had been tortured. His eyes had been burnt out of their sockets and there were scratch marks on the lid of the coffin. He had been blinded and buried alive. Think about it Katalin, he was supposed to have impaled them all in that courtyard. Do you know how long it would take to stake twenty thousand? It would take a lifetime."

"Do you want me to go with you to Gábor's court?" Katalin asked in hope.

"No, Katalin, I want you to stay here with your mother and bring up your children. You have too much of a taste for killing."

"You will need help," Katalin protested.

"Vlad will help me, I am sure he will take great delight in destroying another descendant of Stephen Báthory and I trust him far more than I do you."

Katalin said nothing and turned to go back into the house.

As she did Isabella caught her by the arm and turned her forcibly back towards her. "Be careful, Katalin, I warn you. I have saved you once. I will not do it again. Next time I will leave you to the mercy of the rabble and you should remember what happened to Dorottya." Isabella pressed down hard on Katalin's arm and gave her a taste of the pain that Dorottya had felt. Katalin struggled to get free, but could not until Isabella released her. Katalin was once again scared and as a result, she once more became penitent for her crimes, perhaps for the wrong reasons, but penitent nevertheless.

Isabella was filled with a fresh enthusiasm for life; she would become a righter of wrongs, a corrector of other people's misdeeds. Surely this would help ease her conscience. Isabella realised she needed help in her new plan; she needed help in seeking out these evil doers.

Katalin selected a hierarchy of Slovak Invigilators, as they came to be called. Mostly women, as it was women that were getting persecuted and most at risk. Each Slovak was well-paid and reported back to another within the hierarchy. Each one only knew who they reported to and the person reporting to them, but that was as far as it went. She would sometimes ask for information herself, but she would always leave whoever she had asked with the impression that she was just another member of the hierarchy. Therefore, no one knew who was at the top of the chain. Anyone close to Katalin thought she reported to no one and that pleased Katalin; she never contradicted anyone who thought this.

Isabella's Slovaks would report indirectly to her of people who had beaten the weak, raped, or murdered without just cause. These people would usually fall ill and inexplicably die within days, sometimes even hours. Isabella especially wanted to know about those who sought the help of a witch finder. She would take great pleasure in visiting these people. This new found purpose gave her the opportunity to perfect her sixth sense. She had become so skilled that she could touch the temples of most people and could see their innermost secrets. She could see their worst crimes and their justification, if they had any, to commit these crimes. On an occasion when she was not totally convinced of a person's guilt, if their will was strong and she could not read them, she would extract a confession just to be sure.

Isabella's exertions led to there being very few witch trials in the Carpathians: Moldavia, Transylvania, and Walachia were spared of these atrocities. The Slovaks, however, were now growing a reputation of their own. Isabella would not harm a Slovak even if they where guilty of the worst of crimes and yet, she felt no hesitation in punishing anyone in other communities. Because of this, the Slovaks started to get treated with suspicion. The Slovak Invigilators, unknowingly over time, became the guardians of Vampires.

Gabriel Bethlen had been sent for, and he was worried. He could feel the Prince's antipathy building during the past months. He had spoken out several times against Gábor Báthory's treatment of his own people. He had been chief counsellor to the previous prince and was well respected throughout Hungary and the Carpathians. At first, Báthory had respected his opinion and had curbed his cruel instincts, but yesterday something had happened to inflame Báthory's true nature.

The day before, the two statesmen had been parading through the centre of the city, Báthory sitting on the royal golden coach and Bethlen behind him, in a slightly less extravagant carriage. The crowds were packing in through the gates of the city centre to see the young Prince. Bethlen was worried; some of these people may be crushed as the two coaches pushed through the cheering onlookers. Báthory as usual was unconcerned about anyone apart from himself.

Fireworks were exploding, lighting up the night sky. One of the fireworks exploded prematurely and a spark ignited the others that were still on the ground; a small fire started and a few loud bangs from the fireworks followed. The horses attached to the two coaches were frightened by the noise and veered up. As they fell back to the ground they struck a beautiful woman. They trampled her and blood could be seen soaking through her clothes. Bethlen started to shout at Báthory.

"Keep the horses away from her," Bethlen shouted.

"Carry on," Báthory said calmly to his guards, not paying a moment's heed to the injured woman. Bethlen jumped off his coach and ran to her. He could not tell if she was alive or dead. He lifted her up in her arms; her body was limp and cold. He feared the worst. He tried to climb on Báthory's coach but Báthory pushed him back. Bethlen looked up at his Prince in amazement. He knew the Prince was not a kind man, but to let one of his own people die if there was a possible chance of saving her? Bethlen quickly placed the injured woman on one of his own coach horses. He climbed up behind her as quickly as he could and rode out through the crowd to the city gates. Bethlen until now had been totally oblivious to the crowd but as he turned the horse around he saw Báthory staring at him with venom. Bethlen returned the venomous stare and as he rode out he heard the crowd starting to chant.

"Bethlen… Bethlen…"

As Gabriel Bethlen rode away he wondered if had he just sealed his own fate, but he could not stand by and watch as his sovereign indirectly murdered one of his innocent subjects. He rode back to his house as fast as he could. His wife had taken ill and he knew his doctor was at home, looking after her.

He arrived at his home quickly and pulled the woman off the horse as gently as possible and rushed into the hall, laying her carefully on the floor.

"Zsuzsanna," he called to his wife. "Zsuzsanna," he called again. Zsuzsanna came running down the stairs to her husband.

"What is it?" she yelled.

"Is the doctor still here?" Bethlen said panicking.

"Yes, I will run and fetch him, he is in the kitchen." Zsuzsanna returned with the doctor at her side to see the bloody victim.

"Is she alive?" Gabriel asked. Before the doctor got a chance to feel if the woman was breathing she opened her eyelids to reveal dark, viridian eyes. Gabriel and Zsuzsanna laughed in relief. "I guess she is," said Gabriel. Isabella sat up, not letting the doctor touch her. "Not so fast, take your time," Gabriel said.

"I'm fine," Isabella insisted.

"You couldn't possibly be," Zsuzsanna said. Isabella had forgotten that as far these people were concerned she had been through a horrific accident. So she cautiously climbed to her feet and when she was standing upright she clutched her forehead and pretended to swoon. Gabriel caught her as she fell and said.

"I think we should take her upstairs to let her lie down, and then you can examine her properly," Gabriel said to the doctor. Zsuzsanna and Gabriel walked Isabella up the stairs to one of the spare bedrooms. The Doctor followed behind, Zsuzsanna and Gabriel lead her to the bed and set Isabella down on it.

Zsuzsanna gave Isabella a nightgown and asked, "Do you need anyone to help you get changed out of those clothes?" Isabella shook her head. "Then I will leave you and let the doctor take a look at you."

Zsuzsanna and Gabriel left the room. The doctor approached Isabella. Her dress was very torn and quite a lot of blood had stained the ragged cloth. The doctor looked at Isabella's back and he was shocked to find no wounds.

"There is not a mark on your back," the doctor said. He looked at her arm and again despite the blood stains there was no wound to be seen. "I don't understand—where did all the blood come from?"

Isabella was ignoring him. She was looking at the door and listening to see if Zsuzsanna and her husband were far enough away so they could not hear what she was about to do. As soon as they were out of earshot Isabella lunged at the doctor, holding him still. He was now frightened for his life.

"Are you a good man?" Isabella asked.

"What do you mean?" he spluttered.

"I mean, have you led your life to a standard that I would approve of?" Isabella tossed the Doctor onto the bed and kneeled one leg on his chest. She placed her hand on his forehead and looked at his misdeeds. The worst thing that this man had ever done was put an old man who was crippled with pain out his misery with some laudanum. This was an act of mercy, but this man still felt guilt over it. "It appears you have led a good life. What a pity. I was getting hungry."

She released her grasp of the doctor. He sat up on the bed rubbing his neck. "Now, I want you to go out and let the Bethlens know that I was very badly injured but will recover. Do you think I can rely on you to do this for me?" The doctor, who was still terrified, nodded his head. He got instinctively up and went towards the door. "Doctor," Isabella called after him. "I want one last thing from you."

"What?" The doctor enquired.

"I want you to believe that that is exactly what happened."

As the doctor closed the door his mind was filled with pity for this woman. Her injuries had been terrible but he believed she would recover. He went to tell the Bethlens exactly what he now believed to have happened.

The Bethlens left Isabella to rest and the next morning, Zsuzsanna went to the room to check on her. She was surprised to see that the woman had gone.

"Gabriel," she shouted, "she has gone." Gabriel ran up the stairs to see the empty room and he, too, was shocked.

"Where could she have gone in the condition she was in?" asked Gabriel. At that moment there was a knock at the door. It was a messenger from court. Gabriel Bethlen had been sent for.

※

Bethlen waited outside the palatial wooden doors of court anxiously awaiting knowledge of what would be done to him. He had seen Báthory kill people over much less. The doors finally opened and he entered the court. It was full of Gábor's loyal dignitaries. It was to be a public trial—he was to be made an example of a warning to anyone else who tried to curry favour with the rabble.

Bethlen approached Gábor's throne. He looked around, hoping to see one friendly face among the sea of enemies. He was astonished to see standing in the crowd the young woman he had saved the day before. She stood, elegantly clothed, her arm interlocked with one of the nobles. He didn't recognise her presumed husband; he hoped they both were friendly faces. Isabella reassured him by smiling when she caught his glance and pressed her finger up to her lips to signal for him to keep quiet and not alert anyone to her presence. A thought came into his head, a comforting thought. It told him to be quiet about the woman, and it told him that he should say that the girl he had saved was taken back to her family and that was all he knew of her.

A few hours of questioning passed by and Bethlen was condemned. But still Bethlen was not concerned. He walked out of the biased court, his head held high. The reassuring feeling that emanated from this woman had stayed with him as he was escorted out of the hall and down to a dungeon of the castle.

Gabriel Bethlen waited in his temporary prison, for he knew she would be coming to speak to him. Isabella did not keep him waiting long.

"I suppose you require an explanation?" Isabella began.

"I think I do."

"I have none to give you. What I will tell you, I suspect you already know. Gábor Báthory is a hellish man; you as your actions proved yesterday are not. He has ordered many men and woman slaughtered for no good reason just as he would kill you, given the chance. I myself am no better than him, probably worse, but I have decided to mend my wicked ways."

"If as you say, you are just as bad as him, what concern is all this to you?"

"I don't think you should be questioning someone who is intent on saving you from execution, so be quiet and listen. Your Prince is a powerful man and his death will mean that many people will be spared and that is what I am concerned with. I staged the accident yesterday to see what sort of man you were and also if you were the right sort of man to rule. I need to know that I am leaving my people, that is, the Slovak people who live in this region, in good hands. I want no burnings; this method of execution should be outlawed. I do not want to hear of anyone being burned at the stake, no matter what their crime."

"I have constantly protested against this form of punishment."

"That is another reason I have chosen you. You will have to muster up an army. The Turks will accommodate you."

"What about Báthory?"

"I will take care of him." Isabella kicked open the door and said, "What are you waiting for? Go and come back a Conqueror!" Gabriel fled straight to the Turks as Isabella had told him to do.

Isabella knew that the Turkish regime was not to be trusted to depose Báthory and put Bethlen in his place. She knew they would put in place whoever would be the most useful and Báthory would prove more useful, as he would do anything to save his own skin. He needed to be taken care of.

※

Csaba was worried for his daughter, Ella, for she was late returning home from court. He had quarters within the castle and his daughter was a servant. She was very young and he constantly worried about her.

It had been years since Erzsébet had been punished for killing hundreds of girls. He had witnessed first hand both Erzsébet's and Gábor Báthory's treatment of people, for like his aunt, he was cruel and malicious. Csaba had, years before, gone to seek out his sister and had stumbled onto the massacre that Erzsébet had been responsible for. At Erzsébet's trial he had remembered the descriptions of the awful crimes for which she was guilty. He had sought to get away from such barbarity. But he had not escaped anything; he now witnessed Gábor's cruel treatment of his people. A few months before, he himself had witnessed when a young girl had been trampled nearly to death by Gábor's horses and the Prince had done nothing to help her. When his daughter was put into service within the castle, he couldn't refuse. To refuse would probably condemn his whole family. So he let her go, but kept a watchful eye on her.

Just that night he had been ordered away by the Prince, for there had been a banquet and there was no need of him there. Csaba had watched in the early part of the evening as Gábor, who had already drunk quite a lot, got more and more boisterous. He had slapped one of the other servants, slicing her cheek open with his ring. All she had done was spill a drop of his wine and only because she had been pushed by Gábor.

Csaba sat up watching the door to his daughter's chamber, hoping that she had returned safely. In the early hours of the morning one of his Ella's friends came running up to where he was sitting, waiting and worried.

"Hurry, come with me," the young girl cried out.

"What has happened?" Csaba said anxiously.

"He beat her," she answered. Csaba's stomach sank; his worst fear had been confirmed. The pair ran into the banquet room which was now deserted except for his unconscious daughter. She was lying face down in a pool of blood. Her father ran to her and threw himself down onto his knees.

He rolled his daughter over to look at her face. It was swollen and purple; she had been so severely beaten he hardly recognised her.

"How did this happen?" Csaba said to the other girl.

"The Prince must approve all marriages of his soldiers; your future son-in-law came tonight to ask for your daughter's hand. The Prince asked who the girl was and Istvan pointed to your daughter. The prince said she was pretty and asked was that the reason he was marrying her. Istvan answered back that that was one of many reasons. The prince then asked him if she wasn't pretty would he still be marrying her. Istvan replied of course. The prince then said he wished he could have proof of this unconditional love.

"Unfortunately, sir, you cannot," your future son-in-law responded.

"Cannot is not a word to use with Princes," said Báthory in response.

"You are quite correct sir. I apologise." Istvan then left and everything seemed fine.

"However, from that moment Gábor was watching your daughter. He asked his friends how they could prove this man's loyalty and devotion. One of his friends foolishly, stupidly suggested that if she was ever disfigured only that would prove his loyalty. This man regretted his words as soon as he had uttered them.

"Gábor said that was an excellent idea. The first thing he did was trip her up but Ella jumped quickly back on to her feet. She was unscathed and carried on with her work. She tried to get away and slip out back to the kitchen, but Gábor leapt up from his seat and chased after her. She dropped what she was doing and tried to run but he soon caught her, and yanked her back by the hair. She fell to the floor and Gábor dragged her back into the room by the hem of her skirt.

He left her in the middle of the room for all to see and started kicking her in the face. His guests, who up until this time were egging him on, were now stunned by the Prince's violence. The raucous laughter that had been coming from this room now quickly quieted to an eerie silence. All you now heard was the sweeping sound of Gábor's leg as it bludgeoned your daughter's face. Gábor looked round to see the stunned and now sobered faces. One by one the soldiers asked for their leave. This made Gábor stop and he shouted in a foul temper, "You can all go then." He left the room in a rage.

The room soon cleared of everyone except her and that is when I came to get you."

At this Istvan ran into the room. 'I just heard what happened,' he said. Istvan was appalled when he saw his future wife lying on the floor bleeding. "I am going to kill him," Istvan icily stated.

"I will help you," said Csaba.

One of the servants who had witnessed the gruesome beating was a Slovak and had gone to tell Isabella what had happened. Isabella now entered the room as the two men were plotting the death of their sovereign. They marched out of the room, stern and determined. Isabella ran after them.

"Stop!" she shouted. The two men ignored her. "Stop!" she shouted again. Still ignoring her, they marched on. Isabella ran quickly and got in front of them. "What are you doing?" she asked.

"We are going to kill Gábor Báthory," Istvan stated, not caring who knew.

"No, you cannot, not tonight."

Csaba pushed Isabella from his path and Isabella quickly got in front of him again. She placed her hand on his chest stopping him walking any further and said. "You remember me Csaba, don't you?"

An inexplicable urge made Csaba stop trying to get past Isabella and he looked at her face. He suddenly remembered her; he had seen her several times before. She had been there when he had discovered his sister's body. She had also been at Erzsébet's trial and he had seen her more recently; she had been trampled by a horse. "You remember, don't you, I am letting you remember me so that you will trust me," Isabella continued.

"How can you still be so young?" Csaba asked.

"Never mind, that it is just a detail. You know me. You know I influenced Erzsébet's trial." Csaba's head was now filled with memories that had been blocked out. He remembered this woman standing in the crowd at Erzsébet's trail. He saw Isabella throwing off a body from the battlements so that Erzsébet would be discovered. She was letting him see these things.

"If it was not for you, Countess Báthory would have killed for many more years."

"I don't know if that is true or not."

"It is true; you saved many girls' lives."

"I want to save more people. You must trust me."

"Who are you?" Csaba asked.

"Who I am is of no consequence. But I tell you, you cannot kill Gábor, not yet."

"Why not?"

"Because who will take over from him, another tyrant? Just like him, worse perhaps."

"That doesn't matter. Even if we wait, someone just as bad still could take over."

"No, I know of a man who is good. Gabriel Bethlen is raising an army; you know he is a good man, Csaba,"

"He is," Csaba acknowledged.

"Then give him a chance. If you wait, he will take over and bring tolerance to this land," Isabella pleaded.

"I want to kill Báthory," Csaba said. "I have a right to kill him."

"You will, but just not yet, I promise you that." At this point Istvan interrupted.

"Csaba, why are you listening to this woman?" Istvan protested.

"I know her and trust her, and she is right. We will wait for Gabriel Bethlen to return."

"Listen to Csaba and you both will come out of this unscathed. If you kill Báthory you will also be dead by morning. His soldiers would not tolerate an assassination," Isabella said.

"Do you have healing powers?" asked Csaba, thinking about his daughter.

"No, I don't, I'm sorry, but let me see her." Csaba led Isabella back down the corridor to see his daughter. The girl was badly beaten but Isabella could smell no signs of death. "She'll live," Isabella stated.

"What about scarring, will she...." Istvan asked.

"Will you allow me to touch her face?" Isabella asked.

"Yes if it will help."

Isabella touched the girl's head and took her pain. The girl opened her eyes and Isabella smiled. Not her usual wry smile, but a warm comforting smile. She then felt her cheek bones and nose. "I don't think there are any bones broken that will not heel. She may have some slight scarring from the cuts, that is all, but her mind may never recover from such a viscous attack." The girl smiled at her future husband and he wept; he could hardly bring himself to look at her. Istvan clasped her hand and held it to his chest.

"How long do we have to wait to kill him?" asked Istvan.

"Not long," Isabella answered.

※

Gabriel Bethlen was already on his way home. He had gone straight to the Turks as Isabella had suggested and found the Sultan more than willing to support him. He had raised an army and was now nearly home. Isabella was waiting for him. Unfortunately, while he had been away his wife Zsuzsanna had died. She had been very ill before he had left, but she had hidden how serious it was from him, not wanting to stop him from fulfilling his destiny.

Gabriel stationed his new army a few hundreds yards outside the Hungarian border. Gabriel, wanting to see his wife, sneaked in under cover of darkness to his old home. A Slovak informed Isabella that he was on his way and she, Csaba and Istvan went to his house to wait for him.

He opened the door quietly, not even wanting to wake up the servants. Csaba lighted a candle, alerting Gabriel to their presence.

"Did you do as I asked?" Isabella asked and Gabriel nodded.

"Where is my wife?" Gabriel asked.

"I am afraid she is dead."

Gabriel sat down in shock.

"You can weep for her later. We have no time now," said Isabella.

Gabriel tried to compose himself as best he could. "Who are these men?" he asked.

"They are the men who will assassinate Báthory."

"Why assassinate him?" Bethlen asked. At this Istvan interrupted. He slammed his fist down on the table.

"I have waited long enough," he shouted. "I want his blood."

Isabella smiled. "You are not the only one," she said. "But you must wait just until tomorrow night. Everything is in place. You attack tomorrow and I will ensure that Báthory dies."

"Why does he have to die?" Gabriel asked again, sensing that Istvan was slightly calmer.

"He has to die because the Turks cannot be trusted; if after tomorrow he escapes he could flee to the Sultan and they may be just as accommodating with him as they have been with you. Their loyalty is to whoever can give them the most power. The Turks know you are a strong-willed man and you will do as much for your people as you can, whereas Báthory will grant them anything to regain his throne. That is why he must die. And these two men have most definitely earned the right to kill him,"

"Till tomorrow night," Gabriel whispered.

"Tomorrow night," Isabella answered.

⁂

Isabella sat waiting for Vlad's return. He did just before sunrise.

"Is everything in place?" Isabella asked.

"Yes. Bethlen has surpassed himself; that is a mighty army he has raised. I noticed quite a few Slovaks."

"I sent out word that they should join with him."

"You are becoming a very powerful woman. Isabella."

"I am getting to be more than that, I am becoming a very powerful Vrolok," Isabella smiled. "You will fight with him tomorrow?"

"I will, but I don't think you need me."

"I do. If I was not needed here to ensure Báthory is dead, I would be fighting with you."

"You are a leader of men, Isabella."

"No, the allies that I have do not know where their instructions are coming from. No doubt they would not follow me if they knew who or what was commanding them."

"I think you are wrong. The Slovak people respect you or they would not be fighting with Bethlen otherwise."

"Perhaps, but I believe they may turn against me yet."

"Walking among them tonight I realised they would sooner kill their own kin instead of you. They call you Alexandru, the defender of mankind."

"They presume I am a man."

"They do."

"How archaic of them."

"If I go and fight them tomorrow they will presume it is me, you realise this," Isabella smiled.

"It doesn't matter. In part it has been you, and I don't want any glory. Go and fight with them, for they need you." Vlad walked towards Isabella, took her hand and kissed it. He turned and headed towards the door.

"Vlad," she called out after him. Vlad turned back towards her.

"Yes?" he answered.

"Make sure you only kill Báthory's troops." Vlad smiled and bowed at Isabella; she knew him too well.

"As you wish, my lady."

Isabella waited to hear the first explosion of gunpowder. Within a few moments of the start of the fighting, Báthory came running through the hall half-dressed. Isabella tripped him and he smacked his head on the stone floor. He quickly got back up onto his feet and turned to face the Vampire.

"That was the first cruel thing you did to this man's daughter," said Csaba, who had been standing in the corner.

"What are you talking about?" Báthory answered. "I will have you executed for this!"

"I am afraid you will not be in the position to do that," Isabella stated, and she knocked Gábor to the ground again. This time he did not get up so quickly. Istvan came running into the room, rage surging through him. He kicked Gábor in the face. Isabella touched him on the forehead and gave him the pain of the girl he had beaten. Istvan and Csaba started to kick him in the face over and over again. The vengeful father and husband beat Gábor to death. When the two men had exacted their revenge Isabella asked.

"Do you feel better?"

"I will never feel better, but I feel relieved that he will not be able to do this to any other child," Csaba answered.

"I am glad he is dead and I am glad I killed him. If I could have caused him more pain I would have," Istvan said firmly.

"I must ask you one last thing," Isabella whispered.

"What?" Csaba responded.

"You must forget I was ever here." There was a sudden explosion outside and Csaba and Istvan were distracted as the whole castle shook. Csaba immediately looked round to where Isabella had been standing, but she was already gone and they had already forgotten her.

Isabella climbed up to the battlements to watch the fighting. She saw Vlad and Bethlen leading the charge. A mixture of Slovaks, Turks and Hungarians loyal to Bethlen followed them. Her plan was certainly working. She considered it her greatest achievement yet. She had gotten rid of a tyrant and replaced him with a true Prince and if her new Prince fell short of his potential, she would always be watching him.

Isabella thrust herself off the battlements and flew towards Vlad. He had single-handedly killed hundreds and when Isabella stood by his side, the pair swept through Báthory's army with ferocious and deathly speed. After a few hours a man ran from Báthory's palace dragging Gábor's body behind him. Gábor's face was not recognizable but his royal seal was still on his finger. Bethlen's army started to cheer; the battle had been won.

Isabella looked up from her current victim and smiled. She ran to Vlad and kissed him, placing her hands on his temple, but as she touched his face, she was able to read some of his thoughts and see his darkest secrets for the first time. She had become so skilled that Vlad could no longer block her out of his mind. She saw Kit, she saw Vlad talking to Thomas Walsingham influencing him. She saw all of it.

However, Kit's murder was not his darkest crime. It was only the beginning of her vision. She was about to see much worse than this. Vlad was there the night Nicolae had died. When Katya had gone to get the sword he had poured the Dhampir's blood on the blade so that the sword would slice through Nicolae's neck. He had killed her Nicolae.

Isabella let go of Vlad's face and backed away from him. Vlad knew at that moment he might never see Isabella again, for he had read her thoughts as she had kissed him. He felt her elation as the battle was over and for the first time he could see, for just an instant, how in love she was with him. Then he felt these feelings turn sour. He felt her utter devastation at what he had done to Kit and her complete loathing at what he had done to Nicolae. In that moment Vlad felt Isabella's love turn to hatred. He knew as she backed away and became obscured by the celebrating troops that it might be the last time he would ever see her. She would not come back to him, not after this. He had only in the past felt a slight taste of her resolve to not see him again. Vlad fell to the ground and wept, blood red tears streaming from his eyes.

Isabella was distraught but there was one last thing she had to do. The following day she went to see Gabriel Bethlen as he sat on his new throne. Isabella approached him and curtsied.

"Prince," Isabella started.

"The woman who made all this possible—I have to thank you."

"I am not here to receive thanks," Isabella said. "I just want you to make me a promise."

"Anything."

"I want you to bring tolerance back to this land. Do not get corrupted by the power you now have."

"I won't."

"I hope you won't, for I will be watching you." Isabella left him with this. She kept her promise she did watch him and a few years later she visited him again when he was King of Hungary.

"I want you to relinquish this throne, Gabriel," she began.

"Why?"

"It is too much power."

"It's not."

"I am not here to argue with you. Go back and be Prince of Transylvania, and give Ferdinand the throne here. You do not need it. It has already corrupted you."

"It hasn't," Gabriel protested.

"It has. Are you not planning to burn Anna Báthory at the stake?" At these words Gabriel knew she was right; he had been changed by his newfound power. "Let her go and relinquish the throne of Hungary."

"I will."

Gabriel went back to Transylvania and was a great and tolerant prince till the end of his days.

Isabella sat on a mountaintop in the middle of Carpathians; she could just about see the candlelight flickering in Vlad's castle. She would never go back there. She sat staring off into the distance. Surely she had done enough, she thought, for fifty years. She had not killed anyone that she thought did not deserve it. She had avenged hundreds and probably saved hundreds. She wanted to know could she now die. Could she now find peace at last? Isabella stood and looked at the long drop at her feet and the rocks on the ground below. She threw herself off the top of the mountain. She did not control her motion as she could to save herself from injury. She hit the ground at a tremendous speed bashing her skull on a rock which knocked her unconscious.

She was awakened by someone dripping water on to her forehead. She opened her eyes and looked up at the man who was reviving her. Could it be? She thought. Isabella saw Nicolae's handsome face looking down at her. Isabella was elated she had done enough; Nicolae had come to take her to heaven.

"Nicolae."

"Yes," he answered. "How did you know my name?"

"Nicolae, it is me," Isabella grabbed his face and frantically started to kiss him. She stood and hugged him, not ever wanting to let him go.

"Nicolae, have you forgiven me?" she asked.

"I don't know what you are talking about!" he said. Isabella hugged him tighter still. The moon was covered by a cloud and they were in total darkness. Isabella drew herself back from him. She placed her hands on his shoulders. She could not believe it…her Nicolae was standing in front of her.

She was right not to believe her own eyes. She noticed her fingers were starting to tremble. She had not fed in days; searing pain started to shoot through her body. Isabella could hardly stand it. She saw the bulging vein on this man's neck. She couldn't control herself; she plunged her teeth into the vein and drank. When the pain stopped Isabella let go and the young man fell to the ground. Isabella fell with him; what had she done? She had killed Nicolae again, she had watched him die. She had to do something; she couldn't watch this again, even if it meant him hating her forever, as she feared it would. She slashed her wrist open and let him drink. As he drank she noticed his hair; it was not brown like Nicolae's but black like her own. She then noticed his eyes; they were green but dark like hers, not clear and bright like Nicolae's. Isabella realised in torment what she had done. She had not only killed her own descendant. She had made him into a Vampire.

WENN DU FRAU SIEHST, DENKE, ES SEI DER TEUFEL, DIESE IST EINE ART HOLLE
WHENEVER YOU SEE A WOMAN, THINK, IT IS THE DEVIL, THIS IS A HELLISH BREED

CHAPTER FOURTEEN

Isabella waited for her descendant to awake. He opened his eyes in the early hours of the next morning.

"Can you hear me?" Isabella asked. The youth nodded.

"What happened?" he asked. Isabella hesitated. She didn't want to tell him what she had done.

"I thought you were Nicolae," she said, obviously distraught.

"I am. How did you know my name?"

Isabella sighed. "You are named after an ancestor."

"A distant one."

"Has it been that long?" Isabella reflected.

"What is wrong with me? I feel different."

"You *are* different," Isabella responded.

"How, how am I different?" Nicolae looked up at Isabella. There was no anger or bitterness in this man's face; he was an innocent. He looked at her and the emotion he was visibly expressing was trust. He so resembled Nicolae she didn't want to immediately alter this look to one of hate, but she had to. She had to tell him what she had done.

"I have made you different," Isabella began.

"How?" the young Nicolae asked again. Isabella hesitated. She needed more time. How could she possibly tell her own descendant who she was and what she had done to him? Unfortunately for Isabella, time was running out. She watched in trepidation as Nicolae's fingers started to shake and his body started to contort and convulse in agonising pain. He needed to feed.

"What is happening to me?" Nicolae cried out. Isabella ran to get him food. She ran through the woods desperately listening for some sign of life. She heard horses—someone was travelling close by. Isabella approached; she saw a family. As it was a warm evening, they had fallen asleep underneath the stars. Isabella quickly ran around them touching each of their heads in turn, trying to see who had committed acts worthy of being mortally punished. She touched the father's head first, nothing; he was a poor man but he hadn't as much as stolen food to keep away his hunger, but when Isabella read the mother, it was quite different.

Leila had watched Istvan from afar, but when she heard he was going to marry someone else, she was devastated. She knew Csaba's daughter, Ella, a pretty girl, but not good enough for her Istvan. When she heard Ella had been injured and the wedding had been delayed, she decided it was time for her to her tell Istvan how she felt.

Leila approached Istvan cautiously.

"Who's there?" Istvan asked. He had been drinking constantly since Ella was hurt, trying to block out his own guilt. He blamed himself completely for what happened to her.

"Leila," she answered softly.

"What are you doing here Leila?" Istvan asked. He was aware of her affection for him.

"I came to keep you company," Leila said.

"I don't want any company."

"You need company…you need to talk to someone." Istvan looked up at Leila.

"I do?" Istvan said, already exasperated by Leila's presence.

"You do," Leila affirmed, undeterred by Istvan's attitude.

"I don't feel like talking," Istvan said through clenched teeth.

"Then I will just sit here with you."

Istvan sighed but he lacked the energy to tell her to leave him. They sat quietly for a time until Leila caught Istvan looking at her. Istvan leaned in towards her, looking at her face, looking at her untarnished young face; she was looking back at him with only love. Istvan knew then that Leila adored him and as anyone knows, one of the greatest aphrodisiacs there is, is to feel completely adored by someone else. Sometimes even just for a moment this complete idolization can be intoxicating and contagious. Istvan then said something he should have never have uttered.

"Kiss me."

Leila was overjoyed. She foolishly believed that it was really this easy. She kissed him so passionately that for that exquisite moment Istvan saw himself through her adoring eyes and he returned her affection fleetingly. Leila sat on his lap and Istvan pushed his hand up above the skirt of her dress. He wanted to feel something different than the guilt he felt over Ella. He wanted something or someone to eradicate the feeling, if only for a moment.

The next morning when Istvan awoke he was repulsed by his own actions. He had now betrayed his future wife—this was another cross for him to bear. Leila in turn was overjoyed; she thought that after the events of last night Istvan was sure to marry her instead.

"Good morning," Leila said a glowing and hopeful smile upon her face.

"Get dressed," Istvan snapped, taking his own guilt out on Leila.

"I suppose I should, but I just want to lie here a little longer."

"Get dressed now. This should never have happened."

"What are you talking about? It was meant to happen," Leila said, not yet realising the brutal truth of the situation she was in.

"Meant to happen?" Istvan said. His brief infatuation with Leila was completely over. He now could not stand the sight of her; she was just a reminder of his betrayal of Ella.

"You love me," Leila cried out in desperation.

"Love you? I don't love you; I love Ella and only Ella. You were just a distraction when I needed it most."

"Why are you saying these things? You love me!" Leila cried, pounding her fists on Istvan's chest. Istvan clutched her wrists to prevent her from striking him any more.

"I am surprised I can even remember your name," he said, cruelly. He let her go. He had now delivered his final blow.

At this Leila lashed out at him again but Istvan was too strong for her and violently threw her back away from him. She struck the back of her head on the bed post. She was badly hurt but she would receive no sympathy from Istvan.

"Get dressed and get out!" he shouted. Leila quickly got dressed and ran from the room sobbing.

A few months later, Ella's face had almost healed completely but Istvan's wounds were still far from healed. He was still as guilt-ridden and morose as he had ever been. As Csaba watched the pair be married, he felt uneasy. Istvan had not been the same since Ella's injury. Csaba was distracted from these thoughts as he saw a young woman running towards his daughter. He suddenly became frightened as he realised this woman was brandishing a knife.

Leila lunged forward and stabbed Ella through the heart. Ella was dead almost instantly. Istvan quickly took the knife from Leila and slashed Leila across the face with it, but he did not kill her. Overcome with grief he fell to the floor and lifted Ella up his arms, holding her close, not wanting to let her go. Leila, who was still holding her bloody cheek, was enraged and picked up the knife that had fallen to the floor from Istvan's hand, plunging it into Istvan's back. He took a little longer to die but die he did. He slumped down on the ground looking at Ella, not wanting to take his eyes from her. She looked so beautiful so peaceful, that with his last ounce of energy, he placed his hand on her pale white skin and closed his eyes, never to look upon her again. The crowd was numbed by the events they had just witnessed. Leila was icily calm as she stood up and was escorted to prison.

Isabella had found her years later sleeping quietly with the man who had helped her escape. He loved her, but she was not capable of loving him back and had become a bitter and miserable woman with an unsightly scar on her face to be a constant reminder of Istvan's harsh rejection. Isabella thought that her crimes were monstrous enough and she carried her back to Nicolae for him to kill her and feed.

Nicolae did not hesitate. He was in too much pain and he bit down hard into Leila's flesh. After Nicolae had finished he was still somewhat disoriented and Isabella took him to where she was staying, leaving Leila for dead.

Nicolae slept all that night and all through the next day. Isabella watched and waited for Nicolae to open his eyes again. He awoke with a jolt.

"How are you feeling?" Isabella asked.

"I had an awful dream; I dreamt I was a Vampire."

Isabella shuddered. "You are," she said coldly.

"I can't be."

"You are a Vampire."

Again Nicolae's body started to convulse; he was hungry for the second time since his death. The pain suddenly made him remember the events of the previous night. He remembered with complete distaste.

"What sort of creature are you?" Nicolae asked.

"I have told you I am a Vrolok and now, so are you," Isabella said, and went to take his hand, but Nicolae wrenched it away from her. His actions brought too many painful memories back to Isabella. Nicolae's convulsions were getting worse. He needed to feed and quickly.

"What's happening to me? What is this pain?" Nicolae screamed at Isabella.

"You need to feed," Isabella answered him.

"Feed on what?"

"You know already...blood." These words issued out of Isabella's mouth like a death sentence. Nicolae was appalled to realise that he had been brought up to hate and despise the creature he was now forced to become. His pain was intensifying until he could stand it no longer.

"I have to kill someone to make this stop?" he stated through his anguish.

"Yes, but I have discovered that there are ways you can kill and keep your conscience clear," Isabella tried to reassure him.

"I don't need a creature like you telling me how to keep my conscious clear." Nicolae struggled to his feet and ran from Isabella. However, Isabella was too fast for him. She grabbed his arm but he shrugged her off and threw her back, causing her to fall. Isabella lay where she fell, watching Nicolae as he ran out of her house. Isabella dragged herself up; she knew she had to follow him. She found him sitting by a dead body which he had obviously killed. "I couldn't stand the pain anymore," he whispered.

"I know, I understand." Isabella again tried to put her hands on his shoulders to comfort him. And again Nicolae shrank back away from her as if her slightest touch was completely repugnant to him.

"Don't touch me... why did you do this to me?"

"It was an accident, I thought I was dead; I thought you were my husband for just an instant and then the pain started and I had to feed. Just the way you had to."

"Why didn't you just let me die?"

"I couldn't watch you die again."

"But I am not your husband; I am not your Nicolae."

"You look so like him I couldn't watch even a remnant of him die again." Nicolae walked away from Isabella and watched the flickering lights of the village below.

"So who are you to me?"

"A distant ancestor, just like Nicolae."

"At least we are keeping it in the family," Nicolae said sarcastically.

Isabella smiled through her torment. There was a silence between the two of them. Isabella hoped by his last comment that he was not totally lost to her and saw her as something more than just a Vrolok.

Nicolae turned back towards the body and said, "Is this what my life is going to be from now on, waiting until the pain starts and then killing someone to suppress it?"

"It doesn't have to be. I can see if people are decent—I only kill those that deserve to be killed."

"What about me—did I deserve to be killed?"

"No, it was just a slip, a moment of madness."

"You should have let me die,"

"I told you I couldn't. Do you have any children?" Isabella asked.

"No, not yet. And now, not ever."

Isabella was pleased that he did not have children and a wife of his own waiting for him to come home. She felt a little bit better at least knowing this.

"Can I go and see my mother and father just to tell them I am all right?" he asked.

"But you are not all right," Isabella answered.

"I would like to see them one last time."

"You are under no obligation to me. You can do what you want," Isabella said. "I cannot stop you. Be warned though, your mother and father will not look at you the same way. Believe me, they are better off thinking you are dead." There was a brief silence between the pair.

"So where will I live?" Nicolae began again.

"Wherever you want to live. I am going to England next week. If you want to, you can come with me."

"I will... what else can I do but go with you?"

"If you go with me I can teach you how to only punish the guilty."

"I don't want you to teach me anything. I am staying with you until I can think of somewhere else to go."

Isabella had had enough of this conversation. "I will leave you to sleep now. You will not get any sleep in the light. It is best to find a place where you can sleep in total darkness; light will be a constant irritation to you."

※

The pair left for England a week later. Nicolae wanted to find a place where he could exist were no one knew him. Nicolae was civil to Isabella, even polite on occasion, but whenever she would come near him, he would flinch away from her. He did not despise her but he did despise what she was and what he had become. He understood that she was not completely to blame for her own situation, but still, he could not forgive her.

It was hard for Isabella to remember he was not the husband who died so many decades before. He was so like Nicolae, not just in his appearance, but his character as well. He was incapable of hating, or she at least hoped he was. Isabella convinced herself that this person would react the same way that Nicolae would have eventually reacted to her. It was like a second chance for her to make her peace with her husband.

They travelled through England together. Isabella taught him as much as she could, but she soon realised he was not as powerful as she was. He was not as strong; he did not have the skill that Isabella had. Also, any exposure to sunlight burnt his skin. She wondered whether it could be that the powers decreased from Vampire to Vampire. If so, then how strong must Vlad be?

England was not the same place she had left fifty years before. It was not as opulent and extravagant as she remembered. The country had been plunged into civil war and witch trials were rife. Isabella was still sickened by these trials and the persecution of women who were just slightly different from everyone else. But at least they were not burning these girls here. They were getting hanged, which was slightly more humane to Isabella's mind than burning. But a lot of people were dying and Isabella was determined to stop as much of it as she could. The killing of innocents was totally abhorrent to her now.

Meanwhile, Nicolae was growing to like the kill, perhaps a little too much, but Isabella was never one to judge another Vampire. She felt she did not have the right to do so.

They had been in England for a few years and had decided to settle in the south of the country. One morning, when Isabella wandered a little further than she usually would, she happened upon one of the public hangings. An eighty-year-old man was condemned. He was standing on the scaffold and he turned towards the crowd and shouted at the top of his voice, but he couldn't be heard over the shouts of the unsympathetic mob. Isabella wanted to hear this man's final words as only she could.

"My name is John Lowes and I am the Vicar of Brandeston. I am innocent of these crimes of which I have been accused. I know my words will not save me but I demand a Christian burial. I commit my body to the ground in sure and certain hope of the resurrection of eternal life." As these last words left his lips he was pushed off the scaffold and struggled until his neck broke.

Isabella could not stop this, for there were too many people around, but she could not stomach it either. She turned and walked away from the jeering crowd.

"You don't want to watch this display of modern justice?" An unfamiliar voice was addressing Isabella.

"Is this justice?" Isabella responded.

"It seems to be and that is the real tragedy of this civilised world."

"Do something about it then," Isabella responded, challenging the young man.

"Oh no, I value my neck. I do not want it stretched at the hands of Mathew Hopkins."

"Mathew Hopkins?" Isabella enquired.

"The Witch Finder General. His quest is finding these revolting witches out. He's hanged three score of them in one shire, some only for not being drowned."

"Really," Isabella said nonchalantly, not wanting to let this man know she was in fact very interested in what he was saying.

"He is a man who deserves to suffer like those he has accused."

"He may some day," Isabella answered. "What is your name?"

"Samuel Butler," Samuel answered.

"Have the courage of your convictions, Samuel. Mr Hopkins is not long for this world." Isabella left. Samuel Butler never saw her again.

Isabella went home and told Nicolae about what she had seen that day and her plan for Mathew Hopkins.

"Can I help you?" Nicolae asked.

"Help me what?"

"Help you kill him."

Isabella was pleased that he wanted to help; in the years they had been together he had stayed by her side but had not let her touch him. He talked to her on occasion but that was the only interaction the pair had.

"Of course," she replied. She stood and full of hope rested her hand on his arm, but Nicolae batted it away. Isabella left to go to her room; she could not stand this much longer. She turned back towards him and said.

"If I disgust you so much, you should leave." Isabella banged the door behind her.

※

Mathew Hopkins had made a fortune, but he knew it was coming to an end. The last few times his service had been called for there had not been the complete compliance that there once had been. In these ever-changing times a resistance had now developed within the communities he frequented. Theologians like John Gaule and Bishop Hutchinson were now starting to condemn the witch trials publicly. More people were standing up for themselves; it used to be that they could extract a confession out of a suspected witch just by looking at her, but now there was defiance in people's faces. They were not confessing so readily and witnesses were not as easily manipulated.

Mathew, who had earned enough money through the trials to last him the rest of his days, was quite happy to give it up. He knew things were changing; it was inevitable that this would not last, but there was another reason that he was now compelled to stop. During the last few witch trials, Hopkins had sensed a presence that he did not like. He had seen a woman in the crowds, the same face several times, and she scared him. The first time he saw her he was determined to accuse her of witchery, but just before he did, she looked over at him, smiled and shook her head. From that instant Mathew knew that to accuse this woman would cause him great harm. He was now starting to see this woman everywhere. Yet when he tried to approach her, he would always be distracted by a noise or something that would interrupt his line of vision and when he looked back she would be gone before he could speak to her. This made up Mathew's mind for him; he would not do this work anymore.

"I don't understand it," said John Stearne, his fellow witch finder. "We are making a fortune."

"I think if we carry on we will have a price to pay," Mathew replied.

"Nonsense."

"We have killed hundreds. Enough is enough. The Devil's list has no more names on it."

"You should be careful what you say," John said. "You are talking of sensing danger and the Devil's list—that is witch talk."

"Watch what you say, John," Mathew replied.

"Watch what you do, Mathew," John answered not backing down from a potential confrontation.

"I am going home. I have had enough. That is the last I have to say."

Hopkins left after this. Isabella, who was listening, went over to sit opposite John.

"Is he a witch?" Isabella asked.

"As much as anyone else we have accused," John stated. "He has noticed you."

"He was meant to," Isabella affirmed.

"What do you want me to do?" John asked.

"I want you to accuse him publicly of witchcraft."

"Why does he deserve your hatred?" John Stearne asked.

"Why does he deserve yours?"

"He is stopping what has been a very lucrative business. I don't want to let it go just yet. By accusing him I could start up for myself."

"You really are a despicable man," Isabella stated.

"Be careful; I may also accuse you."

Isabella stood and quickly flipped over the table that separated them. She kicked the chair John was sitting on and it flew back up against the wooden ballast behind him.

"Try it!" Isabella said letting John Stearne feel her strength. The next day Isabella went to see Peter Clarke, a relative of one of Mathew Hopkin's first victims.

"Everything is in place," Isabella began.

"Good, thank you for helping us."

"Don't thank me yet; wait until it is over."

Hopkins returned to Mistley, set to live a quiet life from then on. He had been troubled slightly by consumption, but it had not developed so much that it was life-threatening. And with the money he had earned he could live in comfort, and he suspected that this slight illness would fade away.

Hopkins had dabbled with potions and astrology but he had kept this a secret from every one except John Stearne. Stearne had caught him several times with various herbal remedies that they both would have considered enough to accuse a woman of being a witch, if she had them in her possession. John had kept this information to himself until a time when he could use it, and that time had now come.

Hopkins was sitting in his new home when they came for him. John broke the lock, breaking the door open. Hopkins jumped to his feet and looked over at Stearne.

"We have come for you, Mathew," John began.

"I half expected it," Mathew stated, but when he went outside he did not expect to see what he saw. He saw the families of his victims. He saw Peter Clarke, the nephew of Elizabeth Clarke, the first woman he had killed. He saw Martin Cocke and Henry Moone, husbands of women he had condemned to death. He recognised them all and he was afraid.

The crowd marched him down to the river and stripped him. Each one of them took a knife and slashed his skin as Hopkins had done to their relatives. If the wounds bled he was innocent and if they remained dry he was a witch. Every person here wanted him to be a witch. The wounds bled but they chose not to see it. They tied a rope round his waist and just before they threw him into the river Isabella whispered into his ear.

"Remember, Mathew, you have to sink; if you float, it will prove you are a witch." As the icy water hit, Mathew made no effort to swim; he knew it was pointless. He had to sink like a stone or else he would be hanged. He looked up through the murky water and saw the faces of the crowd, so like the faces of the people he had condemned to death. There was no sympathy on any of these faces, and as he lay there motionless trying to hold his breath he felt that he deserved this. He was pulled up out of the water just before the point of drowning.

"We are not going to just let you drown," Isabella stated. "You are to suffer every indignity that you put each one of these people's families through." Isabella left them and walked back towards Nicolae, who had been watching the sinister events. He continued to watch as each one of Hopkins' indirect victims dipped him into the river. Nicolae did not have Isabella's insatiable appetite for retribution.

"What good is this?" Nicolae asked.

"It is their moment of retribution; they have a right to it." Isabella answered.

"I don't see the point in this. Is this what you do? Is this how you justify your life? You are still killing without remorse."

"I have remorse over the people I killed," Isabella answered, her voice loud.

"How can you look at this and not be ashamed of what you are? A man is being tortured. It is irrelevant what he did or how he led his life, this is wrong."

Isabella turned to face Nicolae. "It is completely relevant. How can you have the audacity to talk this way to me? Let me show you how I can watch this." Isabella dragged Nicolae down to the lake where the crowd was "swimming" Mathew Hopkins. Nicolae still could not read people as Isabella could, but Isabella could help him see. She placed her hand on the first person she came to, Margaret Landish. She had confessed to witchcraft but her confession had been tortured out of her. Nicolae felt her pain as her hands were placed in the thumb screws. She had endured two days of this before she confessed.

The next one Isabella came to was a man. She again let Nicolae feel this man's pain. Stephen Weste had lived in a house that was full of caring women and he had been happy. He used to come home and listen to their laughter, but one day his wife, who worked as a midwife, was sent for. A child that she had helped bring into the world had died, under the direction of Mathew Hopkins. All the women in his family had been tortured. When they would not confess, they had been hanged. Nicolae felt this man's heartbreak as he now returned to a house that was empty.

"No more!" Nicolae shouted. "I have had enough."

"Enough? You have not had nearly enough! Look around you at all these people; there are hundreds, and they all have similar stories. Now do you have pity for him? Do you want this to stop? These people have a right to this and who are you to decide they cannot have it?"

"I'm sorry, I cannot see the things that you see them," Nicolae said, blood-red tears welling up in his eyes.

Isabella stared at Nicolae. She felt sorry for him. His senses and his strength were no match for her own. She sat down beside him and placed her arm around his shoulders and for the first time he did not shy away from her touch.

"Do you ever kill anyone that does not deserve it?" Nicolae asked.

"I try not too… but I killed you, didn't I."

"You did. Why did you?"

"I have told you before. I thought you were my husband."

"Why?"

"Because I thought I was finally dead."

"What happened to you? How did you end up like this?" Isabella decided to share some of her memories with Nicolae. She placed her hands on Nicolae's temples and Nicolae's mind was filled with a few of Isabella's selected memories.

He saw her as a young girl, the rejection she had received from her family and the love she had felt for Alexei, Katya and Nicolae. He saw Vlad killing her and Isabella killing her sister. He felt her sadness as she watched Nicolae dying in front of her and her joy when she realised that she could save him. He felt her complete devastation at Nicolae's rejection and then he saw her years with Vlad. He saw everything through Isabella's eyes and he realised that she needed him to forgive her for the things that she had done because if he did, she believed her husband would have done so and with all her essence, she needed to believe this.

Nicolae took Isabella in his arms and kissed her. Isabella was glad to feel his touch and to feel his forgiveness, but it also filled her with a sense of foreboding. She realised that she could not keep him with her…she was too afraid for him. If Vlad ever found him with her, she was sure he would kill Nicolae. She had to send him away from her.

"You have to leave here," Isabella began.

"Where will we go?"

"No, not me, just you."

"Why?"

"You saw my memories and you saw what a dangerous man Vlad is."

"That does not matter."

"I can only presume that because you do have not as much power as me that Vlad has much more power than even I have."

"But together we could kill him."

"No," Isabella retorted, "I would never conspire against him with anyone."

"Where will I go?" Nicolae said realising that she would make him leave her.

"Somewhere far away from me," Isabella thought for a moment. "The new world! I am constantly hearing about how well humans do when they go out there. It should be easy for a Vampire to succeed."

"Will I ever see you again?"

"I don't know… I hope so." The crowd that were inflicting their retribution on Hopkins had finished and Hopkins was dangling at the end of a rope. John Stearne walked towards Isabella.

"It is finished," said Stearne.

"It's not."

"What do you mean?"

"I mean you are just as responsible for the deaths that occurred."

"So what is going to happen to me?" Stearne said nervously.

"Nothing…yet, but I will be watching you. Never forget that."

"I am not afraid of you." At this Nicolae jumped up and struck John. He fell to the ground, blood pouring from an open wound.

"You should be," Nicolae stated.

"I will be watching you," Isabella reasserted. John stood up and started to run away from Isabella and Nicolae. "John!" Isabella shouted after him. He paused in spite of himself and turned around to face her. "I promise I will be back for you." John, petrified by the two Vampires, began running again. This time he did not stop.

Years later John awoke up in the middle of the night; sweat pouring from his brow.

"She is coming for me," he said to his wife, Mary.

"Who?" his wife asked him.

"The Vampire," he answered. His wife looked at him in amazement. She thought he had gone mad.

The next day she called the doctor to examine him.

"I think he is losing his mind," she began. "He is constantly whispering about a Vampire and that she is coming for him." The pair's conversation was interrupted by screaming coming from his room.

"She is here!" In response to the terrified shout the doctor and John's wife ran upstairs. "She is here," he repeated. John's wife and doctor looked around the room.

As far as they could see it was completely empty. John's eyes were darting about all over the room as if he was following something with his gaze, but yet the other two people could see nothing.

"A madness has come over him, just as it did with his father," his wife said.

"He looks absolutely terrified of something," the doctor said.

John quickly got up out of the bed, grabbed a knife from his breakfast tray and started slashing the air. He came within inches of cutting his wife.

"You can't live with him like this," the doctor warned. "He will have to go to a place where he can receive proper care."

The next day the doctor returned, he brought with him two other men to aid him in restraining John. When John saw them he was frightened, even more frightened than he was of Isabella. He was suddenly filled with memories that he thought were completely forgotten. His father had been sent to the madman's prison, as his mother had called it. He remembered the smell of it, the dark dismal corridors, and the iron gates keeping the mad in. His father had died there and for the first time John Stearne, like Mathew Hopkins before him, knew his own fate. Isabella was there of course, although she had let only John see her. When she had met him so many years before, she had known just how to punish him. As he was forced to walk down the stairs he heard Isabella laughing. His wife, the doctor and the other two men were still completely oblivious to Isabella's presence.

"You are going to die in the madhouse like your father," Isabella shouted.

"No!" he screamed out.

"Believe me you are going to die surrounded by madness and lunacy, alone and forgotten." Isabella left the broken man to his punishment. It was an unwilling penance for his life, which had been dedicated to the persecution of those who had done nothing.

※

Isabella watched as the boat pulled out of the harbour with Nicolae on it. She was sorry to see him leave, but she knew he could not stay with her. The previous day he had begged to stay but he knew it was pointless. Isabella believed Vlad would hunt him down and kill him if he stayed with her. Isabella lay beside him watching him sleep. She so wanted him to stay but she could not watch Nicolae die again. She lay with her head on his chest listening for a heartbeat that was no longer there.

The next evening Nicolae awoke before Isabella did. He lay there watching her sleep. When Isabella awoke, he smiled and kissed her.

"This is stupid," he insisted. "I am quite sure I can take care of myself."

"I know you can, but I have tried and failed too many times to protect people close to me,"

"So it is the Americas then?"

"It is, and believe me, I have no doubt that you will soon forget me."

"I will try to forget you; it should be easy," Nicolae said with a smile. Isabella returned his smile; he was trying to be humorous for her sake as well as his own. They got dressed and walked to the pier. Nicolae left with the money Isabella had given to him and he climbed up onto the boat.

As the boat pulled away from the harbour, Isabella was heartbroken. She knew it was the right thing to do, but it meant several more lifetimes in which she would be completely alone. She projected her thoughts into Nicolae's mind: "*I love you.*" Nicolae jumped onto the side of the boat and blew her a kiss.

Isabella turned away. It was too hard for her to watch anymore. As she turned, she saw a face she recognised standing in the crowd. She could not believe her eyes. The woman was younger, but Isabella still recognised her—it was Leila, Nicolae's first victim. How had she survived?

QUIA MORTUI NON MORDENT
FOR THE DEAD DO NOT BITE

CHAPTER FIFTEEN

Isabella could not believe her eyes. When Leila died she was not the young woman Isabella saw before her. The woman Isabella had taken back for Nicolae to kill was a woman in her forties. Now as Isabella looked at her, she looked twenty. Leila smiled at Isabella, which enraged her and Isabella ran to face her. Leila started to run away but Isabella was much swifter and soon caught up with her.

"What has happened to you?" Isabella knew the answer to her own question but she asked it nevertheless. Leila made no vocal response but lunged out at Isabella trying to bite her neck. Isabella was almost amused by Leila's attempt at an attack. Before Leila could get within biting distance Isabella struck her cheek. Leila was thrust back through the air and landed fifty feet away. Isabella was back by Leila's side again before Leila could even get back up. "Don't be stupid!" Isabella said fiercely and pressed her foot on Leila's stomach, keeping her on the ground. "You couldn't possibly hurt me. Vlad must not have told you very much about me or you would not have dared to confront me." Isabella said.

"He told me enough," Leila answered sharply.

"Did he? Why are you here? Have you been sent to spy on me?"

"No, he doesn't care what you do or where you are."

"Good… then why are you here?"

"I came to track you down."

"Track me down," Isabella laughed. "What on earth for? You must know you can't kill me."

"I can—I have the Dhampir's blood." These words resonated through Isabella's mind. Had Vlad sent this creature to try and kill her? She couldn't believe it and she seized Leila's arm, dragging her on to her feet.

"Tell me the truth." Isabella said, twisting Leila's arm behind her back. Leila screamed out in pain. "How did you get the blood?"

"He gave it to me."

"You lie." Isabella tried to read her but couldn't. Vampires were always hard to read.

"It's true, he wants you dead." At this the crowd who had been going about their business suddenly noticed the two women fighting and came running up to them, pulling Isabella back. Isabella could easily have overpowered them but she did not to demonstrate her strength so publicly. Several members of the crowd started to enquire if Leila was all right, as it had looked to these people that Isabella had been attacking Leila with complete malice. Isabella was still being held back watched as they led Leila away. Isabella knew Leila was no match for her but if Vlad did want her dead he would find a way to kill her, and she would not be able to stop him. Isabella would have to be careful. For the first time in a long time Isabella was frightened. Surprisingly she wanted to live; the possible threat of death had made that apparent to her. She wanted to hang on to this existence, lonely though it was.

Years before Vlad had stumbled across Leila's nearly dead body.

He had been watching Isabella from a distance. He had seen her jump off the cliff and wanted to make sure she was all right. He saw a young man find Isabella and watched with delight as Isabella killed this man, but his delight soon turned to fury as he witnessed her saving his life by turning him. He continued to watch as Isabella ran to get a victim for Nicolae to feed on.

Isabella had left the young man alone, something she would not have done had she known that Vlad was watching her. Vlad was determined to kill him but as he approached him, his determination dissipated. Nicolae, who was writhing in agony, was completely oblivious to Vlad's presence. When Vlad saw his face he noticed a striking resemblance. He realised why Isabella had chosen to save this man, when she had sworn she would never try to turn anyone else. Vlad did not see Nicolae, only Isabella—he saw her raven hair and her green eyes staring up from this man's face. Vlad could not bring himself to touch a hair of his head. He crept back into the woods and watched for Isabella to return. He saw her carrying a middle-aged woman who was kicking and screaming. Vlad continued to watch

VROLOK

as Isabella slit open Leila's wrist and let Nicolae drain the blood from her body. After Nicolae's appetite was subdued, the pair left.

Vlad approached the woman and leaned down to look her, her eyes were shut. Vlad presumed she was dead. Then suddenly the woman's eyes opened. She clasped Vlad's wrist and bit down hard. Vlad was amazed but he did not pull away; he let her drink, he needed a companion as well and if it wasn't to be Isabella, one woman was as good as the next. As she drank she grew younger and a scar that was on her cheek started to smooth and heal before Vlad's eyes. She was now fully revived and smiled up at Vlad, a nefarious smile. This woman was no innocent creature—blackness and jealousy surrounded her. Vlad led her back to the castle and when she entered she looked around Vlad's home with enthusiasm. Leila felt she finally was where she belonged in this world.

"Is this to be my home?" she enquired.

"If you want it to be," Vlad answered. He was truly ambivalent as to whether she stayed or left him.

"I do, I really do," Leila said with eagerness. Vlad was pleased to see a woman that was enthusiastic about living with him even if he knew she was only enthusiastic about him because of what he could give her.

"How did you know to drink from me?" Vlad asked out of curiosity.

"I had been raised here and in Hungary. I have heard rumours and whispers about Vroloks as long as I can remember. I knew to drink your blood would restore my own life and grant me immortality."

"So in spite of Isabella's efforts to the contrary we are still renowned throughout this region."

"Isabella—who is she?"

"She is the woman who killed you." Leila's near constant smile melted away.

"She left me for dead."

"She did, but never mind, you didn't die." Leila kept silent. She was filled with thoughts of revenge and she wanted to kill this woman, but she kept silent. Even after her brief acquaintance with Vlad, she knew he would never let her exact her revenge on the woman who had killed her.

The days passed, still quite slowly for Vlad, but he was finding comfort in this woman's company. She took pleasure in the kill as Isabella had once done and best of all she did not argue with Vlad; she was there when he wanted her and left him alone when he didn't. She was a perfect consort for him, but yet she was still not his Isabella and never would be.

Vlad constantly toyed with the idea of chasing after Isabella but he knew it was pointless, but as time went by his longing to see her overcame his will and he couldn't stand it anymore—he had to find her. He heard a rumour that she had gone back to England and he decided to try and find her there. He eventually tracked her down to an inn in Plymouth. He paid the innkeeper to gain access to her room and when he entered he saw her lying in the arms of the man she had saved. Vlad was devastated, but still he knew enough to know that if there was ever the possible chance of Isabella's forgiveness he would have to leave this man alone. He left in torment and returned to where he was staying with Leila. He went into his room grasping at a bottle of ale as he walked through the door.

"Did you find her?" Leila asked.

"I did," Vlad shouted back at her angrily. "What business is it of yours?"

"What has upset you?" Leila asked.

"It is none of your concern what has upset me," Vlad said, still angry. Leila paused for moment before she replied to him. Vlad by now had finished the bottle he was drinking and went to get another one.

"You have seen her?" Leila asked again.

"I have!" Vlad shouted, throwing the second empty bottle against the wall in frustration. It narrowly missed Leila's head.

"I take it she was well?" Leila said sarcastically.

"She has taken up with one of her own descendants. It's incestuous."

"The man who killed me?"

"Yes." Dracula took another drink; he was quickly losing his reason and his self-control.

"Well what are you going to do about it?"

"What do you mean?" Vlad asked taking another drink.

"How are you going to pay her back for her disloyalty?"

"I can't do anything to him. Unfortunately, Isabella completely overreacts when I kill her acquaintances," Vlad smiled wryly.

"Not to him, to her?" asked Leila.

Vlad looked over at Leila and waved his bottle of ale in her direction before replying. "I should... I should take the Dhampir's blood and end her life as she has begged me to do before." Leila's was now very interested in Vlad's drunken rambles- Dhampir's blood—he had never talked about this before.

"What did you say? Dhampir's blood, what do you mean?" she asked.

Vlad leapt from where he was sitting and snatched at Leila's throat. "Why are you asking me so many questions?" Vlad tightened his grip and Leila could feel his strength. It was far greater than her own and he was causing her great pain. She yelped out and begged him to stop. Dracula relinquished his grip on her and she dropped to the floor.

"You disgust me." said Vlad. "Your constant chattering and asking questions. Do you know what you look like with your fine hair, your pale eyes, your thin lips? I should have let you die. Why can't you be more like her?" With this Vlad fell back and struck his head on the floor, knocking himself out.

Leila was devastated by Vlad's cutting speech. She had never been a woman who could tolerate being rejected for another. Her hatred for Isabella was once again confirmed.

Leila searched their lodgings for the blood and she soon found an old ornate dusty bottle. She dabbed her finger into its contents. A sharp pain seared up through her whole hand as if she had dipped her finger in acid. This must be the secret, she thought, and she poured out a little into an empty bottle of ale. She knew enough to know that Vlad would follow her if she took all the contents. Leila left the inn with the intention of never seeing Vlad again; she had had enough of him. The next day she went searching for Isabella. She eventually found her walking with Nicolae, delivering him to the boat to America.

AMERICA, THOU HALF-BROTHER OF THE WORLD WITH SOMETHING GOOD AND BAD OF EVERY LAND

CHAPTER SIXTEEN

Isabella and Simon descended from the ship onto new soil. They had traveled in a state of luxury that Simon had never known. The long sea voyage had resulted in an outbreak of an unexplained illness that left the ship's doctor baffled. A loss of colour and fatigue were the only symptoms but death was very often the result. As Isabella and Simon walked from the pier onto dry land, ten coffins were being carried after them.

Isabella looked around this strange new world. She was never one to be overly affected by new places, but Simon was in awe. The streets were crowded with people busily attending to their business, not stopping for a moment, everyone in a hurry rushing towards their next destination as if once they got there, the sooner they would be able to start towards the next, for they had not a moment to waste.

Simon was amazed by the place and the sights he saw. He was distracted from the fast moving crowds, by the buildings that lined the outer edges of the streets. They were more than five stories tall and were not narrow like the stone houses and halls of Europe but fat, long and wooden, towering up into the sky. No two buildings were the same; each had its own character and texture. Simon looked ahead of him at the people who had gotten off the ship before him. They seemed to be just disappearing into the crowd; it was as if once you walked off the pier you became an American.

"I think you will need me more than five years," Simon said.

"What do you mean?" Isabella asked.

"There are literally thousands people in this place."

"More like hundreds of thousands," Isabella answered.

"How can we possibly find one man in the vastness of this country?" Simon stated; still trying to get to grips with what his eyes were seeing. Isabella walked towards a young boy heralding the news and asked for a broadsheet. She smiled and showed Simon the headline.

"Death toll reaches one hundred thousand in Civil War."

"There is where we shall find him, where the fighting is," Isabella stated.

"Why are you so sure?" Simon asked.

"One thing you have to learn about Vampires, they go where death is."

Isabella was right; Nicolae was in the thick of the fighting. He had come to America two hundred years before and seen it change before his eyes. This was a country whose short history was steeped in violence, the perfect place for a Vampire. When he arrived it was not long before the French Indian Wars started. He witnessed the implementation of the Stamp Act which made the colonists rise up against the British because of the heavy taxes. The War of Independence soon followed and after America had rid itself of British authority, its people soon turned on their neighbours in the Mexican War. Then finally they turned on each other in the Civil War. Nicolae moved from place to place and war to war, not wanting to stay too long in one vicinity. Isabella had taught him this in their brief acquaintance and her nomadic lifestyle had rubbed off on him. Isabella had told him to go where there was war, famine or disease, places that were steeped in death.

"Who would miss one hundred when thousands are dying?" Isabella had said to him. But even if she hadn't, Nicolae enjoyed wars and America had had her fair share of them.

Nicolae had fought on all sides. Many years before he had abandoned Isabella's principals of only killing those who deserved it. He could not read people like Isabella and enjoyed the kill far too much to be bothered to find out who his victims were and whether they deserved the death he was giving them. His own conscience was appeased by the fact that none of his victims suffered, for he did not draw out their deaths. But even if this were not true the sensation that feeding gave him was far too much pleasure. He felt alive when he fed—he felt omnipotent.

Nicolae had stayed alone, not turning to anyone for companionship. Isabella had told him how to infect a human with vampirism but he had chosen not to propagate any Vampires. He wanted to drift with no one following after him and he didn't want Isabella, if she ever came looking for him to find him with anyone.

Nicolae would stand at night and look out across the wide-open spaces of America, searching the skyline for some sign of Isabella, but she never came, she was never there, not even in the distance.

Even though he had watched for her for two hundred years and had seen no earthly sign of her, he was convinced she was now close. For a year ago something had changed within him. He had always been stronger than he was in life, much stronger and he had selected abilities that no mortal could ever possess. The sun however could burn his skin very quickly and irritated him greatly. He could not expose himself to it at all as his skin would blister and burn, but that had now changed. He could freely walk around in the sunshine. His sight was still impaired, but that was all. His strength had increased as well and he had several new abilities that he had not possessed before. Among them, he could control the weather. When he touched people, if he concentrated, he would get glimpses of their lives. Nicolae thought that this newfound strength and resistance to the rays of the sun must mean that Isabella was close to him. The only time he had seen other people's thoughts before was when she was with him. He hoped that this meant she was trying to find him. He made his actions as obvious as he possibly could, letting those who knew such things existed be aware of the fact that he was a Vampire.

※

Nicolae had been involved in every major battle in the Civil War and Gettysburg was no exception. He was travelling with the Confederate Cavalry, eagerly anticipating the next battle. His troops were searching desperately for shoes when they came across a hub of union soldiers. A battle broke out and it was the most feral one in which Nicolae had been involved. The night after the first day of fighting Nicolae walked through the campsite; he was looking for his next victim. He headed towards the makeshift hospital. The smell of death engulfed the tent, Nicolae smiled; he knew there would be plenty to curb his appetite, judging by the screams of the soldiers. Some might even be willing victims. Nicolae crept in under cover of darkness and meandered in-between the victims, drinking his fill. He had become a merciless killer and little did he know Isabella was watching him.

"He is killing everyone," Simon stated. Isabella and Simon were watching Nicolae fight in the continuing battle the next day.

"He is, isn't he?" Isabella said; she was pleased by his insatiable appetite.

"You approve?" Simon asked.

"I most certainly do. Remember, you are consorting with Vampires, Simon. Your human morality has no place here."

"I know, but he kills with such savagery; you are more humane." Simon said, trying to convince himself that this was true.

"Humane, that is one thing I certainly am not. Don't be fooled Simon, I am worse than him." Isabella turned towards Simon to face him. "Much worse," she emphasized. Isabella's words were so chilling Simon broke out into a cold sweat. He was suddenly reminded of what sort of a creature Isabella was. They both turned back towards the fighting and continued to watch the brutal scene.

Nicolae was running from union soldier to union soldier, slashing them with his sabre and catching the body before it had time to fall to the ground, drinking as much blood as he could before anyone noticed him. His face and Confederate uniform were soaked through with blood. The field was filled with smoke from the explosions of the cannon. The echoing bangs of gunfire were heard in every corner. A stray bullet struck Nicolae, it only managed to knock him off his feet and in seconds he was standing again. A few more seconds passed by and he was killing again. Isabella watched with pride. His blood lust was even greater than her own used to be; he was perfect, she thought.

"He will suit fine for my purposes," Isabella smiled again. "Come on, we have seen enough." Isabella waited for the battle to be over and then approached Nicolae.

Nicolae had walked away from the field exhausted and drenched in blood. He approached a lake, stripped off his blood-soaked uniform and dived in. He swam underneath the surface, not needing to come up for air. He swam through the clear water cleaning the blood from his body that he hadn't managed to consume. Nicolae ultimately brought his head back above the water; he had not seen her, yet. Isabella was sitting on a tree stump behind him.

"You have forgotten everything I taught you," Isabella scolded. Nicolae did not turn around completely; he merely turned his head slightly in the direction of the voice. Nicolae smiled, he knew who the voice belonged to.

"I knew you were here," Nicolae answered.

"You did?"

"I could sense you," Nicolae answered.

"You could?" Isabella smiled. "I don't know that I approve of your method of killing. It was so open, not exactly inconspicuous."

"Do you realise how long I have been waiting for you?" Nicolae stated ignoring Isabella's meagre attempt at chastising him.

"Two hundred years," Isabella answered. Nicolae now turned towards her. He wanted to look upon her unchanged face. He climbed out of the water and Isabella tossed him a fresh uniform. "It was a Union Uniform. I am presuming you do not care what uniform you have on," Isabella continued.

"You presume right."

"I thought so," Isabella said, shaking her head, feigning exasperation with her young protégé.

"What about you, still only killing those who deserve it?" Nicolae asked as he was getting dressed.

"No, I have reverted to my former wicked self," Isabella smiled. It was as if they had never been apart.

"What made you revert to your old ways?"

"I will explain everything, but not tonight." The pair left the battlefield arm and arm. Nicolae believed only death would ever separate them again.

※

Isabella had found her Nicolae in America, Simon was no longer needed and Isabella was happy to send him back to his family. His debt and their debt had now been paid in full.

Simon awoke to an empty room, free from Vampires. On his bedside table was a letter from Isabella with an envelope beside it. A train ticket and a ticket for the ship journey home were both in the envelope, along with several bank notes totaling a thousand pounds. Isabella had taught Simon how to read; she had joked that no husband of hers was going to be illiterate. Simon had been more than keen to learn, as it was something he could pass on to his children. Simon impatiently started to read the letter.

"*Simon,*" it began. *"As you know I have found the person I came here to find. Your debt to me has been paid. I thank you for your companionship and you can travel home to your family with no fear of any Vrolok threat ever again. I promise you that neither I nor any of my kind will ever harm you or any member of your family. When you get home, look for a blue ring of fire and dig up the box underneath the ground, the money you find in it is your second reward. Take it with you, with my gratitude. Look after your family, Simon, and have a good life."*

Simon read the letter with just a little sadness in his heart; he had grown to admire Isabella. She had treated him with nothing but respect. He had to often remind himself that she was a killer. Now she had made it possible for him to return to the Carpathians with money, pride and honour. He would have a good life and he swore to honour her memory and if she ever called on him again, he would willingly help her, no matter what she asked.

FOR MERCY HAS A HUMAN HEART

CHAPTER SEVENTEEN

It had been twenty years since Isabella had put Nicolae on the boat to America. She had abandoned Katya's family during this time and felt that she had to go back. She was incredibly lonely, but even so she was loathe to go back to the Carpathians. She never wanted to be close to Vlad ever again.

Isabella knew Katalin would have been dead for a long time; therefore, Isabella entered the house not knowing who she would find there. It was night and the family which now occupied the place were all asleep. Isabella walked into the back room of the house and looked at the man and woman who were sleeping there. She remembered that Katalin had told her that she had had no daughters. Isabella placed her hand on the temple of the man lying with his arm draped over his wife. She wanted to see if this man had inherited any of his mother's murderous instincts. She was relieved to find that the worst thing this man was guilty of was lusting over a woman that was not his wife. Isabella leaned down and whispered in the man's ear.

"Wake up." He woke up instantly and looked at Isabella. "Follow me outside," Isabella asked. The man got up without any resistance and followed the Vampire outside his home. Isabella could sense he was somewhat nervous but that he had known this day would eventually come and he had been prepared for it. "What's your name?" Isabella asked.

"Havel."

"Do you know who I am?"

"Yes I do," Havel answered.

"Good." Isabella looked up at the castle. "Is he up there?" Isabella asked.

"No one has seen him for years," Havel answered.

"Are any bodies being found?" Isabella enquired.

"No, not that I have seen, definitely not any Slovaks." Isabella found this somewhat surprising but she was still pleased that no Slovaks were being killed. She knew they were useful to Vlad as guardians of Vampires and no doubt that was the only reason that Vlad was not killing them. It was certainly not through any loyalty to her.

"Good."

"What do you want from me?" Havel asked.

"Nothing that will tax you too much. I want the Slovaks to be loyal to Vampires, even him; and none of you will ever be harmed, I will make sure of it."

"We are loyal," said Havel.

"Good, continue to be." Havel was trying to gather up the courage to tell Isabella what he needed to.

"It is causing us some trouble…"

"Trouble?" Isabella enquired.

"Yes, the other people in this region accuse us of colluding with the Devil."

Isabella smiled. "I suppose you are."

"They curse our name; we are becoming alienated from the other settlers here."

"Would you prefer the alternative?" Isabella said.

"No, of course not."

"Then what are you asking?"

"I want you to visit us a little more often."

Isabella sighed. "I don't want to come back here anymore than I have to. I have had enough of this place."

"Isabella, you owe it to us." Isabella looked at the man who dared to confront her. There was nothing of his mother about him but he had a faint look of Katya that shone through in his defiance and Isabella smiled.

"You dare to tell me what to do?" Isabella took a step towards him and Havel stepped back. His courage momentarily left him.

"It was only a request," Havel said nervously. "I am well aware that I can't tell you to do anything." As Havel continued talking his voice was getting stronger, his conviction getting more resolute as he spoke. He was determined to stand up to the Vampire and say his piece. "We have given you so much and you have not given anything back to us."

"I have let you live," Isabella said to test if he could be intimidated by her. She took another step towards him so that she was practically touching him. Havel stood his ground determined to have the courage of his convictions. "You certainly did not get your courage from your mother; she would have sold her kin to save herself."

"Please do not speak ill of my mother," Havel said a nervous tremor echoing through out his voice.

"You are quite right. I should not denounce her in front of you; she was your mother after all."

"Thank you."

Isabella shrugged as if she was completely nonchalant about his thanks. "Well, I have been put in my place," Isabella said sarcastically. "I will visit you at least every two years," she relented.

"Thank you again."

Isabella nodded. The pair stood for a moment in silence; since they had come outside, Isabella had not been able to pull her gaze away from the castle.

"I have decided I want a favour from you in return," Isabella resumed.

"What is it?" Isabella motioned up to the top of the woods. She wanted to see it one last time but she did not want to face that place alone.

"Will you go up to the castle with me?" Isabella said, revealing a vulnerability that she had never revealed before.

"I will." Havel nodded. He was curious to see it himself and he would have never ventured up there with anyone other than Isabella, for he knew she would protect him.

Isabella walked slowly up through the forest, towards the castle, with Havel at her side. The wind rustled through the trees; the icy nighttime breeze blew against her skin, as if even the very winds were telling her not to go back there. She went into the courtyard and remembered the first day she had come through these gates and saw the wolf. She remembered how innocent and naive she had been and asked herself if she had to do it all over again, would she? She smiled to herself, realising she probably would.

"The first time I came here must be more than two hundred years ago," she began. "Your ancestor Katya was with me. She warned me never to come back here, and she was, as always, right. I never should have come up here again. My life would have been so…different."

"And so much shorter," Havel interrupted.

"When you have lived the life that I have, you realise that time is the only thing that belongs to you, and it is an empty possession."

"I am not so sure. Having only another five, perhaps ten years left of my life, I think I would give a lot for another lifetime," Havel answered. "I would like a little more time to see some of the things you have seen." Isabella did not respond. She got up and walked through the stone archway.

The door was lying open, and Isabella continued cautiously into the grand hall. She ran her hand over the armchair that sat in front of the fire; she had sat here so often, at first reading by herself and then with Vlad. It was now a cold and icy place. Dust and cobwebs had gathered in every corner. Vlad had not been here for years. Isabella looked up over the fireplace to see her portrait but it was missing. She wondered where it had gone; he had probably destroyed it she thought, as he had destroyed the picture of his wife.

"Are there any rumours as to where he is?" Isabella asked. Her voice echoed through the empty hall.

"None."

"No doubt he will turn up eventually," Isabella responded.

"Why did you leave him?"

"He would not let me have any company but his own; he went to extreme lengths to ensure that I didn't have any other."

"Surely his company would be better than this total isolation?"

"It probably would, but I am a stubborn woman."

"Surely it is not just stubbornness that keeps you away?"

"You are right; the truth is he did something to me that I can never forgive him for even if I wanted to."

"What did he do?"

"He killed my husband, and in doing that he didn't let me have a chance to see if Nicolae could have forgiven me for what I had done. I will never know if he could have learned to love me again."

"My mother told me you killed your husband."

"No, I tried to save him. Vlad killed him and now he is trying to kill me; he sent a woman to kill me a few years ago."

"Has he made any other attempt?"

"No, not yet, but I wait for him to finish what he started." Wind rustled through the hallway and a door blew shut. Havel and Isabella were now standing in total darkness. The castle just stood as an empty relic; there was nothing here for Isabella anymore. "I have seen enough of this place," Isabella said. Havel and Isabella left the castle.

Isabella was true to her word and she visited Katya's family every two years without fail and made sure they were content and safe from harm. Havel passed his duty on to Josef, his son. Josef passed the mantle to Rada, his daughter and Rada passed it on to Nadezhda, her daughter.

Nadezhda was a young and pretty girl, full of joy. She touched the heart of everyone she encountered. Isabella, like the others who knew Nadezhda, was bewitched by her. Nadezhda looked upon Isabella with nothing but either sympathy or kindness. All the other members of Katya's family, even Katya herself, had looked upon Isabella with a certain amount of fear and mistrust. Isabella always knew that none of them ever forgot what she was, but Nadezhda was different. She didn't even act afraid of Isabella. She was as close to being a perfectly good person as Isabella had ever known. Isabella had never known her mother, Clara, but had always imagined that if she had known her, she would have been just like Nadezhda, seeing goodness in everyone and everything.

Nadezhda had a young family and was loved deeply by her husband. Such a soul could only be deeply loved by anyone she knew. Isabella visited Nadezhda a little more often than any other member of Katya's family. Nadezhda made her feel like part of this family and she enjoyed this feeling.

One winter Isabella had decided to visit Nadezhda a month before she was expected. Nadezhda greeted Isabella with a smile and brought her into the house as usual. Nadezhda motioned for Isabella to sit down. Isabella sat on the seat and Nadezhda placed her young baby son on Isabella's knee. Isabella was amazed at the trust Nadezhda placed in her. Isabella bounced the child on her lap and the child giggled to himself. Nadezhda watched Isabella and made an observation.

"You are good with children," Nadezhda commented. "You had child of your own, didn't you?"

"That was a long time ago," Isabella answered.

"I don't think it was so very long ago in your eyes," Nadezhda answered.

"It was several life times ago and I only saw my son three times."

"That must have been awful for you, not seeing your own child."

"It was better than the alternative."

"Nonsense," Nadezhda scolded. Nadezhda was incapable of seeing any maliciousness in anyone, especially not Isabella. There was a knock at the door and Nadezhda went to answer it. When she opened the door there was no one there.

"That's strange," Nadezhda said.

"Who was there?" Isabella asked.

"No one," Isabella listened. She heard whispering coming from outside. Two women were talking.

"I am hungry," said one.

"So am I," the other hissed.

"Shut the door," Isabella called out suddenly to Nadezhda. Nadezhda did as the Vampire asked, sensing the urgency in Isabella's voice.

"What is wrong?" Nadezhda asked.

"Be quiet," Isabella said trying to listen to the pair out side.

"Isabella, what is wrong?" Nadezhda asked again.

"Take your child into the back room and don't make a sound," Isabella said firmly. Isabella continued to listen to the two whispering outside.

"So hungry, come out of the house, come out of the house." There was a hypnotic quality in these women's voices that only Isabella could distinguish. Moments flew in complete silence. Isabella was getting increasingly nervous; she thought that Vlad had sent these creatures for her. If she went outside, would they be holding Dhampir's blood, lying in wait to kill her? The silence was soon to be interrupted by a smash coming from the room that Nadezhda and her child occupied. Isabella shuddered; she now feared for Nadezhda.

Isabella quickly ran into the other room; the shutter that was covering the window was flapping in the breeze. Isabella could hardly bring herself to look at the floor. She lowered her gaze and she saw the unthinkable. The baby was lying on the floor crying for his mother and there were two Vampires feeding on Nadezhda.

"Get away from her," Isabella shouted. The two Vampires looked up at Isabella, astounded that anyone was daring to tell them what to do. Isabella lunged at the demonic pair and dragged them both back by the hair. The two Vampires were clawing at Isabella trying to injure her. They felt Isabella's strength and when she let go of them they ran from the house and back up to the castle. Nadezhda's husband, who had heard the raucous and the baby crying from outside ran into his bedroom. Isabella was sitting beside Nadezhda, stunned by what had happened. Nadezhda's husband lifted up his dying wife and looked at Isabella.

"Did you do this?" he screamed at Isabella.

"No, it was not Isabella," Nadezhda said her breathing getting fainter, her life slowly ebbing away.

"I can save her," Isabella stated in desperation.

"How?" Nadezhda's husband asked.

"By making her... like me." Nadezhda's husband looked at his dying wife and she shook her head.

"No, she does not want that," he said. Nadezhda let out one final gasp and shut her eyes forever. "No," Nadezhda's husband cried out. Isabella got up and left the room. As she was about to go out through the door Nadezhda's husband asked.

"Where are you going?"

"To kill the Vampires who killed her," Isabella said.

"I am coming with you."

Isabella turned to face Nadezhda's distraught husband.

"No. I will not be able to protect you from them. Think of your child—who will look after him?"

"I don't care; I have to avenge my wife. I can't just stay here and raise my son as if nothing has happened."

"I will avenge her for you; none of them will live through this night. Stay here and raise your son." Nadezhda's husband took hold of Isabella's hand before she could leave.

"You will show them no mercy?" he asked.

"I will show them no mercy. For mercy has a human heart."

Isabella left the Nadezhda's home. She ran up through the forest; as she grew close to the castle she heard voices, all female. Isabella ran through the courtyard and approached the solid wooden door. She threw out one fist against the door and it flew off its hinges, hitting the ground with a thud and then sliding across the stone floor until it came to an eventual stop.

The Vampires inside the castle all heard the door slamming down against the stone floor. They quickly gathered in the hall to face Isabella. There must have been twenty of them, all hissing at Isabella like frightened cats. Isabella ran to fetch her grandfather's sword which was standing by the fire. And there on top of the fireplace was what remained of the Dhampir's blood. Isabella smashed the top off the bottle and poured the blood over the blade of the sword.

The Vampires were circling her, they were not afraid yet. Isabella was ready for them. The Dhampir's blood dripped off the edge of the blade. Isabella stood with her sword out in front of her.

"You cannot harm us," one of them hissed at Isabella.

"We'll see," Isabella answered them. She spun round, and a few loose droplets of blood flew off the sword and hit some of the Vampires. It burnt their skin and they stepped back from Isabella; pain was a sensation they had not expected. One of them, a little braver than the others, tried to jump at Isabella. Isabella retaliated by striking out with the sword and she slashed through this Vampire from the waist to the shoulder and the body fell to the floor in two pieces.

The others looked at their dead sister and were amazed. They began to get frightened now and some of them tried to run, but Isabella was too fast for them. She swung the sword around above her head. Two of the Vampires' heads fell to the ground. Isabella continued killing them with what seemed like little effort. The last one ran up the stairs and Isabella chased after her and caught her by the leg. The pursued Vampire fell to the ground and Isabella plunged the sword through her neck. She pulled the blade from the Vampire's body with such a force that her head, now completely severed, rolled down the stairs.

The last of these creatures was dead. Isabella, drenched in blood and exhausted, heard someone move behind her. She spun round with the intention of cutting whoever it was to ribbons but she stopped inches before the blade could strike their skin. Isabella froze as she caught sight of Vlad Dracula.

"You hesitate. Believe me, I would not," Vlad said.

Isabella just stared at him, thoughts racing through her mind. It was as if she had just seen a ghost from her past; a chill ran up her spine. She was tempted to kill him; she was tempted to end it. Isabella drew back the sword and Vlad closed his eyes fully expecting Isabella's next lunge to kill him. A few moments passed. Vlad felt the rush of air as Isabella spun around again. But then he heard a clatter as the sword struck the floor.

He opened his eyes and saw she had gone. The sword with the Dhampir's blood lay motionless on the stony floor. Vlad wiped the blade clean. There was no more blood to poison Vampires. No more Vampires could die; Isabella and Vlad were both safe from harm forever, or so he thought.

S'IL Y A DANS TOUT LE MONDE CELUI HISTOIRE EXAMINÉE ELLE EST CELLE DES VAMPIRES
IF THERE IS IN THE WORLD ONE ATTESTED STORY IT IS THAT OF THE VAMPIRES

CHAPTER EIGHTEEN

After her confrontation with Vlad, Isabella left the Carpathians determined once again never to return. She started to travel again, always looking over her shoulder to see if Vlad or Leila was chasing her. She didn't regret letting Vlad live but she suspected that he would follow her and when he caught up with her, he would not show her the same consideration that she had showed him. Isabella did not know who he was anymore; perhaps she never had, but she was now sure that she could not predict his actions and she had to be constantly on her guard.

Nadezhda's death had hardened Isabella. She realised the truth about what she was, that she was a cold-blooded killer, a Vampire, a Vrolok. Even when she behaved, in her eyes without question she was still a danger to those around her. The only thing she could offer anyone was death. She would no longer try to appease her conscience by discriminating between those she killed or didn't kill. What good did it do? Isabella willingly and quickly returned to her old ways, the altruistic period in her existence completely over, and once more she killed without feeling or conscience. She learned to enjoy it again.

Isabella travelled west, up through Hungary, through Switzerland and then to France. After a few years had passed she chose to live in Versailles. She had always influenced her way into court and the court in Versailles was no exception. She had with little effort become a regular attendee at the French palace. It was the most ostentatious court Isabella had ever seen, even more so than Elizabeth's court in England, so many years before.

The hall of mirrors had been commissioned by the "Sun King" a century earlier. It was exquisite, stretching the length of the palace, and crystal chandeliers hung from the fresco covered ceiling. The east wall was veiled in mirrors. Each mirror was framed in marble and the marble was set in gold. It was a place that only the truly beautiful, or those who thought themselves truly beautiful, could appreciate; as they walked through seeing their reflection from all angles. It made Isabella slightly sad that she couldn't see her likeness in such a place. Isabella only walked through it at night when no one else could see either her, or her lack of reflection. She sometimes would stare at the mirrors hoping for just glimpse of her own image, but it never appeared to her and she knew it never would.

Despite its beauty and elegance, the court of Louis XVI and Marie Antoinette was very different from any she had been in before. Isabella had hardly been noticed at all. This place was concerned with much graver things than a beautiful stranger. There was a visible sense of uneasiness than ran throughout the court and it was obvious to any visitor. But Isabella could see deeper and lying beneath this uneasy surface there was a deep sense of fear. Every day, more and more people, were deserting this place. Kings and Queens loved to surround themselves with people but this palace was now nearly empty. Even the King's own brother the Comte d'Artois, sensing the danger that everyone who belonged to the hereditary nobility felt, had fled.

Isabella, not finding enough victims within the court to quench her insatiable blood lust often ventured a little distance away, out into Parisian streets. The people of Paris were bitter and disaffected; Isabella heard resentful thoughts going through the minds of the people she came in contact with. Some thoughts were even murderous. Isabella knew that these thoughts were fueling and building hostility that would ultimately burst out into the open and show its malevolent face, and when it did thousands would die. This nefarious atmosphere convinced her to stay; what better place was there for a Vampire than a city that was about to erupt into mass slaughter.

France at this time was divided into three estates. The First Estate consisted of Nobles and the King, The Second Estate consisted of the Clergy and the rest which consisted of over nine-tenths of the population was included within the Third Estate. The Third Estate was not just the poor; it also consisted of the Bourgeoisie, a group that was quite wealthy and well-educated but who did not have the same rights as the First and Second Estates. The Bourgeoisie were extremely resentful of the privileges of the church and the nobility, as were the other people within the Third Estate. The poor were starving and this made them more than just resentful, it made them desperate. France was in a crisis like no other she had endured before. The King was not doing anything to appease the volatile political situation; rather, he was ignoring it. There had been various outbreaks of violence. Wives and mothers were robbing barges and wagons, stealing grain to feed their families, and some of these robberies were resulting in violence and death. The nobility had started to get frightened, but none of them were anywhere near frightened enough.

On the advice of Jacques Necker, the King's Minister for Finance, the King called a meeting for representatives of all three estates in a last ditch attempt to stop the violence. The Estates General meeting took place at Versailles and did not go well. The Third Estate had been slighted all through the meeting, and when the King talked of the changes that he was going to put in place he did not address any of the demands of the Third Estate, still continuing to ignore them. These men were outraged and refused to be intimidated, they decided to form the National Assembly and do away with the feudal system of the three Estates. It was their turn to ignore the King. The King then refused to acknowledge the National Assembly, even though members of his own Estate had voted for it. This outraged members of the National Assembly and they confronted the King. Isabella had watched everything with relish, waiting for it to explode into violence, secretly longing for that to happen.

In early July 1789, Isabella's wait was over. She was standing in court when the National Assembly gathered at Versailles to confront the King, Isabella was watching all of these events unfold. She could not wait; she was baying for blood. The King ordered that the National Assembly disperse, but one man called Mirabeau objected.

"We are here by the will of the people and we shall not be interspersed except at the point of Bayonets!"

Isabella looked out the window she saw thousands of people gathering outside in support of the National Assembly. The officers in charge were now starting to fear that a riot may break out and ordered the soldiers to open fire on the crowd. The soldiers hesitated; they dropped their bayonets and stood with the crowd.

The King, frightened and anxious, conceded. "Very well, you can stay…but I will send for foreign troops and they will show you no mercy."

The King's words echoed through the crowd and quickly news spread of the King's threat to France.

Isabella returned to court the next day and she was disappointed. The tension of the day before had somewhat dissipated and there would be no violence that day. The Queen, however, was just as edgy as she had been the day before. Isabella noticed her watching the Vampire, and soon she approached Isabella to confront her.

"Who are you?" she asked imperiously, for she was getting suspicious of every one who was not a relative.

"Lady Isabelle, my Lady."

"Of where, I do not remember you in court before."

"I have been in court my Lady every day for the past year," Isabella answered.

"Nonsense, I would have remembered you," Marie Antoinette retorted.

"I am not that memorable, Your Highness," Isabella answered, trying to resolve the situation without an obvious display of violence.

"Now, that is a lie. Guards, march her to the Bastille!" Marie Antoinette shouted.

Isabella smiled at this dramatic statement. The Bastille was a good few miles away. This woman wanted no potential enemies in Versailles.

Isabella, of course, could have easily escaped, but as she was marched away. She realised coming back to court was not an option, so she would let these soldiers accompany her to Paris. The soldiers marched her out onto the streets of Versailles; they tied her hands and placed her on a horse with the intention of taking her to Paris. She was to have a public escort to the Bastille. When they arrived at the gates of Paris, the guards dismounted their horses and started to talk amongst themselves.

"Necker has been dismissed," said one of the soldiers. Isabella said nothing, she simply listened.

"Dismissed, because he made public the King and Queen's extravagance," said another. All around Isabella could hear crowds gathering. She heard windows being broken in the distance and people shouting, phrases like *"Live Free or Die,"* and *"To the Bastille."* Isabella sensed that what she had felt brewing was going to happen that day.

A horse and rider galloped up to the guards.

"Where are you going?" the horseman asked.

"And what business is it of yours where we, the King's Imperial Guards, are going?"

Isabella could tell this man was not a native of France. His French was somewhat clumsy and disjointed. She took a chance and decided to talk to him in English.

"Sir," she began, "please can you help me? These men are taking me to the Bastille!"

"You are English?" Isabella sensed that if she said she was English it would only discourage this man from helping her. Isabella through her travels had learned that anyone who despised the English was either likely to be French, Irish or Scottish. He was not French; she thought quickly and answered him.

"No sir, Irish," Isabella responded.

"Irish, you say." Isabella could sense he was suspicious of her but he was prepared to give her the benefit of the doubt. "Well, you can come with me, then."

Isabella pulled apart her tethered hands with ease, took the Irishman's arm and leaped from her horse on to the back of his. The guards tried to stop her but the Irishman unsheathed his sword and pressed the tip at the chin of the nearest soldier to him. "I would not touch her if I were you. Look around you, do you think if you drag a woman to the Bastille, this crowd will show any restraint?" The soldiers, frightened of the angry mobs that were gathering around them, let Isabella and the Irishman ride away.

"My name is Joseph, Joseph Kavanagh," the Irishman said, introducing himself formally to Isabella. Isabella tried to remember any Irish names she had heard. She remembered a story about a warrior princess who was the mortal enemy of her sister. Aoife was her name and it meant beauty. It seemed the perfect name for Isabella.

"Aoife," she said.

"Aoife! You must be Irish. No English woman would know that name."

"Did you doubt me?" Isabella asked.

"I have to say I did. Well, Aoife, would you like to join me? I am on my way to fight and with a name like Aoife you should be able to look after yourself."

"Don't worry about me," Isabella said with a smile.

"I am getting the feeling I do not need to." As the pair rode through the crowd Joseph was shouting to the mobs that were gathering. "Foreign troops are at the gates of Paris." He rode a little further and then again he shouted down to another group of people. "We need gunpowder; the Bastille is the only place in Paris with stores of it. Hurry! Prussian troops are approaching and they will kill us all."

This man was lying, Isabella thought. When they were within walking distance of the Bastille he let Isabella down from his horse.

"Thank you for getting me away from the guards," Isabella said with genuine gratitude.

"I have the feeling you needed no help."

Isabella smiled; she liked Joseph, for he was perceptive and could not be fooled easily, even by a Vampire. "You may be right, but why did you lie to the crowds on the way here?" she asked out of curiosity. "There are no foreign troops at the gates of Paris."

"I was given the task of stirring up the mob." Joseph looked away from Isabella he wanted to survey the scenes of destruction that were going on around him. His mind's eye chose to ignore the chaos, and his glance was captured by a child sitting on a doorstep shivering with cold. The little girl glimpsed a half-eaten rotten apple lying in the dirty street. She ran to it and started to eat. When she glanced up and made eye contact with Joseph, she smiled gleefully. Joseph returned her smile but his smile was not gleeful, it was poignant. "People are starving, It is worse than at home."

Isabella sensing the change in mood, tried to divert the conversation back to something that would lighten his spirits again.

"Why were you given this task?" she asked. Joseph turned his gaze back to Isabella and smiled at her with relish.

"Do I need to tell you? You should know we Irish are the best at starting a fight," Joseph tipped his hat, leaned down and placed a green cockade in her raven hair. "This is what the friends of the revolution are wearing—wear it, it'll keep you safe."

"Thank you," Isabella said accepting his gift.

He smiled once more at Isabella and then rode to the forefront of the mob and therefore into the forefront of danger. It was about to happen. The French citizens were about to storm the Bastille and the violence would begin.

Isabella watched on as Joseph and the others broke though into the courtyard; they demanded the surrender of the Bastille. The governor of the prison, De Launey, tried to negotiate and invited the leaders of the commonalty into the prison to talk to him. Several members of the crowd went in, which placated the mob, but only briefly. Hours drifted by and the crowd grew restless again. Rumours circulated that De Launey had imprisoned the men he had promised to negotiate with. These rumours mostly emanated from Joseph, who was maneuvering his way through the rabble and whispering in the right people's ears. The people again wanted blood and so did Isabella; she was thirsting for it.

A shot from a bayonet rang out. Isabella could see everything as night was fast approaching. Joseph was standing beside a smoking bayonet; he had fired the shot to incite the rabble. On hearing the shot De Launey lost his head and ordered his troops to fire on the crowds. Shot after shot rang out from the guns of the royal troops, but the mob just kept on coming. Cannon fire and an armed assault were not going to frighten them away.

The soldiers were terrified, even though they were picking off tens of these people with their guns; the mob was relentless—it would not be stopped. They surged forward and broke through the gates into the inner courtyard. De Launey, seeing the imminent danger, surrendered and pleaded for mercy, but he was not shown any. When the drawbridge was lowered the mob again surged forward through the gates, and now the table was turned on De Launey's men. The crowd started to fight back and several of De Launey's men were cut down. Joseph headed straight for the governor; he reached him within seconds and brutally attacked him. De Launey kicked out at him purely in self-defence. Joseph squealed out in pain. Isabella could see that he was not really hurt but the crowd around him used this act of violence as an excuse to beat De Launey to death. When they were finished Joseph lifted back his bloody matted hair and sliced off his head. He placed it on his sword and paraded it through the crowd. Isabella watched him, admiring him from a distance.

Joseph was killing for a cause he believed in, but this was not the reason for Isabella's admiration; the way in which he killed impressed Isabella. He was just as vicious and malicious as she was.

Isabella played her part in the storming of the Bastille. She ran through the crowds killing as many as she could, not really caring if they were troops or commoners. Joseph caught sight of her fighting; he thought she was fighting with the Bourgeoisie. He smiled over at her, blood dripping from his face, and Isabella returned his gaze. The pair fought on. When it was over, Joseph lifted his sword, which still had De Launey's decapitated head upon it. He climbed up the Bastille wall and secured it onto the battlements. The crowd watched as he climbed and cheered when the head was in place. Others in the crowd followed suit and all the dead soldiers' heads were stuck on the spikes and swords and tied to the battlements of the Bastille, for all to see.

Isabella surveyed the jubilant crowd. She too was for a moment swept away by this euphoria but it was fleeting, for Isabella caught sight of an old enemy. Leila was standing amongst the crowd, watching Isabella.

Isabella spent the next few years in Paris. There was not a better place for her in the world. People were being killed by the hundreds, sometimes even a thousand a month. She had not seen Leila since that day. She had disappeared from sight but Isabella sensed she was close; she could feel her malevolent penetrating essence all around her. Isabella knew she would confront her eventually and she watched and waited. Isabella sadly, had not seen Joseph again, either... until one day in early September, 1792.

"Aoife!" Isabella responded to one of her many pseudonyms by turning around to see Joseph, in uniform.

"Joseph, have you become respectable?" Isabella asked a mocking tone resonated through her voice.

"Respectable enough to have three meals a day."

"Always important; it appears the revolution is giving us both sustenance," Isabella grinned.

"Walk with me a ways?" Joseph said.

"I will," Isabella complied.

"Do you miss Ireland?" Joseph asked.

"I can't say I do. And surely you do not, when you are getting fed so well."

"My stomach may not but my heart does. I miss home...I miss the wide-open spaces, the green valleys, the stone and thatched cottages."

"The starvation, the poverty," Isabella said sarcastically.

"Still... I want to go home," Joseph said, gazing off into the distance. Something was bothering him.

"But you have found so much prosperity in Paris."

"I have found prosperity in Paris that's true, but at what cost? I used to be fighting for something I believed in, but now I am not."

"What do you mean?"

"I am on my way to slaughter priests, some of them Irish, all of them Catholic. This is not what I set out to do."

Isabella was stunned. This was not the same man who had speared De Launey's head on his sword and had placed it on the gates of the Bastille. The revolution had changed him.

"That is the problem with causes; they are always lost before the end. Just don't kill them. You don't have to."

"But you see I do, I have been ordered to, and I don't want to starve ever again."

Joseph stayed silent for a moment and then continued, "After I do this I can never go back home."

"Who has ordered you to kill priests?" Isabella asked.

"The Committee of Twelve Revolutionaries... may their hands be stained red by the time the night is over." Isabella was struck by these words; they reminded her of a dying man's last words.

"The Twelve Reds," she whispered.

"What did you say?" Joseph asked.

"Nothing. I have to come with you though. I have to see it."

"Why? I don't even want to see it."

"I can't explain it but I have to see it."

Isabella walked with Joseph. Their steps were heedful and hesitant. Isabella felt as if this dead French man was haunting her now, pressing her to make good on her promise to him. Joseph entered the prison with a heavy heart. The slaughter had already begun.

Isabella was for once was not interested in the killing. She climbed up the stairs. She had heard that the King was being held in this prison. She took the keys to the King's cell and went to talk to him.

"Who are you?" asked Louis Capet, as he was now known.

"No one," Isabella answered.

"What is going on downstairs?" he asked. Both Isabella and the King heard screams coming from the dungeons below.

"They are executing some of the prisoners," Isabella stated. The King wiped sweat from his brow.

"Am I to be executed?"

"I believe so, yes."

"They have executed my complete ruin." This too was a phrase Isabella had heard before.

"What did you say?"

"I am ruined and now I am to be executed."

"You have only yourself to blame," Isabella scolded, totally lacking in sympathy. "You and your whole class walked through the streets displaying your extravagance while your country starved. You are now paying for centuries of complacency." The King sat down, his head in his hands and wept, waiting for the inevitable. Isabella left him and went back downstairs to Joseph.

"Are you finished?" she asked.

"I am," Joseph answered disgusted by what he had just been a part of. Isabella glanced at the floor of the prison; it was red with blood. She was distracted by a man running towards them.

"We are men of the cloth," the man shouted. At this Joseph drew out his sword and slashed the man's neck. He was dead immediately, and blood seeped onto his clothes and his white priest's collar. Isabella looked at the floor again. Twelve priests lay bleeding. Isabella's head was filled with memories. She felt as if she was destined to be here—the twelve reds—that phrase echoed in her mind; the twelve dying priests that lay on the floor before her. Another phrase entered her head—'the great seized' was Louis Capet, the once king of France.

"Under murder, murder will perpetrate itself," Isabella whispered. She had witnessed this for years. This turbulent city was going through constant upheaval and every regime that took over was more bloody than the last.

"What did you say?" Joseph remarked.

"Under murder, murder will perpetrate itself. I have to stop it," Isabella answered.

"What are you talking about?"

Isabella looked at Joseph and smiled; she had a new purpose. Mark Nosterdames's words were finally understood.

"Do you want to atone, Joseph?" Joseph considered this proposal for just a few moments. He looked at the evidence of the carnage all over the floor and he answered honestly.

"Yes, more than anything."

"I can give you a chance to atone. I am no righter of wrongs, I know that, but it was a dying man's wish that I would stop this reign of terror, and I will," Isabella said, determined to make it so.

"It would take a miracle to stop this madness," Joseph stated.

"Then a miracle is what will happen," Isabella concluded.

※

Charlotte Corday watched from a distance as Louis Capet was led to the guillotine. His hair was cut from his head and then he was pushed up the steps. They dropped the blade on Louis' head and he screamed in agony—the blade had only partially severed the back of his neck. The guillotine like everything else in France in the end had let him down and inflicted more suffering upon him than his crimes called for. The blade was pulled up again and was let fall; this time it was successful. The executioner lifted the head of the former King to show the crowd. At first they were stunned. France had just killed her King, but then the stunned crowd erupted as somewhere someone shouted.

"Long live the Republic!" An air of celebration once more echoed among the people who were packed into the Place de la Révolution.

Charlotte could not stay and watch any longer. She did not want to be a part of this anymore. She was a revolutionary and a republican but she had seen too much murder in her short life. She wanted a republic, but not at the cost of needless waste of life.

VROLOK

She turned and walked away as the crowd cheered. She glared up at Marat; he was smiling while watching this brutality. He was a staunch republican who incited and perpetuated this violence by the writings in his newspaper, *The Friend of the People*. Charlotte was disgusted at the hellish scene. She showed her disgust visibly and Isabella was there to see it.

"Charlotte?" Charlotte was startled. No one here knew her. She turned to face the Vampire.

"How do you know my name?" Charlotte asked.

"I know many things about you, Charlotte," Isabella answered. "I feel your hatred towards that man." Isabella motioned towards Marat.

"I don't hate anybody," Charlotte said.

"I think you do."

"What business is it of yours?" Charlotte sharply enquired.

"I can help you."

"Help me do what?"

"Create a miracle that will end this carnage."

"A miracle?"

"Yes but that will come later. First, I want to help you do something that I know you want to do."

"And what is that?"

"I want to help you kill Marat."

⁂

Charlotte knocked on the door; she looked back behind her and saw Isabella and Joseph out of the corner of her eye. *"Trust me."* Isabella projected this thought into Charlotte's mind. Charlotte nodded just as the door was opened.

"Who are you?" the man who had come to the door asked.

"My name is Marie Anne Charlotte Corday d'Armont. I am, or at least I was, a Girondonist." The girl's remarks had sparked this man's curiosity; why would a Girondonist be coming to Marat's door?

"What do you want here?"

"I want to see Marat."

"Why?" asked Marat's servant.

"I have in my possession a list of all the names of all the Girondonists in Paris." The servant was very aware that his master would want this list. Marat was persecuting Girondinists; they were too moderate for his liking.

"Wait here." The man shut the door and within a few minutes returned. "Come in."

Marat was wearing a dressing gown, which was obscuring a horrific skin condition. He was a fat, pallid, middle-aged man. His house was filled with treasures stolen from guillotined aristocrats. He was living a very opulent lifestyle, a lifestyle that Charlotte had been brought up to resent. He would be easy to kill, Charlotte thought.

"You are interrupting my bath," Marat remarked.

"I am sorry, sir."

"Don't be sorry, just be quick. What information have you got for me?"

"I have a list of all the Girondinists in Paris."

"And why have you decided to give me this information?"

"I feel it is my duty. The Girondinists are too constrained and violence is the only answer we have to kill all those that oppose the bloody revolution."

"I am not sure I am convinced," Marat answered.

"I do not know what I can do to convince you."

"You can't do anything to convince me but I will take the list anyway." Charlotte was getting anxious and impatient. She reached into her bag, took out the list of fictitious names and handed the pages to Marat. Marat scanned the list and rang a bell summoning his servant. The servant scurried into the room and Marat asked him to run his bath. Charlotte did not know what to do; she couldn't leave before she had the opportunity to kill him. The servant bowed and Charlotte went to follow him out the door. Marat started to speak.

"Where are you going?" he asked.

"I was leaving," Charlotte answered.

"No, you are not. Do you not have confidence in your convictions? You stay until I have had a chance to look over this list properly." Marat got into his bath and examined the list. "This looks genuine."

"That is because it is." Charlotte was hesitating. To kill a man...even this man... was proving difficult. A thought, not her own, entered her head. "*Have courage—do it now*!" Charlotte felt around in her skirts and pulled out a knife. She lunged forward and pushed the knife into Marat's chest. Marat gasped for air and reached out for his bell. He only managed to knock the bell over. Charlotte leaned in close to him and whispered.

"Death is too good for you, how does it feel? I hope it is a painful end to a painful life." Marat looked into Charlotte's cold harsh eyes in shock as he watched his own blood pour into his bath water. In seconds he was dead. Marat's servant ran to get soldiers to arrest Charlotte. Charlotte calmly sat down and waited for them to return. The soldiers burst into the room and arrested Charlotte. Charlotte made no attempt to resist arrest and walked silently away with them. She looked to all observers proud at what she had done.

※

A month earlier, a few days after Isabella had first approached Charlotte, she decided to confront her again. Charlotte had not been as enthusiastic about killing Marat as Isabella had hoped. Isabella decided to stage an arrest so that Charlotte would be forced to listen to her.

Charlotte was awakened in the middle of the night by soldiers banging on the downstairs door.

"Open up in the name of the Republic!" It was the shout that every one in Paris feared hearing in the early hours of the morning. Charlotte was frightened. She knew what these shouts probably meant; she would be tried quickly and then sent to the guillotine. The soldiers were getting louder; they were starting to break through the door. Charlotte was frightened but she was courageous too, and she would face her fear.

She went downstairs and opened the door, letting the men into her house, men whom she believed had been sent to begin her hasty walk to the grave. The troops pushed their way in and dragged her out into the street. They walked a few steps and then one of the soldiers went over to a woman in a long black cloak. All Charlotte could see of her was a few locks of raven hair curling around the hood of her cloak and just a glimpse of her white skin. Isabella smiled at the soldier who had approached her and then pulled down her hood so that Charlotte could see and recognise her. Charlotte did recognise her immediately. Isabella approached the bewildered Charlotte.

"You have great influence to have republican guards in your employ," Charlotte said.

"I have great influence but not in the way you believe," Isabella stated.

"You have had me arrested! Why?"

"I haven't. I just arranged this, so that you would listen to me." Charlotte looked over at the soldiers; they were laughing and joking with Joseph. She no longer felt threatened by these men.

"Who are they?" Charlotte asked.

"Irish," said Isabella.

"Never trust an Irish man to stay loyal; it is not in our nature," Joseph chipped in. Charlotte laughed in nervous relief.

"I thought I was dead," Charlotte said.

"You still may be. I have to talk to you. Walk with me."

"What do you want from me?" Charlotte asked.

"I have a plan to end the cycle of murder; I know you want that, Charlotte."

"How?"

"Nothing less than a miracle will do it."

Charlotte just stared blankly at Isabella, having no comprehension of Isabella's elaborate plan.

"You will kill Marat and you will not resist arrest and you will go to the guillotine," Isabella said.

"I have told you I can't do it. I am young…I do not want to die."

"You will not."

"How will I not if I am going to go to the guillotine?"

"The blade will bounce off the back of your neck. It will not even break your skin."

"That's ridiculous. Believe me, I will not be placing my head underneath the guillotine blade for you or anyone else. And if I ever look up at the steel rushing down at me, I will expect it to end my life!"

Isabella smiled. "Life does not have to be such a fragile thing that can end by the slice of a sharp blade. Joseph! It is time to show this woman the power of immortality."

Joseph held his sword aloft as he was about to strike. Charlotte stunned, stepped back thinking that the sword was about to strike her. The sword plunged down through the air and struck not Charlotte but Isabella. Joseph was thrust back as the sword struck Isabella's neck without making a mark on her.

Joseph found himself sitting on the dusty street; his arm had been hurt by the demonstration. He dusted himself off and stood, his sword was still lying on the ground. Charlotte ran over to it and picked it up, believing that she had just seen some sort of trick. But the sword was authentic and sharp, as Charlotte soon realised when she cut her fingers on the blade.

"I want you to take that sword and try and kill me," Said Isabella.

Charlotte looked at Isabella in amazement. She had no idea what sort of creature she was.

"Try and kill me Charlotte, if you don't believe your own eyes," Isabella said, with such conviction that Charlotte felt compelled to try to kill Isabella. She plunged the sword into Isabella's chest. This time the blade went right through. Charlotte, still holding the hilt of the sword, let it go. Isabella clasped her hands around the hilt and pulled it out of her chest. Isabella stared intensely at Charlotte. Charlotte watched in complete amazement as the open wound healed before her eyes.

"How is this possible?" Charlotte asked.

"You know Rousseau's writings?"

"Yes, of course."

"He wrote that if there is in the world one attested story it is that of the Vampires and he wrote that after he met me. I am a Vampire, an immortal. I can give you this gift that I possess. You can live forever and you need not be afraid when they lead you up the steps of the guillotine."

"How can I become like you?"

"You have to die," Isabella said; she was not going to lie to Charlotte.

"How do I know I can trust you?" Isabella touched Charlotte on the temples. Memories flowed into Charlotte's mind. And when Isabella took her hands from Charlotte's head, she knew she could trust this woman. She held out her wrist for Isabella to kill her and she willingly became a Vampire.

Weeks later, Charlotte was getting taken in the cart to the guillotine. She was not nervous and had every confidence in Isabella and her newfound immortality. She stood proud, her head held high; she had killed a tyrant and the world was better place for him having left it. She had not seen Isabella since the night Marat died and she was pleased to see her in the crowd. Isabella nodded reassurance.

Joseph who was now always at Isabella's side asked, "Will this work?"

"Of course it will," Isabella said in complete confidence.

"It seems a great risk."

"No, believe me, it is not. When they can't kill her they will see it as a sign that Marat should have died and this will all end... I wouldn't worry. There is more chance of you dying today than Charlotte."

"If you are sure."

"I am." Isabella was keeping a watchful eye on Charlotte, keeping eye contact with her to reassure her that everything would be all right. Charlotte's hair was cut from her head and she was led up onto the platform, her hands bound, still a proud look of defiance across her face. A priest stood at the side of the guillotine and was offering redemption in the form of prayer. Charlotte turned to face the crowd and shouted.

"I killed one man in order to save thousands!"

Isabella was proud of Charlotte; everything was going exactly to plan. Isabella looked at Charlotte's supposed executioners that were standing on the platform with her. Isabella saw a woman on the platform with the priest; she thought it strange to see a woman there. She had been at many of these executions and had never seen a woman take part. She could not see her face, for the sun was too bright. Isabella watched as the woman handed the priest a bottle of something and he was sprinkling the contents onto Charlotte's neck. As the liquid hit Charlotte's skin she screamed out in pain.

Isabella knew something was wrong; she drew a cloud overhead to blot out the sun so that she could see. Isabella was horrified to discover this woman standing on the platform was Leila. Isabella panicked She ran to the platform trying to signal to Charlotte that something was wrong. Charlotte did not see Isabella. The Dhampir's blood was eating into the flesh on her neck and she was placed under the guillotine. Her eyes were wide open as the blade plummeted towards her throat. In those last few moments Charlotte knew she was going to die, that the plan had failed. Isabella ran to the platform and up the steps but she was too late. That feeling that had surged through her when Nicolae and Vincente had died blasted through her again. Isabella now longed again for that peaceful feeling. The guards took Isabella away and lead her to prison, thinking she was some sort of insurrectionist trying to stop the execution, and they threw her in jail. She was so grandly dressed that she was soon condemned as an aristocrat.

Isabella's execution day came quickly but not quickly enough for Isabella. She now again longed for death and fully expected to see Leila on the platform; she was not disappointed. Isabella looked at her, willing her to do it. Leila gave the blood to the priest and again and he sprinkled some of the liquid onto Isabella's neck. It seared her skin; Isabella felt it eat at her flesh. She didn't care anymore. She let the soldiers place her in the guillotine without resistance and waited for the blade to come down and slice through her neck. Isabella closed her eyes. She felt the rush of air as the blade fell towards her. It was finally over, or so she thought.

Isabella awoke to find Joseph sitting at her bedside, waiting for her to stir.

"You're awake," he began.

"What happened?"

"We saved you."

"Why?"

"Because you never finished what you started."

"What?" Isabella asked.

"You told me you would help me atone; you said you would end this reign of terror. It would have been Charlotte's wish."

Isabella sat up. Her first thoughts were of Charlotte. Charlotte had trusted her to protect her, but she couldn't. Isabella was angry. Leila had killed Charlotte out of spite. Isabella rubbed her neck; her skin was no longer smooth, the Dhampir's blood had scarred her.

"As scars go, it is quite attractive," Joseph said a mischievous tone in his voice. Isabella managed a slight smile and then Joseph asked her. "Will you end it, Isabella?"

"I will, I will end it," she said. "And it will end for Leila, too, whenever she dares to show herself."

There was a malevolence in Isabella's face. A malevolence and a grim determination that Joseph had never seen before. In that moment she scared him more than she had ever done.

Joseph left Isabella and went downstairs and out into the cobbled street below. He walked a few steps to the corner and the rain began to fall. He ran to the alehouse on the next street and cautiously entered with a certain amount of trepidation. He had not come into this place merely to seek shelter; he had a greater purpose. His steps were slow but deliberate, for he knew how dangerous this man was that he was going to see. The portentous, mysterious man was sitting in the corner staring out the window, watching the rain fall from the sky. Joseph sat down beside him and ordered a tankard of ale. The man did not look around at Joseph, but he knew he was there.

"Is she awake?"

"She is."

"Does she remember anything?"

"Nothing," Joseph confirmed.

"What has she resolved to do?"

"To finish what she started."

"Why?" This man knew Isabella well, but she still managed on occasion to baffle even him.

"She says a dying man made her promise to end it," Joseph stated.

The man sighed and said, "I should have known; she was never one to resist a final wish." The two men sat in silence and then Joseph resumed his conversation.

"Doubtless, you want to see her?"

The man leaned his head back against the wall behind him and looked up at the ceiling and said, "I see her often… I watch her always."

"Then surely you want to speak to her?" The man then for the first time that evening looked at Joseph face to face.

"No, she must not know I am here," he said with finality.

"But you saved her; whatever has happened between you she would forgive, knowing that if it was not for your sake, Leila would have killed her."

"No!" the man said fiercely.

"But—" Joseph tried to protest. Isabella's savior slammed his fist down on the table beside them. The table broke in half. He pushed his face towards Joseph. Joseph was terrified of this man, the black eyes that stared out from an emotionless face.

"She must never know. She would never accept help from me."

"All right, all right," Joseph said. Vlad backed away from Joseph and sat back down. "Jesus, Mary and Joseph, I have the strong feeling there are two too many Vampires in my acquaintance."

"Well, how is she going to proceed now? No more elaborate plans to fabricate acts of God, I hope," Vlad said.

"Judging by the look on her face when I left her it appears she is going to kill everyone."

"That is the best way to end things."

"God help the leaders of the revolution."

"Do you care? From what I can gather, they made you do something that you are totally ashamed of," said Vlad.

Joseph's expression darkened. He did not like to be reminded of what he had done. He drank the last of his ale and got up to leave.

"Yes… definitely too many Vampires in my life. They can see too far into a man's mind." Vlad smiled as Joseph left; he could see why Isabella liked him.

✢

Isabella watched as Herbert and Danton climbed up the platform to their deaths.

"This is only the beginning of the end," Isabella remarked.

"At least it is the start of the end," Joseph answered.

"Are you going to see Robespierre tonight?"

"I am."

"Be careful."

"I always am," Isabella stated and turned to leave as the blade fell to sever Danton's neck from his body.

✢

Isabella had met Robespierre soon after Charlotte Corday's death. She was of use to him because she was a killer, a killer who, if she wanted to, could kill without any sign of violence. Robespierre was waiting for

Isabella the night Danton died; she was his eyes and ears in the crowd, as he refused to attend any of the executions.

"You were there today, as I asked?" Robespierre asked.

"I was."

"Danton and Herbert were quite brave in the end?"

"They were. It would be hypocritical of them to have been anything else, as they have sent so many to the guillotine."

"Did you hear his last words, Danton's I mean?"

"I did. He said that you would follow him and his death would drag you down."

"A fool."

"Perhaps."

"No one can drag me down, I have absolute power now. You were right to advise me to turn on Danton there is no friction in the committee now. I have complete control."

"Well, use your control wisely."

"I will."

"Good." Robespierre walked over to the mirror that was hanging in his room to look at himself.

"Good, everything is good when it leaves the Creator's hands; everything degenerates in the hands of man. Do you know who said this?"

"Rousseau," Isabella answered.

"A great man."

"He was. I met him once a long time ago," Robespierre still examining his own reflection took an orange from the top of a pyramid of oranges that sat on a plate on top of his mantelpiece. He started to peel it.

"I am going to start a new religion for France based on his theory of deism. It will be the called *The Cult of the Supreme Being*."

Isabella looked at him, bemused by this revelation. "I will leave you now," Isabella said. She had enough of his egocentric ramblings.

"Yes, go. I have no need of you anymore." Isabella left and met Joseph, who was waiting outside.

"Well?" Joseph said.

"I think our job is done."

"You do?"

"Danton will become a martyr; he died well and his support was only increased by his death. And that man in there is mad; he will hang himself soon enough, but I will stay just to watch his unravelling."

On a beautiful summer's day in July, Robespierre was intent on giving a speech before the National Convention. Guards lined up in front of the door to stop him from entering the building.

"What are you doing?" Robespierre objected.

"We are arresting you, sir," said Joseph, who wanted to be there in the final days.

"Arresting me? You don't have the authority."

"I am afraid we do." At this moment guards from Robespierre's Paris Commune flooded the streets; they had expected something. The French victories abroad had made the Jacobins, of whom Robespierre was a leading member, fear for their own safety. Robespierre's soldiers were suspicious; they had expected a coup, and soon.

When Robespierre saw them coming he smiled and said to Joseph, "Go home. You will not be arresting anyone today, but believe me there will be consequences to your actions."

Isabella now came out from the crowd and walked towards Robespierre. The Paris Commune Guards were pointing their guns at Joseph's soldiers. Joseph's soldiers were pointing their muskets towards the Paris Commune Guards and there in the middle of it all were Isabella and Robespierre. Joseph looked on anxiously. He did not see a way out of this for any of them. Isabella lifted up her hand and whispered to the soldiers, *"Don't see me,"* excluding Joseph and Robespierre from her deception.

"Do you see a way out of this?" Isabella asked Joseph.

"I don't," Joseph laughed, keeping his sense of humour as he faced his own death.

"Well, I promised you a chance to atone."

"I don't know that I wanted to atone this badly," Joseph smiled, but he was prepared to meet his maker if that is what it took for him to atone. Isabella smiled as well; she always saw through his flippant words. She turned to Robespierre; he was standing there his head held high. From his outward appearance he looked unafraid of his impending death. Isabella leaned over and whispered in his ear.

"He who pretends to look on death without fear lies. Do you know who said that?" A single trickle of sweat slid down Robespierre's forehead as he immediately recognised Rousseau's words. Isabella wiped the sweat from Robespierre's brow; he reacted jerkily to her touch. The soldiers who could not see Isabella thought that Robespierre was signalling to them. Joseph's soldiers were also prepared to shoot. A young soldier in the Paris Commune guards fired, and then others rang out. Isabella pushed both Robespierre and Joseph to the ground, veiling them both from the crossfire of shots. The commune guards were soon overpowered by the

Joseph's troops and the brief state of panic was over. Isabella got up and dragged Robespierre up with her; blood was pouring from his jaw. For the first time in his life Robespierre had been silenced, and by an errant shot from his own loyal guards.

"Are you in pain?" Isabella asked. Robespierre looked at her and made no attempt to tell her anything. "I know you are," said Isabella. She herself had been shot several times, but the bullets had left her body as quickly as they had entered it. Joseph, who had been protected by Isabella, was unscathed.

"Take him away," Joseph stated, and his soldiers led Robespierre to prison. Joseph looked over at Isabella. "Why did you save him?" he asked.

"He has sent so many to the Guillotine I would not deprive him of the pleasure of experiencing it for himself. I want him to hear the shouts of the Bourgeoisie ringing out through the air, shouting *Long Live the Republic*" as he gets led up the steps of the platform. I want him to know that the revolution was always bigger than him. It didn't need him for it to survive."

"All right, then, why did you save me?"

Isabella turned to Joseph and smiled. "What would I do without you turning up to bestow your Irish wisdom upon me?"

"Good point"

Isabella smiled again. "And besides, you saved my life; it was only right that I returned the favour."

"Isabella, I have to tell you something. I didn't save...." Joseph turned to face Isabella. As he did so, he saw Vlad out of the corner of his eye. Vlad was staring at Joseph intently; Vlad shook his head to stop Joseph from telling Isabella what really happened that day.

"Well," Isabella said. "What do you really have to tell me?"

"I tried to kill Leila, but I couldn't."

"Is that all? I wouldn't have expected you to be able to do that."

"She holds the remainder of the only thing that can help me kill her."

"She doesn't. I smashed the bottle, and now none of you can die. We shall see. If there is another way, I will find it. Leila will not occupy her space on this earth for too much longer."

Joseph and Isabella watched as the soldiers and Robespierre disappeared into the skyline. "They are going now to arrest the others St. Just, Labas, Henriot—all of them. It's finally over," said Joseph.

"I will make sure of it," Isabella said.

"What about me, what shall I do?"

"Go back to Ireland with a clear conscience."

"How can I go back and face the people there?"

"You can." Isabella placed her hands on Joseph's face and whispered, *"Forget me, forget all of this."*

Joseph woke up the next day with no guilt at all, just an overwhelming desire to go home, and that is what he did.

Isabella went to the prison the day after Robespierre was executed. She wanted to make sure all those who supported Robespierre would follow him to the Guillotine. She used her influence to infiltrate the prison and she walked from cell to cell checking to see who was condemned and who was not and who should be. She soon espied a young man, a soldier condemned to death. He was insignificant looking, short and chubby, and there was nothing in his appearance to recommend him.

"What has he done?" Isabella asked the prison guard.

"He is traitor to France," the prison guard answered.

"No, he is not, let him go, surely there has been enough needless killing?"

"There has, you are right," the prison guard quickly agreed, with no idea why he was agreeing with this woman, just following the compulsion to do so. "Do you hear that, Bonaparte, you have been granted a reprieve." The prison warden opened his cell and the young soldier walked out and bowed in gratitude to Isabella. Isabella stretched out her hand and the young soldier kissed it. Isabella saw glimpses of his future when he touched her. She saw the resurrection of France and the end of the revolution. She saw the French flag marching across Europe. This man would restore France to a greatness it had never even come close to before.

"Stand up," Isabella said. "I can see you have great things ahead of you." The soldier bowed and then left Isabella.

Everything was as she had predicted. Robespierre had been killed; he had been unable, because of his shattered jaw, to address his people. But he soon realised they were not his people any more. Robespierre's supporters fell. All their clubs were shut down and ninety were executed the day after Robespierre. More moderate revolutionaries, the Thermodoreans, took over and France began to rebuild itself. The reign of terror was over. Isabella had fulfilled her promise to Marc de la Nostredame and she now felt it was time to leave Paris and find some other country to inhabit.

DENN DIE TODTEN REITEN SCHNELL
FOR THE DEAD TRAVEL FAST

CHAPTER NINETEEN

With no Joseph at her side, Isabella was alone again. She left France and traveled east again. She had not seen Katya's family in a generation and felt honour bound to return, for she felt she had abandoned them. She travelled expeditiously, but her swift journey came to an end before its destination. She arrived at Bistrita, needing time to think.

What was she going to say to Nadezhda's son? What was she going to say to her husband, if he was still alive? She was afraid of the reception she would receive there. Nadezhda's child would be a man by now with a family of his own. Isabella would not have blamed him if he held her totally responsible for his mother's death, for she felt completely responsible. These thoughts troubled Isabella's mind.

Isabella sat in the inn at Bistrita, staring at the fire. There was a storm brewing up outside. Every time the door opened the flames flickered, but Isabella was paying no heed to who was coming or going, so she did not notice when a man sat down in front of her. He stared at the Vampire, recognizing her, but she did not even lift her gaze to acknowledge him.

"Isabella."

She raised her eyes. It was Nadezhda's husband. He had aged, but Isabella recalled his face.

"Vilem, it is good to see you," Isabella said.

"Is it?" he asked.

"Of course. How is your family? I was on my way to see them."

"I don't know."

"What do you mean you don't know?"

"I left soon after Nadezhda died," he answered.

Isabella looked curiously at Vilem. "Why, what about your son? I told you to stay with him," she scolded.

"I could not, after what happened."

"You should have stayed with your family! Do you not realise how important family is? What have you been doing all this time?"

"Hunting Vampires,"

Isabella was astonished, even though Vilem had said this in earnest.

"What good would that do? You can't kill them when you find them."

"But you can."

"I can't."

"You did before."

"I don't believe this; you have been searching for Vampires you couldn't even kill. You can't have found many—my kind are few."

"Even so, another Vampire occupies this town."

"Who, Vlad?"

"No, a woman." Isabella stepped forward, leaning into him. Vilem pulled back from her, but Isabella continued to confront him. She could feel his hot, shallow breath on her skin.

"Where is she?" Isabella snarled.

"She's close by; she has been following you."

"Vilem, you have to stay away from her. She will kill you, especially if she sees you talking to me. Tell me precisely where she is," Isabella demanded.

"She is staying near here."

"Where, Vilem tell me where? Be specific, and then go home," Isabella said anxiously. She was determined that no members of Katya's family would be hurt again.

"I will show you."

"All right," Isabella relented, sensing Vilem's determination to go with her. "But then you must go home." Vilem made no response. "You must go home, Vilem," Isabella repeated, until he finally nodded to placate her.

※

Isabella beheld Leila. She had taken a house that was not her own. If Isabella was being honest with herself she could not fault Leila for this, for she had done the same thing many a time. Isabella did not know how long she had been living there. She wondered the extent of Leila's power. If she was following Isabella, how was it that Isabella had not sensed her presence? Could she cloak herself from her? Isabella could identify a

Vampire simply by looking at them. She could even sense them when they were close.

It worried her that she could not discern Leila from the multitude of humans who surrounded her, but she would not think about that now; her thoughts turned to what Leila possessed. She had to know if there was any more of the Dhampir's blood. Joseph had told her he had destroyed the rest of it, but Isabella wanted to be sure that Leila had not escaped with any of it. Isabella waited for Leila to leave and then she went into the house. Leila had obviously lived there a long time. There were no mirrors in the house and no candles for light. In the wardrobe there were clothes of all different sizes. Obviously they had been stolen. Isabella searched the house completely, and she found no trace of the Dhampir's blood. She had now confirmed what she had already suspected, that Leila had none left or else she would have already tried to kill Isabella again. Isabella wanted to confront Leila, so she waited for her to return.

She waited for hours, but still there was no sign of Leila. The sun rose, set and rose again the following day and still Leila did not appear. Isabella decided to leave; Leila was obviously was not coming back here. As she left her reflections turned to Vilem; she wanted to make sure he was safely home. Isabella began to walk the path that led her to her old village.

As the night fell, when she was just a short distance from the village, Isabella heard fighting a little further along the road. She began to run, chasing the origin of the sounds. She paused in her stride to listen and heard a man shouting in Slovakian, so she knew it was her duty to protect whoever it was, and she ran over the brow of the next hill. Isabella could finally see the scene of the struggle; Leila was assaulting Vilem with murderous intent.

Leila leapt at Vilem, pushing him to the ground. He fell, capable of little resistance. Vilem was now an old man; he could not sustain this sort of punishment for much longer and Leila knew it. She was playing with him, drawing out his death.

Isabella pounced on Leila. Leila hit the ground and Isabella kneeled on her back keeping her face down in the dirt as long as she could. Leila was strong but not stronger than Isabella.

"Run Vilem," Isabella shouted. Vilem ran he did not need to be asked twice. Now that he had felt the strength of a Vampire he did not want to feel it again. He ran for his life and when Isabella saw he was a safe distance from them she let Leila out of her vise-like grip. The two women circled each other, enmity mutually emanating from each Vampire. They were ripe for this confrontation.

"This is pointless," said Leila. "We can't harm each other,"

"That's not exactly true; we just can't do any permanent damage," Isabella snarled.

"All right, if that is what you want." Leila ran at her and threw her body against Isabella's. Isabella fell to the ground and laughed at Leila.

"You are going to have to be faster than that," Isabella shouted. She leaped to her feet and slammed her fist into Leila's face. The thrust of the blow sent Leila's body back through the air and seconds later she was lying on the ground writhing in agony. Leila pushed herself back on to her feet, blood dripping from a broken jaw. Leila rammed her jaw back into place. The pair paused to look at each other once more, Isabella grinned at Leila, enticing her to try and strike another blow. The two Vampires flew at each other, each clasping the other by the throat. They spun around, both trying to squeeze out the other's life's breath, but this pair had breathed their last many years ago.

Appreciating this was futile, Leila was the first to let go, and then Isabella relinquished.

"You are right—this is pointless," Isabella said.

"I know what would not be pointless."

Isabella waited for Leila to continue, wondering whether her next threat would be something she could deliver on. "That man, who is he? Why did you save him?"

"I didn't save anyone," Isabella responded.

"No, you did, you called out his name. He is Slovak isn't he? One of your people. Well, he won't be alive for long." Leila chased after Vilem. Isabella, who knew these paths far better than Leila, slipped into the woods to get to Vilem before Leila did.

"Vilem," Isabella shouted. Vilem was still running despite the injuries that Leila had inflicted. Isabella caught him by his coat and whispered, "She is chasing us."

"What should I do?"

"I don't know Vilem; she will catch up to us soon, that's one thing the dead can do."

"What?"

"We can travel fast."

At this Leila leaped from behind, bashing Isabella's skull with such a force that she knocked Isabella to the ground. Isabella fell, blood gushing from the open wound at the back of her head. She reached out and grabbed Leila's leg. "Run Vilem, I can't hold her long." Isabella held tight but Leila was going to quickly get free. She reached behind to her wound; it was still bleeding, Isabella wondered why it hadn't healed yet. She was firmly clasping Leila's foot but the wound was concerning her. She felt ill and drowsy; this was the worst she had ever felt since the night she had actually died. Leila was still writhing around, trying to get free from Isabella's strong grip. Pain suddenly gripped Isabella—shooting pains seared through her body. She let go of Leila's foot. She could not hold on any longer.

Leila stood, towering over Isabella, who was unable to lift herself up. Then Leila knelt down and spoke to Isabella.

"I have killed you," Leila said. "And I promise I will kill that farmer you were trying to protect." Isabella tried to speak but could not. "Still trying to stay alive?" Leila asked. "Well, I will have to make sure you are dead."

Isabella watched as Leila took a tiny bottle of what Isabella knew was the Dhampir's blood from her dress. She placed the last two drops of the blood on the knife and stabbed Isabella in the heart with it. Isabella choked; she could taste blood in her mouth. Her eyes were not closed but her sight was melting away and blackness filled her vision. Leila stared at Isabella; finally she had exacted her revenge and was watching Isabella die. Leila then wanted to make sure she kept her promise to Isabella and chased after Vilem, intent on killing him.

Vilem was still trying to run but his injuries were beginning to be too much for him. He fell onto his knees and even they could no longer support him. He fell to the ground. Vilem had passed out but was awakened by the sound of a child playing. A little girl named Anna was merrily skipping along, not suspecting the danger she was in. Vilem opened his eyes to look at the child, who by this time was sitting at his side. She was stroking his forehead, pushing the hair from his eyes. Vilem clutched at her dress and drew her in close to him. He recognised something in the child. He saw Nadezhda's eyes staring down at him.

"Go," he whispered. "Leave me, for the dead travel fast." The little girl was frightened and ran from him, not looking back, unaware that she had just been warned away from danger by her own grandfather.

Leila was watching from a distance, but was close enough to smell the scent of death surrounding him. She had fulfilled her promise to Isabella; this man was dead. She turned and left him to die in the middle of the road like an animal.

※

Isabella awoke lying in a bed that was unfamiliar to her. She heard a conversation in the next room.

"Look after her—she will wake soon." Isabella was not completely lucid and did not recognise the voice although she should have. She fell asleep again and forgot the fragment of the conversation she had overheard. A few hours later the door opened and someone came in, and the movement awakened her again.

"How do you feel?" the stranger asked on seeing her eyes open.

"Considering I thought I was dead, well enough."

"I am Vilem's son."

Isabella remembered the baby she had bounced on her knee. Then she remembered Vilem.

"Where is Vilem, is he all right?" Isabella tried to get up but she was still very weak.

"I am afraid he is dead."

"I am sorry; I tried to save him."

"I know, he told me…."

"I am so sorry."

"Don't be on my account. I cannot grieve for him, I did not know him."

"That is my fault as well; I should have let him come with me the night your mother died. He needed his own retribution, not just the promise of it."

"It was his own choice."

"We often make choices we shouldn't and they seem totally insignificant at the time of making them, but they can change our lives forever."

"It doesn't matter."

Isabella felt the back of her head her wound was now healed but she felt another scar underneath her hair. "How long have I been unconscious?"

"Weeks." Isabella was frightened if she hadn't fed in weeks—was she old now? She felt her face, it still felt smooth she looked at Anna's father.

"Have I fed?"

"You have."

"How?"

"I would rather not say; it was not the most pleasant experience of my life."

"I can understand that, thank you. What about Leila?"

"No one has seen her; the house that she occupied has been abandoned."

"I am determined to find her now; I have to find a way to kill her," Isabella promised.

"You are not the only one who has promised this."

Thinking that he meant himself, she scolded him, "Are you going to abandon your family like your father did?"

"No, I didn't mean me."

"Who did you mean?"

"No one," Anna's father said nervously. Isabella tried to read his thoughts but she couldn't. She needed to touch him, his will was strong, but Anna's father stepped back away from her touch. Isabella was not surprised by his shrinking away from her. She felt responsible for the demise of both his mother and father. She did not realise that this man was not letting her touch him because he had been warned not to. She decided not to try. She didn't want to touch him if he flinched away from her and it really wasn't that important. Another person in the world who wanted to kill Leila was a good thing.

"How can I find her?" Isabella said, thinking aloud.

"I don't think she will be far behind you when she realises you are still alive."

"You are right, she won't be."

"I think you should find a way to kill her first, before confronting her again."

"I should and I will."

"There must be a way."

"There is. I need a Dhampir's blood."

DHAMPIR
THE CHILD OF A VAMPIRE AND A HUMAN

CHAPTER TWENTY

Vlad was Isabella's consummate protector. He ceaselessly watched Isabella and as a consequence of this, Leila was never far from his sight. He had stopped her from killing Isabella on several occasions, in Paris and most recently near Bistrita. He had fallen behind, just moments behind the pair and when he arrived he saw Isabella lying on the ground, her eyes closed. He feared he was too late, but when he touched her he sensed there was still a glimmer of life left to save. He picked her up and carried her to Vilem's old house; Vilem's son willingly took her in. Vlad stayed with her, letting her feed from him, for this was the only thing that would restore her, his blood acting as an antidote to the effects of the Dhampir's poison. He let her drain him until the pain would have been too much for anyone to bear, Vilem's son watched, amazed as Vlad rapidly aged in front of him. Day after day he repeated this behaviour until her eyes started to flicker and open, but he was gone before she could look upon his face.

Vlad left that night. He had to stop Leila, he understood that now. He feared that one day he would not be able to save Isabella from her. The fact is, if she had had just a little more of the Dhampir's blood, Isabella would have died. Vlad had to kill Leila and to do this he had to create a Dhampir and only Vlad knew how to do this.

He had not told Isabella the complete truth about his reincarnation as a Vampire. The pair constantly kept secrets from each other and this was no exception. It was true he had been resuscitated by a Dhampir, the last Dhampir, to be precise. Vlad had kept one last secret from Isabella about these events, and this last secret was the real reason that the Dhampir's were dying out. A Dhampir was the child of a mortal and a Vampire. Few Vampires now occupied this earth, but there use to be thousands of them. Mircea the Great had helped the Dhampir's hunt them until only he was left, and when he died the Dhampirs had no one left to sire them. And that was Vlad's plan: he would have a child and then he would kill it. Only the blood from this child could kill Leila.

It was a simple but unsettling plan and he had waited until he was sure that there was no alternative. Vlad pursued this course of action with a heavy heart; after all he was about to create something that could kill both Isabella and himself. But Vlad was determined…Leila had to die and this child could never be a threat, as it would not be allowed to reach an age where it would be a danger to any Vampire.

He decided to travel quite a distance; he wanted his child to be born far away from Isabella. He had visited Leila before he had left and told her to leave the Carpathians in a way that only he could. She would initially obey him; she would not return until she gathered up the courage to face him again and that would not be for a long time. He would be back before she would dare to return. Vlad also took comfort in the fact that he had left Isabella in good hands. That family would always be loyal to Isabella because she was always loyal to them.

So Vlad left her—confident she would be safe. He travelled up to the top of Europe and settled in Holland. He began the search for the mother of his child. He wanted a rich woman. His supercilious nature did not want this child. Brief as its life might be, born into some back street hovel. He wanted a woman who would raise the child without fear of society's judgement of having an illegitimate child. A baby whose mother displayed their child in the open and was not hidden away from people would be easier to find and kill. So therefore Vlad concluded he wanted a married woman, a woman who could pass off her child as legitimate.

Vlad entered Dutch society easily; he made himself known to the social elite and introduced himself as a Count and that was all it took to earn their curiosity. Soon a steady stream of invitations to soirées and receptions in the most elegant of houses, started to flow through his transient letterbox. After a few months he was invited to supper hosted by Boris and Sofia Van Helsing.

He arrived on time and Boris Van Helsing greeted him and welcomed him into his home. He introduced him to the other guests one by one. Vlad being the courteous gentleman that he was, kissed the forehand of all the women there. He was of course using this traditional introduction to assess their personalities and what would happen was he to take up with anyone of them. The first woman was too needy; this woman would be in danger of actually leaving her husband for him. No, he thought, she wouldn't do. He was introduced to the next woman and then the next and still some flaw made itself apparent in each one. The host of the party then introduced him to the last woman there.

"And finally, this is my wife, Sofia," Boris said. Vlad leaned down and kissed the woman's hand. She was completely devoted to her husband but yet she was still unhappy in her marriage; she was perfect. Vlad looked into her eyes and she coyly looked away. She was instantly attracted to Vlad and something in her good nature attracted Vlad to her.

He stood watching her the whole night; she was walking about the party, greeting her guests with an obliging smile. She was somewhat uncomfortable, for she knew Vlad was staring at her. Sofia left and went into the garden and Vlad followed her.

"It is a cold night—I have brought you a shawl," Vlad began.

"Thank you," Sofia said. As Vlad placed the shawl around her shoulders she accidentally touched his icy cold hand. His touch excited her and this scared her. She never wanted to betray her husband.

Sofia was dedicated to her husband, but she had never loved him. He had always been so good to her, and she had known him all of her life. They had grown up together and when he asked her to marry him she was reluctant but she knew no other man would ever treat her as well as Boris did. So she finally consented and had been relatively happy, but her life lacked passion and she longed for a child. She had borne a son who had been named after his father but he had died and that loss had very nearly consumed her. Boris insisted that they would have another child but she would not have another child of his. There was an inherit weakness in the children in his family; out of eight brothers he was the only one who had survived to manhood. She could not risk going through the heartbreak of losing another child.

When she saw Vlad that night she was instantly drawn to him; she had never felt such a feeling before. He was handsome, that was obvious for all to see, but there was an added attraction for Sofia, a strength that emanated from him, Sofia knew that it was not a strength of character, it was a strength of will. There was a mystery that surrounded him. When she looked into his eyes she saw something she couldn't quite fathom, it was as if he had lived a dozen lifetimes and this intrigued Sofia. She was captivated by him.

"Why are you depriving your guests of your company?" Vlad asked.

"They are my husband's friends. I am sure they will not miss me."

"I think you underestimate the allure of the company of such a gracious hostess." Sofia smiled. He was trying to charm her in a very blatant way. The mystery that had intrigued her quickly dissipated and she was disappointed but relieved by his very obvious flirtation.

"I think you are right. I will have to go inside and attend to my husband's guests." Sofia walked towards the back door of her house. Vlad sighed. He did not want to use mesmerism to seduce her, he wanted her to fall for him of her own free will as then she would find it easier to let Vlad go and stay with her husband. He would have to do better than he had done tonight—she had just dismissed him as a charming fool. Vlad watched and as she was about to enter the house, she turned back towards him and smiled. Not a knowing smile but a genuine, sincere, innocent smile. Vlad smiled in return; perhaps all was not lost yet.

During the succeeding next weeks Vlad made it his business to see Sofia as often as he could. Every time they met, Sofia treated him with nothing more than kindness and a friendship blossomed between the pair, but Sofia was determined that it would never be anything more than that. Vlad despite himself was actually starting to enjoy Sofia's company. She was a good person and Vlad had forgotten what that meant until he had met her. She had bewitched him with her kindness and generosity of spirit. Vlad made up his mind that he would not corrupt this woman she was too good for him, she would not be part of his hellish scheme but he would go and see her once more just to say goodbye.

He arrived early at Sofia's house before he was expected, but he wanted to leave as soon as he could. Sofia greeted him with a smile.

"It has been some time since I saw you last; I thought you had forgotten about us, Abraham," Sofia said when greeting him at the door.

"No. I have just been occupied with other things."

"Too busy to pay friends a visit?"

"Yes, I am afraid so, and my business unfortunately is taking me away. I must go home," Sofia shuddered. She felt as if her heart had dropped into her stomach. She did not want him to leave; she couldn't bear the thought of never seeing him again. She tried desperately to keep her feelings from him.

"Home, where is home?" Sofia asked her voice quivering.

"Far away from here," Vlad answered.

"Oh... I will miss you." Sofia got up and stared out at the garden so Vlad could not see her face. Tears were welling up in her eyes.

"Nonsense, no sooner will I have left than you will forget me," Vlad said sensing her feelings towards him and trying to convince her that it was just a momentary infatuation.

"I think you are quite wrong." Vlad was still reluctant to involve her in his plan, such a good woman did not deserve so harsh a treatment. He decided he had to go now; he should never have even come to say goodbye.

"I am not wrong; it is better that I leave now," Vlad answered. Tears were now steadily falling from Sofia's eyes. Vlad got up and approached Sofia; he placed his hand on her shoulder and said. "It is far better that I leave and you have nothing more to do with me, trust me in this." Sofia could not stand it any longer. She turned towards him, the tears flowing from her eyes.

"You can't go." Her voice was broken and little more than a whisper.

"I have to." Sofia took his hand and pulled him close to her. Vlad made one final attempt to pull away but he was reluctant to leave this woman. He longed to look into the eyes of a woman who loved him and did not hide her love like Isabella always had.

"I cannot bear the thought of being parted from you," Sofia begged.

"Where is your husband?" Vlad asked

"He is gone for the whole day. Please stay with me?" Sofia was completely in love with him. Vlad could not help himself. He kissed her and felt her exhilaration at kissing him. For the first time in two hundred years all thoughts of Isabella momentarily left his mind.

Their relationship lasted months; they met several times a week and each meeting was less happy than the last for both of them. Sofia felt guilty at betraying her husband and Vlad now constantly remembered Isabella; he was haunted by Isabella's face and what he was going to do to Sofia. It had to end soon. The next meeting was to be their last.

Sofia was obviously very upset when she came to see him on the last day.

"Come in," he said.

"I am not going to stay long," Sofia said.

"Why not?"

"We must end this," she said.

"You're right."

Sofia turned to face him. Vlad was relieved at her words. He did not want to hurt her and hopefully not too much damage had been done.

"You are taking this better than I thought you would," Sofia replied in a cool manner.

"What do you want me to say?" Vlad asked.

"I expected at least some protest from someone who has told me that they love me."

"You are wrong Sofia. I have never told you that I loved you."

Sofia thought for a moment. "That's right, you never have. I guess I presumed you did." Vlad realised at her words that he knew he had to hurt her to end this completely.

"The truth is I never loved you. I never made you any promises. You were just a distraction for me."

Sofia was both shocked and hurt by his words. "You felt nothing for me?" she spoke in a fractured whisper.

"I would not say nothing, I felt something for you, what we had was quite pleasant and that is why I let it last as long as I did, but I will never feel anything more for you than that."

"I don't believe you."

"Believe it." Sofia launched herself at Vlad pounding her fists on his chest.

"How can you say these things to me, after I have deceived my husband to be with you?"

"That was your error in judgement."

Sofia stood back from Vlad in disbelief. This was not the man she had fallen for. She now realised that the man that she had loved had just been a dream and the man before her bore no resemblance to him whatsoever. Sofia wiped away her tears; she had lost enough dignity in front of this man. She stepped back and walked towards the door.

As she opened the door that lead back out onto the street she took a deep breath and said, "I never want to see you again."

Vlad was glad it was over before it was too late, but then he felt completely iniquitous as Sofia spoke her last words to him. "And the child that I am carrying will never know your name." With that Sofia left. Vlad was devastated. It was too late; the damage had already been done. Vlad's heart sank. He should have been happy, for he had done what he had set out to do, but his heart was heavy and he did not want to hurt Sofia any more than he had already done.

A few years passed. Vlad went back to check that Isabella was all right and of course she was. He watched her from a distance, trying to remind himself what he had done this for. When he looked at Isabella he remembered why he had done what he had—to preserve her precious life. Vlad knew what he had to do but he delayed the inevitable as long as he could. He had meant to stay away only months but had stayed away years. Five years passed before he finally returned with the intention of killing Sofia's child.

He gazed at Sofia from afar. She looked so happy with her child. It was a boy. She was walking with him to the market. She was laughing and her son was laughing, too. For the first time in her life she was completely happy; she had found someone to love completely and who loved her completely in return.

How could Vlad take this away from her? But he had to. It was the only way. He waited until the boy was outside his house playing on his own. Vlad approached him and the boy unknowingly greeted his father.

"Hello," said the boy. Vlad didn't answer him. He just stared at the child he was about to kill.

"Abraham, Abraham," a voice called from behind Vlad; it was Sofia.

"Coming, mother," the boy shouted. Vlad was amazed Sofia had named him Abraham—the name he had used when he had met her. Abraham ran to his mother and hugged her.

She greeted him with a smile and said, "Go into the house and get ready for dinner."

"All right," he answered and ran to his home.

Sofia went over to Vlad and said, "What are you doing here?" Vlad ignored her question; he had one of his own.

"I thought you said he would never know my name?"

"I thought I hated you when I said that, I even tried to hate you but I realised I couldn't, because you gave me something that I will always treasure." Vlad could not do it; he could not kill this woman's son.

"You have raised a good boy; he will be better off without my influence."

"I don't doubt that for a second," Sofia said seriously. Sofia watched as Vlad walked away from her forever.

Sofia would never realise how lucky she was and how close her son had came to danger at such an early age. Vlad left never to return. He knew Sofia would never tell anyone of her affair, so he knew no one could possibly find out that her child was a Dhampir. He would find another way to kill Leila. There had to be another way. He would never try this method again.

ABRAHAM VAN HELSING THE MOST FAMOUS OF ALL THE DHAMPIRS

CHAPTER TWENTY-ONE

Isabella would completely recover from the wounds that Leila had inflicted. However, she now had two more permanent scars, one on the back of her head underneath her hair and one on her chest just above her heart. Her recovery would be slow, and she would stay with Vilem's child, Jakub, until it was complete. His wife Rayna, was not happy about the situation but Isabella knew her hostile attitude was only because she was concerned about her children. Isabella understood this and put up with the somewhat repressed animosity that Rayna infrequently displayed.

Jakub's eldest child Anna interested Isabella. She was a strong, wilful child and Isabella liked her. Anna revered Isabella and followed her around, imitating every mannerism Isabella displayed. Isabella was flattered by the child. Unfortunately, the skills of reading and writing that had been passed from generation to generation within this family had stopped with Katalin. She had no interest in learning and no interest in teaching. Isabella decided to correct Katalin's mistake and used her time at Jakub's to teach Anna how to read. It was her payment for Jakub's family's kindness and toleration.

Isabella was enjoying her recovery; she felt as if she was part of a family again. Even though the parents within this family feared her, they also respected her and Anna, not knowing how her parents felt, loved Isabella like an older sister. Despite this, Isabella knew her stay with them was to be relatively short-lived and when five years had passed and she was fully recovered, Jakub approached her.

"How much longer are you going to stay?" Jakub asked.

"You are not sick of me already, surely not, for it has only been a few years?" Isabella smiled as she said it. She had been expecting this conversation for the past year.

"We are not sick of you," Jakub answered.

"No, you are not sick of me. You are just scared that I will kill your children." If Isabella was going to be flippant, Jakub was as well.

"I know you won't kill my children, I am worried for the neighbour's children."

Isabella laughed. "Fair enough, I will leave soon."

Jakub detected sadness in her eyes, and he regretted the previous conversation.

"Stay as long as you want, Isabella, I mean that."

Isabella turned to him and smiled poignantly.

"I know you do and that is why I must leave, for some day the thirst will over take me and I will kill someone and it could be someone you care about," Isabella answered.

"I don't believe you would do that."

"Rest assured I would and it would not be the first time."

Sensing her remorse, Jakub replied, "I am sorry for you."

"Don't be. I know what I am; don't let sentiment make you forget."

"You are quite a woman."

"I was. Not any more—now I am quite the Vrolok." There was a lull in the conversation.

"Isabella I mean it, you can stay as long as you like," Jakub reiterated.

Isabella ignored Jakub's comment and asked, "Do you remember your mother?"

"Not at all. I sometimes think I remember what she looked like but how could I?"

"You remind me of her."

"I do?"

"Yes very much so. I have to say she was the most honest and pure soul I ever knew."

"Thank you for telling me that, I would give anything even to remember what she looked like or what her love felt like." Isabella turned and placed her hand on Jakub's shoulder.

"Your father should have told you." With this, Isabella went back inside the house with the intention of leaving that very night.

"My daughter will miss you dreadfully," Jakub shouted after her.

Isabella turned back towards Jakub and said, "She is a good child. Say goodbye to her for me." Isabella stood for moment looking at Jakub;

she wanted to give him something. "I have never given you anything for letting me stay here. I would like to." Isabella walked back towards Jakub placed her hands on his temples and Isabella gave him a memory, a long since forgotten memory. Jakub was amazed; tears started to flow from his eyes.

"I remember her," he simply stated. Isabella wiped his tears away with the tips of her fingers and left him.

Isabella traveled north through Germany and then through Holland. Since she had left Jakub's home she could sense she had company. Leila was always close but never showed herself. Without the Dhampir's blood Isabella was too strong for her. So Leila chose to follow her without confrontation, waiting for an opportunity to arise to either end Isabella's life or inflict some great harm. Isabella let her follow her, for she too was looking for some way to kill Leila and Isabella was sure that she would eventually find it.

Isabella had practically traveled as far north as she could without crossing an ocean. She had halted in Rotterdam and was walking along the bank of the port. She paused for a moment to gaze out across the Mass River. She was only fifteen miles from the North Sea. She longed to cross it and chase after Nicolae, but she knew she could not. She stood on the dock beside a dilapidated and abandoned ship. It caught her eye for a just a moment as she turned. The ship was old and weather beaten; it had been tied to the pier where it would eventually sink, a once magnificent ship that had been forgotten when it had outlived its usefulness.

"The last of the Flying Dutchmen," a voice spoke at Isabella's side. "I came here to see it."

"A Flying Dutchman?" Isabella queried. She was glad of the conversation; it had been ten years since she had spoken to anyone.

"Do you know the story?"

"No, tell me." Isabella turned to see who was talking to her. He was a little more than a child and a little less than a man.

From the instant she saw him Isabella discerned that there was something very different about this very young man. She sensed an inhuman quality. If she didn't know better she would have sworn he was another Vampire, but she knew he couldn't possibly be; he was far too young. Hopefully not even Leila would have turned one so youthful. This creature was something new, something extraordinary, neither human nor Vampire. This new being continued to speak.

"Legend says that Captain Van der Becken was determined to achieve what no other captain had before. He wanted to sail around the Cape of Good Hope. So dogmatic was he in his quest that he did not observe, or chose not to observe, the dark clouds looming overhead. The captain sailed straight into the eye of the storm; the ship was doomed and started to sink. The captain, however, would not give up and would not let a storm so baneful that it must have been sent by God himself to beat him. He yelled out and cursed God for sending such a storm. He yelled he would round the Cape even if he had to keep sailing until doomsday. And with his own words he had sealed his fate, and that is where he is until this day, sailing his ship totally alone, his crew having abandoned him. So if you ever see a ship only manned by one sailor, look away quickly, as whoever looks upon the Flying Dutchman will die a most terrible death."

"That is a grim tale," Isabella said.

"It is not a tale, it is the truth,"

Isabella smiled. "Of course it is."

"Abraham!" A voice in the distance echoed through the summer air.

"That is my mother. I better go."

"You had better."

The boy bowed as a courtesy to Isabella. He had been holding a paint box, tightly in his hands the whole time they had been talking.

"Are you a painter, Abraham?" Isabella asked.

"I am, but not for long. I start medical training next winter."

"I take it you are not happy about that prospect."

"No, not really, but it is what my mother and father want me to do."

"Medicine is a good profession, an honourable one."

"I suppose."

"Abraham!" This time his mother's voice was sharper and more determined.

"I better go."

"You better." As Abraham turned and walked away Isabella knew that she would meet this boy again, but when he was fully grown.

※

Isabella did meet him again several years later in Germany. He had lost a little of his romantic nature and was now a man of science.

Isabella was walking along the bank of the river Neckar when she came across an advertisement.

"Goethe's *Faust* now showing at the Heidelberg Theatre," it read.

"You know the story." A familiar phrase and a familiar voice came out of the darkness. Isabella looked around and saw Abraham. He had matured and was now a handsome young man, his adolescence several years behind him.

"As a matter of fact, I do," Isabella answered.

"Is it a good story? I am considering going to see it." Isabella smiled at Abraham, but he did not recognise her.

"You don't remember me, do you?" Isabella enquired.

"No, should I?"

"You should, I flatter myself that I am not usually so easily forgotten."

"When did we meet?" he questioned.

"You told me a story about the Flying Dutchman."

Abraham looked at Isabella and now he recognised her. "That must be ten years ago; you look as if you haven't aged a day."

"Appearances can be deceptive."

"You look well; anyway, I can't believe you remembered that, I was just a boy then."

"You are not a boy any more?"

"I try not to be."

"An honest answer, a rare thing from a young man."

"That's a bit harsh; you must never have known the right young men."

Isabella laughed and answered, "I mustn't have."

"Well we can correct that; if I go to the play tonight will I see you there?"

"Perhaps," Isabella said, and a promising smile occupied her face.

"I hope I do." Abraham bowed his head and left Isabella. She still felt that unfamiliar aura but it seemed a good deal more human than it had done before and so she dismissed it as a simple paradox.

Vlad and Leila looked on as Isabella was talking to Abraham. Vlad was not close enough to recognise his own son. When Isabella left the young man she still sported her smile for a few hundred yards. Abraham had made an impression on her and this fact was evident to both Leila and Vlad. Leila decided there and then that if she could not kill Isabella she would kill anyone else that Isabella held dear, so she would wait until this impression grew deeper. Vlad also tried to fight off similar instincts; old pangs of jealousy were starting to well up inside him. He saw Leila following Abraham and he knew what her plan was but he hesitated from stopping her; he briefly considered letting Leila kill this young man.

Leila kept watching the pair for the next few months, looking for some sign of growing affection on Isabella's part. Leila had waited to kill him until she was certain that Isabella would be hurt by his death, and unfortunately for Isabella she was growing fond of Abraham.

Isabella was relishing the company of this young man. He was someone to talk to and who was eager to talk to her. She was asking him plenty of questions, about his life and what he wanted for his future. He was from a prominent Dutch family and he was attending Heidelberg University studying medicine. He was an enigma. To Isabella he was just a normal man, with a normal upbringing, but yet still there was something about him that captivated her. When he touched her she felt a sharp tingling sensation run through her. It was not unpleasant, but it felt unusual and out of place, as if her body was warning her to stay away from this man and that ironically was what made Isabella stay close to him. Isabella could not read him at all, she could not see what he was thinking, and even when she touched him she could not enter his mind.

Isabella had been keeping company with Abraham for almost a year. Abraham requested to see Isabella regularly, but today was different. He had made such a formal request to see her, he had even gone to the measures of sending a note to her apartments, and this was something he had never done before. He wrote that he wanted to ask her something important and because Isabella could not read him she had no idea what it was.

"I'm glad you came," Abraham began when they met that evening.

"Well, how could I not when I was so formally requested to do so. Your note said you wanted to ask me something important. I had to know what it was." Isabella realised Abraham was very nervous, for when he had taken her hand in greeting it was clammy and hot and yet it was a cold night in February. "What is wrong with you?" Isabella asked. "Why so nervous?"

"Nothing, nothing," he answered. "Nothing at all," he repeated quickly again.

"All right, I believe you, why all the mystery and the written invitation?"

"I will tell you later."

"All right, where are we going then?"

"For a walk along the river bank—it is a beautiful night." Isabella pressed out her arm for Abraham to take and the pair started to walk across the bridge on to the river bank.

"This is where we first met," Abraham stated.

"Not quite, remember the Flying Dutchman?" Isabella corrected him.

"Oh, yes." Abraham remained silent for a few seconds. His nerves had momentarily settled as the pair had started their stroll but he was becoming skittish again.

"What is wrong with you?" Isabella asked.

"Nothing," Abraham retorted. "Stop asking me what is wrong!" he shouted.

"I will if you tell me why you have brought me here," Isabella snapped. She was not one to tolerate being shouted at.

"All right, all right, I asked you here because I wanted to ask you to…"

"To… what?" Isabella stated getting increasingly more and more impatient.

"This is not how I envisioned this happening."

"I am going home; I am tired of your riddles." Isabella turned to leave. Abraham caught her hand and pulled her back. At that moment Isabella was struck by how strong he was. She had not put up much resistance but what little she did should have been enough to make him relinquish his grip on her.

"I asked you here because I wanted to ask you to marry me," he said. Isabella forgot momentarily about his strength because she was amazed by the content of his outburst. She started to laugh out loud. All this time he thought he had been courting Isabella and she had not even realised. He was always so courteous and gentlemanly, Isabella had dismissed it as being due to his upbringing, not ardour; her heightened vampiric perception was of no use to her with Abraham.

"Marry you?" she said through her laughter. "You must be mad."

"I didn't think that I would ever have a lady laugh at me when I asked her this question. This is not how I imagined it." Isabella was still laughing at the absurdity of the situation she was now in. Abraham was now hurt by her reaction. "Isabella, please stop laughing." The sincerity in his voice curbed Isabella's blithesomeness, and her laughter was immediately silenced. Abraham began to speak again reiterating his proposal. "I love you and I want you to marry me."

"Abraham," Isabella began.

Abraham quickly jumped in before Isabella could speak; he sensed that she was going to say no. "Before you say anything, at least think about it." Abraham took Isabella's hand in his and pulled it to his chest, pressing her hand to his heart.

To Leila and Vlad, who were still watching, this was the first sign of any sort of passion between the pair. Leila thought to herself that this was the night to act. She would kill this man in front of Isabella to ensure that Isabella knew that the only future she would have was one of constant misery.

"What I mean to say is..." Abraham continued. "I am from a good family, I am going to be an important physician, and I will work all the days of my life to ensure that you have everything you desire."

Isabella was touched by his words. "Abraham," Isabella said, still trying to interrupt him.

"No, I am not finished yet," Abraham protested, but Isabella had to speak. She would not let Abraham continue on.

"Listen to me, Abraham!" Isabella took both his hands in hers and said, "I care very deeply for you, but I cannot marry you."

"Why not? What possible reason could you give me to refuse me? I have every possible answer to any excuse you could give me—I have been thinking about this for a very long time,"

Isabella smiled at Abraham, a warm heart-rending smile.

"Believe me, there is nothing I would like better than to live out my life with you, raising a family; it would be like a dream come true."

"Perfect, then you cannot refuse me."

"I have to."

"Why?" Isabella tried to think of an excuse that would stop his persistence. "Tell me, give me one legitimate reason," Abraham continued. Isabella turned away from Abraham.

"Believe me, I am tempted more than you will ever realise."

"I can convince you if it takes a decade, even a lifetime, I will convince you."

Isabella turned to Abraham. "Stop," she said trying to silence Abraham. "I can't marry you," she cried.

"Why? Why not?" Isabella was feeling the pressure of the constant questioning by Abraham.

"I can't," she retorted.

"Why can't you?"

"I can't...because."

"Because?"

"Because I am already married." Abraham stepped back from Isabella.

"Married?"

"Yes."

"But you don't wear a ring."

"When I left my husband, I chose not to wear his ring." Abraham walked a few steps away from Isabella.

"Tell me he is an old man and might die soon," Abraham flippantly pleaded.

Isabella smiled again. "That is not very charitable of you," she said.

"I am not in a charitable mood."

"Well, he is not old and is unfortunately in perfect health; you will probably die before him."

"Well, I am so glad he will outlive me. Why did you leave him?" his sardonic tone becoming more earnest.

"He hurt someone very close to me and let me believe he had nothing to do with it. When I found out he did, I could not stay with him."

"But you wanted to stay with him."

Isabella looked at Abraham, shocked by how perceptive he was. "I did."

"You still have feelings for him?"

"Yes… I will always have some feelings for him; that is my curse."

"And I can't change your mind?"

"No."

Abraham got up and bowed to Isabella. "If you ever reconsider, I will be waiting."

Isabella watched as Abraham slowly walked away. At that moment she was struck by the thought that her last chance of happiness was walking away from her. Isabella could not let him leave; she deserved some happiness, she needed some, she had spent so many years alone she could not stand it any longer. Just a few years, she thought, and then she would leave him.

"Abraham, Abraham!" she called after him. Abraham turned back towards her. She ran to him flinging herself into his arms. "I lied," she said. "I never married him. I was supposed to but never did; I am free to marry you if you will still have me." Abraham returned her embrace, and whispered in her ear.

"Of course I still want you," Abraham said. Isabella's eyes were shut, her head resting on his shoulder. She was holding him so tightly, fearing that if she let go he would slip away. Isabella reopened her eyes to see someone running towards them. It was Leila; brandishing a knife, intent on killing Abraham. She was running at tremendous speed. Isabella pushed Abraham back from her in an attempt to save him. It was too late; she could do nothing but watch as Leila slashed her knife deep into Abraham's back. Abraham reached out for Isabella trying to speak her name. He fell to his knees and then collapsed completely to the ground. Isabella looked away from Abraham towards Leila; she too had fallen to the ground. She had been injured and was screaming in pain.

Leila was holding her face wondering what was wrong and where this pain had come from. Isabella launched herself at Leila and pushed her over to see why she was screaming out. Her face had been scarred by Abraham's blood. Isabella couldn't believe what she saw. Along one cheek it looked as if she had been very heavily burnt, like someone had poured acid onto her face. Isabella let Leila go and left her to writhe around in misery. She was in great pain; she dragged herself up onto her feet and ran away. Isabella went back to Abraham; he was lying on his stomach. She pressed the tip of one finger into his blood. A pain seared through her and her finger wizened slightly into a tiny scar.

"Dhampir," she whispered. Abraham's wound had partially healed. She rolled Abraham onto his back and looked at him. Colour was starting to return to his cheeks. The wound that Leila inflicted should have been mortal, but there was no scent of death surrounding him. He was going to live. Isabella looked again at his wound; it was starting to heal rapidly now. It was not as quick to heal as it would have been if Isabella had received it but it was healing very quickly, nevertheless. Isabella wondered what to do. She realised what she should do. She should kill him and take from him enough blood to finish off Leila. But Leila would be granted a reprieve tonight. Isabella picked Abraham up, being careful not to let any of his blood come in contact with her skin, and carried him back to her temporary home. She placed him on her bed and waited for him to awaken.

Days passed and he still had not woken but on the night of the fourth day as Isabella sat beside him, Abraham took a deep, sharp breath and opened his eyes with a start. He was bewildered and confused, but when he saw Isabella his mind settled. He felt safe with her, but he shouldn't have. Isabella smiled at him; she believed there was no point telling him what he was and what she was at this point. She would wait until he was fully recovered before she did that, to at least give him a fighting chance.

Weeks passed and soon Abraham had completely healed. They hadn't talked about that night but Isabella knew he would soon start asking questions.

"I am fully restored," Abraham began.

"That is good," Isabella answered Abraham, smiling as she did.

"I think I owe my speedy recovery to you."

"I did nothing; you healed so quickly yourself. Do you ever remember being sick in your life?" Isabella asked.

"No I have always been quite healthy; in fact this is only time in my life that I can remember being even remotely ill."

"I thought as much."

"What are you talking about?"

"I can't marry you," Isabella stated.

"Surely we have been through all this."

"Now I am certain. You cannot convince me otherwise and you will not want to when you know what I am."

"Isabella you are talking nonsense."

"I am a Vrolok, a Vampire and you are my opposite, my nemesis, you are a Dhampir."

"A Dhampir?" Abraham staggered and clutched his head. "I feel quite light-headed all of a sudden."

"You should, because I have drugged you; you will soon pass out and when you awaken tomorrow I will be gone." Abraham was slowly losing consciousness but he would stay awake long enough for Isabella to tell him what she had to. Isabella took a knife and slashed her arm. Abraham watched in amazement as the wound healed almost instantly before his eyes. She then took the knife and pricked his finger with the tip of the blade. She pricked her own finger and instead of healing it withered her skin into a scar.

"You are poison to me. I am a Vampire and you are destined to be a Vampire hunter, as you are the only one who can be."

Abraham was stunned by what he was seeing and hearing.

"We will meet again," Isabella stated, sure that they would. "But I fear the next time we meet one of us will have to die. I am leaving you now but I want something from you first." At this point Abraham blacked out and Isabella slashed his wrist to take some of his blood. She could kill Leila now, and she wanted to use her grandfather's sword to do it.

※

Isabella had left the sword with Vlad; he had had it long enough. She wanted it back. It was hers and the only thing left from her grandfather that she possessed. She called into see Jakub before going to the castle. He was an old man now but Isabella was glad to see an old friend.

"Are you well, Jakub?" Isabella asked.

"All the better for seeing you," Jakub had always been kind to Isabella.

"That I am sure is a lie, but it is nice to hear your sweet lies again,"

"No, it is the truth; I have been looking for you."

"Why?" Isabella asked curiously.

"That place is filled with Vampires again," Jakub tilted his head up towards the castle.

"Are they killing any Slovaks?"

"No, not yet."

"As long as they are not killing Slovaks I have no quarrel with them."

"I thought you might say that, but the Slovaks of the village are getting nervous. They are scared; they know what happened to my grandmother and my father. They think you have abandoned us."

"Abandoned you? You know that it is not true."

"I know it, but the people of the village are not so certain."

"What do you want me to do? I can't go around to every Slovak and promise them I will always protect them."

"No, I am not asking you to do that. I just want you to visit a bit more often."

"I visited Nadezhda very often and look what happened."

"You were not to blame for her death and if you had not been there I would have probably been killed as well as my father."

"All right. I will visit more often... how is Anna?"

"Very well. She is a mother now. She has a son and she named him after me."

"So you are a grandfather?"

"I am a proud grandfather." There was a pause. "What brought you back?" Jakub asked.

"I am back for my grandfather's sword."

"Do you want me to come with you?"

"No, this is something I have to do it myself."

Isabella waited until nightfall to go up to the castle. She crept up and peered through the window. No one seemed to be about but she saw her grandfather's sword leaning up against the fireplace. Isabella suddenly became distracted by a noise from behind her. Isabella turned around to see Anna.

"Anna, what are you doing here?" Isabella scolded.

"My father was worried about you."

"So he sent you up here after me?" Isabella asked suspiciously.

"Oh no, he would have never have sent me up here; he realises how dangerous it is, I wanted to come here, and I wanted to help you."

"Anna this is not a game. You are a mother now; you should take better care of yourself and not be doing stupid things like this." Isabella studied Anna. She was still so young that it was hard to believe that she was already a mother.

"Do you want me go back?"

"No. I want you to stay where I can keep an eye on you." Isabella was slightly concerned for Anna but if truth be known she wanted a friendly face with her. Isabella opened the door and stepped into the castle. Anna followed her in.

The large hall was as she had left it. There was a fire still burning in the fireplace but the room was empty and cold. Isabella walked over to the fire and Anna crept in behind her. She turned around to watch Anna, who was walking on her tiptoes. Isabella smiled at her.

"There is no need to try and be quiet. If a Vampire was here it would have heard you already." Anna looked a little embarrassed and began to walk normally. Isabella went over and picked up the sword. It was the only thing in the castle that had been looked after. It must be worth something, Isabella thought, or why else would Vlad have looked after it so well. A gust of wind echoed through the hall and the door slammed shut. Isabella was startled; she knew the wind was not strong enough to blow the heavy wooden closed. She realised she was not the only Vampire in this room.

"Anna, stay close to me," Isabella whispered. Anna, who was now frightened, did what she was told.

"Who are you?" A voice echoed through out the darkened hall. Isabella could not pinpoint where it was coming from.

"My name is Isabella."

"Isabella. He has talked of you," the voice responded.

"I'm sure he has," Isabella cynically responded.

"What do you want here?" the voice responded.

"Nothing. I just came for my grandfather's sword."

"Is that all?"

"Yes."

"He misses you. Will you not wait till he comes back?"

"I will not and that information is of no relevance to me."

"I know that is not true."

"Who are you?" Isabella asked, and the other Vampire finally revealed herself. She appeared at the top of the stairs. She was a very young-looking girl; she must have been only sixteen, perhaps seventeen, when she was turned. She descended the stairs with so much grace she looked like she was floating down them. Her golden hair and blue eyes shimmered in the moonlight.

"She is beautiful," Anna whispered, unable to contain her awe at this vision.

"Yes she is," Isabella agreed. There was a ghostly quality to her as if she was not of this earth and never had been.

"I am Olya. I am a Vampire but not a very strong one. I was turned too late. I was dead when he changed me. I had been dead for just a few moments; I saw a light and I reached out towards it. I think I nearly touched heaven before I was yanked back from it into this dark world again."

Isabella felt pity for this heavenly creature.

"I can end it for you—I can send you back towards that light," Isabella stated.

"No, not yet, I believe I was brought back for a reason and I will not leave until that reason has presented itself."

"You are brave," Isabella stated.

"No not really."

Isabella turned to leave.

"Will you ever come back to him?" Olya asked.

"Never. I can't."

"I see only blackness ahead for all us if you do not," Olya answered.

"Blackness is not just our future, it is our present, as well."

"This life is not so black for me and it need not be for you."

"Do you have to feed?" Isabella asked.

"No, I don't have to kill."

"You are a wonderment; can I touch you? I want to see if you are really real."

"You can." As Isabella touched Olya's hand an energy surged through her. She recognised it. It was the feeling she had felt when Nicolae, Charlotte and Vincente died. Isabella did not want to let go but Olya pulled back her hand. "You must let go—it exhausts me."

Isabella let go, not wanting to cause Olya any pain.

"Isabella, if you don't want to see him you should leave now, for he is near."

"Thank you," Isabella stated.

Isabella turned to leave and as she was just about to go out the door with Anna behind her, Olya called after her. "Try to forgive him, Isabella. He loves you and he knows he hurt you greatly, but he is truly penitent."

Isabella smiled back at this angelic creature. "Do you know what your name means?"

"Yes, it means a holy one."

Isabella looked at Olya. A serenity surrounded her. Isabella felt as if she had been touched by an angel. She shut the door behind her and left the castle. As she walked down through the woods with Anna to the village below she saw Vlad on a horse galloping up towards the castle. Each was struck still by the presence of the other. Vlad and Isabella gazed upon each other's faces for the first time in half a century.

"Who is that?" Anna asked.

"No one," Isabella answered. "Come on, Anna, I better make sure you get safely home." The horse that was carrying Vlad veered away and galloped on. Isabella also journeyed on, neither one of them taking the time to glance back at the other.

Isabella made sure Anna was safely home and then left to look for Leila.

※

Vlad had held Leila back from Abraham the night she was wounded; he knew she was going to kill him. He should have stopped her months ago but his old nature made him reluctant. But Vlad knew that he must try to save Abraham, for if he did not Isabella would be hurt and he had hurt her enough. He watched with a firm grip on Leila that night. He was standing behind her. She had wanted to strike out at Abraham since he had arrived to meet Isabella. Leila knew by the way Isabella was looking at him that she felt great affection for him. She had been about to run towards Abraham when Vlad had wrenched her back.

"Where do you think you are going?" Vlad asked.

"Let me go," Leila screamed.

"No," Vlad shouted. "You have caused her enough harm."

"Not nearly enough," Leila screamed. Leila was struggling trying to get loose from his grip but it was useless.

"Stop struggling; it is pointless." Vlad said, for he was much stronger than Leila.

"You can't hold me forever."

"Maybe not, but I can break your arms and legs. That should slow you down,"

Vlad had never been to close to Abraham. In fact that evening was the closest he had ever been. He was watching the pair and as Abraham stood to leave he turned directly towards Vlad. Vlad now facing him for the first time was amazed. He saw what he knew were his own son's eyes staring back at him. Vlad started to laugh and let go of Leila.

"Go, Leila, try and kill him," Vlad said. Leila pounced on Abraham and Vlad saw her shrink back when some of his blood splashed onto her skin. He saw the realisation on Isabella's face as she discovered Abraham was a Dhampir. After a few minutes Leila stood and began to run away, but she did not get very far. Vlad stopped her.

"So for once you have felt what the Dhampir's blood feels like."

"Leave me alone," Leila shouted.

"It is quite fitting that you have ended up this way—that scar will never heal."

"Stop it, let me go!"

"I will let you go, but she won't," Vlad pointed to Isabella. "Now that she has a Dhampir's blood she will be relentless in the pursuit of you."

※

Isabella had turned the tables on Leila; she was now chasing her. She had easily tracked her down. Leila was not as cautious as Isabella was about covering her tracks. The path Leila took was littered with abandoned bodies. Leila's scar was as prominent as it ever was. Isabella confronted Leila for what she hoped was the final time.

"Leila," Isabella called out. Leila was chilled to the bone when she saw Isabella. She knew Vlad's prediction was about to become true. Leila shrank back from her. She wanted to hold on to her pathetic existence, miserable though it was.

"Get away from me!" she yelled.

"You are finally scared of me," Isabella said. Leila was by now running from Isabella. Isabella chased her and within seconds caught her. She had always been faster and stronger than Leila. Isabella tripped Leila and she fell onto the dirt.

"I am not afraid of you," Leila said very nervously, jumping back onto her feet, trying to show Isabella that she still had some courage left. Isabella pulled Leila close to her so that she could see her own reflection in Isabella's eyes.

"You should be, you should have always been." Isabella placed a drop of the Dhampir's blood in her eye. As soon as the blood touched Leila's eye it was petrified and the skin that surrounded it hardened into a callus.

Leila wrestled free from Isabella's grip and screamed out, "Are you going to torture me?"

"Should I torture you? Should I let you live, only to slowly and painfully take your life bit by bit?" Isabella lunged at Leila again and took another drop and placed in it in the other eye, blinding Leila completely.

"Why?" Leila shouted.

"You ask me why? You killed Charlotte, you tried to kill Abraham and you killed Vilem, one of my kin."

"You killed me," Leila shouted back.

"I didn't do a good enough job; I should have made sure I had finished you off."

"Well, make sure you don't make that mistake twice—finish me." Leila was crawling around on the ground, feeling for Isabella. Isabella knew she did not want to grant Leila the peace that she had witnessed, which every other Vampire had gained when they had left this world.

"No, I am not going to kill you; I want you to suffer for what you have done. I will not grant you the serenity that comes with death."

"If you leave me here I promise you I will feed on nothing but Slovaks for the rest of my days."

"You will never feed on anything ever again!" Isabella clutched Leila's jaw and poured some of the Dhampir's blood into her mouth. Isabella pushed her jaw together. The quantity was not enough to kill her but her mouth started to burn, Leila squealed and that was to be the last sound she ever made. Isabella pushed her mouth shut again and her skin seared together. Isabella pushed her jaw up towards her nose, crushing her bones, fusing the bottom and lower part of her jaw together. Isabella turned from her, leaving Leila in agony. Leila grasped out for her trying to listen for an indication of where Isabella stepped but she couldn't find her. She was gone.

Isabella had left Leila blind, disfigured and unable to feed. She would now spend the rest of her existence in constant pain, she would age and she would die, but not for years.

Isabella did not know it yet, but she would come to regret letting Leila live.

RENFIELD
A SANE MAN FIGHTING FOR HIS SOUL

CHAPTER TWENTY-TWO

Renfield watched as they carried the coffin down the street. The skies had opened and were weeping, quite fitting on this day. His daughter was in that wooden box, cold, still and lifeless. They said she died of natural causes but Renfield knew that not to be true. He had killed her, the same as if he had stabbed her through the heart. He had sold her in a marriage that he knew would suffocate her. Her husband had money and Renfield wanted money more than his daughter's happiness. This was the result, a funeral. The sights seen on this day would haunt him forever. How could he face Saint Peter and plead for his soul when he had done this? His guilt-ridden tears were hidden in the rain.

Vlad was watching Isabella when she finally confronted Leila. He saw how strong she had become; Leila was no match for her. As he watched, he came upon the realisation that she did not need him, at least not any more. She did not need his protection; no one on this earth was a proper match for her, not even another Vampire. He wondered, was he capable of beating her? He doubted that he could now. Vlad turned his back on Isabella; he was filled with sadness. He now felt totally alone—he was no longer her distant guardian.

Isabella had had every intention of killing Leila, but on seeing her pathetic existence she had decided it would be a worse punishment to leave her alive. Isabella spent the subsequent years the same way that she had spent so many others, completely alone. But after two decades, she heard Anna calling her home.

Anna's son was getting married when Isabella returned; a girl named Catherine was his bride. Neither Isabella nor Anna thought much of her but Anna's son was in love. Anna had changed in the years since Isabella had seen her last. She was not the young impetuous girl that had followed Isabella everywhere she went. Her second child had died of consumption and since then moroseness had penetrated her mind. She ached for the daughter that was no longer there.

Isabella was still very fond of her and she was possibly one of the only humans that could have any influence over the Vampire.

"There is a lot of activity going on up there," Anna said, looking to the castle.

"What do you mean, activity?" Isabella asked.

"People have been coming and going."

"People, what sort of people?"

"Some Slovaks and some Szgany Gypsies have been hired to work there and there is one other person who lives in the castle now, a foreigner."

"A foreigner, from where?"

"England."

"England, he always loved England; I wonder what he is planning. Do you know why the Englishman came here?"

"All I know is that he was a British solicitor. He told the innkeeper that he was here to finalise the paper work on the Count's purchase of some property in England."

"Purchasing property? Isabella said bemused. "We Vampires do not purchase property, we... acquire it," Isabella said with a smile.

"Well that is what he is doing, according to all reports."

"If Vlad wants to purchase property, he has to let him return home."

"A coach came for him a few weeks ago, but he never got on it."

"I think I will go up and talk to Olya and see what is happening. Have you seen her recently?" Isabella asked.

"No not at all."

"That settles it. I want to check that she is all right. I will go up tonight."

"Will you let me know what happens?" asked Anna.

"I will, I'll be back before morning," Isabella concluded.

Isabella walked through the forest up to the castle. All the torches that surrounded the castle were now lighted. These torches had not been seen for two hundred years, perhaps even longer. Isabella was puzzled by this. Vlad had no need of light. Was he trying to pass himself off as human in front of this Englishman? Isabella hesitated before she pushed open the heavy wooden door. She did not want to see him, but she wanted to see Olya. So she somewhat reluctantly continued and crossed the threshold. The entrance hall was empty, but Isabella could hear whispering coming from upstairs. She slowly ascended the staircase, apprehensive as to what she would find there. She opened the door to her old room to discover that Olya now occupied it.

"I knew you would come back," Olya began softly.

"I am not staying," Isabella said, not wanting to give Olya false hope.

"You should. The danger that I spoke of before is much closer now." As Olya spoke, Isabella realised she felt it too. There was something…life felt finite again.

"I think you are right. I feel it, too, the end for all of us feels near," Isabella answered.

"Then you must come home."

"This is not my home; it hasn't been for a very long time, no matter what happens I can never live here."

"Isabella…" Olya began, she was trying to plead with her, but Isabella cut her off before she could continue."

"No, never," Isabella said firmly.

"Well will you do me one other favour?"

"Anything else."

"Will you help me go outside? I rarely get to go out anymore. I want to feel the fresh air on my face."

"Of course." Isabella practically had to carry Olya outside, for she was very weak. The glow that had enveloped her had gone, and it had taken with it the serenity that radiated from her heart. Isabella did not know if she was dying or becoming like her.

"Why are the torches lighted at the gate?" Isabella asked when they were both outside.

"A man arrived a few weeks ago."

"Yes, I know, an Englishman."

"Renfield is his name."

"Why is he here?"

"He is helping Vlad buy a house in England."

"But why does he need to buy anything?"

"He wants to live in England respectably."

"Respectably?" Isabella smirked as she spoke.

"Yes."

"That is the most ridiculous thing I have ever heard, is he deluded? He is a Vampire; he cannot be respectable."

"He is trying. He has stopped feeding."

"Completely?"

"Yes."

"What has affected this change in him?"

"I'm not sure. His visits to this place used to be rare—sometimes it would be years between visits. Then twenty years ago he came home in a deep melancholy. He was inconsolable and didn't leave this nebulous place not even for a moment, and then a few months ago he decided he wanted to leave forever." Isabella stooped down and took a fistful of dirt in her hand.

"He will not leave forever. In life this is the land he fought for. He would have died for this land; it will never let him go." As these words left her lips, the earth started to heat in her hand. Isabella unclasped her fingers and let it fall to the ground. As the sod hit the forest floor the heat spread throughout. Without realising it, Isabella had released a mighty power.

"Are you going to go with him?" Isabella asked Olya.

"No. Whatever extra life I was granted is soon to end," Olya cried. Isabella was sorry for her. Isabella's thoughts were interrupted by a loud banging coming from deep within the castle.

"Who else lives here now?"

"There are three other Vampires; they are vicious and malicious creatures. Renfield occupies the upper rooms."

"I'm going up to him," Isabella stated. At this the wooden door at the entrance of the castle banged shut.

"Vlad is back," Olya whispered.

Isabella was reluctant to go back inside. She did not want to occupy the same space as he did, but she felt she had to know what Vlad's plan was. For, like Olya, she too now felt the darkness that was about to encapsulate them. Isabella crept silently up the second staircase to the higher chambers where Renfield was being held. She peered in through the gap between the hinges and the open door. For the first time Isabella was watching Vlad without his knowledge.

"Renfield," Vlad began and Isabella listened, "I want you to return now to England, and send someone else to finish off your work here. A young man. I want to know a different man's outlook on English living." Isabella looked over at Renfield. He was anxious and scared. Vlad had obviously been torturing him. "Will you send me this man, if I let you go home?"

"I will," Renfield vehemently agreed.

"Very well, you will leave tonight."

"Thank you, thank you," Renfield groveled.

Isabella was shocked. Renfield obviously knew what Vlad was and yet he was letting him go home. Isabella knew this was completely foolish and when the coach came for Renfield that evening she would make sure that she was on it. For she would have to kill him.

※

Renfield stumbled onto the coach. He wanted to get away as fast as he could and his haste was making his steps clumsy. Isabella was already sitting inside. Sweat was dripping down Renfield's brow. He kept looking at his watch. Isabella did not have to strike up a conversation with him, for he started to speak to her before she had a chance.

"How far are we from Bistrita?"

"Twenty, perhaps thirty miles," Isabella answered.

"That far?" Renfield asked nervously.

"It should only take a few hours to get there," Isabella said, trying to reassure him in an effort to gain his confidence.

"A few hours, surely not that long?"

"Why are you in such a hurry?" Isabella asked.

"I'm not, I...I just want to get home."

"Your business in the Carpathians is concluded?"

"I have done all that I can do," Renfield answered.

"What was your business?" Isabella asked. At this Renfield raised his glance to look up at Isabella's face. During their whole conversation he had not lifted his eyes from his watch.

"Why are you so curious as to the nature of my business?" Renfield demanded.

"No reason at all, just making conversation."

"I am sorry," Renfield apologised. "I just want out of this place."

Isabella moved over beside him and touched his head. Isabella saw jumbled images in his thoughts. A lost daughter, a fear of death, a fear of hell, and an eventual betrayal. He would not stay loyal to Vlad—he had to die.

Isabella stayed with him until he got the boat to England from Varna. She watched the ship until it was out to sea. She turned her back on it and looked up to the skies stirring up the winds. A storm engulfed the boat; Isabella believed the ship would be swallowed by the sea. Unfortunately, the ship was sturdier than Isabella had hoped and Renfield arrived in England unharmed. Renfield kept his promise to Vlad and sent Jonathon Harker to finish what he had started.

※

Isabella was satisfied that Renfield now occupied a watery grave, that he could not tell a soul and he could not send anyone else. She returned to the castle to appease Olya. As she entered her old room she was struck by how pale Olya looked; she would not last much longer.

"It is all right, Olya, he will not tell anyone anything." Isabella did not tell Olya that she sent the winds to kill him. For Olya would have felt in some way responsible, and that was too much for her good heart to stand.

"That's good," Olya struggled to get the words out.

"Olya, I am afraid to leave you."

"Then don't."

"I have to. But will you not come with me?"

"No, a force that is beyond whispers to me that I must stay here."

"All right, but if anything should happen, get word to Anna and I will come back." Olya nodded. Isabella got up to leave.

Olya called out after her, "Thank you, Isabella, for all you have done." Isabella nodded and left.

A few months went by and Isabella stayed in Bistrita, for she wanted to be close if Olya called for her. During this time, to Isabella's dismay, another man arrived from England. Renfield had survived to tell the tale.

Jonathon Harker stayed in the Golden Krone hotel, and even before he arrived there was a letter waiting for him from Vlad. Isabella paid one of the hotel workers to let her see it but it had nothing of any importance in it. Isabella watched Jonathon for a few days from a distance. She decided that he probably posed no threat whatsoever. He obviously did not know anything of Vampires, but just in case she would try and scare him into not going. Isabella waited for the landlady of the hotel to come down from Jonathon's room.

"Well?" Isabella enquired. "Did you frighten him?" Isabella asked.

"I did, but not enough. He still has every intention of going," said the landlady.

"He is a fool."

"He may be...he scribbles everything down in a diary."

"A diary. This may prove useful to me, thank you." Isabella gave the landlady some money and then left. She observed Jonathon the next day as he was waiting for a coach. Vlad had sent his own coach to collect him.

Isabella had decided to travel with him. She climbed the steps into the coach and as she did she caught sight of the landlady from the night before. She was obviously talking about her to the villagers who were there. They all made a sign of the cross as the coach pulled out. Isabella thought to herself how stupid these people still were that they believed that their foolish suspicions could ward her off. Isabella glanced over at Jonathon; he was looking at the villagers as well. He was getting increasingly frightened of what was ahead of him. Isabella thought that he should be scared. She had no idea what Vlad had planned for this man, but she suspected he would not be allowed to leave the castle as Renfield had, so she would let him carry on with his journey.

Isabella sat with the other passengers, who were anxious and agitated—they knew who she was. That was the wonderful thing about the Carpathians. It was the only place in the world that Vampires were known and recognised, despite Isabella's efforts to the contrary.

The coach was traveling at a horrendous speed. Isabella knew what the coach driver was up to; he was trying to out run Vlad, he was afraid for himself and those who travelled with him. It would never work. As the light was fading the other passengers were terrified of Isabella, afraid she would strike out as soon as the darkness engulfed them. The coach came to abrupt stop and the coachman jumped off his seat and pushed his head through the open window to talk to Harker.

"I see no sign of another coach," he said quickly. "He has not sent anyone to get you. I suggest we go on to Bukovina and you can see what has happened to him from there." His words were interrupted by the sound of another carriage approaching from what seemed like nowhere. Isabella smiled; she knew Vlad would have predicted this.

"I don't think you have to be moving on to Bukovina," Isabella stayed inside the coach; she did not want Vlad to see her.

"Mr Harker, my master sends his compliments and will ensure that the rest of your journey is as comfortable as possible."

"Thank you," Jonathon answered. Jonathon climbed onto the other coach and went with Vlad towards the castle. Isabella was slightly reassured; Vlad had not changed that much; he would not be foolish.

Isabella stayed in Bukovina and waited for word. Six months went slowly by and there was nothing, until Anna sent a message to Bukovina asking for her to come home. Isabella hurried home. She feared the situation that awaited her there.

"I am so glad you are here," Anna began.

"Why, what has happened?" Isabella asked, a certain amount of concern in her voice.

"Soon after you left the castle a baby was stolen from one of the villages near by."

"A baby?"

"Yes. Just an infant, no more than a few months old."

"Was it a Slovak?"

"No."

"Then I have no grievance with whoever took it."

"I know that, but you will have a grievance."

"Why?"

"You should come up with me to see Olya; she has something to tell you." Anna would not tell Isabella anything more than that. The pair walked up to the castle in silence. Isabella was astounded at the thoughts that were running through her head. She worried not for herself and her own safety. She was worried, desperately worried, for Vlad. She tried not to be; she tried to tell herself she did not care but she could not lie to herself anymore.

When they arrived at the castle, Isabella made straight for her old room. Olya was lying in her bed exhausted and dying. Isabella smelt death around the room Olya's time was very close to being over.

"Olya," Isabella began. "What has happened here?"

"Isabella," answered Olya, her voice weak and fragile "sit down, please."

Isabella looked over at Anna, who looked as if her world was starting to come apart. Isabella had tried to touch her arm on the way up to the castle but she would not let her. She knew Isabella could read her if she let her take her hand. Isabella sat down on the bed and waited for Olya to relate what she had to tell her.

"I helped the Englishman Harker to escape," said Olya.

Isabella was relieved when she heard this. "Is that all?" Isabella said. "I don't care. I have helped many a human in my lifetimes. I realise that we can sometimes feel pity for them. There was a time when I would not have killed a human without good reason."

"Isabella," Anna said loudly, silencing Isabella. "Listen. She has more to say."

Isabella continued listening, her brief sense of relief completely dissipated.

"I let him go for a reason," Olya continued.

"What was your reason?" Isabella asked.

"I saw his future," Olya answered.

"What did you see in his future?"

"Start earlier than that Olya, she must hear everything to understand completely," Anna interrupted again.

"A month ago the three other Vampires that occupy this castle brought a child up from the village below. Just a child, an innocent; they slaughtered it without any sign of conscience. I was disgusted. From that instant I knew this all had to stop. Those women, the abomination that they had become, it all had to end." Isabella now realised what she was about to be told.

"Continue," Isabella said firmly. Her concern had changed to anger.

"Dracula left the three Vampires behind him when he left; they fed on Harker every night. I could hear him crying when they left him and screaming when they returned the following night. They were slowly torturing him, prolonging his life for the sheer enjoyment of it. I couldn't stand it, Isabella. Every time I closed my eyes I saw the baby they had killed. I had to stop it…I had to."

"So what did you do?" Olya now sensed that Isabella would not be sympathetic.

"I went up to see him. He was exhausted, barely alive, as I was trying to make him more comfortable. I touched his arm… I saw a vision of the future."

"What did you see?"

"I saw the blackness that I have been sensing for years but now I saw what it was and how it would come about. I saw the three Vampires being killed and I saw…"

"You saw?"

"I saw an end to it all."

"An end?"

"Yes, I saw Vlad, I saw him dead, I knew if I helped Jonathon escape it would set off a chain of events that would mean the end to all Vampires."

"So you let him go just because three Vampires killed a baby?"

"I did." Isabella got up and walked towards the window. She was standing with her back to the two women and she said, "You let that man escape from here when you knew it would result in Vlad's death?"

"Yes, Isabella, don't you understand, I had to." These were the last words that Olya would ever utter. While Isabella was standing with her back to the two women. She had unsheathed her grandfather's sword and poured some of Abraham's blood on the blade. Isabella spun around to face Olya and thrust the sword through the air at tremendous speed. The tip and then the full blade went through the middle of Olya's throat. The sword was thrust with such strength that it penetrated the head board behind Olya's back. Only the stone wall behind the bed was able to stop the sword's motion. Olya touched the blade with the tips of her fingers. She was trying to pull it out of her throat but she could not. A few seconds later her head slumped and she was dead.

Anna had sat frozen, unable to even close her eyes or pull them away from the gruesome scene. After a few seconds, when the numbness had passed, Anna ran to Olya, crying out her name. Isabella walked calmly over to Olya's body and placed her foot on her stomach and pulled out the blade from Olya's neck. This last action severed the head completely and Anna collapsed in grief.

"Why?" Anna shouted, begging Isabella for an answer. Isabella now coldly wiped off the blood from her sword.

"You know why."

Anna, who was still sobbing on the floor, said, "She knew this would be your reaction—she told me."

"She was right then, wasn't she?" Anna was shocked at Isabella's callousness.

"I said that it was not true you could never kill her," Anna said, still not really believing what she had just seen.

"Anna, I have never lied to you; never forget I am a Vampire. She let a human who will kill Vlad escape. I would never have let her live under any circumstances."

"You don't understand, I am not crying for Olya," Anna said. "She said if what she had seen started to come true, my son... would also die."

"I am sorry Anna; I will try my best to stop it," Isabella answered. "You must tell me everything she told you."

"She did not tell me much more than that. She told me that Harker and an American would slay Vlad."

Isabella saw a glimmer of hope in Anna's words. "That is impossible, humans cannot kill Vlad. Did she say anything else or mention anyone else?"

Anna tried to think and remember, but she was still in shock. "She did she mention a Dutchman named Abraham."

Isabella fell onto the bed in shock. "The Dhampir! Vlad really is in danger!" Isabella ran for the door and turned back towards Anna. "If I can save your son, I will, I promise you that."

THE EARTH IS FREE FROM A MONSTER OF THE NETHER WORLD

CHAPTER TWENTY-THREE

Isabella journeyed as quickly as she could. For the first time in her conscious permanence she had not a moment to spare. She got a coach to Bistrita and then a coach to Varna. She boarded the first ship she found and stirred up the winds to let the ship sail to its greatest capacity. She had to rescue him…she couldn't let him die. She felt responsible for the danger that Vlad was in. She should have killed Van Helsing when she realised what he was. She left the Carpathians with the firm intention of correcting her original error. She arrived in England a week later and swiftly travelled up the coast to Whitby.

Whitby was the perfect setting Isabella reflected. If she did not know for certain that Vlad was somewhere here she would have known as soon as she saw it. The ruined Benedictine Abbey looked down on to the village below, as his own castle looked down on the forest and the many villages that had settled on the forest edge. But unlike his home, Whitby's population had grown and flourished. It manufactured Jet, which was the only respectable jewellery worn by ladies in mourning. In a world where death was always abundant, anyone who could profit from it always had infinite custom.

On seeing Whitby Isabella knew that Vlad would have settled up the hill a certain distance so that he could look down on the busy port below him. As Isabella walked up the path, she noticed a clipping from a newspaper flapping in the breeze. She picked it up to read it.

The article was from the *Daily Telegraph* and spoke of an accident that had happened the previous month; a ship had run adrift on to the shore.

> The people of Whitby had watched it as it came hurtling towards the bay at great speed. Crowds had gathered because a storm had started suddenly out of nowhere. Then the fog started to roll in, almost obscuring all of the boats that were still out at sea. The people of Whitby were frightened and feared for the crews of these vessels that were now completely obscured by the fog, which was made worse by the rushing winds of the storm.
>
> All of the ships except one arrived back safely, but this ship was still in difficulty. No one recognised it. It was obviously a foreign ship just coming into port. As it approached, people in the crowd noticed that there was a dead man lashed to the wooden steering wheel of the ship. A few people ventured out and approached the ship when it ran onto dry land, and within seconds the black clouds above them had dispelled, the fog and the rains swiftly rolled back out to sea. The onlookers gasped as a wolf jumped from the ship onto the English shore and ran away from the crowd.

Isabella finished reading what was left of the article. She knew the wolf was Vlad. She smiled to herself, almost laughing, thinking about what Olya had said. "He wants to be respectable?" Isabella stated under her breath. She had sat down to read the article; she stood up again and walked up the path to look for Carfax Abbey, Vlad's new home.

Isabella soon found the abbey, though she did not find Vlad there. She waited for his return. A few hours later she heard men shouting outside. She walked over to the window to see who was shouting and why. Five men were approaching the outside of the house. They were brandishing torches and various weapons. Isabella recognised Abraham as one of their number. Since she saw no sign of Vlad she began to worry: was she too late?

She continued to watch these men, hoping that Vlad was close behind them; the men entered the chapel at the front of the house and were partially obscured from her sight. She could see them opening the crates that lay inside the chapel. They were sprinkling some sort of liquid on the contents of the crates. Isabella knew it was Dhampir's blood. She wondered what was in these crates that these men felt that they would have to poison them. An hour had passed; Van Helsing and the men left as abruptly as they had come. Isabella sat down again and waited anxiously, yearning for Vlad's return, hoping that he would return to her unscathed.

Just before sunrise he did return, not quite unscathed. He had a cut on his forehead and the wound looked old; it had not healed and showed no sign of healing, His eyes were not their usual black but red and piercing; they almost looked as if they were on fire.

Isabella sat in the corner of the room in silence; she hesitated before she alerted him to her arrival. She had not talked to him in two centuries and she did not know how to start.

"Vlad," she said gently, he turned towards her. The pair looked at each other, each one not knowing how to react to the other's presence.

"Have you come to witness my ultimate demise?" Vlad said. Isabella had not expected a response like this.

"So you know you are danger?"

"I do."

"You recognised Van Helsing as a Dhampir?"

"Oh, I recognised him."

"What do you mean?" Isabella asked.

"I mean I recognised him because he is my son."

Isabella looked at Vlad; she was completely confounded.

"Your son?"

Vlad sighed.

"That is what a Dhampir is Isabella…the child of a Vampire and a human." Isabella could not believe what she was hearing. She quickly unsheathed her grandfather's sword, which was hidden as always amongst her skirts. She hurled it at Vlad. It cut straight through the palm of his left hand and pinned him to the wall behind. The sword was now lodged in both Vlad's hand and the back wall of the room; mortal strength could not have freed him. Vlad looked over at Isabella and sighed. "So in two centuries you have not learned how to control your temper," Vlad said.

Isabella confronted Vlad; she raised her hand and struck him. Vlad freed himself and pushed her back, pinning her to the opposite wall. Repressed passion was bubbling up to the surface of both Vampires. Vlad pulled back on Isabella's hair and kissed her. Isabella pushed him back; he fell to the ground. She stood over him, he clasped his hand around her ankle and she fell to the floor. Vlad rolled on top of her, restraining her with the weight of his body, Isabella tried to push back but she could not. She struck him again; a cut appeared on his lip, Vlad smiled. He lowered his mouth to touch hers. Isabella bit him. She was still putting up the pretence of resisting him. Vlad was undeterred as Isabella struck him again and this time Vlad struck back. Isabella was outraged. She kicked out trying with all her might to get him off her. Vlad fell back from her and Isabella rose to her feet, heading for the door. Vlad threw out his hand clasping Isabella's ankle and pulling her to the floor again. As she fell Vlad ripped at her bodice to reveal her flesh. Isabella's passion for him took over, but she was still defiant and she struck him again. Vlad took hold of each wrist and held them over her head. She struggled and succeeded in getting one hand free from his grip. This time instead of striking of him she ripped open his shirt. She wanted to feel his cold flesh touching hers once more. Isabella kissed him again. Vlad unfastened her skirts and Isabella could feel his cold flesh penetrating hers.

Hours later they lay in each others arms.

"I am sure your reaction to such news would be more controlled…" Isabella was first to speak continuing their previous conversation. "But you are telling me you have fathered a child, a child that can kill us both. Why?"

"Because…." Vlad rose to his feet. He did not want to tell her why, why should he? "It doesn't matter why, it just happened."

"You have killed us all," Isabella retorted.

"I may have," Vlad nodded. "Why did you come here?" he asked.

"Olya foretold that we would all die. Some of her predictions have come true. I thought if I could save you then it would prove her prediction to be wrong, and perhaps I would live through this," Isabella lied. She was not telling this man that she had come to save him, with not a thought for her own safety. The pair had not talked to each other in decades and within moments of seeing each other they had slipped into their old destructive pattern of lies and deceit.

"I think I will stay here and face them." Vlad said.

"Don't be ridiculous! You will die here, and according to Olya if you die I will be next, and dying is not something I am planning to do for a very long time."

"So where do you suggest I go?"

"I suggest we go home; if they follow us, there are plenty of Slovaks who will protect us from the English."

"Are you asking me to go home with you?"

"I am," Isabella responded. She felt this was a moment to be honest.

"All right, I will go with you."

"We must go now," Isabella said as she went over to the window to see if their way was clear. As she looked outside again she was reminded of the boxes that the men had poisoned. "What is in the crates outside?" Isabella asked.

"Earth from home."

"Why did you bring it with you?" Isabella asked. Vlad looked into Isabella's eyes and realised that she truly did not understand why he had to bring it here.

"Isabella, do you not know how powerful you have become? You told the land, my land, to never let me go and it appears, it listened." A memory flashed into Isabella's mind. She was talking to Olya and earth had heated in her hand.

Isabella looked up at Vlad in disbelief and thought, could she have caused this?

"I cannot go anywhere without it. I do not get a moment's peace unless my land is close to me."

Isabella could not believe his words.

"And that is not all, Isabella; it seems your influence over me is truly great. I cannot enter a building without being invited; that is one of your futile principles, isn't it? I believe, for almost a year now, no Vampire has been able to enter any building with out an invitation." Vlad's eyes dropped to the floor. "I am losing my powers. They seem to be slipping from me. Those men you saw earlier tonight—I have made a Vampire out of one of their women, Mina Harker. I can feel her in my head; I cannot block her out. She visits my mind every sunrise and sees things I cannot control."

Vlad approached Isabella and looked deep into her eyes.

The newfound red fire of his eyes seemed like a warning to Isabella and she asked him. "What has happened to your eyes?"

Vlad sighed. "That is another thing. I remember Mircea, my grandfather, vaguely. What I do remember of him are his red eyes. I asked my father when I was just a child...did he always have eyes like fire? My father told me no, that when a special man like your grandfather is dying, the last remnants of his life burn out and we can see these remnants burning in his eyes."

Vlad was convinced he was about to die, but Isabella was still determined to save him. "We should go as soon as we possibly can," Isabella stated.

"When we get home will you stay with me...until it is ended?" Vlad asked.

"I will stay until the fire in your eyes has been chased from you."

"We will leave tonight," Vlad stated.

⚜

Isabella sent a letter to Anna as they left England. After receiving this letter, Anna spoke to her son.

"They may need the Slovaks to help them to get away from the English. She wants the Slovaks to greet her and Vlad at the ship docks," Anna told her son.

"I will leave tomorrow," he answered.

Anna shook her head. "No you can't. Look at her letter; she has said that you should not. She does not know if she can keep you safe."

"I have to go... mother, she would not hesitate to save me even if she believed that saving me would kill her. You told me that...remember? I have to show her the same loyalty."

Anna nodded. She let him go, but she was grieving, for she knew she would never see her son alive again.

Anna's son, Trajan, had arranged for a coach to meet them. He had gathered together a small army to protect them. Some Slovaks had responded to Isabella's request and he also brought Szgany Gypsies with him—as they would do anything for the promise of money.

Isabella was feeling calmer, for she had not seen any sign of the Van Helsing and the English who accompanied him. She hoped they had not followed but she knew in her heart that they had, for Vlad's burning eyes were still bright and there was not a trace of black to be seen in them.

The two Vampires travelled the rest of the journey by coach and when they were a few miles from home there was still no sign of any danger. Isabella stopped the coach.

"I am going to go ahead," Isabella began. "You stay here until I send for you, when I know it is safe."

"What about you, Isabella? If the English are there I don't want you to face them alone."

Isabella grinned. "I can take care of myself."

Vlad placed his hand to her face and gently ran his fingers down her skin. It was a welcome expression of affection. He got back into the coach and whispered to himself.

"I know you can, Isabella, I know you can." Vlad signalled to the coachman to take him to the nearest inn.

Isabella walked the rest of the way. She didn't want to draw attention to herself. As she approached the castle, she called into see Anna.

"Has anyone been up there?" Isabella asked.

"Yes, a few days ago a man and woman arrived. He has killed the three Vampires that were left up there."

"Well, that is no loss," Isabella said. "It must be Abraham; he wants to kill us all and he is the only real threat to us."

"Do you think you will be able to change Olya's prophecy?"

Isabella went over to Anna and squeezed her hand.

"I will try Anna, I promise you I will try." Isabella spoke these words with conviction but she suspected it was hopeless. Yet she had to try, for she could not imagine a world without Vlad in it. Despite everything, he was the other part of her and without him she would always be wanting.

Isabella went back for Vlad. She had to tell him that their worst fear had been confirmed; Van Helsing had followed and was waiting for them somewhere.

"There is no sign of them," Isabella began.

"Well, that is good. Perhaps they have not come after us."

"They have. Abraham has already been up to the castle and disposed of your three…concubines."

"Well, that is no great loss to the world."

Isabella smiled. "That is what I said. I think the best thing to do is go back to the castle and wait for them there. I think that is our best chance."

Vlad and Isabella travelled home together. Isabella was wrong. It was the worst thing they could have done; the English were waiting for them. The coach ascended up through the forest and when they were nearly at the castle gates, Isabella heard horses starting to chase after them.

"They are coming," she shouted to Vlad. Vlad grabbed Isabella and pulled her close to him.

"Go!" he said vehemently, staring deep into her eyes. "Save yourself."

Isabella shook her head in defiance but Vlad tossed her from the coach and sped on towards the castle.

Vlad had thrown Isabella with such a force that she was now out of sight of the English and well away from their path. She stood looking up in horror and desperation, trying to think what she could do. As if her situation could not get worse, she saw someone else there that day—she saw Leila.

Leila's other senses had become more acute and despite her blindness she was breaking the necks of any Slovaks she could find with ease. The Slovaks saw that they were being slaughtered by a Vampire and they started to retreat. Only the Szgany remained.

Isabella ran towards the castle as fast as she could, defying Vlad. Perhaps she could still save him. Leila was not killing the English, so they were not paying too much attention to her. Anna's son was there, calling, beseeching the Slovaks who were retreating to help in the fight. One of the Englishmen crept up behind him and ran his sword through his stomach.

"No!" Isabella cried out from a distance, willing this event to have not taken place, but it was too late: Olya's prophecy was coming true. Isabella continued to run towards the castle. She was frantic and for the first time in her life she was unconcerned by the slaughter of Slovaks. Anna's son was already dead and she cared nothing for the rest of them. Let them run. They would not be running for long. Her only concern now was Vlad.

She had by this time reached the castle. She saw Abraham. He was about to strike and Vlad was trying to escape. Isabella had never seen him run from anyone. One of the men, Isabella presumed he was one of the English, plunged a knife into Dracula's chest and another was about to slit his throat. Isabella unsheathed her grandfather's sword and plunged it into the side of one of the men.

"*Don't see her,*" Vlad whispered. As the other men watched, they thought it was Szgany Gypsies that had wounded the American called Quincy. Isabella summoned up all the power she could muster.

"*Time, slow for me.*" She ran through the crowd that seemed to be almost frozen by her words. When she reached Vlad, the wound was not healing—the knife obviously had Dhampir's blood on it. Isabella slumped down and knelt at his side. She had little time. She could not hold off his would-be murderers for long.

"What can I do?" Isabella asked, frenziedly trying to think of a way to stop the wound from growing.

"Nothing, Isabella, let me go," Vlad said. Tears welled up in Isabella eyes. She had not cried since Nicolae's death, but today she could not hold back. Her tears flowed from her eyes in a mighty red gush.

"No, I can't," Isabella cried. "I will never be able to let you go."

Vlad lifted up Isabella's hand and placed it on his temple. Vlad's memories flowed into her mind. She saw Vlad saving her from the guillotine; she saw him letting Nicolae live because he looked so much like her. She saw him carrying her back to Jakub's home after Leila had attacked her. She saw him nursing her back to health; she had nearly died. He had saved her by letting her drink from his blood and it had caused him hours of agonising pain. And finally she saw why he had fathered a child—to save her from Leila.

Isabella was completely distraught; she couldn't let him go. "We could have been happy," Isabella said, but Vlad smiled slightly.

"No, we couldn't," Vlad whispered. Isabella was unable to contain her grief.

"I love you." Isabella whispered. "You and no other. There was never anyone else but you, it has been always you and always will be."

Vlad tried to smile but his life was ebbing away from him. He wanted desperately to speak his final words to Isabella. "All I ever wanted to do… was share eternity with you." Vlad saw Jonathon Harker kneeling down to deliver the final blow. His knife was covered in Dhampir's blood; he was one of the first to break free from Isabella's spell. Vlad used what remained of his strength to push Isabella back and out of the way. Isabella screamed as the blade sliced through Vlad's neck and struck the stone floor below him. Phosphorescence that only Isabella and Van Helsing could see now shot out of Vlad's body. It was that feeling of serenity again but it was stronger this time, stronger than Isabella had ever felt it and she felt more powerful than she had ever done. It was like an energy surging through her. She could see and hear things much further than she ever had before. She felt her strength increasing tenfold and she could feel her influence was much greater. Her scars melted away and her power was greater at that moment—she felt invincible.

And her greatest gift of all, her daylight vision, was given back to her. The sun was shining brightly and she could see, oh so painfully and clearly, as Vlad's body turned to dust and he gave her all that remained of his omnipotent power. The surge of energy knocked Isabella to the ground and the cobblestones beneath her broke. A light like a thunderbolt ricocheted from her and a scar on the head of the woman that the English had brought with them disappeared; this woman was now free from Vlad's curse.

Abraham, who was resistant to both Isabella's and Vlad's power, approached her.

Isabella stared up at him.

"Isabella," he said. "You said when we met again one of us would have to die," Abraham continued.

"I did," Isabella answered.

"I think there will be a third meeting, don't you?" Isabella almost smiling at him said.

"Yes I think there will." Isabella looked beyond Van Helsing and saw Leila approaching. "Once again, sir, I need something from you." Isabella slashed her sword across Abraham's arm, and leapt at Leila. Isabella swung around and took off Leila's head with one last blow. Vlad's influence still resonated through the crowd of perpetrators and onlookers. No one apart from Abraham could see Isabella, but now she wanted to be seen by her own people. The people that she had protected for centuries had now repaid her by running from her when she needed them most.

"*Slovaks see me!*" she shouted.

The fleeing Slovaks now all looked up at Isabella who was standing on top of the battlements. "Mark my words, for letting Vlad Dracula die, you, your families, every one of you will all die, I promise you." The Slovaks knew Isabella meant every word.

TOMBSTONE, ARIZONA
FEW PEOPLE THERE DIE IN THEIR BEDS

CHAPTER TWENTY FOUR

Simon walked the dusty path towards the inn where he had left his family. Isabella had given them enough money so that they could stay there indefinitely, and it would be easy then for Simon to find them when he returned. Simon was within a mile of home; he was hoping and longing to see a glimpse of his family. He heard children playing in the distance and he wondered whether they were the voices of his children. He strained to hear, hoping, listening for a familiar tone. That familiar tone that he sought soon found his ear; he dropped his bag and started to run. Moments passed, his vision still obscured by the distance and foliage of the forest, but then all of a sudden he saw his wife. She was sitting with her back towards him. Simon had longed to see his wife again, for all the three long years that he had been away. But on seeing her now Simon's running was instantly halted. He was now hesitant. Questions started to race in his mind. She could have presumed him dead; after all, he had left with a Vampire. No one would have blamed her for making such an assumption. Simon's heart sank even as he was just fifty yards away from home.

Simon's wife was sitting watching her children play. A feeling came over her that she was being watched. She was not frightened; she knew the eyes that were watching were not going to cause her any pain. She stood and looked in front of her, lifting her hand over her eyes to shield her vision from the sun; there was no one there. She sat down again, thinking she had just imagined it. She tried to dismiss it but couldn't; the feeling was still with her and it had grown stronger. She stood again and peered in front of her and still did not see anyone that she recognised. Then something deep within her heart told her to look to the woods. She twisted around her head as far as she could and she saw her husband standing watching her. She looked forward again her heart pounding; a single tear ran down her cheek. She couldn't believe her eyes. Could this be a dream? Was this image behind her a welcome figment of her own imagining? She was now frightened. If she looked back again would the image of her husband be gone forever.

Simon was still watching as his she caught his eye. His heart dropped as she looked away, in his eyes his worst fear had been confirmed by her immediate glance away from him. He turned to walk away from her; he would not come back to ruin her life if she had moved on. He turned away with a heavy heart, but then Simon had to turn around again because his wife was calling his name.

"Simon, Simon!" she called. Simon turned to face his wife. She was smiling at him and at that moment Simon was reassured. When his wife was but steps from him she threw herself into his arms. She threw herself with such a force that Simon fell backwards and they both fell to the ground. Simon and his wife lay clutching each other, both laughing, not wanting to take their eyes off the other, not wanting to even blink for fear that their happy reunion was just a dream. When Simon's children saw their mother running from them they thought it was a game and started to chase after her. The children were only steps behind their mother and also threw themselves on top of their parents. Simon was now sure that his future life would be happy and it was; Simon lived out the rest of his days in sweet prosperity.

Isabella had always planned to wait before her return to England. She wanted to wait partly because of Olya's prediction and partly because she wanted to spend some time with Nicolae. She did not want to march him back to a place where only death would greet him. She and Nicolae both deserved some time and a little happiness. There was also a more sinister reason for her wait and it was the most important of all her reasons. She wanted the English to put the events behind them, to begin their lives again, to even forget what had happened, and when they had forgotten, when they were able to have a good night's sleep with dreams free from Vampires, that was when Isabella would strike.

She knew Van Helsing would come after her eventually and she would be ready for him, but he would take time to find her and until he did she would spend this time with Nicolae.

So Isabella with Nicolae at her side joined the battle at Gettysburg and fought with the Army of the Potomac under General Meade. A woman in this army was not such a strange occurrence; there were many women fighting under the guise of being men.

The battle of Gettysburg which the confederacy was winning changed its direction, as the union on the second day fought back ferociously, thereby winning the battle. This was surprising to everyone apart from Isabella and Nicolae. Isabella and Nicolae stayed with the Army of the Potomac for the duration of the war. They witnessed the New York draft riots and eventually they witnessed the surrender of the confederacy.

After the war was over the pair travelled out west. They followed so many other veterans who had been involved in the war, whose homes had been destroyed and who had no other place to go. Isabella loved the lawlessness of the west. There were still marshals and sheriffs and courts and trials but they were not imposing and were often killers themselves. The appearance of law, as Isabella had learnt, far too often meant that law neither existed nor was enforced. The truth was that the west was far too big a place to govern and no one really wanted to tame its wildness, not yet, anyway.

Isabella was sick of covering up her long raven hair under an army cap. She had had enough of tents and walking everywhere. She wanted to get back into her beautiful elegant dresses again; she wanted to return to her grandiose lifestyle that she had become so accustomed to having.

Rich women and their husbands did not choose to travel out west— usually only gamblers and reprobates did. As Isabella did not want to be thought as a reprobate she decided to let people think that she was a gambler, and judging by her clothes, a very successful one.

Isabella had spent the last years travelling through Kansas, Okalahoma and Colorado. She spent her days sleeping in her hotel room and she spent her nights looking for food and occasionally playing poker. She had acquired quite a competent amount of skill. Seeing into the minds of her fellow gamblers was quite an advantage. Isabella and Nicolae had stayed in Dodge City for almost a year when a new assistant marshal had been appointed in the city. Isabella had only had a few brief glimpses of him, but she sensed she would have trouble with him and she had no tolerance for anyone wanting to disrupt the contentment that she had achieved in her new life with Nicolae.

Isabella was sitting in the corner of the Comique saloon with her back to the wall. She enjoyed playing poker; it appealed to her. Nicolae had learnt to deal Faro and was at another table. Isabella liked to observe the goings on of these saloons; she had never seen anything like the cow towns in any part of the world. They were dens of inequity and Isabella relished being part of them.

A storm was starting up outside. The storms in Kansas through the summer were dry and dusty and stung the eyes of anyone who walked in them. They started without warning and could often result in a tornado. Isabella did not like tornadoes; they were too powerful for her, though she would try and control them as much as she could.

Isabella sat in the Comique, Nicolae dealing Faro just across from her. The wind was gathering up outside and the candles were flickering in the saloon. She was trying to control the storm but as she was inside she did not really care that it got out of her control. She started to hear the footsteps of a man approaching the open entrance of the saloon. The reason this man had caught Isabella's awareness was because every few steps were interrupted by his own coughs.

He turned to come inside and Isabella watched him. He was quite striking, and he was obviously ill. His skin was as pale as Isabella had ever seen on a human. He had clear blue eyes that shone from across the room. His lips were blood-red like a Vampire and his hair was brown, but the Kansas sun had dusted it with blonde. He was dressed in fine clothes and had the elegant deportment of a gentleman. He looked very out of place in the saloon. Isabella with all her finery also looked out of place, so they were a perfect match. She looked him over wondering what his story was, why he was out there. He had the look of another time about him. Isabella could see him living twenty years before he did, she could see him sitting on the porch of a grand southern mansion surveying his land, not thinking about the darkness that was to come in the shape of war. He was a remnant of another world that the war had ended forever.

Isabella continued watching him as he approached the bar. He signalled to the bartender to get him a drink. The bartender did so; he poured him a shot of whiskey and then went to take away the bottle. The man grabbed the bottle before he could take it and took the shot glass and bottle with him, laying a few coins for the bottle on the bar. He looked over at the Faro table and saw Nicolae dealing there. He then caught Isabella's glance. She smiled at him and he returned her smile and tipped his hat out of courtesy.

The man then started towards the poker table. Nicolae was watching the interaction between the pair. Isabella knew he was and she quickly broke her glance with this man and gave a reassuring glance to Nicolae. Not

VROLOK

that she needed to, Nicolae knew she loved him and he was never jealous, a quality he had inherited from his ancestor of the same name. The man approached Isabella and asked.

"Would you mind if I sat in that chair?" he asked, motioning to Isabella's seat.

"I can't say that I mind but that does not mean that I will give you this seat." Isabella answered.

"I would be eternally grateful if you did."

"Eternally grateful? All right, if you tell me why?" Isabella asked out of curiosity. The man pulled Isabella's new seat out for her to sit down.

"Gentlemen in my profession like to sit with their backs to the wall."

"Why?" Isabella was now slightly intrigued.

"In these volatile times, gunfighters, and poker players such as myself, should always sit with their backs to the wall. So they can see any men who are likely to shoot them before they do. If Bill Hickok had followed this rule, the events of last month in Deadwood would never have happened."

"So you are not very brave," Isabella said, mocking him slightly.

"No. I just want to hold on to my life as long as I can." The man coughed again, he lifted a handkerchief to his lips and Isabella noticed a few spots of blood on the white linen cloth, she also observed the initial H was embroidered into the corner. Isabella could smell death biting at his heels but he was fighting it. He would not let go of this world until he was entirely sick of it.

"I would never have suspected that a man in your condition would be so determined to hold on to your life." The man was slightly insulted by this remark and Isabella could tell her words had hurt him. She tried to take it back or at least give her words another context. "What I mean to say is that a man who is in your profession is not the type to worry about getting shot in the back of the head …that is surely just an occupational hazard." The man smiled at Isabella.

"You didn't mean that, but thank you for extending me the courtesy of suggesting that you did," he said and extended out his hand to Isabella, "Tom McKey."

Isabella took his hand and said, "Isabella Hawthorne."

"Very pleased to meet you, Miss Hawthorne."

"Likewise." At this moment another man came into the Comique. He approached Tom and said.

"Tom, how are you; I heard you were feeling poorly?"

"Nonsense, Wyatt, I am the picture of health." He paused mid-sentence to cough again. "I never felt better."

Wyatt turned and walked away. He went over to the bar and started to drink shot after shot of whisky. He, unlike Tom, as Isabella was soon to find out, could not hold his liquor. After about an hour Isabella and Tom were still playing poker. But Wyatt was drunk and as a consequence, bad spirited—he seemed to be spoiling for a fight. He was watching Isabella intensely, but she chose to ignore him. She could handle him if he tried anything and would be happy to dispatch him given the opportunity. He poured out one more shot of whiskey and drank it back before coming over to stand beside Tom.

"How is the little lady doing?" Wyatt asked Tom. Isabella was not one to tolerate being referred to as a little lady. She threw him a supercilious look. Nicolae, who was listening intently to all that was going on, decided to stop dealing Faro and watch Isabella. He loved to watch her when her temper was about to break. He went over to the bar and started to watch the events unfold. If Isabella was to snap he wanted to have a ringside seat. He sat on the stool at the bar looking over at her... watching, smiling, content to wait the few moments until she would blow her very short fuse.

"The lady..." Tom recapitulated, "is doing very well, as I suspect the lady always does." Tom smiled at Isabella as he tossed in his hand into the centre of the table. Isabella leaned forward to pull her winnings over to her side of the table. Isabella had been winning all night and the two other poker players were starting to get suspicious.

Wyatt was prepared to incite their suspicions. "I think she may be cheating."

Tom shook his head. He was disappointed in Wyatt, who was always shooting his mouth off and causing arguments when there was no need to cause one.

"She is not cheating, Wyatt, she is just a good poker player," Tom said firmly.

"I don't know, a stint in the jailhouse overnight may bring her lucky streak to an end," Wyatt threatened. Wyatt approached Isabella and grabbed her arm. Isabella looked at his hand and then drew her gaze to his face.

"Remove your hand," Isabella said firmly.

"Why should I?"

"I asked you to." Isabella said her voice low and determined.

"Do people usually do what you say?" Wyatt asked.

"They do," Isabella said calmly. Isabella knew Nicolae was watching her with a childish grin on his face. Tom McKey went over to the bar and stood beside Nicolae, also watching the pair.

"Are you that woman's husband?" Tom McKey asked.

"I am," Nicolae answered.

"Do you not think you should intercede?"

"I wouldn't dream of it." Nicolae patted Tom on the back and answered. "Watch for yourself—she can handle herself."

"You are sure?" Tom asked trying to ensure that it was the right decision to leave the pair alone. He knew how hot-tempered Wyatt could be. His mouth was always getting him into trouble and he feared he might lash out at Isabella. "I mean to say I know Wyatt, he has a hot temper and he may do something rash, he could hit her." Nicolae laughed. He poured Tom a glass of whisky and turned back towards the scene.

"Let him try..." Nicolae said. "Let him try."

"You are not acting very concerned for your wife's safety."

"No...I can't say that I am." Nicolae turned and poured himself and Tom another drink. Tom was looking at this man with amazement. He was displaying no concern for his wife; he looked as if he wanted Wyatt to hit her.

"Are you unhappy in your marriage, sir?" Tom asked.

"No, I am very happy with my wife?"

"You don't act like it."

"Tom, is that your name?" Nicolae asked.

"It is."

"Tom, I would be more concerned for your friend. If he does not remove his grip from my wife's arm very soon, she may kill him." Tom looked at Nicolae astonished. "If he is lucky she may just break a few bones, but knowing my wife, she'll probably kill him." Tom was still standing dumbstruck: he looked over at Isabella's face, and there was a feral look upon it. He looked back towards Nicolae, who nodded with a smug look now upon his face. It was the look of a proud husband.

Tom now realised that Isabella was in no danger and actually feared for Wyatt. He went back to the poker table. "Wyatt, perhaps you should leave the lady alone."

"Tom, don't tell me you are afraid of a woman."

"Something tells me, we both should be afraid of this one." Wyatt tightened his grip on Isabella's wrist. Isabella joined the conversation.

"Let go of my arm," Isabella said again firmly.

"No, you are coming with me." Wyatt was now being obstinate. He was now determined to arrest Isabella.

"Remove your hand from me, sir," Isabella commanded again.

"Or you'll what?" Wyatt asked. Isabella leaned in close and whispered in his ear.

"I will break your trigger finger; you'll never be able to work as a marshal again." Tom was getting very anxious about the situation again, but this time his concern was directed at Wyatt.

"Wyatt, leave it, what will it prove to overpower a woman? It won't do your reputation any good," Tom said.

Wyatt, sensing there was no good way out of this situation but still determined not to be upstaged by a woman, did not relinquish his grip.

Isabella had had more than enough. She grabbed Wyatt's hand, removing it from her arm, and bent it back towards his upper arm. Wyatt was in terrible pain; he couldn't believe the vise-like grip this woman now had on him. He tried to pull back but now it was Isabella who would not relinquish her grip. He then tried to back away from Isabella but she would not let him.

Tom tried to intercede on Wyatt's behalf. Isabella looked around at the crowd that was in the saloon; they were all watching her. She did not want to leave this town just yet and such a public murder would ensure that she had to leave. So Isabella let Tom intercede on Wyatt's behalf.

"You will have to forgive Wyatt, Mrs. Hawthorne…" Tom began. "He is not used to dealing with a woman of quality."

Isabella let go and Wyatt fell to the floor clutching his hand. Isabella got up to leave. Nicolae quickly finished his drink to accompany Isabella back to their rooms. When Nicolae was at the door he leaned down to Wyatt and helped him up. As he did so he whispered in his ear.

"Your friend saved your life tonight, Wyatt." Wyatt pushed Nicolae away from him. Nicolae started to laugh and said, "Don't ever underestimate a woman, especially that woman." Nicolae left with a smug grin on his face. Wyatt was a man who continually told stories about his exploits and who normally exaggerated his part in these exploits. This was a story he never told a soul.

Isabella and Nicolae stayed away from the Comique for a few weeks; it was the saloon which mostly the law makers and gamblers would inhabit. Nicolae, always the voice of reason, convinced Isabella to stay away.

"If you kill him, we will have to leave here." Isabella said nothing. "I know you like it here."

"All right." Isabella was exasperated because she knew he was right.

"Just wait until you can look at him without wanting to kill him."

Isabella smiled and said, "That may take a long time."

Nicolae laughed. "I know it may."

Isabella and Nicolae had stayed away from the Comique, but Isabella was itching to go back; she missed it. No other saloon in Dodge had the same atmosphere and the sense of imminent danger just bubbling under the surface; it was an exciting place to be.

After a few weeks had passed, Isabella had almost convinced herself and Nicolae that she could control her temper. When they walked into the Comique that evening it had not changed. Tom McKey was there but this time he had a woman with him. He was acting totally uninterested in her but she was sticking to him with a sense of urgency. It was as if she was convinced that if she turned her back on him she would lose him. Isabella went over to the table and asked to join the game. Tom McKey's lady friend was the first to respond.

"No women are allowed to play."

Isabella was insulted and she raised her gaze to look at this woman's face. When Isabella saw the desperate look in the woman's eyes she was inclined to feel sorry for her. Tom responded to his companion's outburst, first with a sigh followed by a vocal response.

"Now, Kate, you are not being civil, you should listen to this woman, you should study her. For she is something you are not." Tom McKey coughed and then continued. "For she is a lady."

Kate looked down at Tom. She was hurt by his words but she did not walk away or cry. Her hurt sensibilities welled up into a fury. As Isabella would come to find out, this was always Kate's standard reaction to Tom's hurtful words. She smashed Tom's bottle of whisky and pressed it to his throat. Tom slapped her across the face and she was thrust back to the floor. Kate immediately stood up and grabbed a gun from another man's holster. She pointed it at Tom her hand was shaking; Kate wanted to hurt him as he had hurt her.

Isabella's sympathy rested totally with Kate and she knew that if Kate succeeded in killing Tom, even though at least in Isabella's eyes he may have deserved it, Kate would be lynched and she did not deserve that. Isabella reached out her hand and touched Kate's arm. Tom was laughing at Kate, maliciously trying to provoke her to follow through on her threat. Kate looked around at Isabella and Isabella smiled a comforting warm smile.

"Come with me, Kate." Kate immediately calmed. A sense of serenity swept over her. Kate held her head up high, dropped the gun, and walked outside the saloon with Isabella.

The two women walked down the street together. Kate's serene mood was leaving her and she turned towards Isabella.

"I know what you are up to."

"What am I up to, Kate?" Isabella asked.

"You are trying to take him from me."

"After the way he behaved tonight I would not want him; besides I have a husband and I have no need for another. I am no threat to you in that regard." Kate believed her, which was one of Isabella's gifts; Isabella could make people believe her, especially when she was telling the truth. "Why do you stay with him?" Isabella asked. "He obviously treats you with no respect."

Kate pulled her shawl in tight around her shoulders and simply said, "I love him."

Isabella smiled. She of all people could not blame this woman for loving someone she should not.

"Well, Kate, I hope you can be happy with him..." Isabella smiled at Kate and continued. "Or at least I hope you kill him before he kills you." Isabella looked at Kate and even she smiled and started to laugh slightly. "Go home and get some sleep," Isabella said.

"I can't," Kate answered.

"Go on. I will keep an eye on him; he'll behave himself. I'll make sure of it." Kate smiled at Isabella in gratitude and then turned to go home.

Isabella returned to the Comique and by this time Wyatt had arrived. He was staying well away from Isabella. He did not want to embarrass himself again. So he hardly acknowledged her presence.

Tom was wiping the whisky that Kate had spilled off his lap when Wyatt approached him.

"Trouble?" Wyatt asked.

"Just Kate," Tom replied.

"I have told you many times you should be able to keep that woman under control," Wyatt said. Isabella could not help herself; she had to at least say something.

"And how would you control her, Mr. Earp?" Isabella enquired.

"When I hit her she would not be able to get up so quickly."

"You certainly could not control me," Isabella cut in. "I doubt you would have any better luck with Kate."

"She has you there, Wyatt," Tom said. "Let's leave it at that."

Wyatt walked out of the Comique in a fury. The next few hours swept by quickly and then Morgan Earp, Wyatt's younger brother, entered the Comique and went straight over to Tom.

"Have you seen Wyatt?" Morgan asked.

"No, not in a few hours?" Tom responded.

"Doc, I'm hearing he is in trouble."

"That wouldn't be like Wyatt," Tom said sardonically.

"Tobe Driscoll and Ed Morrison are looking for him."

"Do you want me to help you find him?" Tom asked.

"I do." Tom immediately downed the rest of his whiskey and went with Morgan without a minute's hesitation. Another few hours passed and in the early hours of the morning. The Comique was brought to an eerie silence as shouting was heard coming from the street outside. A few shots were fired in quick succession and then there was silence again. The people inside the Comique figuring whatever argument which had started had now finished and continued on with what they were doing. Then the noise started up again, but not one of them was concerned that someone may have been shot dead outside.

Isabella, unlike the people around her, was at least curious about the incident and went outside to see what had happened. The gunfight was far from over; Wyatt was facing off ten men. Any shots that had been fired had just been into the air. Isabella stood watching. She had absolutely no inclination to help Wyatt, but she was slightly impressed that he was facing all these men by himself. Nicolae came out to join Isabella. She recognised Driscoll and Morrison—she had seen them about the town.

"You have to admit he is brave," Nicolae began.

"Not brave enough to face me," Isabella said.

"Who would be?" Nicolae answered. "He is not going to live through this." Nicolae continued.

"We'll see," Isabella answered.

"Do you know something I don't?" Nicolae asked.

"I suspect this man has a lot of luck on his side and perhaps even a few good friends."

"You are referring to a gambler who can't seem to stop coughing?"

"Perhaps."

"You came out here to save him, didn't you?"

Isabella looked at Nicolae with a smile. "Would you mind if I did?" Isabella took his hand.

"Not at all." Nicolae smiled; he was telling the truth and Isabella knew it.

"I don't deserve you, Nicolae, but then again, I never did." Nicolae turned to go back into the Comique. Isabella caught his arm, not letting him leave her. "Stay, Nicolae, things are just about to get interesting." Isabella pointed over to the other side of the street. There was Tom taking a swig of whiskey from a canteen, just before he made himself known to the group that had confronted Wyatt. There was no sign of Morgan yet, but Tom had no intention of waiting for him.

"Do you…" Tom paused as if trying to think of a collective word to call these men "gentlemen… have a problem?" Tom said superciliously.

"This is nothing to do with you, McKey," Driscoll shouted.

"I beg to differ," Tom shouted. Tom struck a match on his boot which was resting on the wooden hitching rail across the street. The light from the match was the only glimmer of illumination in the whole street. Tom was obscured by the darkness, and only Isabella and Nicolae could see him clearly. He lit his cigar and threw the match away; and then slung his other leg over the rail and jumped onto the dusty street, making his frame visible to all. Tom started to walk slowly over to the group. The men who were squaring off to Wyatt obviously did not want Tom involved. Wyatt and Tom were both killers, and these ten men did not want any of their number killed and they knew that Wyatt and Tom would take a good few of their number with them.

Tom approached the gang slowly. One man getting nervous started to pull out his gun cautiously. Isabella and Nicolae saw him, but so did Tom. Tom quickly drew out his own gun and shot a bullet that, struck the man's shoulder. He fell to the ground—he would be of no more use to his friends.

"Who's next?" Wyatt asked. He too had his gun out and was swiftly pointing it at each man in turn. None of the men made any signs to move; they were starting to get nervous. They could have faced one gunfighter alone, but toss Tom into the mix and they were backing down. "You are all under arrest," Wyatt shouted. It was a mistake to shout this as the men were perfectly prepared to back down and walk away but they were not prepared to spend a night in jail.

"Stupid," Isabella whispered under her breath.

"There is no way out of this for him," Nicolae whispered. "Should I help?" he asked Isabella.

"That's up to you," Isabella answered.

"I think I will." Nicolae hopped over the hitch rail and started to point a shotgun at the aggressors.

"Let's rush them," Driscoll shouted. "There are only three of them."

"Four," Isabella shouted back. Driscoll started to laugh when he saw Isabella holding a shotgun. One of the others started to laugh and said.

"There is still only three...women can't shoot for shit." Isabella without a moment's hesitation shot the man through the skull. All the men including Tom and Wyatt were shocked by Isabella's actions and the accuracy of her aim. The initial reaction to this event was a stunned silence, but then laughter emanated from Nicolae and Tom.

"Does anyone else want to question the lady's shooting?" Tom asked. The nervousness that these men had briefly experienced came flooding back again. With one man down and one man dead they now decided enough was enough and were prepared to leave to fight another day.

Isabella walked down the steps onto the street, going closer to the men in an attempt to intimidate them. Isabella was getting bored with the standoff and sent another shot into the air.

"Let's go, Driscoll, another day," Morrison said. After a few seconds the men started to back away. Isabella shot again before they could completely retreat.

"Take those two with you," Isabella said calmly. The men picked up the body and left the street, with the injured man hobbling along behind them. When it was safe Tom McKey lowered his shot gun and said.

"I think I need a drink." At this point Morgan Earp came running up the street.

"What happened?" Morgan said in surprise.

"The excitement is all over for this evening," Tom declared to Morgan. "You missed it," he continued.

"Did you kill anyone?" Morgan asked.

"Just one," Tom replied. Morgan laughed.

"If I had been here the death count would have been higher."

"I believe you, Morgan," Tom patted Morgan on the back and headed back into the Comique for a drink with the others. Isabella decided to leave. She had had enough of company of these men for one night, but she returned to the Comique the next night and was greeted with a smile by Tom McKey.

"Where did you go last night? I wanted to say thank you." Tom asked.

"Thank me for what?" Isabella asked.

"You saved my life last night, you and your husband."

"Did we?"

"Yes, you did, you know you did. Why did you?" Tom asked.

"Why are you questioning what I did, you're alive, aren't you?"

"You're right. No more questions. I thank you for helping us and let's just leave it at that."

"What I don't understand is why you did it..." Isabella asked. "Why did you risk your own neck to save him?" At this point Morgan entered the Comique and tipped his hat towards Isabella and Tom.

"You ask me why I saved him?"

"Do you have some sort of death wish? Do you want to go out in a blaze of glory?"

"No I want to live; I want to hang on to this life as long as I possibly can. Desperate though it may be..."

"What age are you now?"

"Twenty-four."

Isabella looked at him suspiciously; she knew he was more than twenty-four.

"All right, I am a few years older than that. When I was eighteen years old I was told I had two years to live I have eked out ten more years and hope to live another decade or two."

Morgan, who now was standing at the bar, interrupted the pair. "Can I buy you a drink, Mrs. Hawthorne?" Isabella smiled at Morgan. In their brief acquaintance Isabella was struck by how different Morgan was from his brother. He was filled with an enthusiasm for life. Wyatt was only filled with an enthusiasm for himself. His enthusiasm for life was only equalled by his attitude to gunfights. He loved them. He had a nonchalant attitude to danger and loved to be in the thick of it.

"I will have a drink," Isabella answered.

"Doc, I know you will, too."

"You'd better leave me the bottle," Tom said. Morgan smiled and walked away.

"Why does he call you, Doc?" Isabella asked.

"It is a nickname; you see I used to be a dentist before I discovered this more suitable and I have to admit, more profitable profession."

"So you never told me why you were compelled to save that man?" Isabella pointed towards Wyatt.

"Well the reason is simple; I stepped into the fight last night because Morgan asked me to."

"So your loyalty lies with Morgan?"

"It does."

"Why? No, don't tell me…he saved your life?"

"No, not quite."

"Then what did he do?"

"He saved a woman's life."

"A woman's, surely not Kate."

"No, not Kate, heaven knows why she stays with me; the woman he saved was nothing like Kate."

"Then who was she? Tell me I am interested."

"Her name is Mattie Holiday, I was engaged to her and there is nothing I ever wanted more than to be her husband. But fate was not on our side I was sent to Baltimore to learn dentistry. My father said we could not marry until I had some sort of business and was earning a decent wage. So I was packed off and sent to East. My father did not know but the whole town was full of consumption and there I was, all day, every day, staring into the mouths of these people, letting them breathe their contaminated breath on me. Needless to say I returned home coughing out my insides. When my father saw me he said I couldn't marry anyone, let alone Mattie."

"What did you do then?"

"I knew my father was right, I didn't want to condemn Mattie to be a widow before she was twenty. So I left. Mattie was devastated and so was I…. I left hoping one day if I didn't die, to go home cured. I headed out west to the dry weather to see if that could cure it. A few years drifted past and Mattie was writing to me regularly. I should have let go of her, not let her write. It was hard for both of us and she couldn't stand to be parted from me any longer." Doc took another drink and smiled a poignant grin. "God bless her, the meek, polite little southern belle came all the way out here to find me. She hitched a ride on a bullion run that Morgan was working for, Wells Fargo. The bullion coach was regularly robbed and this particular run was no different. The coach was held up and when Morgan would not give up what he was paid to protect, the cowboys started to shoot into the coach.

Mattie screamed and came out of the coach with her arms in the air. Morgan was shocked to see a woman; he thought she was a man since she was wearing trousers and he hadn't looked too closely at her. He wasn't interested in who was travelling. Another couple of shots rang out. One struck Mattie on the side of the head and she fell to the desert floor. When Morgan saw her fall he dropped his gun immediately; he would not risk getting this woman killed.

The gunmen took the coach and horses and left Mattie and Morgan in the dessert to die of thirst. Most men would have left her there to die and, but not him. He wrapped his coat around her and dragged her behind him. They were lucky they were picked up by another coach and brought to Denver. After a few days Morgan came to look for me. He told me what had happened and I have been thankful to him ever since. So when he asks me for a favour I oblige him, no matter what it is."

"What happened to Mattie?" Isabella asked.

"I sent her home. This is no place for her. It was then I decided to become Tom McKey. McKey is my mother's maiden name. I didn't ever want any news of my unlawful exploits getting back to Mattie."

"What is your real name?"

"John, John Holiday, Doc to my friends."

"It is a good name, and you are a good man despite all your efforts to the contrary."

While the pair were speaking, another man had entered the Comique. This man had a purpose and as soon as he espied Isabella he raised his gun and shot Isabella four times in the back. Blood gushed from Isabella's wounds and she fell to the floor. Doc, stunned by what had happened, looked over at the man. It was one of the Texans from the previous evening. The man ran away but he did not run far, Nicolae chased him down, and the last thing this man saw was a Vampire biting into his neck. After he was dead Nicolae ran back to the Comique.

Doc kneeled down beside Isabella. Blood running out her wounds formed a pool across the floor. She was dead or dying and Doc knew it, even if he didn't want to believe it. He lifted up her head onto his lap. Her body was limp; he felt for a pulse and he couldn't feel anything. He was just about to place her back on the ground when Isabella's eyes abruptly opened; she grabbed the lapel of Holidays jacket.

"Get my husband!" she whispered and then she let go again and let her arm fall limply back to the ground. Doc looked frantically about the Comique for Nicolae but he wasn't there, but suddenly Nicolae rushed into the saloon and ran over to Isabella. He picked her up and walked out with her cradled in his arms.

"Be careful, I will run and get the Doctor." Nicolae looked back at Doc.

"I think you know it is too late for that," Nicolae answered him solemnly.

Doc couldn't believe it. For once in his life he did not want to spend all night drinking. He started to wander through the streets of the town with only himself for company. Doc walked to the edge of town and out of the corner of his eye he saw two people mounting horses in a hurry to get away. Doc ran over to them. He had not seen Nicolae dispatch the man who killed Isabella and he presumed that these men were involved or at least would know where the man was. Doc grabbed one of the men as he was mounting his horse and spun them around. This gesture knocked off the man's hat and Doc was amazed to see Isabella's raven hair falling down around her shoulders. Doc could not believe his own eyes.

"How?" Doc asked. Isabella looked up at him and said.

"It turns out I wasn't hurt at all." Doc looked at his hands. Isabella's dried blood was still on them.

"I know that isn't true..." Doc said. "You were dead."

"Not quite dead. It's takes a lot more than a few bullets to kill me."

Doc smiled. He did not know by what miracle she was still alive but he was glad she was. Isabella mounted her horse again and turned back towards Doc.

"Doc, I can call you Doc, can't I?" she said.

"You certainly can," Doc said through a smile.

"No one will remember my bloody demise in the morning except you."

"You're an amazing woman," Doc answered.

"She definitely is," Nicolae interrupted. Isabella smiled at the both of them. Isabella once more turned to leave. But then something made her turn back towards Doc again.

"Doc," she said, "try and take care of Kate a little better; you will lose her if you don't and you need her."

"I will try, I will probably fail miserably but I will try." Isabella turned the horse around again and both Nicolae and she rode off into the Kansas desert towards the sunset. Doc Holliday watched the pair as they left. He was bewildered, amazed, and somewhat amused by this couple. He walked back down the street with a newfound spring in his step and every few strides he would spin round to look at the backs of the two Vampires, wondering what their secret was and wanting to see them again and somehow he suspected he would. He knew that this woman's involvement in his life was far from over.

Tombstone was a prosperous mining town and was producing a steady amount of gold and silver. People were flocking to it. After they had been forced to leave Dodge, Tombstone's prosperity and lawlessness attracted the two Vampires. In Tombstone, Faro dealers and gamblers were rife and earning a fortune. Isabella knew that the Earps and Holiday would eventually come here, for Wyatt was greedy and Morgan and Doc would follow him.

Isabella was in the Oriental saloon the first time she saw Doc Holiday again. The Oriental was always empty and Isabella and Nicolae had just gone into get out of the hot sun; the new blue-tinted spectacles that Isabella had acquired for Nicolae were of no use today as a shield to the sun's rays. They were standing at the bar when they heard an argument in full swing behind them. Nicolae turned to see who was arguing and why.

"Look who it is," Nicolae said. Isabella turned around to see Wyatt Earp and Doc Holiday arguing with the Faro dealer. Wyatt then dragged the dealer out the door by the ear. One of the Faro dealer's friends reached down for his gun, but before he could even touch it, Doc thrust a knife at his gun hand, slashing it open. He would not be able to use that hand for quite some time.

"This is an argument between Mr. Tyler and Mr. Earp," Doc said. Not one of the other men made a move to help their friend. Isabella looked Doc over. A few years had passed and they had taken their toll on him. He was thinner and even more pale, if that was possible. However, there were two things that had not been marred even slightly by time or his failing lungs; he still had the power to intimidate the men around him and to Isabella's delight his clear blue eyes were still as electrifying as ever and still shone from across a darkened room. Doc saw Isabella out of the corner of his eye and smiled at her, tipping his hat as he did so.

When he knew Johnny Tyler's friends would not stand up to him, Doc followed Wyatt outside. The pair told Johnny Tyler to leave town. On seeing that both Wyatt and Doc were squaring up to him, he placated them and got all the way to county line before he reputedly stopped running. For years after this incident, hecklers would shout at Johnny Tyler.

"Stopped running yet, Johnny?" This was a true testament to these men's reputations and it was something that they both were proud of.

After Doc had rid Tombstone of Johnny Tyler, he returned to the Oriental and called out to the bartender, "Get that lady a drink, she is a friend of mine." Isabella looked over at Doc.

"Still risking your neck for Wyatt, I see," she said.

"I am not risking my neck for anyone. Johnny Tyler is no threat. He's just full of bluster."

"A bit like Wyatt," Isabella said.

"You could say that; the only difference is Wyatt can usually take care of himself."

"And when he can't you step in because of Morgan?"

"That pretty much sums it up."

Isabella smiled, "Is Kate with you?"

"She is, regretfully; she begged me to let her come."

"And you still don't think that a woman who loves you that much is worth anything?" Doc made no response.

Wyatt then entered the Oriental and joined the conversation. Wyatt actually looked pleased to see Isabella.

"I never got to thank you for what you did in Dodge," Wyatt said to Isabella.

"I think Doc is the one you should be thanking," Isabella answered.

"Oh, I do, daily," Wyatt answered.

Isabella still did not think much of him, but at least he was talking to her with some civility.

The Earps and Holiday slipped into the same a pattern that they had done in Dodge. The oldest brother Virgil became Sheriff and occasionally he would deputise Morgan, James, and Wyatt, if there was trouble. And there was trouble often in Tombstone. The Earp wives were a bit like Kate; they seemed to like none of the Earps except the one they were married to and sometimes they didn't even like their own husbands. Plus none of them seemed to like Isabella. She was not liked because she frequented the Oriental. This was a place where they were not allowed to be, and of course they did not blame their husbands for their lack of admittance, they blamed Isabella. However, over the past few weeks their enmity had shifted to another woman, Josephine Tull. They believed Wyatt was paying her too much attention. Josephine was the sheriff of Conchise County's fiancée, so Wyatt's attentions were causing trouble within another faction, the cowboys, and this was dangerous for all concerned.

The sheriff was never one to face the Earps in person. Instead, he tried to get at them through their wives; he had little success with the Earps, but Kate, on the other hand, was quite a different story. He had gotten her drunk and convinced her to tell him her woes; she told him that Doc had threatened to kill her, but this was no surprise to anyone. Doc regularly threatened to kill Kate and she regularly threatened to kill him. However, Behan, the sheriff, convinced her to swear out a warrant against him and a month later in retaliation Doc returned the favour and swore out a warrant against her. This was the last straw for them both and the pair parted company. But before she left him Doc gave her a large sum of money to start a new life. He told everyone that she had blackmailed him into giving her this money, but Isabella knew this not to be true. He had given her the money out of guilt and some latent affection that he still had for her.

Doc's health deteriorated after Kate had left and he realised how much she had done for him when she had been with him. Doc's health got so bad that every few nights he had to take a night off to rest and he hated having to do that. As far as he was concerned, by doing this he was admitting he was ill. Every night that he was able to come to the Oriental he stayed until the sunlight and crept through the curtains. Morgan was the only one who could make him go home to rest.

Ironically his luck had never been better. He was winning every night, so much so that people were starting to say he was cheating, but although he had cheated in the past, he was not cheating now.

"I only cheat when I am losing. Why would you cheat when you are winning?" he said to Isabella one night in jest.

The cowboys spurred on by the county sheriff were still causing trouble for the Earps. Up until now the confrontations had just been minor arguments, nothing life-threatening, but when the Bisbee stage was robbed, accusations started to fly about Tombstone and these minor arguments were steadily getting more and more violent. No one really knew who was involved, for the cowboys were blaming the Earps and the Earps were blaming the cowboys. It seemed that every night there was fight about it and Virgil was under pressure to issue warrants for the arrest of those involved.

The rains had come very heavy that year and it had rained so hard that it pounded and bruised everyone's skin as it fell. This did nothing for Doc's condition or his humour; he was irritated very easily and flying off the handle even with Isabella. At a time when remaining cool and rational was crucial Doc, not Wyatt, was losing his temper.

Doc was sitting in the Alhambra when he would have the fateful argument with Ike Clanton a cowboy known for his bad temper which often led to violence. Ike came in and sat beside him. Isabella had not seen Ike in a few days. Not that he was someone who warranted her attention, but today she was very attentive to him. She wondered why he had chosen to sit down beside Doc. Doc had beaten him too many times at poker for there to be any benevolent feeling between the pair. Isabella wanted to hear what they were saying. So even though she was sitting across a busy room filled with people, she used her unique ability to listen.

"Doc?" Doc looked over at Ike and as he took a drink said, "Ike…what have I done to deserve the pleasure of your company?"

"Enough of your smart talk," Ike said in response to Doc's belittling tone.

"I forgot I was not conversing with an equal; I will lower the tone to suit you." Doc was not even looking at Ike as he was talking; his eyes never left his poker hand.

"Look at me when you talk to me!" Ike shouted. Doc ignored Ike completely and looked only at the cards he was now being dealt. Ike infuriated, lifted up the side of the poker table and overturned it. Doc, who was still sitting in his chair, finally looked up at Ike and said.

"You have my attention, what is it?"

"Your friend has framed Frank Stillwell."

"And what friend would that be?"

"Wyatt Earp, the whole town knows he was behind the Bisbee robbery."

"Nonsense," Doc protested.

"I don't think so; everyone knows he was in on it, him and his brothers." Doc stood to face Ike. He staggered as he stood, and his legs nearly gave way underneath him; he hadn't slept in days.

"You are a liar, Ike Clanton."

Ike squared up to him, "Am I? We'll see. We'll see, Holiday."

VROLOK

Doc set his hand on his gun. Ike could see that Doc was very ill. He leaned forward, pressing the tips of his fingers on Doc's shoulders. Such a little amount of force was enough to send Doc crashing to the ground. Morgan who was having his lunch now became fully aware of the altercation. He leaped over the table where he had been sitting and hit Ike over the top of the head with his gun butt; Ike fell but got up again as soon as he hit the floor. Isabella knew not to help Doc up; he wouldn't accept help from anyone. He was embarrassed enough that he had fallen in the first place. He struggled back on to his feet. Morgan had gone out to the street and was surrounded by John Ringgold, Ike Clanton, and the Hick boys. Doc, sensing the urgency of the situation, came out to help his friend, even though he knew he was in no condition to fight.

"We'll be coming to get you; we will be coming to get all you Earps," Morgan shouted, drawing his gun.

"You come near any of us and I'll kill you. I will kill y'all!" Morgan shouted.

Isabella came out and was standing behind Doc. She happened to notice one of the other men was reaching cautiously for his gun. She whispered in Doc's ear, *"Look to your left."*

"I'd put that gun away Frank McLaury or you will be first to die," Doc shouted. At this sheriff Behan came from around the corner.

"Don't cause any trouble today, boys; there'll be plenty of time," he said. With that the crowd broke up and walked away from the scene. Doc walked back towards his hotel and when he got to the door, using the last of his strength he shut it behind him. He could not stand up any longer. He collapsed to the ground, coughing up blood.

From then on there was a deep sense of tension on the streets of Tombstone. There had been no more confrontations between the Earps and the cowboys but everyone knew that the enmity between them would erupt, and when it did the result would be bloody.

When no one had seen Doc for days, Isabella was concerned for him, so she went to see him. She knocked on his door. There was no answer, but Isabella decided to go in anyway; after all, he had invited her many times to come to his rooms. She pushed on the door and opened it as gently as she could. When Isabella entered the room it was in darkness.

Doc was lying on the bed in the dark, opened letters lying scattered on the floor beside the bed. The letters where crumpled and yellow; they had obviously been read many times. Isabella opened the curtain and Doc opened his eyes.

"Ah, it's the lady who cheats death," Doc said. The stench in the room was vile. Isabella proceeded to open a window to let in some fresh air.

"I haven't ever cheated death—I have just avoided it," Isabella corrected.

"Avoided it. I see. You will have to teach me how to do that someday."

"Perhaps I will…someday. Who are these letters from?"

"Mattie."

"Why don't you go back to her?"

"Go back to her to cough and spit all over her?"

"She has already seen you the way you are now, when Morgan rescued her and brought her back to you."

"She couldn't bring herself to look at me."

"I am sure that is not true."

"No, I sent her home. I didn't want her to know who I am. I wanted her to remember the eighteen-year-old that I used to be, before my lungs started to rot."

"She still writes to you. Do you think she would do that if she couldn't look at you?"

"She is too kind to stop; she writes to me only because she pities me."

"Nonsense. You are the only one who pities you…get up and go outside. I think your friends are going to need you soon."

"What are you talking about?"

"The McLaurys and the Clantons are threatening to kill Wyatt and his brothers. He has caused yet another fight."

"He will get himself killed one of these days," Doc said.

"Or worse…he will get someone that is close to him killed," Isabella said as she left.

When Doc had a few minutes to think about what she said, he knew she was right and he was worried for Morgan. So he got up, got dressed and went outside. As he walked down the street he met Morgan, Wyatt, and Virgil; he joined them and headed towards the OK Corral. Isabella watched as they disappeared from her line of vision and went down the next street. She listened for the gun shots and waited and watched to see who would survive.

"Why aren't you going over to see what you can do?" Nicolae asked.

"Have you forgotten I am a Vampire? I am not supposed to help humans—I am supposed to kill them."

"That has never stopped you before."

"I have saved him once—perhaps that was one more time than he deserved."

"There is more to it than that; you are not telling me something."

"The truth is he has a woman who loves him somewhere and he is too afraid to go home to her. He would rather stay here and defend Wyatt; even if it kills him."

"And that reminds you too much of yourself." Isabella looked over at Nicolae and walked over to him; she laid her head on his chest and put her arm around him.

"You are so like him."

"Who?"

"Nicolae, my Nicolae, I try and remind myself that you are not him but the things you say. So like the things he would have said."

"And that is a bad thing?"

"No. I suppose not. But you differ in one aspect; he would never have forgiven me."

"Yes he would have, Isabella, you underestimate yourself." The shooting stopped and Isabella went back over to the side of the road to watch the survivors coming around the corner. Wyatt and Virgil were first to appear, Wyatt was holding Virgil up, then Morgan appeared; he had also been hurt but was able to walk by himself. Isabella's grip on Nicolae tightened; there had been many shots fired, Isabella was frightened for Doc. Perhaps she should have helped him. But then off in the distance she heard a cough. She released her tight grip on Nicolae and ran across, leaning over the hitching rail to see Doc walking around the corner. It seemed that Doc was never going to die in a gunfight.

The gunfight at Tombstone did nothing to dissipate the tension; in fact, it made it worse. For Vampires the threat of violence was always a good thing. If a few people died there were always plenty of people to blame. But for Doc and especially for Morgan the threat of violence was far from a good thing.

Morgan was in Campbell and Hatch's billiard parlour the night he died. Doc, Wyatt, and Virgil were with him. Morgan was in good humour, but then he always was. He relished the danger and loved Tombstone.

"Stillwell and Clanton have been threatening us again," Virgil began.

"You worry too much. We are more than a match for any of them," Wyatt answered. Morgan was up on his feet to take his shot.

"We can kill them all, and the world would be better off without them," Morgan laughed. Doc's coughs could be heard from the other side of the room. "Or Doc can give them all consumption and we can get them that way." Doc would have never allowed anyone else to say this except for Morgan.

"For you, Morgan, I will try and cough on them as much as possible."

"Don't bother Doc. Knowing our luck they would probably last as long as you have," Morgan answered. The whole group of men started to laugh and Morgan bent down over the table to take his shot. The men jumped as they heard the glass of the front window break. It was raining heavily outside and Doc ran over to see why it had shattered. Whatever or whoever had smashed the window was no longer there.

"I can't see anything," Doc said. But his words were ignored.

"Morgan!" Wyatt cried out. Doc turned around slowly, afraid of the scene he would see behind him. Morgan was lying on the floor, collapsed at his side.

"He has been shot in the back!" Virgil said. Doc was devastated his best friend in the world was dying. He tried to think how he could save him. Then a memory ran through his mind. He had been in this situation before, sitting beside someone who had been shot in the back.

"Isabella," he whispered. Doc left the bloody scene and searched for Isabella. He found her on the outskirts of town but he was not happy when he saw her, for that was the night he found out what sort of creature she was.

※

Isabella was calling over to a young-sixteen-year-old boy when Doc found her. An inner voice told Doc not to make Isabella aware that he was nearby.

"Daniel, come over here, there is something I want to give you," Isabella's voice sounded like an angels, no one could have resisted her call. Daniel walked over to her, his eyes full of admiration. Daniel walked to his death. When he was within reaching distance Isabella grabbed his throat and lifted him up. She bit down hard on his neck, Daniel was now struggling for his life; the admiration that had been in his eyes was now replaced by terror. Isabella eventually let go and Daniel's limp, lifeless body fell on to the dusty street.

Isabella looked up to see Doc; blood was still dripping from her mouth. Doc was horrified it was not some wonderful magic that Isabella possessed, that it was a disease far worse than his own. She was some sort of ungodly creature; whatever way she cheated death could not help Morgan. He was a far better being than Isabella ever was. Doc returned to the place where Morgan was dying in utter devastation.

Isabella watched as Doc walked away. Doc had liked Isabella; he had even held her in great affection, until he realised what she was. For Doc was a man who could not tolerate a woman's failings, no matter what they were. Isabella had not felt this type of disgust for what she was in a long time

VROLOK

and it hurt her, but she would go and see what had upset him so utterly. She walked over to the billiard room. The scene was desolate; Morgan's wife was crying at his side and he was in dreadful pain, totally aware that he was going to die. His last minutes on this earth would be spent in tortuous agony. Isabella acknowledged that Morgan did not deserve this.

"John?" she said to Doc, for she did not feel she was entitled to call him Doc anymore. "I need to speak to you."

"What do you want?" he retorted, barely able to look at her.

"I need to talk to you."

"I have nothing to say to you."

"I have something to say to you. Come with me." Isabella used her influence and Doc followed her out into the street.

"My friend is dying in there, and you have dragged me out into the street to explain the creature that you are."

"I brought you out here to offer you something."

"Offer me what?"

"I can take his pain away."

"By making him like you?"

"No. Just by touching him. You have to trust me."

"I will trust you this one last time, because of Morgan...do it." Isabella went into the room Doc followed her. Isabella sat down beside Morgan and held his hand; the pain flowed through her. Morgan was now content and could die in peace. Isabella got up and left the Earps to their grief.

Isabella had had enough of Tombstone and made up her mind to leave with Nicolae as soon as she could. Before she had time to leave, Doc came to see her.

"I am sorry for my behaviour the night Morgan died." He said the last part with a slight smile. He was trying to break the tension that now existed between them.

"Don't apologise; your true colours were shown," Isabella said, as always it would take more than a mere apology to win back her regard.

"I am sorry, anyway," Doc said.

Isabella did not want to listen to incessant apologies, so she said, "Never mind, I am sure I will live." Isabella added with a wry smile, "What are you going to do now without Morgan to look after?"

Doc became serious again and said sternly, "Find his killer," Doc stated.

"Do you know who it was?"

"We have our suspicions."

"But you don't know for sure."

"No."

"So what are you going to do?"

"Kill them all. It's the way Morgan would have done it," Doc said, a poignant sense of remembrance echoing through his words.

"That's not very practical; it may get you all killed. I can help you," Isabella said.

"How?"

"One of my many abilities is that I can tell what people have done in their lives by touching them. I can see their worst crimes."

"You can?"

"I can."

"By the merest touch?"

Isabella nodded. "By the merest touch," she repeated.

The McLaurys, the Clantons, and Frank Stillwell were sitting outside the Alhambra. They were laughing and pointing over at the Earps, who were on their way to bury Morgan. Isabella walked beside them with her right hand at her side. She glided past them, and as she did she very gently touched each man in turn. Doc was waiting for her at the end of the street.

"Well, who was it?"

"The one on the end," Isabella answered.

"Stillwell," Doc said under his breath.

"I can do something else for you. I can give him Morgan's pain. He can experience everything that Morgan did in one in one exquisite, agonising moment."

Stillwell was walking by the southern tracks in Tucson when Isabella confronted him. Wyatt and Doc were with her. At first he turned to run but Isabella pulled him back. Wyatt was amazed at Isabella's strength but said nothing.

"Do you remember my brother?" Wyatt asked.

"I didn't do it," Stillwell lied.

"You're a liar, Stillwell," Doc said.

"Do you know what it feels like to be shot in the back?" Isabella asked. Stillwell ignored her; he was more concerned by Wyatt's and Doc's presence. He did not realise that the real danger he was in was from Isabella. She leaned into him and whispered, *"This is what it felt like."* Isabella placed her hand on his heart and Morgan's pain seared through him. Stillwell screamed out and tried to push Isabella away from him, but he was nowhere near strong enough. After a few agonising minutes Isabella let go and Stillwell fell to the ground in a crumpled heap.

Doc pulled him back onto his feet and shouted, "Did you kill Morgan?"

Stillwell looked away from Doc and answered, "Yes!"

"Run Stillwell…keep running—it'll never be fast enough," Doc said as he threw Stillwell to the ground again. The man stumbled to his feet and ran for his life. Doc shot him first and the bullet penetrated Stillwell's back. He fell and then both Wyatt and Holiday put bullet after bullet into his body.

After this day Isabella left Doc's company; this time she had no intention of seeing him again. However, she still heard of his exploits after Stillwell died. He was becoming famous. Wyatt and Doc were killing cowboys all over the west. It got so bad for the cowboys during this period that they were turning themselves into the authorities, too frightened to wait for Holiday and Wyatt to catch up with them.

Isabella met Doc one last time in Pueblo, Colorado. Holiday smiled when he saw her.

"You are carving out quite a reputation for yourself," Isabella began.

"I know; cowboys quiver at my name," Doc said playfully, exaggerating his words. "Morgan would have gotten a kick out of that."

"He would have."

"Wyatt hardly remembers you."

"I know."

"Why have you let me remember and not him?"

"Wyatt has too big a mouth. I believe you can keep my secret."

"I will, I will keep it to my grave." There was a silence and Isabella asked.

"How is Mattie? Do you still hear from her?"

"I do. Would you believe, she is joining a convent?" Holiday said this with a smile but Isabella knew he was devastated by this news. Another silence interrupted the conversation and Holiday began to speak again, "I am going to go to Leadville after this."

"Leadville?" Isabella said. "But the weather there is—"

"I know, hardly any sunshine, rainy days and nights—it's bad for my condition," Doc said nonchalantly.

"It'll kill you," Isabella said seriously.

"I have been dying for years. Maybe it's time to give up and let it take me."

"When are you going to go?"

"As soon as Wyatt doesn't need me anymore. I owe it to Morgan to stay with him as long as he wants me. I have always felt responsible for his death. I could have saved Morgan."

"You couldn't have done anything to stop it." The Holiday Isabella met in Pueblo was a different man, a broken man. With Mattie's announcement that she was entering a nunnery his dreams of her were gone forever. He now for the first time in his diseased-ridden existence wanted life to end. He was staying with Wyatt out of loyalty to Morgan and it was torturing him.

"I have something to tell you," Isabella stated.

"What?"

"You are not responsible for Morgan's death."

"What do you mean?"

"Wyatt conspired to rob the Bisbee stage."

"What? But he always denied it."

"You don't owe him anything. If anyone is responsible for what happened it is Wyatt." Doc was sitting there amazed. The robbing of the Bisbee stage—Wyatt had been involved. Everything that had happened could have been avoided if Wyatt had told him the truth. Stillwell, Clanton and the others had a right to their grievances.

"Even when we killed Stillwell, he never told me," Doc said in shock.

"Well, you know now." Isabella got up to leave. "Well, John, have a nice life, what's left of it."

"Why are you calling me John? My friends call me Doc?" Doc said quietly.

"Goodbye, Doc." Isabella left and never saw him again.

Doc Holiday and Wyatt Earp had an argument in Pueblo. No one knows what it was about, but they never spoke to each other again.

※

A few nights later Isabella was sitting in her hotel lobby waiting for Nicolae. She was watching the hustle and bustle of the activity going on in front of her. She felt a rush of air behind her head. Someone was trying to hit her with something. She heard Nicolae cry out and she turned around. She saw Nicolae holding the arm of the man who was trying to wound her. She looked at his face—it was Abraham Van Helsing.

THIS BATTLE HAS BUT BEGUN AND IN THE END WE SHALL WIN

CHAPTER TWENTY-FIVE

He was watching her as he had done so many nights before; she glided down the empty street, her golden hair glimmered, even in the blackness of night. She was a vision. She looked so beautiful and pure that if he had not seen her kill he would never have believed she was capable of it. He waited for her to approach him before he showed himself. When she was just steps away from him he faced her.

"I was looking for you." Her voice echoed like music through the air. The bewitching creature leaned into to kiss him and he appeared receptive to her embrace. His hands were at his back and he slowly brought them around. To an onlooker it seemed that he was about to hold her in his arms as she kissed him. But then his motion gained speed and he pushed her from him. He reached for his knife and slashed his own wrist. Blood seeped out onto the blade. The creature he had pushed from him ran back towards him with the intention of ending his life but he was to end hers: she ran onto his blade. She screamed out in agony and fell to the ground. She would no longer trouble this world. He walked away satisfied that he had done what he had come here to do, for he, Abraham Van Helsing, had just killed his first Vampire.

Isabella's shock at seeing Van Helsing quickly turned to thoughts of revenge. She saw traces of Vlad in his eyes and it reminded her of her promise to avenge Vlad's death. Her need for retribution had been reawakened. She wanted her revenge. She was filled with fresh hatred for those who had killed him.

Nicolae was holding back Van Helsing's arm. Isabella looked into the old man's eyes. The two Vampires were more than a match for him. He still had great strength but it was not enough; the only way he could possibly kill Isabella was by creeping up behind her and striking before she knew he was there. Thankfully, Nicolae had stopped him on this occasion. Nicolae was about to kill him, but Isabella spoke before he did.

"No Nicolae, death is too good and too quick for him." Isabella had never hated Abraham. At one point in her life she had even grown close to loving him, but he had killed Vlad and Isabella had never been one to forgive, no matter how tempted she had been. "We will let him live."

"Let him live?"

"Just a little longer." Nicolae let Van Helsing go and he scurried out through the door of the lobby. "We must be careful from now on," Isabella said. She was concerned for Nicolae. She had now lived for four hundred years and the threat of death would not stop or even deter her from getting her retribution, but she felt that Nicolae should be free to choose his own path. She would not condemn him; she had no right.

That evening Nicolae asked her, "Why did you let him go? He has the power to kill us both."

"He may well succeed some day; I have to tell you something."

"I was warned that our race of Vampires would die out, and I believe that going back to England to seek my retribution may be the last thing I ever do."

"Then why go?"

"I have to go."

"Then I have to go as well."

"No. Nicolae you have to consider this thoroughly, you have a grave choice to make."

"I have already made my choice."

Isabella was exasperated by Nicolae's response. "You haven't even begun to consider what you are facing."

"Won't you listen to me?" Nicolae protested. Isabella sighed. She had to make him listen to her. He had to understand what he would face. She went over to her dresser and pulled out a bottle; it was all that she had left of Van Helsing's blood. She placed a few drops on her knife, not letting Nicolae see what she was doing. Isabella then turned around and calmly stabbed Nicolae in the heart. Pain surged through his body, pain he had never even been close to feeling that way before. This new torturous sensation was unendurable. Nicolae dragged his eyes up from his wound and glanced astounded at Isabella. She of all creatures on this earth had killed him; he never would have believed her capable. Blackness started to invade his vision and he fell forward into Isabella's arms.

Of course, Nicolae was not dead. For Isabella would never let him die and she knew that she could bring him back from the brink, but she wanted him to taste death so that he understood completely what accompanying her might mean.

A few nights later when Nicolae awoke his room was empty. He had a tiny scar over his heart where Isabella had stabbed him. He got out of bed and looked around for Isabella; there was no sign of her. Nicolae got dressed, went outside and started to wander the streets, not knowing how he would react when he saw Isabella.

After a few hours he found her. She had turned another Vampire, a young girl. Isabella was walking down the street with her. Nicolae stayed back out of sight and watched and listened.

"I'm hungry," the new Vampire said.

"I know, child, and you will feed soon," Isabella answered her.

"But I am hungry now," the Vampire wined.

"Be quiet, Lizzie. Let's go into the public house up ahead. No doubt we will find food for you in there." Isabella went in and she saw the man she was looking for. "Wait here," she told Lizzie. "I will let you kill someone soon, but not until I tell you." Isabella went over to the back corner of the alehouse where Van Helsing was sitting.

"I have been waiting for you," Van Helsing began. Isabella said nothing. "Waiting for you to end it." Isabella watched him in silence for a few moments. He was just a shell of the man Isabella had known so many years ago in Germany. His skin was pale and grey. He was rubbing his hands together at the fire as if he could not get heat into his tired old bones. Isabella finally opened her mouth to speak.

"I have not come to kill you, Abraham," she said.

"You will forgive me if I don't believe you," Abraham responded.

"You can believe what you like, the main reason I have come here is to tell you something."

"What have you come to tell me?" Isabella was silent and Van Helsing was getting impatient. He wanted this to be over. "Tell me."

Isabella leaned forward and looked into his black eyes. "You have his eyes."

"Whose?"

"Your father's."

"How do you know that? You have never seen my father and anyway his eyes were…"

"His eyes were?" Isabella asked. "You have such an unusual colour of eyes. They are so dark, almost black." Van Helsing was nervous; this was the worst thing Isabella could have told him and she knew it. "Do you not realise how alike you are?"

"No, stop telling me this!" Van Helsing shouted, knowing the truth already.

"A Dhampir is the child of a human and a Vampire and that is what you are, Vlad Dracula's son."

Van Helsing, unable to find words, threw his fists out at Isabella, but she quickly subdued his violent outburst and threw him back into the chair.

"I will leave you now to your grief," Isabella said. Isabella walked over to Lizzie and whispered in her ear. "You can kill him now." Lizzie clapped her hands in glee and Isabella watched as she practically skipped over to where Van Helsing was seated. She was like a child who just been told there was a present for her in the corner. No sooner had Lizzie bit into him than she stepped back in agony. Her young skin aging rapidly, she fell back and looked at Isabella, reaching out for her help, but Isabella had none to give her. Van Helsing was not quite dead and Lizzie was going to be dead within seconds. Isabella ran over to Van Helsing—it was not over for him. She slit open her wrist and let her blood drip into Van Helsing's mouth. He tried to struggle and get away but he was powerless. Lizzie, whom Isabella had dismissed as dead, suddenly found what was left of her strength and pushed Isabella away from Van Helsing. Lizzie wiped away the poisoned blood from her mouth onto her hand. She reached out for Isabella's face in an attempt to strike her and at least scar her with this liquid that was just about to kill her. Lizzie's actions had drawn the attention of the other people in the tavern.

Isabella threw the onlookers a nefarious glance. "Go back to your dinner," she hissed. Every person who had noticed the Vampires turned away and went back to eating their meals with no recollection of what they had just seen.

Nicolae now rushed towards Isabella, fearing for her safety. He kicked Lizzie away from her and this final blow ensured she was dead. After he had dispatched Lizzie he continued to help Isabella. He held Van Helsing down while Isabella let blood drip into his mouth. After the vengeful deed was done, the two Vampires let Van Helsing go. Isabella looked at Nicolae and smiled; he returned her smile warmly.

"Tell me this…" Nicolae began, "if I am ever killed, will you do this to avenge my death?" Isabella nodded.

"If you were ever killed, I would be merciless," Isabella answered.

Van Helsing ran about the streets in agony and despair. His father was a Vampire and he was a Vampire. These were the creatures he despised. He saw up ahead of him iron railings encircling a church. He threw himself on to them and by God's grace, he died.

REMEMBER YOUR OATH
CHAPTER TWENTY SIX

Before they departed for England, Isabella and Nicolae searched Van Helsing's rooms; she found several journals, newspaper articles, and a copy of the *Demeter*'s ship logs. This was the ship on which Vlad had traveled to England. When it was pasted together it created quite a detailed account of Vlad's entrance and departure from these people's lives. It was the only thing Isabella took from Van Helsing. But then again, it was the only thing that Abraham had that was worth anything.

Isabella read the accounts over and over again trying to learn about her prey, trying to get to know the Harkers, Arthur Holmwood, and Jack Seaward. She was looking for clues in order to execute her revenge. Isabella promised herself that she would think of the worst possible punishment for each of them.

There were references in these pages to Vampires being repelled by religious symbols, wafers, crosses, and holy water. Vlad had always despised religion and shrunk from it, but there was no mythical power guarding people who hid behind these ancient expressions of faith. The weapons that Holmwood, Harker and Seaward had used were all dangerous weapons to mortals but not to Vampires and Van Helsing knew this. He had placed a few drops of his blood onto the weapons and when the end was near he added a lot more than that to make sure that Vlad Dracula died. He had smeared a drop or two on the wafer that he had pressed on Mina Harker's head. When it burned they all knew that she had turned. Isabella destroyed any reference that existed regarding a Dhampir's blood; she didn't want there to be a written record that held the key to the destruction of a Vampire's existence.

Months later, Isabella was again in London. She had not yet forced herself into the lives of those she hunted. She had to establish herself once again in British society so that she could kill or destroy each one of them in turn, without suspicion. Isabella and Nicolae had to be invited to meet the Harkers, Holmwoods, or Seawards. It had to seem as if they had met purely by chance and that nothing had been prearranged. In the meantime, while she waited for that precious invitation to arrive, she amused herself by hunting through bookstores looking for stories that interested her. Isabella had never lost her thirst for knowledge.

It was a dark winter's day when she found herself in an old and forgotten bookstore near the theatre district. As she was looking through the various books she couldn't help but hear two men standing across from her having a heated conversation.

"I would give it up, Bram; you will never write anything that anyone would be even remotely interested in," one of the men stated.

"Henry, you are being unkind. I will write a great novel someday...I just need to find a story to inspire me."

"Perhaps, Bram, but you won't write anything skulking around bookshops." Henry left the shop and Bram stayed behind leafing through the books, looking for the inspiration for an original idea that so far had eluded him. Isabella was now standing beside him. The Vampire and the aspiring writer both reached for the same short story. Isabella's hand was on the book before Bram's. Bram gently brushed Isabella's hand. Isabella quickly drew her hand back from Bram's touch.

"I am sorry," Bram began. "You take the book; I have read it many times before."

"You have."

"I have it's a great story."

"What is it about?"

"A Vampire."

"I had guessed that from the title."

"Yes but this one is different. He mingles with society, totally free from suspicion. In fact he is quite an alluring Vampire, unlike any other vampiric creatures we have read about before."

"What have Vampires seemed like before?" Isabella enquired.

"They have always been described as parasites with no redeeming qualities whatsoever, no personalities. Skulking around in darkened alleyways, hissing like cats as they pounce on their unsuspecting victims. What makes Ruthven so dangerous is that he can pass for one of the best us..."

"Ruthven?" Isabella queried.

"Yes, Lord Ruthven—he is the villain of the story."

"I know that name," Isabella said, looking at the man before her. He was a middle-aged man. He was quite tall, well-groomed, with a beard and a kind face. Isabella thought to herself that this man deserved to get his novel and she decided that she would give it to him. "I couldn't help but over hear that you are trying to write a novel."

"I am. I have been for years."

"I have a story for you."

"Tell me."

"Not here, not now. Meet me tomorrow outside the British Library."

"A secret rendezvous with a younger woman. My wife would not approve."

"Your wife has nothing to worry about." This woman intrigued Bram Stoker; he would meet her at the British Library at least to hear what she had to say.

The next day Isabella was waiting for him and the pair went inside together. Isabella took him straight over to the historical section of the library. Bram stayed silent. He was trying to indulge the young girl in an innocent, paternal way. Isabella lifted up German texts and showed them to Stoker.

"Have you ever heard of this man?" Isabella asked. Bram looked down at the German text. Although he could not read German, the words somehow seemed clear to him.

"Prince Vlad Dracula." Bram said quietly.

"Yes, a Prince, a great and noble prince, the scourge of his time."

"You talk like you know him."

"I did." Isabella looked up at him with a faint smile, touched his forehead and memories flowed into his mind. He saw what he instantly recognised as a great man, a Prince and a warrior, and he was standing at the top of a battlefield. He saw a young man approach him from out of the darkness. This adolescent bore a strong resemblance to the young woman he saw in front of him. Bram stoker fell back He was amazed at this vision, it was so clear. It seemed to him as if he was actually witnessing these events which he knew had occurred centuries ago.

"In life he was a good man, in death he was the man I loved," Isabella continued. Bram Stoker raised his eyes up to look at this woman again. She was possibly the most beautiful creature he had ever seen; her face was exquisite and Bram knew she had stories to tell, stories the like of which the world had never heard before. "I want to give you a present but before I do, I want to tell you a story," she continued.

At this Bram Stoker got up and took her hand and held it carefully.

"Please I want you to tell me as much as you can."

"Sit." Isabella gestured for Bram to sit down again. She began to tell a story, but it was not one of her stories—it was one of Vlad's.

※

Eighty years before, when Vlad had been in England, he had left Isabella in Jakub's care and was filling time before he had to go back to Holland to kill his son. Vlad had always liked England and he wanted a place to distract him from the grizzly task ahead. He decided to stay there until he had to return.

When he was in this country he had always used the same name, Edward Hawthorne. He did not think this name was appropriate anymore. He wanted a name that suited his morose mood and one that inspired a certain amount of fear. He called himself, Lord Ruthven.

The Ruthvens had been Earls of Scotland; they had a reputation as assassins. The most infamous incident was when Patrick, the third Lord Ruthven, brutally murdered David Rizzio, Mary Queen of Scots' chief advisor. He had been brutally slain in front of the Queen's eyes. His son the fourth Earl had also tried to usurp the monarchy by imprisoning Mary's son, James. After this, their Earlship was taken from them and had never been restored. Vlad took it upon himself to give them back their lordly status, even if it was only for the duration of his stay. He introduced himself as Lord Ruthven, Earl of Gowrie.

He flitted from party to party unimpressed by the superficial society around him. His contempt was obvious at these affairs and yet he kept getting invited to them. No one knew much about him and his pale skin and black eyes always made him stand out from the crowd. There was an air of mystery that surrounded him and he attracted and fascinated most people. Some, however, were more cautious and were suspicious of this lord who came from nowhere.

Vlad was never very sociable and he usually stood in the corner watching the exuberance of the other guests with disdain. He was not interested in his surroundings or the people that occupied them. However, one man kept trying to start a conversation with him. Vlad was reluctant to enter into any sort of dialogue and either snubbed or ignored him, but this man kept persisting. He suspected Vlad had stories to tell and he wanted to hear them. This curious man's name was John Polidori.

Polidori was a young doctor with literary pretensions. He attended these gatherings to see if he could converse with the likes of Coleridge, Wordsworth, Shelley and most especially Lord Byron. Polidori had initially noticed Lord Ruthven, simply because he seemed so unimpressed by these literary giants. While swarms of people gathered around these men like sycophants waiting on their every word, hoping they would break into verse and give an impromptu demonstration of their skill, Ruthven looked through them, not even acknowledging them.

One evening Polidori, who always kept one eye on Byron and the other eye on Ruthven, hoped to one day see some sort of reaction from him. Ruthven had obviously become annoyed earlier than he usually did and he left the party long before midnight. Polidori was compelled to follow him that evening. He grabbed his coat and stayed a few paces behind.

Of course Vlad was well aware of Polidori following him. He had left the reception because his hunger was starting affect him and he did not want to kill anyone so publicly. He wandered through the streets and with each step his pace grew slower. He was waiting for Polidori to catch up with him. They had wandered into a district that had a growing reputation for violence. Vlad had brought Polidori here purposely, with the notion, when Polidori's body was found tomorrow, that it could be easily explained.

Vlad stood on the river's edge waiting for Polidori to come up behind him. He had decided that he would strike him then. Vlad, being very elegantly dressed, was a temptation for any thief who was watching, and one was watching him. This questionable character ran at Vlad, and he had a bludgeon in his hand. His plan was to knock Vlad out and take whatever he could find in his pockets. Vlad felt the rush of air as the thief struck out at Vlad, but of course his blow did not even make a mark. Vlad knew that Polidori had seen these events and was running towards Vlad to help him, but Vlad had no need of help; he had to feed.

The thief had now felt how strong Vlad was and was tempted to back away; he knew he could not subdue this man. Vlad turned around and looked up to the heavens.

"*Rain*," Vlad whispered. Rain started to pour out of the sky and winds started to stir up fog. The street quickly filled with it. Polidori's vision was now unclear. Vlad caught the thief by the neck and bit into him, feeding quickly before Polidori could reach the scene. Polidori was within a few steps of Vlad and the thief was now dead. To cover up his actions and the dead man Vlad threw himself and the body into the Thames. To Polidori it looked as if there had been a struggle and the two men had fallen into the river as a result. The rain stopped and the fog dissipated. Polidori, who was now frantic, stood at the river's edge, desperately looking through the darkness to see Vlad coming up for air, but the water was calm and still; there was no sign of him.

Polidori dived into the murky water with the firm intent of saving Vlad's life. Vlad had stayed underneath so that Polidori would presume him drowned, but Polidori was not so complacent that he would stand by and watch a man drown if there was a possibility that he could save him. Vlad remained limp and still and let Polidori swim towards him. He let him take hold of him and drag him back up to the surface of the water. Vlad made no effort to help him, believing that Polidori would eventually let go and leave him to drift down into the blackness of the water. He was wrong. Polidori dragged and pulled with all his might until he was almost drowned himself. He got onto the river bank and dragged Vlad's body up from the water. He pressed down on Vlad's stomach to try and get the water out of his lungs. He opened his shirt and placed his ear to his heart. There was no sound at all. Polidori was exhausted and scolded himself for not being fast enough. He walked away to try and report the drowning.

"If I only I had been quicker, I could have saved him," Polidori said to the policeman he found. "He is just over here." Polidori pointed and jumped down onto the river bank. The body was gone. "It was definitely here," he said.

"Sir, have you been drinking?" The police man asked.

"Yes, but..."

"Sir, I suggest you go home and stop wasting my time." With this abrupt reply the officer left and Polidori began looking around the riverbank completely puzzled. He started to walk home. It was just an hour before daylight and the streets were silent. All Polidori could hear was the sound of his own footsteps; he did not like this eerie silence. The events of this evening had unnerved him and he ran the rest of the way. He was frightened and he was right to be. Vlad had been watching him, deciding whether to kill him or not. He had eventually decided that this man had saved his life or at least he had tried to. Could Vlad really kill a man who had almost killed himself trying to save him? No, he would let him live for now, he thought.

A few years passed and Polidori had worked hard at becoming a friend and confident of Lord Byron. Lord Byron had taken Polidori with him on a trip across Europe. They were travelling through France together and were invited to a house in which Byron was supposed to display his talent. Polidori as in all such occasions disappeared into the background of the party. He wandered through the building while Byron was entertaining the masses. These performances of Byron had lost some of their appeal for Polidori, for they had grown monotonous; the originality which he had seen in England was somehow lost in these bloated and arrogant exhibitions. However, what he had lost in respect for Byron's literary talent, he had gained in friendship. He heard uproarious applause. It was obviously all over for another evening. Polidori headed back into recital hall and Byron called him over.

"Polidori...come over here, I want to introduce you to someone." Polidori walked swiftly over to Byron and smiled. "You may have met him before in England," Byron continued. The man who was standing with his back towards Polidori started to turn slowly around. Polidori's blood chilled to ice as the man he thought was dead was revealed to him. "Lord Ruthven," Byron stated. "Do you remember him? We saw him at several parties I think, in London."

"Yes, I remember," he stuttered.

Polidori was sick with fear the rest of the night; he knew this man had been dead. He had no heartbeat, how was he still alive. Polidori kept trying to steal a glimpse of Ruthven without him knowing but every time he looked over at him Ruthven was staring back and smiling menacingly. Eventually Polidori could not stand it any longer. He had to get out of this place. He went over to Byron and begged his leave.

"Go if you want Polidori, I will not be leaving for some time yet." He knew this would be Byron's response. He was not one to leave any place that he was receiving such high praise. Polidori went outside and got into the coach that was waiting for him. As he stepped up into the coach there was a sudden change in the weather. A mighty storm stirred in the sky and Polidori said to the coach driver.

"Hurry, please I want to be home before this storm becomes destructive."

"Yes, sir." Polidori heard the coach driver lash the horses with the reins and they sped off. Within a few minutes, lightning stabbed down from the sky to the earth below. Polidori remembered the weather of that other night in London. He dismissed these ideas trying to blank out these thoughts, but he couldn't.

Polidori's mind was racing with thoughts that were only adding to his fear. When they were within a mile from where he was staying one last fork of lightening struck the earth. It split a tree in half and the tree collapsed in front of the galloping horses. The coach grounded to a halt.

"I am afraid I cannot go any further," the coach driver yelled down.

"What?" Polidori retorted. "Nonsense, carry on," Polidori said, scared out of his wits.

"I can't sir, the horses will not move another step... you will have to walk."

"I can't walk," Polidori said now completely distressed.

"It is only about half a mile down the road, sir. You will find it easily."

"I am not worried about finding it," Polidori said underneath his breath. "I am worried about getting there alive."

"What was that, sir?"

"Nothing. Will you go back for Lord Byron?"

"Yes sir, when the storm eases over." Polidori looked up at the sky and the wind seemed to be settling. The lightning had stopped. "It seems to be calming down, sir."

"Yes, it does."

"I will return now for Lord Byron, or do you want me to take you the rest of the way?"

"No, I have a feeling the storm would start again if I got back in that coach." The coach driver looked at him without comprehension.

"Never mind. Go back for Lord Byron." The coach rushed away and Polidori was left to walk on his own back to his lodgings. He walked down the road, but unlike London, there was not complete silence this time: his footsteps now had an echo. With each step that that he took the echo got louder and faster. Polidori now surrendered to it; whatever this creature was he could not escape it, for it wanted him.

He stopped, turned and shouted, "Ruthven, come out and face me!"

Vlad thought to himself how brave this man was and he came out from the shadows to face him. Vlad's face was now emotionless, his black eyes cold and hollow. Polidori watched him coming closer and closer to him. Vlad's black eyes looked through him as if he was a fly to be swatted. Polidori thought it was death itself coming for him, but he stood his ground and watched as this pernicious creature approached.

"You have come for me, then?" Polidori began.

"I have."

"I was always told I would die young," Polidori answered.

"Walk with me a stretch," Vlad answered.

"And delay the inevitable?"

"Are you in a hurry to get to your grave?"

"I suppose not." The Vampire and Polidori started to walk along the road together.

"If I made a bargain with you, would you keep it?"

"It would depend on what the bargain was."

"Say I offered you your life for something in return. Would you do anything to save yourself?"

"No, I would not."

Vlad laughed. "I believe you would. Life is a precious thing to a mortal— I have found that they usually do anything to negotiate for a little more of it... I will let you live, but I ask for someone else to die in your place."

"I would not let anyone take my place," Polidori said with determined resolve.

"Not even that pompous travel companion of yours?"

"Especially not him."

"What about someone that I could guarantee deserved to die? A murderer, perhaps a malevolent soul?"

"No, life has dealt me this hand and I would not put anyone else in my sorry position."

Vlad smiled again and Polidori noticed they were standing outside the inn where he was staying.

"Well, John Polidori, you have saved yourself, but I will ask you one thing." Polidori looked up at Vlad. Relief had not entered his mind yet; he was still sure that he would die by this creature's hand. "Do not be frightened of me anymore. What I ask in return for your life is very little."

"What is it?"

"I want you to never tell anyone about me. If you keep this secret, I will let you live." Polidori thought this was an easy promise to make and he readily agreed.

"Of course."

"Do not be hasty. Keeping this secret may be the hardest thing you have ever had to do."

"I give you my oath, I will never mention Lord Ruthven to anyone."

"Very well." Vlad clasped his icy hand around Polidori. He felt his strength and power and he knew from that moment on if he did not keep this oath he would be sure to die by his hand.

Before Vlad let go he said one more thing to Polidori, "That man you travel with, he is not your friend. Mark my words, he will cast you aside if he sees even a glimmer of anything creative within you."

"You are wrong," Polidori said.

"Am I? We shall see," Vlad answered and with this Vlad turned his back and walked away. Polidori ran to his room hoping that Ruthven would not change his mind. He ran upstairs and looked out the window. When he studied the street below, Ruthven had gone. Polidori hoped it was forever, but something in his heart told him he would see him again.

Sometime later Polidori was indeed travelling with Byron again. This time they had two further travelling companions, Percy Shelley and his wife Mary. They were travelling to Italy but the storms had stopped them dead in their tracks. They took a house on Lake Geneva and waited for the storms to pass.

Shelley and Byron had been almost intolerable on this trip, both of them trying to out do the other. Polidori was becoming increasingly more and more tired of their constant rivalry, while his own talent was never even considered. One evening the storms seemed to have dispersed completely but they were staying another few days just to make sure. That evening Byron and Shelley proposed a contest.

"We should write a ghost story," Byron said. "At the end of the evening when we are done we should compare our stories to each other's."

"Are we all eligible to enter the competition?" Mary asked. Byron laughed at Mary's request.

"Of course, my dear, you can play along if you want too; I doubt you will have anything too much to offer, but you can certainly try," Percy said. Polidori tapped Mary on the hand and whispered, "Don't listen to him Mary. I am sure our stories will be far better than theirs."

Polidori had never spoken a truer word. Byron heard his words but did not say anything; he simply scoffed at them for the moment. The four got to work and Polidori looked out at the bright sky outside his window. This time he was determined to tell a story that would be far better than anything Byron or Shelley could produce. Polidori searched his mind for a place to start and he was suddenly reminded of the dark stranger that had entered his life and he knew what his story was going to be about. The four sat down and each, in turn, started to relate their stories. Polidori was third to tell his tale.

"It happened in the midst of the dissipations attendant upon a London winter...." As Polidori began his tale the bright sky outside his window darkened and a storm began again. It was exactly a year and a day after he had made his oath to Vlad.

Polidori had managed to stun the whole room with his tale of Lord Ruthven, The Vampyre. Shelly and Byron were speechless and they had more to come as Mary began to speak.

"I busied myself to think of a story, a story to rival those which had excited us to this task. One which would speak to the mysterious fears of our nature, and awaken thrilling horror one to make the reader dread to look round, to curdle the blood, and quicken the beatings of the heart...."

The room had been stunned into silence again this evening. Shelley and Byron had been outplayed and outmatched. They were shown to seem like amateurs in this room by a Doctor and a nineteen-year-old girl. Shelley was stunned by the story Mary had related and he turned to Byron and said.

"Do you see what I have, George?" Shelly said to Byron. "She is a goddess." Percy picked up his wife's hand and kissed it. "I will never belittle you again, Mary—you will always be able to impress me."

Byron's reaction to his friend's literary prowess was quite different. The raucous laughter that had preceded the storytelling was no longer there. After Percy and Mary had gone to bed, Byron had a talk with Polidori.

"I think it is time we parted company," Byron began.

"What did you say?"

"I think you heard me."

"I can't believe you are saying this to me. Just because Mary and I embarrassed you this evening…"

"Embarrassed me! How dare you, you could never embarrass me. I want you to pack up your bags and leave."

"I was warned you would do this, but I defended you—I said it would never happen."

"I don't want to see your face again." These were Byron's last words to Polidori.

Polidori packed his bags and returned to England. He watched over his shoulder for months waiting for Vlad to appear. He waited for him to bark at him, *"Remember your oath,"* as Polidori had stated in his story, but it did not happen.

Polidori thought he was free from Ruthven and decided to publish the story. He wanted to get some acclaim as a writer just to show Byron he could. He published the story and it was well received and still there was no sign of Lord Ruthven. After five years had drifted by Polidori thought he was free from the creature, but he was wrong. One night in his apartments Lord Ruthven made one final visit.

Polidori came home to his apartments and was startled to see Lord Ruthven sitting in the corner. Polidori shuddered when he saw him and he knew his time had come. Vlad threw a published edition of his story at him.

"You didn't remember your oath."

"I didn't." Polidori replied.

"Then you realise that I have come for you."

"I do."

"Was it worth it?" Vlad asked.

"Yes, it was. It was worth it to see the look on Byron's face as I relayed a story that was far superior to anything he had ever thought of." Vlad sped towards Polidori and bit down hard into his neck. Polidori's life was over, but his story of "The Vampyre" would live on.

❦

Stoker was still sitting in the chair in the Library as Isabella finished her tale.

"That is unbelievable," he said.

"You still need more proof," Isabella said.

"Your story is unbelievable. Even with the things I have seen today I believe my mind is playing tricks on me."

Isabella snatched a letter opener and plunged it down deep into her arm. Stoker tried to grab the knife away from her. But Isabella pulled it from her arm before Stoker could get to it. She held up her arm and Bram watched in terror as the wound healed instantly before his eyes; not even a scar was left on her white skin.

"Do you believe now?" Isabella asked.

"I do, I definitely do, do not injure yourself anymore." Stoker looked around the library to see if anyone else had seen the miraculous thing he had just witnessed, but to his surprise no one was looking over at them. Every one was doing exactly what they had been before Isabella stabbed her arm. They still had their eyes buried in the books or they were still looking through the shelves, none of them looking over towards Isabella.

"I don't want them to see me," Isabella said. "And the people I choose not to see me don't, it's as simple as that." Stoker remembered the story of Polidori and he now became frightened.

"Are you going to make me promise you never to tell?"

"No quite the contrary, I want you to tell a story—Vlad's story."

"Why?"

"He was a great man and then he was a great Vampire. He deserves what was taken away from him. He deserves his immortality." Isabella handed him the documents, the diaries and the journals. "Here, you can make a story from these, a great story."

"What about you? Can I say anything about you?"

"You will forget me."

"I think you are wrong. I will never forget you."

Isabella laughed. "I have told you, you will forget me. Do you not realise when I want someone to do something they do it?" Stoker started to leaf through the pages of the documents Isabella had given him. Isabella got up to leave.

"Wait a minute. What about these people in this book—they are probably still alive?"

"Oh, I wouldn't worry about them." Isabella's voice seemed quite sinister when she issued these words. Bram Stoker watched as she left the library. But by the time she got to the door of the room Stoker had already forgotten her name, and by the time she got outside the library, Stoker had forgotten what sort of creature she was and he started to believe he was the one who had written the papers on the table before him.

TRULY THERE IS NO SUCH THING AS FINALITY

CHAPTER TWENTY SEVEN

After months of attending galas, receptions, opening nights at the opera and many other trivial gatherings at the homes of social drones of London, it finally happened: Mina and Jonathon Harker, Vlad's killers, were at a reception which Nicolae and Isabella attended. Isabella immediately recognised Mina, she sensed her as soon as she came through the door.

"The Harkers are here," Isabella whispered to Nicolae.

"After all this time, how do you know it is them?"

"Jonathan, I have seen them before and some of Vlad's blood still flows dormant in Mina's veins; it is up to us to awaken it again."

"Shall we make our introductions then?"

"Absolutely." Nicolae pushed out his arm for Isabella to take and they both started to make their way to the entrance of the room, where Mina was taking off her coat. Another man was behind her. He started to help her with her coat. The sight and essence of this other man immediately halted Isabella's motion and she was frozen to the spot.

"Stop," she whispered to Nicolae.

"What is it?" Nicolae asked. Isabella was showing signs of consternation and pressing her fingers into Nicolae's arm. If he had been alive she would have been cutting off his circulation.

"The young man behind her."

"What about him?"

"Can't you sense it?"

"No. I can't feel anything."

"He is a Dhampir!"

"How is that possible?"
"I don't know; you have to leave here. I have to do this alone."
"Isabella, do not start this again; I am staying here with you."
"I can't guarantee you will live through this."
"You never could. I am staying here with you till the end, Isabella."
"But…."
"Isabella, this may be our only opportunity to get close to them."
"All right, but never let him touch you."
"What possible harm can he do me, simply by touching…?"
"Never Nicolae, I mean it, never let him touch you."
"All right."

Nicolae dragged Isabella the next few steps. She was within moments of beginning the completion of the task she had set herself. Isabella realised Nicolae was right, she needed him. She regained her composure, clasped Nicolae's arm tightly and made the final few steps towards them. By this time the Harkers had entered the room and were starting to fraternise with the other guests. Mina was talking to Cicely, the hostess of this particular gathering. Isabella had made it her business to befriend this woman, as she knew everything about everyone and was very keen to let everyone know she knew everything about everyone.

Cicely took pleasure in introducing people she knew to ones whom they did not know. For those brief few moments during introductions Cicely, who could never feel superior to anyone intellectually, felt superior to everyone superficially. It did not take but a moment for Isabella to catch Cicely's eye.

"Ah, Isabella," Cicely turned back towards Mina and said. "I want to introduce you to my American friends." Cicely practically dragged Mina over to Isabella. "Isabella dear," Cicely shouted over at Isabella. Isabella pretended for a moment not to hear her. "Isabella…!" Cicely shouted again.

Isabella turned around and smiled over at Cicely. Cicely beckoned Isabella over and when Isabella was not quick enough for Cicely, she reached out for Isabella's hand and pulled her over. "I want to introduce you to someone."

Isabella walked over with Cicely to Mina and as she did so Jonathon Harker walked over to join his wife. Isabella took Mina's hand and shook it. Isabella's face wore a smile that made it look to all witnesses like her soul shone through with innocence.

"This is Isabella," Cicely continued. "Isn't she just beautiful? But then again most Americans are, although they are usually quite sun-kissed, but not you, Isabella. You are so pale, but then that almost adds to your beauty. Oh there is my friend Julia, you know Julia, she is supposed to be considering leaving her husband... Julia! Julia!" As Cicely left their company, running over to Julia, Mina and Isabella laughed together at Cicely's behaviour.

"I don't think she even introduced us in the end," Isabella stated. "My name is Isabella Hawthorne and this is my brother Cole."

"Very nice to meet you," Mina said. "This is my husband, Jonathon." Jonathon Harker took Isabella's hand and bent over to kiss it. The Dhampir that Isabella had never taken her eyes from was standing with his back to the group.

"Quincy," Jonathon called to his son.

"Father, I am talking to Stephen," Quincy replied without even turning around.

"Quincy," his mother said very gently. No one, not even the most rebellious of sons, could have defied this kind and gentle voice. Quincy turned around and sheepishly looked at his mother. "Your father wants to introduce you to someone."

"Yes, Mother."

Jonathon Harker pointed to Isabella and said to his son, "This is Isabella Hawthorne; she is an American, Quincy." Quincy was not paying Isabella any attention; his eyes were drawn to other things. He bowed out of courtesy and only then did she draw his gaze. From the first moment he saw her face he was enchanted.

"You are beautiful!" Quincy exclaimed. His feelings were so strong that he was unable to hide them.

"Quincy!" his mother scolded. "You should not be so forward. I do apologise for my son, Miss Hawthorne."

"Don't be silly, I could hardly scold a young man for so gracious a compliment." Her words were soft and demure, and she dropped her eyes pretending to be slightly embarrassed by his compliment. Isabella then looked up at him again and smiled coyly and it was with this smile she managed to steal another Dhampir's heart. All this time Quincy was still firmly gripping Isabella's hand.

"Give the lady back her hand, Quincy," his father said to him. Quincy suddenly realised he was still holding it and quickly let go.

"I am sorry," he apologised and laughed nervously.

"There is no need to apologise." Isabella threw him another coy smile to reassure him, and then she looked away, even managing to blush, as if she actually was slightly embarrassed by his constant intense gaze. "This is my brother Cole." Quincy outstretched his hand to take Nicolae's. At this exact moment Isabella dropped her glass of champagne on Quincy's trousers. As Quincy bent over to dry himself off she batted Nicolae's hand away. She was determined the Vampire and the Dhampir were never to touch. "I am afraid it is my turn to apologise; how clumsy of me," Isabella continued.

"Nonsense, I think it was my fault," Quincy stated. Mina and Jonathon looked at each other knowingly. Quincy had never shown any interest in young ladies before; they were pleased by his sudden interest in this one, who seemed like such a well- brought up and accomplished young lady.

"How long are you staying?" Mina asked.

"At least a year." Isabella answered. "I am afraid it is the fashion in America for a young woman to have at least one London season."

Mina smiled. "And you sir, how long are you going to stay here?"

"Our parents are dead and I am my sister's guardian, so I will stay as long as she does," said Nicolae.

"I am afraid Cicely was right about one thing. The London weather is doing nothing for my pallor," Isabella stated, knowing that young women of this time were restricted to conversations about the weather and the latest fashions.

"You should come to Whitby, then," Quincy said enthusiastically.

"Whitby?" Isabella enquired, seeming slightly curious.

"Whitby is where we are from," Mina answered. "It is a seaside town; it would do wonders for your complexion," she continued.

Isabella looked at Nicolae and Nicolae, interpreting her gaze accurately, said, "My sister and I will certainly consider visiting Whitby."

"It sounds absolutely lovely," Isabella enthused.

"Sister, there are the Baileys—we must go and present ourselves to them."

"My brother is right, you must excuse us, and I hope to see you again someday." As Isabella said this she looked solely at Quincy and no one else. The two walked away from the Harkers and Quincy was once again scolded by his father.

"You mustn't act too keen, Quincy."

"Nonsense," Quincy answered back. "If she looks back, she loves me."

"Quincy such foolish talk, you should be ashamed of your behaviour tonight." Mina said not really meaning the words she spoke. Even though both parents had scolded their son, they too watched with him to see if Isabella looked back. The three people watched her for what seemed like an age.

"It looks like she is not going to look back. That is too bad."

"Have faith father just another few seconds." As Quincy spoke these words Isabella turned her head slightly towards him. When their eyes met she smiled and then quickly turned away.

"That's it, Father, it is confirmed she loves me. I bet she will be in Whitby before the end of the month, and when she does come we shall have to get Holmwood to throw the grandest party for her."

Isabella and Nicolae waited three weeks and then made their way to Whitby. When they arrived at the inn at Whitby there was a letter waiting for them.

"Who is it from?" Nicolae asked.

"Need you ask?" Isabella responded. "Quincy welcomes us here and begs us to call on him as soon as we arrive. How long has this letter been here for us?" Isabella asked the innkeeper.

"It is the strangest thing, Miss Hawthorne. He left it for you the day he came back from London. He must have known you were coming before you did."

Isabella smiled. "He must have, thank you." Isabella went over to Nicolae.

"He is smitten." Nicolae said.

"He is."

"It's working then."

"It is."

"We must start distancing ourselves from each other to a certain extent."

"Why?"

"If one or other of us is found out, the other must be in a position to be totally trusted by them."

"How could they find out?"

"Remember we are dealing with a Dhampir; we have no power over him," Nicolae laughed.

"I think you are wrong about that," Isabella smiled. "His infatuation with me will dissipate when he realises what he is. But how can he be a Dhampir?"

"Do you think Vlad had another child?"

Isabella threw Nicolae a malicious look and he regretted saying it. She softened when she realised it was the logical conclusion.

"No, remember his mother was a Vampire for a time. He obviously was conceived when she still was," she said.

"That is another thing I wonder about. How could she have turned back into a human?"

"I don't know. Vlad died before she killed anyone; perhaps that is the answer. As soon as you kill your first you are eternally condemned and if the one who made you…dies first, then perhaps you are granted a reprieve," Isabella answered.

"Do you think there was a chance for us all?"

"There was no chance for you."

"What do you mean?"

"If that is the way it works you would have had to kill me, and love you though I do, you are far from capable of killing me," Isabella smiled, Nicolae reciprocated and a few moments passed in silence. Nicolae was still thinking back wondering if he had a choice.

"Do you remember when you turned—did you have a choice?" Nicolae asked.

"I was not aware of any choice but I would still have chosen the path I did, even if I had known of any alternative."

"Why do you say that?"

"Because my first kill was my sister and I would have endured more then this to watch her die."

From this moment Nicolae understood that there was a coldness within Isabella and that coldness had not just came upon her as a result of being a Vampire.

A few days passed and Isabella and Nicolae were invited formally to the Harkers. They entered the house. It was unpretentious, an understated house befitting a solicitor who had inherited money. They were simple people with no pretensions above their station.

"So good to see you again," Quincy began. Isabella looked to the floor coyly, avoiding his gaze, acting shy but receptive to his compliments. As Isabella was acting like a demure and well-brought up young lady, another young lady entered the room who was not so demure. "This is my sister, Lucy," Quincy said on her arrival.

"I am glad to meet you," Isabella said, extending her hand to Lucy. Lucy sighed when Isabella said this with such meekness. Isabella chose to ignore Lucy's rudeness and said, "This is my brother Cole." Lucy looked over at Cole with absolutely no interest.

"Where are mother and father?" Lucy asked.

"In the drawing room." Quincy was disgusted at his sister's rude behaviour and wanted her away from this company as soon as possible. "Why don't you go and speak to them?" At this Lucy knew her brother wanted rid of her, so she was determined to stay.

"Quincy, why do you want to be rid of me?" Lucy asked. Quincy was now getting angry with his sister.

"Lucy, if you can't behave yourself you should not inflict your company on other people," Quincy scolded.

Lucy sat down in a chair beside Isabella, trying to intimidate her. Isabella acted as if Lucy was being successful. When Isabella looked over, Lucy made a face and Isabella immediately looked to the floor and then looked up at Quincy with an uneasy smile on her face. Nicolae was watching Isabella's flawless performance in front of Quincy and he wondered, did Isabella do this with everyone? Did she show everyone the side of her that they wanted to see?

Quincy and Lucy's mother then entered the room and she knew by looking at Lucy that she was causing mischief. Mina looked at Isabella, who seemed slightly uncomfortable by Lucy's brash nature and at Quincy, who desperately wanted Isabella to feel comfortable in his home.

"Lucy dear, I think your father wants to talk to you in the other room," Mina said gently.

"Mother I am being entertained in this room by Quincy's friends. Although this girl that my brother has taken a fancy to has not said much. Does she ever speak, I wonder?"

"Lucy!" Quincy shouted. "Leave the room!"

"You can't order me to do anything," Lucy retorted back at her brother. Mina had raised her children with such high spirits; she was now wishing she had been a bit stricter with them when they were young, but that was not in her nature.

"Lucy, I think you should go and talk to your father."

"All right, mother. I will excuse myself from this riveting company and leave Quincy to be bored by himself." With this Lucy left the room and slammed the door behind her. Isabella pretended to jump at the loud bang of the door.

"I do apologise for my sister," Quincy said.

"Don't apologise, I admire her vitality... I... I wish I could be more like her."

"Sister, I think it is time we were going," Isabella sensed Nicolae was annoyed.

"Yes, we should probably be leaving." Isabella stood to leave. Quincy practically ran over to open the drawing room door.

"I have asked Arthur Holmwood to set up your ball; he is arranging it for the first of next month," Quincy said as he escorted her out.

"It is most kind of you to go to so much trouble for us, Quincy." By this time Lucy had re-entered the room.

"Oh Lord…save me from such banality," Lucy said.

"I know how you feel," Nicolae whispered.

Quincy threw Lucy a chastising look. Isabella, however, would have to wait to chastise Nicolae.

"Well, thank you again," Isabella said.

"The ball will be the first of the month," Quincy said.

"I look forward to it." With this Isabella and Nicolae left the Harkers' home.

Nicolae sat silent during the coach ride back to the inn.

Isabella was not in the mood to have him sulking for the rest of their stay there, so she asked, "What is it?"

"Nothing," Nicolae replied abruptly.

"Your tone indicates that it is something."

"You see, that is the Isabella I know, a woman with an answer for everything. Yet you turn into this shy meek woman, a totally different person from the one I know, when you are around Quincy."

"I am the person Quincy wants me to be."

"That is exactly what concerns me."

"What do you mean, Nicolae?"

"You do it so well. You trick and manipulate them so well."

"I am a Vampire, Nicolae, I trick and manipulate everyone. I have to and so do you."

"Why don't you kill them and be done with it. I cannot stand this deceit."

"Killing them is not enough."

"Why Isabella? Why is it not enough?"

"Because it isn't."

"Why, Isabella, why?" Nicolae asked.

"Because they have to suffer as I have."

"As you have?"

"I mean as he did."

"No. You said as you have."

"Nicolae, if you want to leave, then leave."

"I don't want to leave you…" Nicolae turned from her. "Not yet, anyway." Isabella placed her hand gently on his shoulder and Nicolae turned back to look at the woman he still loved. Nicolae's heart lightened and he tried to end the tension between them. "I am sorry; I just want to kill someone."

Isabella smiled but her smile was poignant; she knew and Nicolae knew that this issue would come between them again.

"I promise that you can kill someone at this ball he has arranged for me."

"That will make me feel so much better," Nicolae said sarcastically.

"Good."

Arthur Holmwood's house was quite different from the Harkers'. It was a grand old lavish English mansion. Even Isabella was impressed by it. It had thirty bedrooms and an exquisite ballroom. When Quincy saw her he rushed over to her and brought her over to one of his father's old friends to introduce her.

"Isabella, this is Doctor Jack Seaward. Along with Arthur they are my family's oldest and closest friends." Isabella of course recognised the name immediately; this man would be the first to be punished.

"I am honoured to meet such a trusted friend of the Harkers."

"Isn't she stunning?" Quincy added.

"She certainly is," Jack agreed.

Nicolae left Isabella's side; he was sickened by this deception. He went over to the waiter to get a drink, and Lucy followed him.

"Your sister could not be as innocent as she makes out," Lucy quizzed Nicolae. He was startled to have someone talking to him. He thought this was Isabella's show and if truth be known, he did not want to be involved.

"Sorry to disappoint you—she really is that innocent; she has had a sheltered life," Nicolae lied.

"Oh, I am not disappointed," Lucy replied. "Just bored with these social drones," Nicolae smiled.

"You sound like someone I used to know."

"Who?"

"Oh, no one of any importance. So you are bored with Whitby?"

"I am. I was very disappointed in your sister, when I heard you were both from America I thought you both would be something different but it turned out you were just the same."

"Well, perhaps I can prove to you I am not the same."

Lucy for the first time realised how handsome Nicolae was; she had never looked at him before, not with her mind's eye. "I doubt it," Lucy said not wanting to give any hint her new found attraction to Nicolae.

"You could at least let me try," Nicolae said.

"What is your name again?"

"You know what my name is," Nicolae said.

"I don't," Nicolae looked suspiciously at Lucy who was trying her hardest to act indifferent towards him. "I don't," she repeated. Nicolae kept looking at Lucy he was smiling sceptically. "I really don't, Cole."

"Ah ha," Nicolae said. Lucy and Nicolae started to laugh together. Isabella had not noticed Nicolae talking to Lucy but two other people in the room had.

"Look over there," Mina said to her husband.

"It appears we may be getting rid of them both," Jonathon said.

"That's unkind, Jonathon."

"I know the house will be a lot quieter without Lucy in it."

It was the middle of the night and Jack Seaward was petrified. He was running towards the Harker's house, falling over himself, panicking, constantly looking behind him, straining his eyes trying to see if anyone was following him. When Jack arrived at the front door he started pounding his fists upon it and shouting.

"Mina, Jonathon, please open the door!" Slowly the lights started to shine from the house into the gloom of the darkened street. Jack could hear someone coming down the stairs and he shouted again. "Hurry, let me in!" Jonathon let his old friend into the house. As soon as he was inside Jack turned around and locked and bolted the door behind him.

"What is wrong?" Mina asked. Jonathon helped him to a seat.

"It is happening again," Jack said. By this time Lucy and Quincy had awakened and followed their parents down into the hall. Mina looked up at Quincy and Lucy and said.

"Quincy, Lucy, go back to bed."

"No mother, not until we know what is wrong with Jack."

"Nothing is wrong with him—go back to bed," Jonathon scolded.

"But mother, there is obviously something wrong," Quincy shouted.

"Go to bed, children!" Mina shouted. Both Lucy and Quincy were shocked. Neither of them remembered a single time in their lives when their mother had raised her voice to them. All three watched as the two youngest Harkers ascended the stairs and left their parents with Jack.

"I am sorry," Jack said, trying to catch his breath.

"What have you seen?" Jonathon said.

"Him... I have seen him."

"Jack," Mina said calmly and softly. "You know that is impossible. We killed him."

"I know, my head tells me it is impossible but I cannot dismiss the evidence of my own eyes...I saw him!" Jack shouted.

"Think about it rationally, Jack. We saw him turn to dust," Jonathon said.

"I am telling you I saw him."

"You couldn't possibly have," Jonathon stated. Jack opened his shirt collar and showed Mina and Jonathon two puncture marks on his neck.

"Now do you believe me?" Mina stumbled back into a chair and sat down, horrified. Was it truly happening again?

"All right, tell us exactly what happened," Mina said, gathering her composure.

Jack Seaward was not able to sleep that night. He decided to go for a walk in the hope that it would tire him out. He got up and walked to the end of the street. The street was silent and all Jack could hear was the hum of the streetlights above his head. He walked for another mile, but then an unsettled feeling came over him.

He walked a few more steps and then the silence was suddenly broken. He heard someone running, and then heard whoever it was stumble and start running again. The sound of the steps was getting louder and louder. It seemed as if they were just around the corner. But then there was silence again.

Jack decided it was time to go home. He thought his mind was playing tricks on him. He started to walk briskly, refusing to run, thinking that he was being foolish. His head was telling him that there was nothing there and to run would be stupid—he was not a child. When he was within a few steps of home, he began to hear the running footsteps again and they sounded very close, as if they were behind him. He spun around, but nothing was there. All was silent again and he resumed walking, dismissing the noises as just nighttime jitters.

Then once more he heard them. Once more they sounded as if they were just behind him. This time Jack was afraid to turn around. He couldn't make himself look behind—he was too afraid of what he might see. A gust of air touched the back of his neck. When Jack felt this he had to turn around, and again the street behind him was silent and empty.

A strong wind rustled through the trees that lined the avenue. It was so strong that a few leaves started to fall, and then fog poured into the street, engulfing him so that he could not see anything. The running started again and this time he heard voices, first close and then distant and then close again. These voices kept repeating the same phrase.

"Help me!"

Jack reached out, trying to feel for whoever needed his help. He felt nothing. No one was there. "Help me," the woman's voice whispered again. "Help me, Jack."

"Tell me how I can!" Jack shouted.

"Help me! No one else can, Jack."
"I recognise your voice! Who are you?"
"You know who I am, Jack."
"I don't."
"You do, Jack."
"No, I don't, who are you?" Something touched his arm.
"It's Lucy, Jack."
"Lucy Harker? Are you playing a trick on me?"
"No, Jack you know I am not Lucy Harker."
"No, you couldn't be." This time something touched his other arm and he jumped around.
"I am Lucy, Jack, you know I am." At this Lucy's face suddenly appeared before him in the fog. Jack covered his eyes and started to scream and run.
"Jack, there is nowhere to run—he is coming for us both." No matter how fast Jack was running in the fog, the voice followed closely behind him, whispering in his ear, never dropping back, not even a step. Jack stopped running; he realised it was useless and he turned around and faced whatever it was that was chasing him.
"Who is coming for us, Lucy?"
"He is Jack…he is."
"Who, Lucy? Who?"
"Dracula!" The voice was no longer a whisper—it was loud, stern and menacing. Jack was shaken to his very core and he began to run again.
"No, we killed him," Jack shouted.
"You didn't do a good enough job; he has come for all of you." The phantom took hold of Jack Seaward, pulled him to the ground, and bit down hard into his neck. Jack blacked out. When he awoke, he began to run through the streets of Whitby to the Harkers' house.

※

"That is exactly how it happened?" Mina asked.
"I woke up and I ran here," Jack answered.
"What should we do?" Jonathon asked Mina.
"I don't know," Mina answered.
"I am not sure I can go through this again." Jack's hands were still shaking. Mina got up from her chair and went over to him. She kneeled down in front of him, bringing her sweet face in line with his gaze.
"We must do what we must do, Jack. We'll get through it; we will help each other." Jack's tired eyes were comforted by Mina, but he was still dreading the days ahead. Jack Seaward's worst fear was Dracula himself.

※

"Is he asleep?" Mina asked her husband.

"Just," Jonathon answered.

"What are we going to do?"

"First, we shall send for Van Helsing."

"You really think that is necessary?"

"I do, best to be cautious, but..."

"But what?"

"We know Dracula is dead. We saw him die, it could not be him," Mina said.

"Then are there other Vampires? Are there more?"

"There could be, but I am not so sure."

"Why?"

"The Doctor who just checked on Jack said there was no blood loss."

"How can that be?"

"If it was a Vampire then it can't be so. I asked him to look at the marks on his neck. He said they were scratches."

"Scratches?" Jonathon queried.

"Just simple scratches, I don't think we are in any real danger."

Mina and Jonathan went up to their room but before they could they heard shouts coming from Jack's room. Mina and Jonathon ran to his room and when they went inside, they saw Jack standing in the corner and pointing.

"Get away from me," Jack shouted. Mina and Jonathon could only see Jack staring and pointing at something that was not there.

"They can't see me; I have only come for you." The voice that only Jack could hear whispered. Jack did indeed see something, even though Mina and Jonathon could not. He saw a dark, hooded figure. It approached, then retreated, and then approached him again. The dark figure kept repeating this motion. Every time it got close Jack covered his eyes and struck out at it, and then it pulled away. Mina, not seeing the figure or hearing the voice, thought Jack had been struck by madness. She thought years of nightmares and haunting memories had finally taken their toll.

"Oh, Jonathon, I am so afraid for him." Mina went over to Jack and took his face in her hands and said, "There is no one here."

"Yes there is, it's him... *it's him!* Can you not see him?"

"Believe me there is no one there!" Mina begged him to listen to her. Jack stared at Mina and wondered how she could possibly not see this figure. Then what he saw began to disappear and Jack fell to his knees and wept; was he imaging these things, he thought—had his sanity left him after all? He hoped so. Anything was better than the alternative.

Nicolae and Isabella were walking away from the Harkers' home.

"Well, it worked," Nicolae said.

"It's working," Isabella corrected.

"You won't be happy until he is actually mad."

"I won't."

"I don't think I have the stomach for this."

Isabella turned towards him. "I told you to leave."

Nicolae turned back to look at the Harkers' and said, "I will stay for the moment."

※

The next night followed the same pattern. Mina and Jonathon were awakened by Jack Seaward's shouts. Again when they entered the room they could see no one but Jack shouting and pointing at the corner.

"Don't let him take me!"

Mina started to cry.

"Jack, there is no one there," Jonathon snapped. As Jonathon said this Jack's vision disappeared. He was taking longer and longer to calm down. He was breaking out in a cold sweat. His eyes darted about the room looking for the menacing figure to reappear. When he slept his dreams were filled with nightmares and he carried these nightmares into his waking hours. His wife had come to see him and was frightened by the state her husband was in.

"He seems completely terrified," his wife stated.

"We thought it best he stay here," Mina said.

"Thank you. You have always been so kind, Mina," Jack's wife replied.

"There is no need for thanks. He can stay here until he gets well." The truth was Mina did not want Jack to go home; she did not want him spouting warnings of Vampires to frighten his wife. His wife knew nothing of what the group had been through.

That evening, the shadowy figure of Vlad appeared before Jack for the last time.

"Jack Seaward, wake up!" Isabella shouted into Seward's ear. Outside the room Quincy was on his way down to the kitchen. He heard a woman whispering to Jack. He did not hear what she was saying and thought nothing of it at the time. He presumed it was his mother trying to comfort Jack in some way. Quincy was the only person who could hear Isabella, as he was the only person who was not susceptible to her power. When Jack looked at Isabella all he saw was Lucy Westerna. "Jack, why didn't you save me from him?" Isabella asked.

"I tried, Lucy, I tried."

"You didn't. You let me die because you were afraid of him."

"No, I tried to save you."

"You did nothing to save me, you sent for that Dutchman to kill me!"

Jack pounded his hands against his head. "I can't stand this anymore! I can't go through this."

"What did I go through? Consider that!" Isabella snapped.

"No, it's not true."

Jonathon and Mina now heard Jonathon's cries. "Should we go down to him?" Mina asked.

"It does no good. Perhaps we should just leave him tonight and see if it makes a difference," Jonathon said. Mina did not agree with her husband, but they had tried everything else to snap Jack out of his lunacy.

"You have to kill him; you know how it is the only way I will be saved," Isabella continued.

"I can't remember how."

"You know how you need the Dhampir's blood."

"There is no Dhampir's blood! Van Helsing is in America."

"There is another Dhampir.'"

"Who?"

"Quincy."

"Quincy?"

"He is a Dhampir. His blood is the only thing that will kill him. You need his blood to kill Dracula and then we will all be saved. Get the letter opener from the dresser and kill him."

Jack now had a purpose. He snatched the knife and ran down downstairs, knife in hand. Isabella went to Mina's room and whispered in her ear. Mina by this time had fallen back to sleep.

"Mina," Isabella whispered. "Your son is in danger." Mina's eyes opened. Instantly she was filled with a sense of danger and concern for her son. She ran to his room and he was not there; then she heard a noise coming from the pantry. Quincy was rummaging around for something to eat, unaware of the danger he was in. Jack stealthily entered the pantry; he knew only what his weak mind told him to do.

Quincy heard a noise and turned around to see Jack Seaward walking towards him. Quincy did not notice the look on Jack Seaward's face; as far as he was concerned it was a friend that stood behind him.

"You hungry, too?" Quincy asked. Jack made no answer. "Mother hates me doing this, getting up in the middle of the night and raiding the cupboards. Are you feeling better?"

"I am sorry, Quincy." Quincy looked over at Jack strangely.

"Sorry for what?" Jack lunged at Quincy with the knife but by this time Mina had run in with her husband very close behind her. Mina grasped at Jack but she could not hold him back. However, she restrained him enough so that the knife only struck Quincy's arm. Jonathon then pulled him back and threw him towards the wall. Jack struck the wall hard and fell forward onto the floor. The two parents, realising that Jack was beyond causing harm, turned their attentions towards their son.

"What has come over him?"

"Madness," Mina said. "It is the only explanation for it." Mina looked over at Jack, who was still lying on the floor not moving. Mina observed a growing pool of blood seeping out from his body.

"Jonathon, I think he is dead!" Jonathon rolled Jack over. He had fallen on his own knife. With his last breath he whispered the word Dhampir, but because of Isabella's influence only Quincy heard it.

Jack Seaward's murderess attended his funeral.

"I am so sorry, Quincy, I know he was a good friend of yours," Isabella said.

"Thank you. I still do not know what happened."

"It's probably best not to think about it," Isabella answered. The pair strolled around to the church where the Harkers were talking to Arthur Holmwood.

I WOULD GIVE MY LAST DROP OF BLOOD TO SAVE HER

CHAPTER TWENTY-EIGHT

"So what is his worst fear?" Nicolae asked. Isabella was reluctant to tell Nicolae—he would not like the answer. "What is it?" he demanded. "When you shook his hand today, I know you were reading him."

"His family."

"His family?"

"Losing Lucy almost killed him. After Vlad died he became morose and retreated from society, retreated from everyone. His family was concerned for him, especially his cousin Vivian. She went to see him every day. He was resistant to her visits at first, not even wanting to let her in his home, but she gently pushed her way in. Gradually he began laugh again and started to begin to live again, and he was so grateful to Vivian. He soon came to realise that he loved her and he married her. He found happiness. They had two children. Then one died before his sixth birthday and again Arthur retreated, and although Vivian was devastated herself, she managed to bring Arthur out of his melancholy and to seek solace in the child that remained. Loss is his worst fear, the loss of his wife and child. He would never recover from that."

"Isabella..." Nicolae clasped his hands around Isabella's arms and held her in front of him. "You cannot be seriously planning to do this."

"I can, and I will."

"Have you no heart?"

"My heart died four hundreds years ago. I am a Vampire, and so are you."

"The malevolence within you is suffocating me."

"The malevolence within me? Have you not killed people? Am I talking to an innocent? Your blood lust has always been greater than mine. The difference between us is only that I always knew what I was."

"I know what I am; I am what you made me. I may not have a soul but I do still have a conscience."

Isabella turned to Nicolae. "Your conscience has no place here," Isabella said calmly.

"I don't think I have a place here anymore."

"That is your decision."

With this Nicolae left Isabella, but before he departed he said one last thing.

"Isabella," he said softly. "Your eyes, they are red; they look as if they are on fire."

Isabella said nothing, for she was not surprised.

***

After his final argument with Isabella, Nicolae went to meet Lucy Harker, whom he had been meeting frequently. Lucy smiled when she saw him.

"I have missed you, Cole."

"You saw me yesterday," Cole said.

"I know, but I still missed you."

"This certainly is not the rude defiant girl I met that first day at the Harkers."

"You have mellowed me."

"Have I indeed?"

"You have."

"Sit down with me. There is something I have to tell you." Lucy sat down and stared at Nicolae with adoring eyes. Nicolae did not want this woman to look upon him with anything but adoration.

"What do you want to tell me?" Lucy asked.

"Nothing, it can wait for awhile."

Lucy leaned forward and kissed him.

***

Isabella crept into the room of Arthur Holmwood's daughter. There would be no slow death for this victim; her death would be easy and quick. She crept in and bit her neck. Arthur Holmwood's child would never wake up.

Isabella silently crept into Arthur's bedroom; his wife was the next to die silently and without pain. Arthur slept beside his dead wife until the morning. As the first rays of sunlight entered the room, Arthur awoke. He reached over in order to wake his wife but when he touched her arm it was cold. Arthur Holmwood's heart was filled with terror. He turned his wife over to look at her; a pair of dead eyes stared back. He looked at her neck and saw two puncture marks on her neck. He then ran to his daughter's room and saw another pair of dead eyes staring back at him.

Arthur fell to his knees. He was finally a completely broken man.

MY LATEST AND TRUEST THOUGHT WILL ALWAYS BE FOR HIM

CHAPTER TWENTY-NINE

Nicolae and Isabella attended the funerals of Arthur Holmwood's wife and child. Nicolae stayed out of everyone's view, but Isabella knew he was close. Quincy was holding Isabella's hand, and after the funeral Isabella went over to face Nicolae alone.

"Holmwood will probably just kill himself, you realise that," Nicolae said.

"He hasn't the courage to kill himself," Isabella replied.

"I think courage is the wrong word."

"Whatever you may call it. What I read in his heart is that whatever this world has to throw at him...he fears what the next world holds for him even more. He will live in misery for the rest of his days." Nicolae sighed and there was a pause in the conversation.

"One last time, Isabella."

"One last time what?"

"I am going to beg you to abandon this plan."

"I will not," Isabella said.

"I will not ask you again."

"However many times you ask, my answer will still be the same."

"You realise you are going to die here."

"I do."

"You cannot rely on me on any longer."

"I never relied on you, Nicolae. I have never relied on anyone!" Isabella answered.

"That is a vicious and malicious thing to say—all these years and you say you have never relied on me?" Nicolae questioned.

"Never."

"All right. If that is the way you want it…you cannot trust me to stay quiet. I may warn them."

"Do what your conscience dictates." Nicolae left Isabella and this time he had every intention of never going back to her.

※

Isabella had lied to Nicolae when she told him she had never relied upon him. During the twenty years since they had had been reunited he had been her only constant. Reliance and trust had become very important to her. She had never had this with Vlad. Nicolae's leaving was devastating to her, but Isabella was too stubborn to ask him to stay and in a way she was glad. Olya's prophecy still haunted her. Blackness was chasing and for the first time she could feel it biting at her heels. As she watched Nicolae walk away she felt he was walking towards the light. Nicolae had freed himself from the fate that Isabella was inevitably going to face, or so she thought.

※

The next day when Isabella went to the Harkers she found the mood and spirit very sombre, but Quincy still greeted her with a smile.

"Arthur, I take it, is inconsolable?" Isabella asked.

"Of course, but my parents have more bad news today."

"What has happened?"

"News from America. My father's oldest friend Van Helsing is dead."

"I am so sorry," Isabella lied.

"I am afraid the house is not in the mood to entertain tonight, but I will walk you back to your lodgings."

"Thank you." The couple started to walk through the nearly dark streets back to the inn where Isabella was staying.

"My parents are frightened; I don't understand it. I have never seen them like this."

"What are they frightened of?"

"I don't know."

"Your family has been touched by such tragedy of late, it is only natural they would be frightened."

"It's more than that. I have a strong sense that this is far from over, that there is more tragedy to come."

"Don't be silly, Quincy, what else could possibly happen?" Quincy took Isabella in his arms. Isabella wanted to shrink back from his touch not because he was a Dhampir but because she was afraid that she was starting to feel something and that would make the next few weeks harder than they were already going to be.

"Isabella, I love you, do you love me?" Isabella hesitated before she answered. It was too late—she did feel something; she did not want to answer him. She didn't want to lie to him.

"Of course I do," Isabella answered. She was ashamed of herself. She had not felt this much regret since she had seen the mother of one of her victims outside Erzsébet's castle. "Go home and be with your family. I will see you tomorrow."

"Will you marry me soon? Who do I ask for your hand?" Isabella shrugged off Quincy's grip.

"My parents are long dead."

"I will ask your brother, then."

"He has gone back...." In Quincy's excitement he was not really listening to what Isabella was saying and was unaware of the sudden coldness she was displaying.

"I will ask your brother. He is coming to visit my sister tomorrow."

"Cole is visiting your sister?"

"I am sure you have noticed they have struck up a relationship." Isabella eyes hardened and her lips stiffened. Had Nicolae been betraying her all this time? Had she been so blind?

"Isabella you look different, somehow." Isabella looked back at Quincy, restoring her façade with the purest of smiles.

"Sorry, I did not realise Cole and your sister were so close, I have been blind," she said.

"It is those blue tinted glasses you wear now; they do not let me see your pretty eyes...you are not upset?"

"Of course not. I could not be happier for us all."

"I will see you tomorrow, then."

"You certainly will." Isabella watched as Quincy walked away with an added spring in his step. He was a boy in love. Isabella decided at that moment to end this as soon as she could.

❖

When Quincy got home his parents called him into the drawing room. They wanted to speak to him.

"We have to tell you what is happening, you and Lucy."

"I have something to tell you, too," Quincy said with a gleeful smile, for he was happy. "I am to be married."

"That is wonderful Quincy!" Mina said. She was truly happy for her son, but there was sadness behind her smile.

"I am happy for you, too," Lucy agreed. "Although I do not know what you see in that pale excuse for a girl."

"Well, I do not know what you see in her brother." Mina stopped her children's playful bickering and said.

"We are very pleased for both of you but we must tell you something," Mina said.

"Do you remember the night Jack died…?"

"Speaking of Jack, there has been something I have meant to ask you about him."

"Quincy, whatever it is, it can wait," Mina said, but the words had already left Quincy's lips before his mother had a chance to silence him.

"What is a Dhampir?"

Mina stepped forward, taking her husband's arm; anxiety was making her squeeze him tight.

"Where did you hear that word?" Mina asked, a sense of urgency resonating through her voice.

"We all heard it," Quincy said.

"When?" Jonathon asked his son. He, too, was desperate.

"The night he died he pointed at me and yelled the word 'Dhampir'."

"'Dhampir'! How could it be true?" Mina gasped.

"What is a Dhampir?" Quincy asked.

"It is true; he was the only one who heard Jack use that word. He is resistant to the Vampire's power."

"He is a Dhampir!"

Quincy was now afraid at the gravity of his parents' mood. "You are talking nonsense about Vampires. Have you both gone mad?"

"I wish we were. It appears you are a Dhampir."

"What does that mean, mother?"

"You are a Vampire hunter, Quincy. Vampires cannot enter your mind. You are impenetrable to them. That is why you could hear Jack's words and all of us could not."

"Jack tried to warn us but we would not listen." A tear rolled down her cheek. "Then Arthur's wife and child were killed by a Vampire and we knew Jack was telling us the truth. A Vampire is among us again and you may be the only one that can kill it."

"What do you mean?"

"You are a Dhampir. Your blood is poison to them. Van Helsing was a Dhampir too."

"How can I be a Dhampir?"

"Who knows? Some quirk of fate, Van Helsing did not know why he was what he was," Mina said. "He met a woman when he was very young and this woman told him he was a Dhampir."

"How do you know Van Helsing is dead?" Quincy asked.

"We sent a wire to the last hotel where he had written to us. He had gone weeks before and left a forwarding address. We then contacted that hotel and the one after that and the one after that. We ultimately received a letter saying that he had killed himself."

A frantic knock on the door interrupted their grim tale. Lucy, who had been uncharacteristically quiet, got up to answer the door. Nicolae was at the door. He was out of breath, and when Lucy opened the door he fell towards her. She stumbled back, unable to support his weight. The Harkers, hearing the commotion, came running into the hall fearing for their daughter. They saw a weak and tired Nicolae lying on the floor, gasping for air.

"Shut the door," Nicolae whispered. "Shut the door," he said again, gathering up his energy, his voice becoming louder and more determined to scream: "For the dead travel fast." With this Nicolae shut his eyes and did not say another word.

"He has passed out," Lucy said.

"Check his neck for punctures," Mina said. Sure enough when Lucy loosened his collar to reveal his neck there were two puncture marks. An hour passed by and Mina came into the living room. Nicolae was now lying on the couch, Lucy sitting beside him, holding his hand.

"Is he awake yet?" Mina asked her daughter.

"No," Lucy answered. Mina placed her hand on her daughter's shoulder.

"Don't worry, Lucy. The doctor said there has been no blood loss. Whatever attacked him, he was strong enough to see it off."

"I know, Mother. Is Quincy back from checking on Isabella yet?"

"No, but I am sure she will be all right," Mina said.

"I hope so mother. I know I have not made her completely welcome, but I would never wish her any ill."

"Of course not, Lucy, your brother knows that." Lucy's dauntless exterior melted away and she began to sob. Mina was distressed to see her daughter cry; she had not seen Lucy cry since she was about six years old.

"Oh, mother, why is this happening to us? What have we done to deserve it?"

"Nothing, child. It will pass and you will be happy again. I promise you that." As Mina said these words she knew she was incapable of keeping this promise to her daughter. Nicolae opened his eyes and looked at Lucy.

"Lucy," he whispered.

"Cole, you are awake. Thank goodness!" Mina left the young couple to comfort each other. When Mina went out into the hall she sat and watched the door waiting for her son and husband to come back, praying they would be unharmed. Eventually, after what seemed like an eternity but was only a few hours, the door opened and Jonathon came in, and behind him to Mina's obvious relief was Quincy carrying Isabella, who, like Nicolae, looked as if she had been through an ordeal.

"She's unconscious as well," Quincy said "we found her near Arthur's home."

"Near Arthur's?"

"Don't worry. We checked in on him; he is fine. Well, as fine as he can be."

"Are there any marks on her?"

"None whatsoever."

"Thank God," Mina said. "Cole is awake."

"That's good; we need to ask him what happened," Jonathon said. He knocked on the door of the living room, and entered, Quincy following closely behind him.

"Come in," Lucy said.

"Sorry to interrupt, but we have to know what happened tonight."

"Of course," Nicolae answered. "It's all a bit of a blur. When I went back to the inn it was after dark. I had walked because it was a pleasant night. I could hear someone walking behind me but I did not think anything of it at the time. I thought it was someone just going the same way I was. The next thing I know something grabbed me. It seemed to bite into my neck. I kicked and struggled and somehow I got loose, although its grip seemed like a vise on me. And then as soon as I was free I ran as fast I could; I ran to Lucy."

"So you don't know what happened to your sister?" Quincy asked. Nervousness came over Nicolae; a flaw in his plan had made itself apparent.

"My sister?"

"Yes, do you know what happened to her?"

"No."

"We found her unconscious, too, outside Arthur Holmwood's house, but there were no marks on her."

"That's…good. Where is she now?"

"She is sleeping upstairs."

"I would like to see her."

"Of course. Lucy you can show him upstairs."

Nicolae climbed the stairs with a sense of foreboding. He had not betrayed Isabella. He never would…but would she betray him? Nicolae had pierced his own neck and had kept piercing it every time Lucy left him on his own, not giving the wounds a chance to heal. He had tasted loneliness before and could hardly bear it. He wanted a chance at living.

When Nicolae and Lucy entered the room Isabella still had her eyes closed.

"Lucy, can you give us a few moments?" Nicolae asked.

"Of course." Lucy leaned forward and kissed Nicolae on the cheek; she then shut the door on her way out of the room. Nicolae crept over to Isabella's bedside, but he knew she was awake and listening to whatever was being said.

"Open your eyes, Isabella," Nicolae said firmly. Isabella opened her eyes and smiled at him. However, it was a smile tinged strongly with maliciousness. Nicolae had never known what it felt like to be the object of Isabella's hate, and then he did.

"Well, I am surprised to see you here," Isabella lied. "I heard you had a traumatic time, attacked by a Vampire."

"Isabella, do not start playing your malicious games with me."

"Don't tell me what to do. I have never listened to anyone. I am five hundred years old. Do you think I am going to listen to you?"

"No, Isabella you will never change, you are just as bitter and twisted as you always were, both in death and life." Isabella scowled at Nicolae now. He had never spoken to her in this manner. He really hated her.

"What were you doing near Arthur Holmwood's? Surely you have done all you can to him?"

"It is none of your business what I do," Isabella said. Nicolae got up to leave the room.

"I will not tell these people what you are. I couldn't even describe what you are," Nicolae said.

Nicolae's disgust was penetrating. It hurt Isabella, but as always, she did not let her feelings show. She needed to be away from this place before she completed her revenge. She would go home just to see her own land once more. She wanted a reminder as to why she was doing this.

Isabella had promised Anna that she would never come to visit her again; indeed she was not sure if she would still be alive. If she wasn't, her family would be living in the castle and would know nothing of Vampires, but Isabella had to see that place again—she had to remember him. Isabella walked through the forest she had left fifty years ago with the intention of never returning. So many times she had this intention and so many times it had called her back. The castle had actually been kept in good order; someone was occupying it that really cared. She knocked on the oak door and a young adolescent woman opened it.

"Can I help you?" The young woman asked. "Did you want something?"

"Nothing, really, I just wanted to see this place again."

"You can come in if you want."

"Thank you. I will not stay long."

"Stay as long as you like. No one else is here at the moment."

"I won't bother you too much. I used to live in one of the villages down below."

"You did? Most of them are gone now."

"I know."

"Most people have moved to Bistrita or somewhere else."

"So where is your family?"

"They have gone down into town."

"And why did you not go?" The girl looked embarrassed and coy.

"I am waiting for a friend."

"A male friend, no doubt."

"Yes."

"Do your mother and father know that is why you stayed behind?"

"No, they would not be pleased if they did."

"I wouldn't lie to them if I were you. Lies and deception never lead to happiness."

"It sounds like you know what you are speaking of."

"I do, believe me, I do."

"You do not look that much older than me."

"I am older than I seem." There was a lull in the conversation.

"Tell me about the man you love," the girl said.

"Who says I love anyone?" Isabella was shocked at this young woman's perspicacity.

"Your sadness tells me. Oh, please tell me, I love to hear stories that promise of happiness."

"My story, if it promises of anything—it certainly isn't happiness."

"There must have been even glimpses of happiness, or else you would not be so sad to have lost it."

Isabella smiled, she could not think of a single time when she was totally happy; darkness had always seemed to cast a shadow over her. "I can't think of a single moment when both of us were completely happy."

"Then why did you stay with him?"

"I loved him, God help me, I loved him."

"Then there must have been a time when you knew he loved you. There must have been something that made you love him."

"Something that told me he loved me?" Isabella reflected. "The truth is I did not know how much he loved me until it was too late."

"That must have been terrible." For the first time in the conversation this child's inexperience shone through.

"Terrible does not quite seem enough of a word. When he was dying he told me how much he cared for me."

"How did he tell you?"

"We had argued. We constantly argued and I had left him and was determined to stay away for good. I took myself off to another country where no one knew me and I did not know anyone. I lost myself in total anonymity. I did not realise there was someone following me, someone who wished me… harm. Vlad, that was the name of the man I loved."

"That is my ancestor's name…he was a Prince who lived in this castle."

"Yes I know…he started to watch me without my knowledge; he had been my constant protector. This someone…she tried to hurt me many times and each time he did his best to stop her. If I was in any danger at all he saved me from it. He kept me alive and kept himself hidden, not ever letting me know how much he cared. He saved me many times and I didn't even know he was there. He didn't tell me this until he was moments from death." Isabella looked up at the young girl; there were tears in her eyes. "Don't waste your tears on me," Isabella said.

"That story is heartbreaking, and you never knew he was watching over you?"

"Never," Isabella looked at the young girl. "You love this boy whom you are waiting for?"

"I do."

"What would you do if someone killed this boy? What would you do to those people?" A dark look came over the young girl's face.

"I would be merciless," the young girl replied.

"Even if it meant that you would die in the process?"

"I would do anything to avenge him. I would try and inflict the greatest harm that I possibly could to anyone who was involved." Isabella got up to leave.

"Thank you, you will never now how much you have helped me." The girl smiled at Isabella, and Isabella said. "You never told me your name."

"Isabella," the girl answered back, Isabella looked shocked. "I was named after an ancient ancestor. My great-grandmother Anna insisted on it. She said that this woman was a fighter, a strong person and although she did not always make the right decisions, she was a woman who when she made a vow to someone she loved, she never reneged on it. No matter how hard it was for her to keep."

"Anna was a good person."

"She was, or so they tell me."

"The man you loved—do you know he was named after a national hero."

"A hero?" Isabella replied.

"Yes."

"He was a hero." Isabella left and made her way swiftly back to England to finish what she started.

※

"I don't understand it, why did she leave?" Quincy asked.

"What did she say when she left?" Lucy asked.

"She said she had some urgent business back in America to do with her father's estate."

"But Cole, you did not go," Lucy said.

"Isabella was always far more clever than I was… at that sort of thing," Nicolae quickly added on. "Don't worry, she will be back," he added.

"How are you so sure?"

"I know it for a fact."

"I am not so sure," Quincy said.

"Believe me. Don't worry. I guarantee she will be back; she will not leave us alone for long."

※

Isabella arrived back in Whitby in the middle of the night. She made her way straight to the Harkers. She walked by Nicolae's bedroom window; he had taken up residence in a seaside hotel closer to the Harkers' home. Nicolae was sleeping when a chill ran through his blood. He knew Isabella was close to him again. She woke him up by simply walking underneath his window. Nicolae ran to the window and looked outside. He saw Isabella turning around the farthest corner of the street. She looked up and back towards him. Her eyes were gleaming red, brighter than ever and then she disappeared from his sight.

Isabella pressed against the front door and the lock broke open; she went in and silently climbed the stairs. She entered Jonathon and Mina's room with malicious intentions. Isabella crouched down and kissed the neck of Mina Harker, drawing her life's blood. She then slit her wrist and let blood drip into her mouth. Isabella's blood quickly awakened Vlad's dormant essence. Mina's eyes jerked open; she was again a Vampire. A red scar reappeared on her head.

Isabella backed out of the room, jammed the door shut and left Mina with her husband. No one would escape this room until the utmost horror had taken place. Quincy heard a commotion coming from his parents' bedroom; he wandered sleepily to their door. When the half-awake young man saw Isabella he was overjoyed. He cared not to ask why she was here in his parents' house in the middle of the night. He ran over to her, but Isabella shrank back from his embrace.

"I am not worthy of you," Isabella said.

"Of course you are worthy of me."

Isabella pressed her finger to Quincy's lips. Quincy heard his mother screaming from inside the room. His heart sank he pressed gently on the door, but it would not open. Then he pressed as hard as he could, the door opened easily and he was surprised at his own strength. He went into the room and Isabella followed him.

Mina was holding her husband in her arms and was drinking from his blood. What had once before seemed inevitable, now finally years later, had actually occurred. She bit down hard into Jonathon's arm. This time Mina did not have the strength to fight her Vampiric instinct. Then Mina let her husband drink from her and now Mina and Jonathon were both Vampires. Their bloodlust momentarily satisfied, Isabella began to speak.

"Jonathon," Isabella said, her voice was haunting and compelling. "Jonathon, you feel the pain don't you, and you can't stand it. The pain is too strong—it overpowers you. It surges through your body. You can stop it. All you have to do is feed." Jonathon fell to the floor and shrieked out in agonising pain. "To save your father, Quincy you have to kill your mother," Isabella continued.

"What, are you saying, how can this be true?"

"It is true, Quincy," Mina said, who after her hunger was satisfied, remembered her human sensibilities. "You must kill me to save your father." While the mother and son were talking Isabella was still whispering in Jonathon's ear.

"The pain Jonathon—how can you stand the pain?" Isabella asked. "You see Quincy. He is strong; he can spare some blood to stop your pain. He would want you to take it. He would want to stop your pain. Look at the vein in his neck; he is a Dhampir—he will not die."

"Kill me," Mina said to her son. Mina fetched Quincy's namesake's sword and dagger that she and Jonathon had kept all these years. She placed the shaft of the sword in her son's hand; she took his other hand and pressed it on the blade. His skin broke and blood gently flowed onto the blade. Then finally Mina pressed the tip of the blade to her heart.

"I can't do it," Quincy said.

"Yes you can," Mina answered. "I want this to end and you are the only one who can end it."

"Jonathon, you see his blood that can make your pain stop," Isabella whispered continually into Jonathon's ear. Not being able to resist temptation any more, he leaped forward just as Quincy plunged the sword into his mother's heart. Jonathon tasted his son's blood before the knife penetrated Mina's heart. Mina's death was too late. Jonathon had already tasted his first blood and as Mina fell to the ground the pain of death surged through her.

"Your daughter will follow your son to the grave," Isabella whispered into Mina's ear.

The last thing Mina saw was her husband drinking the life's blood from his son. Mina died in absolute misery and absolute pain.

Jonathon was still clamped to his son's wrist drinking his blood. He drank as long as he could but the poisonous Dhampir's blood was killing him. He let go but it was too late for him and his son. Jonathon writhed around in agony. Isabella crept over to him.

"Which is worse, Jonathon—the pain or the knowledge that you have killed your own child?" Isabella knew which was worse, for she had witnessed this scene before. Jonathon covered his eyes. He wanted to block out Isabella's face. He had always known he was not as strong as his wife and could have never endured what she had done, not for a moment. He too died in pain and misery.

Isabella went over to Quincy. He was starting to shiver and he was but moments from death. Isabella kneeled down beside him.

"Why?" he struggled to ask her.

"Because your parents, Arthur Holmwood and Jack Seaward, hunted Vlad Dracula down like an animal and killed him. They did to me the worst they could have possibly done, so I returned the favour. Jack Seaward was terrified of Vlad himself, so Vlad appeared again to him. Arthur Holmwood's greatest fear was loss; he could not stand to lose anyone who was close to him. Your father was afraid that if he was ever touched by vampirism he would not be able to control his impulses, that he would kill someone he loved. Your mother's worst fear was that her husband would not be safe. She said it herself: her latest and truest thought would always be for him."

"So you made their worst nightmares come true."

"I did."

"What about me?"

"You had to die. You are a Dhampir, I let a Dhampir live before when I should not have and I was punished for it. I could not let you continue to occupy the same world that I did, not for one second longer."

"So you have killed me and you never felt anything for me?"

"I wouldn't say I felt nothing for you. If it is any consolation, it is with much regret that I have had to kill you." Isabella went to touch Quincy's face but he batted her hand away from him. Quincy took one last gasp and closed his eyes forever. Isabella took his sword and plunged it deep into his chest. She had to make sure that Jonathon and Mina would never awake from their eternal slumber. With the blood soaked sword she decapitated both them, and in that instant she envied them, for she felt their peace.

Isabella got up and left the bloody scene. She walked calmly down the stairs and out onto the street. Nicolae was running towards the Harkers, but he was much too late. On seeing Isabella, he immediately stopped in his tracks. Isabella walked by him. She did not even care to look at him.

As she passed him she said, "I have left the girl unharmed—my parting gift to you."

"Thank you, Isabella," he called after her. Isabella made no visual or verbal acknowledgement of his thanks. She kept on walking, her held high, but if Nicolae had seen her face he would have seen a blood red tear trickling down her silken ivory cheek.

A year passed in peace for all concerned but there was someone still tormenting Isabella's mind and she decided to return to Whitby one last time. She stood in the grounds outside Arthur Holmwood's house. After some consideration she approached the door and pushed it open. She could see from outside that there was only one light on in this house. It was a solitary, flickering candle on the second floor. Isabella climbed up the stairs and headed towards the light. She entered the room and found Arthur drinking and crying. He had only his misery to keep him company.

"Arthur..." Isabella began "do you remember me?" Arthur looked over at her.

"You are the Vampire who killed my wife and child."

"I am."

"I have not the will or the strength to fight you."

"I have not come here to fight you."

"Then what have you come here for?"

"I have a proposition for you."

"A proposition?"

"Yes."

"What can you offer me?"

"Everlasting peace." Arthur now stopped drinking and looked at Isabella. "That is what you want isn't it?" Arthur looked bewildered and she said again. "Isn't it?" Arthur nodded.

"It is." Isabella approached him and bit into his neck, slowly draining him of his life's blood. He closed his eyes, never to awaken. For him, the ordeal was over. Isabella was glad, because with his death she felt the ordeal was over for her as well. Could this act of compassion have freed her, could she put these grizzly events behind her?

She walked through the grounds and she could feel her melancholy lifting; the cold air began hitting her face. For the first time since Vlad had died she felt free from her task of revenge. Isabella walked down the path towards the street and a smile even dared to whisper across her face, but she was not to smile for long.

"Isabella." A voice shot from out of the darkness, a voice that was shouting her name. It was a voice she did not recognise at first. Isabella turned around to see Nicolae and Lucy Harker staring back at her. "My husband was awakened tonight by a dream and a sense that you had come back. I see he was right," Lucy began.

"Your husband... could always feel me," Isabella said with relish. "We have a connection that you will never be able to break, even by killing me."

"We'll see," Lucy cried out, and she drew out a sword stained with blood. Isabella drew out her grandfather's sword. Lucy and Isabella's swords clashed together again and again. Isabella was far faster than Lucy and stronger, but Lucy was determined. Nicolae stood there, not coming to the aid of either woman. Isabella moved in front of Nicolae and Lucy lashed out at her but Isabella was quick to move out of the way. Lucy's blade was about to fall upon Nicolae. Isabella thrust out her sword arm to stop the falling blade and saved him.

"Are you trying to kill your husband?" Isabella quipped. Nicolae's only thought at this moment was that Isabella had saved his life, after all that he had done... *she still saved my life*, Nicolae reflected. He stared at

Isabella, his beautiful Bella, and realised what he had tried to forget—he loved her.

"Isabella," he called out. "I…" Before he could finish what he was going to say he watched in horror as his wife forced her sword through Isabella's heart. Isabella's mortal wound drew her gaze. She gently pressed her finger on the blade. A pain shot through her, and she whispered with what she thought to be her last breath.

"Your brother's blood."

"Not my brother's, my son's," Lucy answered. Isabella glanced over at Nicolae in amazement and fell back down onto the ground. Blackness filled her eyes and pain surged through her body. Lucy ran to her husband and embraced him. Nicolae, still in shock, saw Isabella lying dead before him. Isabella was without consciousness. She was still, unmoving.

Isabella had not been defeated.

An inner cognition awakened her. From the dark recesses of her mind a voice whispered to her: *"Isabella, you are stronger than this, you are a Queen of the immortals! You are going to build a nation of Vampires as great as there existed so many years before. Are you, Isabella, going to be killed by this human? You have more power than I ever had; it is time you discovered that."* Vlad, Isabella thought.

Nicolae stood frozen. Was she really dead? Could she really be killed? He dismissed these thoughts, for he remembered the power Isabella had. Lucy could not finish her life, not completely, not yet. Nicolae watched as Isabella's eyes opened again and she pulled the sword from her heart. He held his wife tightly so that she would not look around. Isabella pulled herself up onto her feet and smiled at Nicolae. Her life was far from over. In an instant her burning red eyes returned to green. Nicolae propelled all his thoughts into Isabella's mind.

"Did you ever think I could abandon you completely?" Isabella smiled at her Nicolae. *"Besides, I miss the killing,"* Nicolae looked down at the throbbing vein on Lucy's neck.

Lucy pulled herself in close to her husband and said.

"It's over…?"

EPILOGUE

VROLOK

For centuries I have walked among you;
Feeding off you, living off you;
You haven't known I was there;
You have never known the creature that I am;
And to this day you think I do not exist.
Be warned—I do exist.
I am a Vampire, a Vrolok,
a Devil, and a Killer.

I could be there when a storm comes from nowhere out of the sky.
I could be there when you hear a whisper in the wind;
Or see a phantom in the mist.
I could be there when your blood turns to ice
and your hands start to tremble.
There is no escape from me, for…
I am a Vampire, a Vrolok,
a Devil, and a Killer.

I have had three great loves in my existence on this earth.
First was a human, then a Vampire, and then a Vrolok.
Each one was different from the last;
And each one I loved with what was left of my empty heart.
I would I have died to protect them but at times the
only protection they needed was from me. For
I am a Vampire, a Vrolok,
a Devil, and a Killer.

I cannot be harmed by you or your kind.
Only a unique creature can harm me;
This creature is now but a child.
Until that child comes of age,
I will continue to wander the earth, free to be...
a Vampire, a Vrolok,
a Devil, and a Killer.

So how can you distinguish me from the other people of this world?
Look for a woman with raven hair, red lips, and white skin.
She will be cold to touch
and will have a small scar above her heart,
where she once came close to harm,
But, be warned... do not seek me out for
I am a Vampire, a Vrolok,
a Devil, and a Killer,
Will I build a nation of Vampires?
Will they be the greatest race ever to rule the earth?
Will they be like they were before thousands of years ago?
Who knows... only time will tell.
But for as long as I rule the immortals, rest easy in your beds.
For no Vampire can enter your home without an invitation.
So when a stranger insists on an invitation
before they cross the threshold of your home,
Always be cautious ...For they may be
a Vampire, a Vrolok,
a Devil, and a Killer.

Vrolok, published by an anonymous author 1906.

Printed in the United Kingdom
by Lightning Source UK Ltd.
114811UKS00001B/181-249